▼ ▼ ▼ ▼ ▼ ▼ ▼ ▼ ▼ ▼

TRAILS OF DESTINY

BY

NEIL DUKE

▲ ▲ ▲ ▲ ▲ ▲ ▲ ▲ ▲ ▲

Rick,

This story is in a great primitive
land before it was called Montana
and Wyoming. Hope you enjoy it.

Neil Duke
December 15, 1997

"TO SOW THE FALLOW SOIL"

WINSTON-DEREK
Publishers, Inc.

PENNYWELL DRIVE . P.O. BOX 90883 . NASHVILLE, TENNESSEE 37209

PUBLISHED BY WINSTON-DEREK PUBLISHERS, INC.
Nashville, Tennessee 37205

Library of Congress Catalog Card No: 91-65536
ISBN: 1-55523-440-2

Printed in the United States of America

*This story is dedicated
to those who love the West*

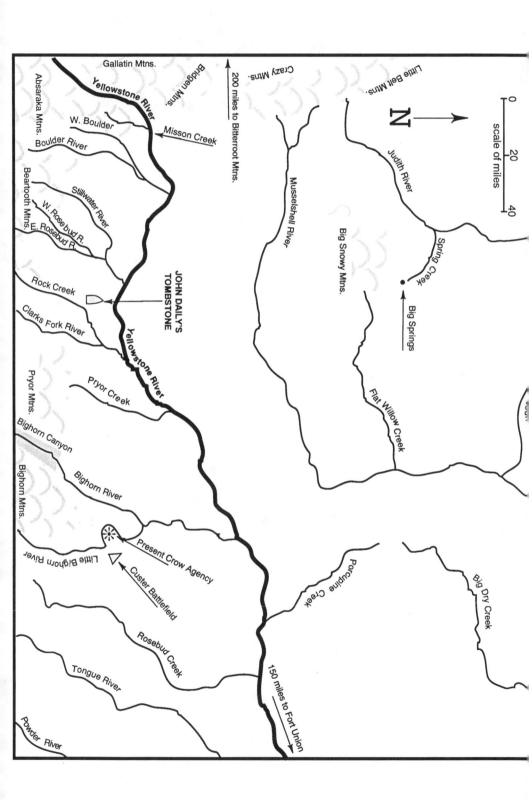

PREFACE

I was inspired to write this story from seeing the obscure, lone tombstone in a canyon in this area. The old ranch owner showed me the stone. The Montana Historical Society has no information about the person buried there. It is evident the stone is authentic because lichen has been growing on the face of the stone for a very long time. The death was nineteen years before the Custer Battle of the Little Bighorn.

This is the area where the Indians and buffalo made their last stand. The Custer Battlefield is on the nearby Crow Indian Reservation, and the tombstone is on land the Crow Indians once owned. I wove fiction and history into a story of the adventures of three trappers while they lived here among the Crow Indians during the 1850s to 1880s. The vision Chief Red Bear saw in the sky was an omen of events to come. In the story, the death of John Daily is a tragedy that could very well have happened as told or in a similar manner. The love story is of uncomplicated, faithful lovers.

The Indians and trappers were a very colorful and interesting people living here in a magnificent land. Their customs and history slowly fade into obscurity, just as the engraving on the stone slowly fades away.

I was born in Greybull, Wyoming, in 1919, and raised in Montana. Some old buffalo skulls could still be found on the prairies then. I have always had a great interest in the early history of this area. I am fascinated by the Indians' life and customs as they lived among the great herds of buffalo and the tragedy of their near extinction.

This story was written for posterity, so others may know of this great primitive land at that time and the colorful people living here. It is meant to be an interesting story of geography, history, and adventure.

▲▲▲▲▲▲▲▲▲▲▲▲▲▲

In a hidden box canyon in the Yellowstone River Breaks, the great silence is broken by the sighing of wind through pines nestled in the rimrocks. There is a low, lonely moaning of wind around the yellow cliffs as it swirls past the sides of a lone tombstone of sandrock at the base of a cliff. This is the scene of tragedy long ago. The shallow inscription on the stone has grown dim after 130 years of sunlight, rain, and wind. Lichen now dots the face of the three-foot stone that had broken away from the cliff. It is marked "R.I.P." for *Rest In Peace*, "JOHN DAILY, BORN 1802, DEATH 1857." Nearly imperceptible at the bottom are the initials "D.D.," the mark of the engraver. This is their story.

1

▼▼▼▼▼▼▼▼▼▼▼▼▼

THE CANYON

▲▲▲▲▲▲▲▲▲▲▲▲▲

Gray hair showed beneath the hat brim of Dan Daily, the rider on the big sorrel horse. The young, dark-haired lad on the gray horse was his grandson, fourteen-year-old Bob Daily. The year was 1896.

The two riders rode across the valley toward the mouth of a big canyon of high rimrocks. The canyon cut deeply through round-topped, grass-covered hills with patches of pine trees on the hillsides. Shorter canyons branched from the sides of the big canyon. The main trunk of the canyon reached another high, long cliff topped by a broad mesa that broke into more canyons northward to the Yellowstone River.

They had followed a wagon trail for several miles from Billings, near the Yellowstone River, to the Clarks Fork Valley. They were headed for home at the foot of the Beartooth Mountains. Ten miles up the Clarks Fork, they turned up Rock Creek Valley a few miles and stopped at the homestead of Carl Alt. Dan noticed many of the high sandstone cliffs across the valley from here that were extremely eroded into strange domes and hundreds of caves and holes.

They found Carl near his cabin. They had met Carl soon after he homesteaded the place in 1893. "Howdy, Carl," Dan greeted him. "We're heading back to the ranch along the West Rosebud."

"Howdy, Dan, Bob," and they shook hands. "How's things in Billings?"

"Well, there's still more people coming there."

After some visiting, Dan said, "If you don't mind, I'd like to show Bob that tombstone up in your box-canyon."

"Sure, that's fine. He oughta see it. You know, I lived here two years before I ever noticed it. Even then, I just happened to be driving a cow along the base of the cliff, or I wouldn't 'ave seen it yet. The sun was shining across it just right to see the writing. Say, when you get back, stop for supper and stay the night."

"Well thanks, we'll do that," and they rode away.

As the riders reached the broad mouth of the big canyon, they turned up the right side into a dead end canyon of high, yellowish-pink cliffs. An opening in this canyon's right side led up another half-mile-long, shallow box-canyon. At the upper end of it they reached a short, steep grassy slope at the base of a cliff. There on a flat spot, fifteen feet from the bottom of a cliff, stood an engraved stone; the same stone Dan Daily had engraved thirty-nine years before in 1857.

"Well, there it is, Bob. Still looks fine."

"Yeah, it's a good one. The letters still show," and Bob got down to look real close. Then, "I don't think anyone will ever bother it here."

As they stood beside the tombstone with bowed heads and hats in hand, Dan softly spoke a short prayer as a light breeze whispered through the pines above, and finished, "—and now he belongs to the Lord, amen."

Dan looked up. In memory he heard shrill Indian war whoops, a rattle of rifle shots, and the pounding hooves of a running battle here long ago.

Dan's thoughts slipped back to his parents' farm near St. Joseph, Missouri, where as a young man of eighteen he was so thrilled when his uncle, John Daily, came to visit them after spending several years in the West. When John returned to the West, Dan had gone with him. Dan remembered their lives with the Crow Indians and how John Daily was killed in this canyon.

He was nudged back to the present time by his grandson's offer of a bouquet of wildflowers to place at the base of the stone. When Dan looked up, he saw a dozen cows grazing peacefully along the mouth of the canyon. It looked just as it had that day in 1857 when he engraved the stone and placed it here, but on that day a dozen buffalo grazed slowly by.

They placed the flowers at the bottom of the tombstone, and then rode in silence down the canyon.

As they reached the valley, Dan said to his grandson, "John's dying was the saddest time of my life, and it still bothers me when I dwell on it. That's why I seldom come back here."

Young Bob nodded, "I'm glad you showed me the place."

As they neared the log home of Carl Alt, the sun dropped behind the mountains and lighted golden edges on wispy, crimson curtains hanging in the sky. The memories of the times he had spent with his uncle John lingered on in Dan's mind.

2

▼▼▼▼▼▼▼▼▼▼▼▼

ADVENTURE TO
CROW COUNTRY

▲▲▲▲▲▲▲▲▲▲▲▲▲

Riding their saddle horses and leading one pack horse each, Dan Daily, his uncle John Daily, and their friend Jake Barnes followed the Oregon Trail as they were starting westward on a long trip in 1852.

The wide brim of a gray felt hat shaded the handsome features of forty-seven-year-old John Daily, and the buckskin jacket hid the smooth strength of his body. He stood five-feet, ten-inches, and weighed 170 pounds. His hair was brown, with a touch of gray at the temples. His movements revealed power and confidence. John had a pleasant personality and an easy smile.

John's wife had died six years ago on their farm near St. Joseph, Missouri. After a while he met Jake Barnes as Jake was preparing to leave St.Joseph for the West.

They first met when John was in the blacksmith shop in St. Joseph one day, and Jake walked in just after the blacksmith had dunked a red-hot horseshoe in the water to cool a little, and then tossed it on the floor still pretty hot, but turned black. As Jake walked in he saw it, but did not know it was still pretty hot as he picked it up to have a look. "Wow," and he quickly dropped it.

"Dang, was that too hot for you, Jake?" asked the smithy.

"Naw, it jus' don't take me long to look at a horse shoe," and Jake grinned.

John laughed with him, and then they visited awhile. After a short time they became friends, and John learned Jake was also a widower. He was a little taller than John, slower moving, and rather course featured. He was just a little older than John. Jake was a friendly old backwoodsman from the Ozarks, and he filled John full of stories of his adventures where he had been in the San Juan Mountains and the Colorado River land.

John took a great interest in his stories of the West, so he went with Jake to the upper Arkansas River and the upper Colorado River. They had a lot of experience there trapping and prospecting before they returned.

Now they were on their way West again, and John's nephew, Dan Daily, was with them. He was riding a few feet in the lead on his four-year-old sorrel stallion. His name was Sonny, and he had a narrow, six-inch stripe on his forehead. Sonny stood fifteen hands high at the shoulders; just a little above the average-sized horse. He was a fast, powerful, barrel-chested horse with great stamina. With neck slightly arched in a proud stance, Sonny's outstanding beauty always drew immediate attention wherever he was seen. He stood on strong, lengthy legs, and hard hooves. Although a stallion, Sonny had a good disposition as he was usually calm and gentle, but always attentive and alert. He was a colt from Dan's best mare, and Dan had raised and trained him very well. Because he was Dan's pet, they had the strongest feelings of friendship for each other.

John and Jake were glad to have Dan with them. They liked this handsome, well-mannered young man. He was also strongly built, and nearly six-feet tall. His trimmed, thick brown hair lay in gentle waves, and alert brown eyes shone in a face of well-formed features. Dan's friendly smile matched his good manners. To Dan, his uncle was just about the greatest character to return from the Rocky Mountain West.

Dan had left his parents, brother, and sister on the farm near St. Joseph. He was eager to see the great mountains and rivers of the West and learn how the Indians lived there. Besides trapping, he hoped to look for gold sometime. Although it was after the early part of the California gold rush, most of the West still had not been prospected. Now they were on their way to the Bitterroot country and the Yellowstone.

At camp one evening along the Oregon Trail, Jake told them of a bad time he had with a bear.

"Sure got a scare from that ole bear. I wus walkin' down a trail in the San Juan Mountains. I looked back an' saw this big ole black bear a follering me, so I hurried along on a trot. I looked agin, and he wus trotin', so I started running hard as I could. When I looked back, he wus lopin' along, and gettin' close. He wus a hungry lookin' ole bear, and I could see I'd never outrun him. Ahead of me wus a tall pine by the trail with the first limb about fifteen feet off the ground, so I made a jump fer it," and Jake paused.

"Well, did you grab it, Jake?" asked Dan.

"Nope, but I caught the limb above it," and they all laughed. "Yup, when we get out there, you'll have to watch out fer the bears, Dan."

Dan and John figured Jake stretched his stories some, but they enjoyed them.

A few days up the Oregon Trail, Jake said, "I believe we can travel by ourselves and not get jumped by the Indians 'til we get past Chimney Rock, almost five hundred miles from here. As we begin to get closer to the mountains in Sioux country, we'd better join one of these wagon trains along the trail, even though we'll have to travel slower with them. There's too many tribes of hostile Indians west of Chimney Rock for us to travel alone if we don't have to."

Every few days they would overtake another wagon train where they would visit some of the people and then ride on. Two days beyond Chimney Rock, the people on a wagon train they overtook reported having seen a large band of Indian braves.

The three trappers found the wagon master, Bill Jones, and John asked, "Would it be all right for us to travel along with you? If we don't head north from Fort Laramie to the Yellowstone, we may want to travel with you as far as the Snake River. We're willing to pay a fee."

The wagon master was very cordial and said, "Yes, we'd be glad to have you along. It would be dangerous for three men to travel alone through this country. Three more men will make more protection for the wagon train. These people are all friendly, so I'm sure you'll enjoy

7

traveling with us. You can earn your fee hunting game for us." They joined the wagon train.

When they reached Fort Laramie, the first range of snow topped mountains stood nearby in the west. The great, white bulk of Laramie Peak dominated the horizon. A soldier told them the plains here were four thousand feet high.

Dan exclaimed, "Wow, what a sight. Looks like we've finally reached the West! Even the air feels different here."

"That's right," answered Jake, " and from here on it gets better."

The wagon train had not had any trouble with the Indians this far, but the commander at Ft. Laramie said to them, "I've been trying for a long time to get a peace treaty with the surrounding Indian tribes, but I haven't been able to, so don't stray too far from your wagons." To John's query about going north, "It wouldn't be safe goin' through Sioux country to the Yellowstone. The Sioux sure don't want any white people in their land. I don't think you'd ever make it to the Yellowstone."

The trappers continued northwest with the wagon train along the North Platte River and around the north end of the Laramie Mountains. About every day, they brought in buffalo for fresh meat for the settlers, and became well acquainted with all of them. For a while the three trappers watched the drama of a young couple on the wagon train.

Ray Miller sometimes hunted buffalo with the trappers. They liked this pleasant, helpful twenty-year-old man. One day, Ray told them, "I sure like Henry Madden's daughter, Shirley. Trouble is, the Millers are goin' to the Willamette Valley in Oregon, and the Maddens are goin' to California. Before we started out here, we had farms near each other near Hannibal. Shirley and I have liked each other for a long time. She's a couple years younger than me."

"Maybe you can get the Maddens to go to Oregon," John suggested.

"I'm afraid not. Henry Madden's got the gold fever for California."

Later, one evening near the wagons, Shirley said to Ray, "This is awful. When the wagons part where the Oregon Trail divides, some will go to California, and some to Oregon, and we're expected to say goodbye to each other. When we get to our new homes, we'll be more than a thousand miles apart, and it's all awful wild country between." With tears in her eyes she continued, "I don't believe we'll ever see each other again, Ray."

"I've been worrying about that for a long time. I can just imagine seeing the fork in the trail and watchin' your wagon slowly fade from my sight as the wagons part." With a hug he asked, "Will you marry me, Shirley, right away? Then we won't have to part; we can always stay together.

"Oh, yes, Ray. I would love to marry you real soon. I'd be sad forever if we had to part."

"Then I'll ask your father."

That night, Ray asked Shirley's parents for their permission to marry Shirley, and Henry Madden answered, "Yes, Ray, you have our consent. We think a lot of you, and we've been expecting this some day. Knowing that we'll be parting in about two weeks, I'm sure is why you decided to get married now. I only ask that you always be kind to her. Now, when the wagons part, it's her mother and me who will be sad, but I guess that's how life is, and we just have to bear it." Then he shook Ray's hand and gave Shirley a hug as a tear appeared in both parents' eyes.

A few days later the wagon train camped a little early one evening, and there was a wedding for the young couple with all of the members of the wagon train attending. There were long summer days now, so it was still daylight for the wedding that was held in the center of the circle of wagons. During the wedding, a few guards had to watch from the edge of the circle of wagons to be sure they were not surprised by an Indian attack, as this was in Sioux country.

Surprisingly, from among the settlers there was a fiddler, a trumpet player, and one to play the guitar, so they were able to play the wedding march as Shirley's father brought her forth. There was a minister to perform the wedding, and the bride wore a white wedding gown. She was very pretty with her sparkling blue eyes, and curled dark hair.

The groom was also handsome in his best trail clothing, and was even ready with a wedding ring at the right time. They were a very happy couple as they were pronounced husband and wife, and then embraced. It was a happy time, and an event to break the monotony of traveling every day.

The settlers had the things that were needed for a wedding because they had planned to bring such things for living in Oregon.

After the wedding, the people were entertained with music, dancing on the short grass, and good food. There was even a wedding cake.

9

As the glow of twilight dimmed, John stood outside of the circle of wagons for a time, and watched the flickering light of the campfires. The sound of music floated softly through the quiet air, and from the black silhouette of the Laramie Mountains, the plaintive wail of a coyote drifted in to blend with the notes of the fiddle. For a time there was a loneliness in John as he remembered his wedding day.

An hour after dark, the festivities ended, for the people always had to rise at dawn to care for their stock and get ready to travel.

There were sixty-four wagons in the train and 284 people. Often men left their wagons to be driven by a member of the family or a friend while they went hunting, but because the trappers were single men without a wagon to drive, they were relied on for a lot of the game needed. The packs on their horses were stored in some of the settlers' wagons so the trappers could bring in game on their pack horses.

Although the former endless herds of buffalo were not so great along the Oregon Trail now, there were still many smaller herds of buffalo and bands of antelope within a few miles of the trail.

The wagon train continued on the trail around the north end of the Laramie Mountains with the south end of the Bighorn Mountains in view far to the north. The wagon master told the settlers, "Watch close for Indians, we're passing through both Sioux and Cheyenne land. I don't expect to be attacked because we're near enough to Fort Laramie that the soldiers would retaliate against Indian attacks on any wagon train, but you hunters be careful away from the wagons. The Indians wouldn't expect trouble from the soldiers just because they killed a few stray hunters."

Only once had a small band of Indians been seen since leaving Fort Laramie, so one day the trappers with four other men rode out toward a herd of buffalo near the bottom of the low hills over two miles away.

Jake said to the men, "When the buffalo are this close, we can try for some if we're careful, but this could be the chance the Sioux 'ave been waitin' for. We're all ridin' fast horses, so if they jump us, we oughta be able to get back to the wagons."

As they rode on, John mentioned, "Other men will follow with the pack horses for the buffalo if no Indians come when we kill the buffalo. If the Sioux jump us, I hope it's before we load the pack horses or we'll lose the horses. If they're hiding out there, I don't think they'll wait that long to jump us. Maybe its kinda crazy, but for some reason, I seem to get a thrill out of this. It's a hell of a lot more exciting than following a plow in Missouri."

One of the men of the wagon train answered, "I'm sure you and the Indians are enjoying it a hell of a lot more than I am."

With a grin, Jake led on, and Dan figured there'd be some excitement on this hunt.

As they neared the buffalo herd at the foot of the hills, Jake said, "I can't see an Indian anywhere. There are none in this close, shallow draw between the hills, so they'd have to come at us from over the crest of the hills."

"That'd give us a quarter of a mile lead on them," stated John.

Dan offered, "That's about a half a minute lead."

Jake said, "I suppose four of us can each shoot one of these close buffalo, but you other three men better hold your fire for the Indians. If they come, we wouldn't have time to reload our muzzle-loaders and get away."

The men dismounted to take careful aim. Each picked a different buffalo, and the four men fired together. The four buffalo dropped, and instantly a dozen Indians seemed to ride right out of the ground from the nearby draw!

"Damn it," Jake swore loudly, "They were in a low place we couldn't see in that big sagebrush," then shouted, "Let's go."

The other three men fired their rifles, and one Indian fell. Many more Indians rode over the crest of the small, close hills. The Indians from the draw were getting very close as the hunters hurriedly mounted and started away.

Dan thought, "This will be close, but I'm sure Sonny can outrun them." He waited to leave until the last men were mounted.

Seventeen-year-old David Green jumped on his horse, and as the horse burst into full speed it fell, then got up and lunged away before David got up. Dan knew he would have to get David. It looked to Dan as though one or two of the nearest Indians could possibly catch him because of the delay. It would be close!

Dan raced to David, pulled Sonny to an abrupt stop, and David jumped on behind him! Before Sonny could gain full speed, the big war-painted Sioux in the lead caught up to them! He screamed and thrust his spear at Dan! Dan struck at the spear with his empty muzzle-loader! The barrel slid down the spear and hit the Indian's hand, knocking the

11

spear to the ground! David had lost his gun and could not help. The Indian's pinto horse jostled into Sonny's side as the Indian raised his tomahawk to strike again! With a harsh squeal, ears laid back, and teeth bared, Sonny bit and jerked the pinto's neck! With a grunt, the pinto stumbled, fell hard and rolled over the Indian! Dan thought he could outrun the other Indians now, although two more were close. Two arrows whizzed by. Dan could feel the strength and speed of Sonny as he urged Sonny on. With outstretched neck and pounding hooves, Sonny rapidly pulled away from the whooping Indians.

John and Jake had looked back and slowed to return and help Dan, but Dan's fight was over so quickly, they only joined Dan as he came by. The whooping Indians chased the hunters back to the wagon train that had just finished forming its circle for defense. Even with two riders, Sonny reached the wagons first. After dismounting inside the circle, Dan patted Sonny's neck and said, "You're the best horse in the world for sure, Sonny. I'm sure you knew I was having a lot of trouble with that big Indian. Thanks, old pal."

David said, "Gee, thanks Dan, and Sonny too, for helping me. I sure thought the Indians would get me. My horse stepped in a badger hole. I'm sure glad he got back all right, but I lost my gun."

The Indians had stopped out of rifle range of the wagons, then returned to join more Indians who had arrived and started butchering the four buffalo.

"These Sioux are plenty cunning," said Jake. They can hide where it looked impossible." Then smiling, "Anyhow, we showed them who has the fastest horses. We left them way behind."

Looking from the circle of wagons, John said to those near him, "I don't think the Sioux are that hungry. They kill all the buffalo they need. They just wanted to show us this is still their land, but we'll get more buffalo in a day or two."

The wagon master added, "The Sioux and Cheyenne don't even like for us to pass through here. They're afraid some of the settlers will see a place where they'd like to stay, so they keep showing us that only dead settlers will stay here. I've been bringin' wagon trains through here for three years since the gold rush in 1849, and already I can see there's a lot less buffalo along the trail. The Indians sure don't like that."

"No one can farm with a herd of buffalo in his field," quipped a settler.

12

John stated, "I came here to get away from farmin'."

Dan agreed, "I'm sure we'll find a lot of things in the West that are a lot more interesting than a corn field."

Soon the wagon train continued on in close formation, and the Indians did not bother them.

Two days later, on a flat prairie without a hiding place for Indians within five miles, the men killed six buffalo, and no Indians came.

One day on the prairie southwest of the Laramie Mountains, the trappers saw many scattered bands of antelope with a few dozen in each band.

"They'd make a good change of meat from the buffalo the people 've been eatin'," advised Jake.

The curious antelope allowed the men to ride just within rifle range. By firing together they were able to shoot one antelope each, most of the time, before the antelope raced away. They carried the antelope to the wagons on the pack horses. Each time after unloading, they returned to hunt.

After the third and final trip that day, while returning to the wagons, John said, "Jake, you never missed one shot today. One shot, one antelope each time. Did they call you "dead eye Jake" where you lived in the Ozarks?"

"No, a lot of squirrel hunters down there are real marksmen. A squirrel is a lot smaller target than an antelope; course an antelope is a lot farther away, so it's about the same. But you have to be careful about shooting up inta the trees down there too early in the mornin', you might hit one of your relatives up there gettin' his breakfast. It's a great country for persimmons, papaws, and mulberries ya know," and Jake could not suppress a big grin.

"I'll bet you never told that one around all those people of yours."

"Aw no, coulda got shot."

Their trail turned westward again as it left the curve of the North Platte River. Far to the west, beyond the vast sweep of the diverging purple sage prairies, reared the precipitous face of a long line of snow-crested peaks.

Pointing, Jake said, "That's the Wind River Mountains way out there. It's one of the highest, longest, ruggedest string of peaks in the West. I haven't been up in 'em, but from near them with an eyepiece, I've seen some of the damndest big vertical pillars, and high pinnacles of anywhere I've been."

13

John replied, "It looks like there's no way through or around them."

"You can't see it now, but at the south end where the smaller Green Mountains begin, there's a gap called South Pass."

"It's fantastic," exclaimed Dan. "It's so much bigger and more remote than you were able to tell us. It would take ages to explore all of it. I can't imagine all the peaks, creeks, and canyons out there, and even way beyond that, where we're goin'! I wonder how the first explorers felt when they saw what was ahead of them here."

"'Bout the same as you do."

John remarked, "These great mountain rimmed, wide open spaces sometimes give me a lonely feeling, or a kinda religious feeling as I marvel at the handiwork of God, but then I have to return from my wonderment and ride on to whatever destiny waits for us in those wild places beyond the far horizon."

For several more days, the wagon train followed the trail westward in the area of the Sweetwater River, then rumbled over the rocks and around the boulders of South Pass, where scattered snow drifts still lingered in the month of June in this high, wide pass between the ends of the Wind River Mountains and the Green Mountains.

At the summit the wagon master told them, "This pass is not the head of a canyon or narrow valley like a lot of passes in the west, but the summit of this long, gradual slope is the Continental Divide."

Two miles down the west slope they came to Pacific Springs, where Dan said, "Looks like this water's running west now. Somewhere it'll find the Pacific Ocean. What a change in just a few miles."

As the wagon train left South Pass, it started into a high, flat basin, and looking ahead John said, "Looks like this is a wide, dry basin. Must be dang few buffalo out there. We still have quite a lot of buffalo meat, but I think we're gonna eat a lot of antelope while we're crossin' this prairie."

Many miles out into the high, wide plains, the wagon train followed the well worn Oregon Trail through a sandy prairie of very short grass and sagebrush. Although there were high mountains far to the west, they were out of sight over the distant horizon. The crest of the Wind River Mountains was still in sight behind the wagon train. Slopes and low ridges of lonely, gray prairie seemed to reach forever into the distance. Far out in the middle of this melancholy space, the wagon train finally reached the fork in the trail where those heading for

California would take the left trail, and those going on to Oregon would follow the right trail.

This was the time of parting that Shirley Madden and her parents had been dreading. The wagon train stopped when it reached the fork in the trail. For more than an hour, the settlers visited and said farewells. The Maddens' hearts were breaking as the wagon train started forward. As each wagon reached the fork in the trail, it turned right or left as the wagon train divided. About half went each way. The three trappers rode on with the wagons going to Oregon, but they watched the wagons divide. As the Maddens' wagon turned south to California, John said, "Well, there they go. Sure is too bad the Maddens have to go so far away from their daughter. She's goin' to Oregon with the Millers now."

As the wagons parted, Shirley sat on the seat at the front of the wagon with her young husband, Ray. She and her parents continued waving good-bye until their wagons passed from view. They were all terribly downhearted.

When the California-bound wagons had faded from view, Shirley looked ahead with tear-clouded eyes as Ray tried to comfort her, and said, "I don't believe I'll ever see my folks again."

With the California wagons, the Maddens were also extremely sad. For an hour after the Oregon wagons had passed from sight over the far rise, Shirley's parents lamented parting with their daughter. They had been recalling the past, and talked of the days when she was a baby and of the time when she was such a pretty little girl. Now she was a beautiful and pleasant young lady, and they expressed the fear that they would never see her again, or the grandchildren that they would surely have some day.

Henry stared westward across the wide prairie through shimmering heat waves to where it blended into infinity. "Good Lord," he exclaimed, "As far as it is across this prairie, how far can it be from way down in California to the Willamette Valley in Oregon? It's just too far, and I'm afraid we'll never see her again. Never is just too long." He pulled the horses to the right and stopped his wagon off of the edge of the trail.

As each wagon passed by, they stopped and talked a minute to see what was wrong, and then said good-bye and went on. Soon Jack, the new wagon master for this part of the train, came back to see what was wrong with the wagon.

Henry said, "We just decided nothing is worth going that far from our daughter. Our other kids don't want to either. We're all unhappy, so we're goin' to turn back and catch the other wagons."

Jack replied, "Well, I can understand how you feel, and I wouldn't say that you shouldn't, but we must have come four miles since we left them. I'm sure they have traveled that far too, and they'll go a long ways yet today. It's ten o'clock already, and I don't know if you can go back and catch them by dark. We don't know if any Indians are out there either. It would sure worry us to see you go back all alone like that."

"Yes, I've considered all of that, and hoped we'd either be lucky or the Lord will help us. I couldn't catch the other wagon train by dark if I go back to the fork in the trail, but I plan to cut across to meet them," explained Henry.

"It don't look too rough to weave your way across what we can see from here, but I sure hope you won't find a deep coulee that you can't cross, or worse yet, get stuck in it."

"I'll just have to be careful," replied Henry.

"I'll get three men to come along and we'll ride our saddle horses with you to the top of the slope," offered Jack. "That's about three miles, and I can still see my wagons from there. I hope we can see yours from there, too."

Jack and three other friends rode the three miles to the top of the gradual slope with the Maddens. Where they stopped at the top, they were unable to see the Oregon wagons or the Oregon Trail anywhere in the distance. The prairie sloped down a couple miles and then sloped up again for over a mile, so they were unable to see over the far slope. The Oregon wagons had to be out of sight on the other side.

Henry's escort wasted very little time in farewells now. Jack cautioned Henry again about crossing gullies, wished him good luck, and started back to his wagon train. After they left, Henry stared determinedly ahead to the top of the far slope over two miles away.

They started down the north slope where there were several patches of high sagebrush, and some big rocks to go around. The first half mile was gentle enough for the horses to hold the wagon back with the neck yoke on the wagon tongue, and the help from the big hand brake for the rear wagon wheels. Two-thirds of the way down, Henry stopped the wagon where the slope suddenly broke into a very steep downhill grade.

Henry's wife, Mae, exclaimed, "Oh, Henry, we can never make it down that place! It's just too steep and rough!"

16

"Looks pretty bad all right, but it's worse everywhere else. We could travel for miles and maybe never find a better place to go down the hill. Besides that, at the bottom of this hill is the only place where we might be able to cross that gully."

"I sure hope we'll not have to unload any of our things to leave behind," Mae worried.

"What we could leave behind wouldn't help enough. Here, Roger," he spoke to his fifteen-year-old son. "Hold the reins while I go take a look around that big ledge of rock down there." Then he walked down a short distance to the big outcropping of rock on the hillside.

When he returned he explained, "It's just goin' to be nip and tuck to get around that turn below the rock ledge. There's enough slope there that it could tip 'er over unless I can go real slow."

Roger stared down the hill, "I wish the trappers were here. They could tie on to the side of the wagon with ropes from their saddle horses and keep the wagon from rollin' over."

"That would sure help, son."

Henry's twelve-year-old daughter, Rose, said, "I'm scared, Pa."

We'll probably make it all right, honey." And then, "Roger, I'll drive down a little ways to where it gets steep. You go wait there, and get a good square-like rock, heavy as you can handle, to chuck under a rear wheel when I stop."

When they were ready, Henry started the wagon down, and at the right place he spoke, "Whoa, whoa," to the big bay horses as he pulled back on the reins. When the wagon stopped, Roger chucked a good, heavy rock that he had picked under one of the big rear wagon wheels.

"There, that'll hold 'er son. Now, will you hold the horses for me again? I've got to rough-lock the wheels to try to hold the wagon back as we go down this bad, steep place.

"How do you do that, Pa?"

"Just watch, and you'll soon know how it's done."

Henry got two log chains from the wagon, one for each rear wagon wheel. Between the front and back wheels, on each outside edge of the wagon box, he hooked a log chain onto an iron ring.

While standing by the wagon, and holding the horses' reins, Roger said, "I always wondered what the rings were for. Now what?"

With the other end of the chain, Henry then made three wraps around the wagon wheel rim and through the wagon wheel spokes. He hooked the chain with enough slack so that when the wagon started

17

ahead, the wheel would lock on top of the wraps of chain and the chain would dig into the ground to help slow the wagon. He locked both of the rear wheels in this manner, and then stated, "That oughta do it."

"Hope so, Pa."

"I'll ride 'er down alone," Henry advised, as he climbed onto the wagon seat, and Roger handed him the reins.

From where Mae and Rose were standing nearby, Rose exclaimed, "You can ride 'er without me, Pa. I'm scared."

Henry spoke to the horses, "Get up," and the wagon started. The big team of horses had to pull the first little ways, and then as the hill became steeper, the wagon tongue had to help hold the wagon back. As the neck yoke pulled on their collars, the breeching of the harness around the horses haunches pulled tight, and held the collars from pushing off over the horses heads. Farther down, at a steeper place, the wagon approached the rock ledge that the wagon must go around. Faster and faster, the wagon slid down the hill as the rough-lock chains dug into the sod, tearing up dirt, screeching and rumbling over solid rock. Then Henry turned the wagon forty-five degrees to the right, and started around the bottom of the rock ledge! The ground flattened just a little along a narrow space below the ledge, but there was a very steep slope on the left where the wagon would roll if it turned over. The reins pulled so hard on the horses bridle bits that it bared their teeth. Now they were losing it! As they started around the corner gaining speed, the horses could no longer hold it to a walk, even though their hooves dug stiffly into the ground. As the dust flew, the right wheels lifted off of the ground!

Rose screamed, "Ohh!" Mae cried, "Oh, no!" Roger shouted, "Oh, God!"

Henry gritted his teeth, and leaned over to the right as he held the horses' reins with one hand and the end of the wagon seat with the other while bracing his legs, ready to jump! Then, slowly, slowly, the wheels came down as the wagon reached flatter ground! With great relief, and a cheer, the family suddenly relaxed, as Henry got the wagon stopped below the ledge. As they reached Henry, Mae exclaimed, "Scared us all to death!"

"I thought you'd get killed," Rose exclaimed, with tears in her eyes.

"It even scared me," admitted Roger.

"Pretty close one, that's for sure. It was worse than I expected, but we'll make it yet," advised Henry.

18

Henry rested the horses a short time as he removed the rough-lock chains. "It's not as steep now, and still quite a ways down, but the brake should hold the wagon now."

"We'll still walk the rest of the way down," said Mae.

At the bottom of the slope they found what they expected—a small ravine that had to be crossed with a very small stream, with a little water running down the center.

"Well, it could be worse," Henry said. "We can fill 'er in bank to bank with rock."

It took the family over an hour to carry enough rocks to fill in the vertically banked little creek. The afternoon had become hot now, so it was hard work to carry the rocks.

Before the work was finished, Roger said, "I sure hope no Indians come while we're down here out of sight of either wagon train."

Henry jokingly replied, "Well, if they happen to come by, we'd better ask if they'll help us carry rocks while we get a little rest."

A very small pond had formed above the crossing, so Henry unhitched his big bay team and led them down the steep slope to the pond for water. He then hitched them to the wagon again, and with the brake set, he drove the wagon down the steep slope to the crossing. The wagon bumped hard onto the crossing, but stayed upright and did not break any wheels.

Henry's family watched from the slope. After the wagon had crossed, Henry stopped and his relieved family got in the wagon.

Mae said, "It was a lot of work carrying all those rocks, but it was the only way we could cross and not break the wagon."

The Maddens rode their wagon a mile to the top of the gentle slope that was covered with short sagebrush. When they reached the crest, Henry said, "Good, there's the wagon train. It's about three miles west of here," and then pointing, "There's the Oregon Trail cuttin' through the sagebrush about a half mile to the right."

"Am I ever glad to see that," exclaimed Mae.

"We'll soon get to the trail, then we can hurry along and catch them in an hour."

Roger spoke up, "I hope what I see a half mile to the right of the wagons are riders from the wagon train, and not Indians!"

"There must be a dozen of 'em" advised Henry. "Don't look like they're hunters from the wagons. There could be Ute or Paiute Indians here. They must be watchin' the wagon train. I haven't heard of them bein' real war-like, but they might take advantage of a lone wagon."

"We have three muzzle-loaders," offered Roger, "If they come after us, we oughta be able to get three of them before they get us."

"We might," agreed Henry, and he urged the horses into a faster trot.

They had gained half of the distance to the wagon train when they saw the Indians turn back from the wagon train toward them. They were coming at a fast trot!

Soon Roger cried, "Look, the wagons stopped," and then, "Looks like seven riders from the wagons are startin' this way at a gallop."

Henry added, "I think the trappers are in the lead, and they're gainin' on the Indians. Looks like Dan, on Sonny, is really gainin' on 'em. There, he took a shot at 'em."

"Catch 'em!" shouted Roger, but a quarter of a mile from Henry's wagon the Indians broke into a hard gallop and started north.

Henry had stopped his horses, and the men from the wagon train slowed their horses to a trot as they came on and soon reached where the Maddens waited.

When they arrived, Henry exclaimed, "By golly, you must know how happy we are that you got here before the Indians! That Sonny can run, can't he? I don't think the Indians were headed over here for a friendly greeting."

"We thought you'd be glad to see us," replied John, with a smile.

They all visited for a while as their horses rested, and then they drove on to the waiting wagon train.

When the Maddens reached the train, their daughter, Shirley, ran to them with open arms, wild with joy. "I'm so surprised that I can't hardly believe it's you!" she exclaimed as she hugged and kissed all of her family. "I'm so happy, I can't tell you how much. Oh, how wonderful, but the Indians nearly got you!"

"Only if three Indians were ready to die, isn't that right, Roger?" and Henry looked at Roger.

In early evening, the wagon master stopped the train to camp beside a creek, and the people all had a good visit. They were so happy to have the Maddens safely back.

John asked, "How did you decide to try to catch the Oregon wagons, Henry?"

"We were just too sad to think we'd probably never see Shirley again. I thought we'd be happier digging potatoes in Oregon with all of the family together, than digging for gold in California. Maybe I would never have found any gold in California anyway. I'm really glad we came back."

"We're glad you made it," stated John.

It was a happy camp that evening.

The next morning, Bill Jones, the wagon master, explained to all the people, "We're followin' the Sublette Cutoff to the Bear River. The California bound wagons took the main trail to Fort Bridger, where they'll continue on to the Great Salt Lake. The main trail follows Sandy Creek southwest to the Green River. Across the Green River, the main trail leads southwest up the Black's Fork to Fort Bridger. From Fort Bridger, The Oregon Trail leads northwest, across several streams, to the Bear River Valley. The main trail is twice as long as this Sublette Cutoff to the Bear River. The Sublette Cutoff is harder to travel because of a forty-mile stretch of waterless prairie that has to be crossed beyond Big Sandy Creek, but we can make it. We'll have to cross at night so the horses can stand it without water."

In the two days after the wagons had parted, the Oregon wagons crossed Little Sandy Creek and reached Big Sandy Creek. Many bands of antelope were seen, even though the vegetation was very sparse on this arid prairie.

The settlers and trappers camped and rested their horses during the hot daytime temperatures beside Big Sandy Creek. The Sandy Creeks were small enough to be forded with the wagons. They flowed from the lower southwest end of the snow-draped Wind River Mountains. This incredible row of white, sharp peaks formed a spiny ridge a hundred miles long, north and south. The settlers and trappers gazed in awe across the sagebrush flats at the full length of these peaks that looked even more prominent on the west side than they had looked from the east side.

Bill Jones explained, "It's said that group of about a dozen peaks near the north end of the range are over thirteen to nearly fourteen thousand feet high. It's one of the greatest mountain ranges in the west."

"Good Lord, they're a sight," Dan exclaimed. "A drink from one of their high, cold mountain streams would taste mighty good right now."

John said, "Those peaks look cool. This prairie is so hot today that it would sure feel good to be near some of that snow."

Jake remarked, "This is the first time I've been on this side of 'em."

As the burning sun sank lower in the western sky, the air began to cool, so the settlers hitched their horses to the wagons and started across the dry, flat prairie. They traveled all night in the light of the moon, with an occasional rest stop. In the cool night air, their horses were able to cross the forty-mile stretch of prairie without a drink of water. Before the morning turned hot, the wagon train arrived at the cool, clear, smooth-flowing Green River.

John remarked to his pardners, "That was kind of a hard, strange trip all night long, but we made it to a real good river. Bill Jones sure knows this country."

The settlers rested a few hours as, one wagon at a time, they crossed the Green River on a ferry. The next day, they traveled a shorter distance over the prairie to a pass around the south end of the Salt Mountains, and farther west, they later reached the Bear River Valley. It was a more pleasant trip down this valley, northwest to Soda Springs. From there, they crossed to the Portneuf River, and followed it northwest to Fort Hall, on the Snake River.

There Dan said, "It's sure a good thing the wagon master knows his way through this country."

John added, "He has to know his way through all these mountain passes, or he'd be sure to have a lost wagon train."

"The first trappers in here had to find the passes," Jake stated.

At Fort Hall, Jake said to his pardners, "We've sure come a long way west; clear to the Snake River. It was pretty easy ridin' with a wagon train. Now, here's where we leave 'em and start north on our own. Bill said the Snake Indians around here have been raidin' wagon trains sometimes, and killed a few settlers that strayed from their wagons. Some of 'em are pretty mean. He told me these Indians that are camped here to trade at the fort are friendly Bannocks that'll be headin' north pretty soon. We'd better see if we can go with 'em."

"We'd sure better," John agreed. "We'll play it safe when we can. I think we'll find a lot of wild country when we go north, but that's what we wanted to see. There's not many white people there either, so maybe there's still some pretty good trappin' left somewhere."

Dan said, "It's sure to be interesting, seein' all that big country. Maybe we can even do some prospectin' for gold."

Next day, the trappers bid the settlers good-bye. They had become good friends on the long trip to the Snake River.

Bill Jones, the wagon master, shook their hands and said, "We've had a good trip together, without any disasters. I'm glad you came with us. You sure supplied us with a lot of buffalo and antelope. We never

22

missed a meal. I'd like for you to come with us to the Willamette Valley in Oregon. I believe you'd like it there. It's pretty country."

"Well, thanks for the offer, Bill. I'm sure a lot of settlers will be farmin' there, but we're really not interested in farmin'," John replied. "We'll go on north to the Bitterroot country."

The trappers got their supplies that had been stored in the settlers' wagons and told them good-bye. Henry Madden said, "We sure appreciate your friendship and help to all of us. Now be careful up there in that big, wild country."

"We will," answered John, and they waved as they left.

The trappers rode northeastward with the Bannock Indians along the south side of the Snake River for over twenty miles to a place where it was possible to ford the river with pack horses. In August, the Snake River had dropped to a much smaller stream than it had been during the early summer runoff of snow water from the great mountainous area to the east. During the spring runoff, the Snake was a mighty torrent of muddy, debris-laden water, whose rolling waves plunged over many waterfalls, and then raced on to join the awesome Columbia in its unhindered rush to the Pacific. Any man or animal caught in these raging waters was sure to be swept away and drowned.

The Bannocks led the way to a river crossing that the trappers would never have believed existed, even during a time of low water. They followed a trail that led them down a long, brown slope for a mile, with a few switchbacks to lessen the grade. Steps of a broken and cracked, eight-foot rock bank allowed the horses to enter the stream. A solid bottom of lava rock, sand, and gravel provided good footing nearly all the way across a hundred-yard-wide stream of nearly clear water, two to three feet deep.

"By the high water marks, I can see what an awful river this is in the spring," John said. "It's pretty big yet."

Carefully, the trappers and the bronze-skinned Bannocks rode their horses across the moderately swift water. In a few places, the water pushed against some of the horses' bellies. A few times, slick, green rock caused a horse to stumble or fall on its side and douse its rider, but with strong hands and legs, hard effort, or friendly help, the rider was always able to gain control of the plunging, splashing horse, remount, and ride on, with water running from black, shining hair, and dark blinking eyes. Very little damage to personal property, horse or rider was incurred, so the incident was treated with humor. The trappers rode their saddle horses and led their pack horse across the river without any incident.

Dan noted that Sonny never made a misstep. He was always a very sure-footed horse.

When they reached the north side of the river, John commented to Chief Snow Bird, "Chief Snow Bird knows the best place to cross the river. It is good that we are with you."

"Bannocks crossed here when I was little Bannock," the Chief smiled.

The Bannocks and trappers followed a trail up from the river to a wide prairie of short grass and mountains in the distance. They traveled unhurriedly northward for several days, and rode past great lava beds to their west. With a point of his thumb, Jake exclaimed, "From the looks of all that black lava, there musta been a hell of a hot time around here once."

With the Bannocks, they continued northward up a creek that was flowing through a grassy plain, and then rode through a gentle pass over the Continental Divide, between the Bitterroot and Centennial Mountains. Several miles farther north, the Bannocks set their tepees beside the Red Rock River, in a pleasant land of grassy slopes, tree-lined streams, and moderate mountains. Once again, the trappers were on the east side of the Continental Divide.

The trappers spent two pleasant days at the Bannock Indian village. When they were ready to leave, Chief Snow Bird drew a map on the ground with the point of a knife.

Northwest of the confluence of the Red Rock and Beaverhead Rivers, he drew the location of Badger Pass, and of Big Hole Pass into the Big Hole Basin, with the Big Hole River turning to the east. He then drew the Gibbon Pass leading west from the Big Hole to the Bitterroot, where he indicated the water runs north to the "Big River."

The trappers understood this to mean the Gibbons Pass was the Continental Divide again, where the Bitterroot would run north to the Clark Fork of the Columbia River.

Jake then spoke, "It is good Chief Snow Bird shows us the way to the Bitterroot."

They gave the chief another small sack of tobacco and a wave as they rode away leading their pack horses.

For a day, they followed down alongside of the Red Rock River. Once, Dan pointed to the River and exclaimed, "Just look at that! Great big white birds! They gotta be trumpeter swans! I've read of them, but this is the first ones I ever saw. There's nine of 'em."

As they continued down along the stream, they were pleased to see several more small bunches of the great, white birds.

"We just keep seeing white-tailed deer all along here, too," John said.

When they reached the Beaverhead, they stopped to gaze down the wide valley, and John pointed out, "There's several good bunches of elk scattered down through the valley. The Indians must eat elk more than they do buffalo, here."

The trappers rode through the Badger Pass, and Big Hole Pass, into the Big Hole Basin. It was a high, cool, wide basin, surrounded by mountain ranges. Along the Big Hole River, the most abundant wildlife the men saw were elk feeding on lush meadows and moose feeding on the willows.

As they wove their way across several miles of low, flat ground that was covered with high, green grass, sedges, and willows, they saw many big, dark, hump-shouldered moose. The bulls had enormous, broad, flattened antlers, large muzzles, and a dewlap under their chin.

Jake said, "Ain't they purty," and laughed. "Gol-danged big ugly things are bigger'n a horse. It's dangerous riding through these thick willows in moose country. We may have to outrun one of these ol' cow moose that has a calf or two. Some of these big ol' broad-horned bulls can get real upset, too."

"They could sure surprise us in these thick willows," Dan agreed, but they never came closer than a hundred yards to a moose as they crossed the brushy areas along the streams.

Out on the grass again, John gestured back with his thumb, "If we was here in the winter with the snow butt deep and thirty below, a big ol' moose would taste purty good."

"Prob'ly about all that'd be here ta eat in the winter, too," answered Jake. "I've heard it's a basin of awful deep snow and long winters. Snow can be four feet deep here all winter long. This is real snowshoe country, and the first trappers have it about all trapped out."

While passing through scattered clumps of willows in a wide, low area in the Big Hole, the men suddenly met a band of twenty Indians on pinto horses. The Indians were wearing buckskin clouts, leggings, and moccasins. They were bare from the waist up, and were not wearing any war paint. A few eagle feathers were standing in the braided hair of some of the braves. They were armed with bows and arrows, and two old muzzle-loaders.

Dan grabbed for his gun, but Jake said, "Wait, maybe they're friendly. I don't think they're Blackfoot," and raised his hand.

The Indian in the lead raised his hand in peace, so the Indians and trappers slowly met.

With sign language, a little bit of English, and a few Indian words, Jake learned the Indians were from another tribe of Bannocks.

John took a small can of tobacco, and a small sack of beads from a saddle bag and gave it to the Bannock sub-chief.

The Bannocks had the quarters of a moose and a deer on their pack horses. They gave John the hindquarters of a deer. It was a token of their friendliness. Soon, the Indians left and headed north.

Jake said, "I think they understood my thanks, and that we're goin' to the Bitterroot."

"We can't always be lucky enough to find friendly Indians," Dan offered.

The trappers crossed the wide prairies of the Big Hole country, then crossed over low, pine-covered mountains through St. Joseph Pass and Gibbons Pass to the East Fork of the Bitterroot River. At the confluence of the east and west forks, they found the Bitterroot Valley. This was the country they had traveled so far to reach, and it was as great as they expected.

Looking north down the valley, John exclaimed, "So this is the Bitterroot. What a good lookin', long, wide valley it is. Must be ten miles wide, and a hundred miles long, and lots of grass."

Dan offered, "That has to be the high peaks of the Bitterroots running down the west side. I think it's the Sapphires along the east side. Sure is a timber country in the mountains."

"Must be the best valley we've found," Jake stated. "I've wanted to see this for a long time."

They traveled northward down the valley to Fort Owen. At the fort, the trappers met the congenial owner, John Owen. He was operating a good trading post that he said he bought from the Jesuit Priests who had founded it in the Flatheads' land. He said the Indians had become Christianized, but they didn't like the priests when they attempted to Christianize the Flatheads' bitter enemies, the Blackfoot Indians.

John Owen said to the trappers, "I hope you'll stay in this area. You'll like it here. There's still some trapping here, and maybe prospectin' would even pay off sometime. Somebody should start a sawmill, too."

"We'll try the country for a while," promised John.

John Owen said, "The Flatheads are friendly. They don't understand how we got started calling them Flatheads. They're really Salish Indians. They don't practice the custom of flattening their infants' heads as it has been told about them. The Chinooks and Killmucks on the Columbia are the ones who do that."

When the trappers associated with the Flatheads that were camped near the fort, they saw that they were a light-colored, medium-sized people. Their black hair was allowed to grow long and fall loosely down the back, and in front of the shoulders. Often, it was tied with a buckskin ring or ornament on each side of the neck, near the jaw. The hair at the top of the head may be pulled back or combed to the side, but not usually parted at the center. One or more eagle feathers were thrust erect at the back of the head, protruding high above the hair.

The men wore long, buckskin leggings, reaching from the ankles to the hips, and overlapping in the front. They were fastened by rawhide strings to a leather belt. The loose-sleeved buckskin shirt and leggings were fringed at the outside seams. They wore moccasins, but had no cover for the head, except in bad weather when they used a buffalo robe over head and body. The women were wrapped in a robe of buckskin reaching from the neck to the feet, and ornamented with fringes, beads, hawk bills, and variously carved bones. The apparel was regularly cleaned with clay.

As they became acquainted with these Indians, the trappers found them to be amiable among themselves and the white people. They had been friendly to the Lewis and Clark expedition in 1804, and claimed they had never killed a white person. However, these Indians and the Blackfoot practiced horrible torture and cruelty upon each other when they took prisoners. In spite of the terrible torture, the victims never whimpered, but tried to aggravate their tormentors. The trappers did not care to witness it.

Many of the Flatheads could speak English quite well, and during the trappers' visits with them, they learned much about them. The great herds of buffalo ranged on the plains east of the Rocky Mountains. The Blackfoot lived at the eastern edge of the Rocky Mountains, and the Flatheads lived just across the divide on the west side. They were age-old enemies. The Blackfoot claimed the land east of the mountains, but the Flatheads claimed buffalo hunting rights there because their ancestors had always hunted buffalo there. This kept them in constant conflict that had developed into great hatred. The Blackfoot even threatened to kill white people in the Flatheads' area. The Blackfoot had not liked American whites ever since they were included in the Louisiana Purchase. Their first meeting with Lewis and Clark had been violent.

27

Due to the greater numbers of Blackfoot and the greater numbers of guns they were able to obtain from the traders in Canada, the Blackfoot were slowly reducing the Flathead population, even though the Flatheads fought with intense valor.

This was the situation the three Missouri pardners found at the time they arrived in the Bitterroot Valley.

One day the trappers visited the Flathead village of Chief Grizzly Standing, twenty miles below Fort Owen. The trappers were met near the village and escorted to the chief's tepee. Suspended on a pole beside the chief's lodge were a dozen Blackfoot scalps. The trappers entered the lodge where the chief sat at the honored position at the back and center of the lodge.

The trappers sat on each side of the chief while he passed the pipe around. He understood English, so they were able to tell him about the areas they had passed through to get to the Bitterroot Valley. He was familiar with those areas as far as the Snake River. The chief described the surrounding area to the trappers. Before the trappers left, the chief said, "If you want buffalo, come with us to Missouri River. We get many buffalo there for food and robes this winter. Maybe you shoot some Blackfoot. We go in two days."

Two days later, the trappers left the Flathead village with Chief Grizzly Standing, and nearly two hundred braves with their squaws and children. Other such groups would go hunting after this group returned. There were about eight hundred people in the group.

There were not enough horses. There were only forty more than one horse for each brave, and most of the horses would be used to haul the dried buffalo meat and hides home. Most of the Indians had to walk. The trappers brought their pack horses with them.

As the trappers, leading their pack horses, rode away with the Indians, Jake stated, "I reckon when we start back from the Missouri, these pack horses are gonna be loaded down with all the buffalo meat and hides they can carry."

"That's pretty sure," John answered.

"Wonder if we'll see any Blackfoot," Dan commented.

"We could," John answered.

From the village the hunting party traveled down the Bitterroot Valley a few miles, and then passed around a small mountain and reached the Clark Fork of the Columbia River. In September, the water in the river was rather low, and very blue. The stream was about fifty yards wide, and quite swift as it flowed between shores of gravel, sand bars, and four-foot sod banks. Occasionally there were small rapids.

The sky was blue, and it was a pleasant trip as the Indians and trappers traveled southeastward up the Clark Fork for seventy miles. Very little noise was made by the group as they moved along. Only a dull thudding of the horses hooves, the sounds of breathing, a slight rustle of a travois or pack, and an occasional quiet conversation by the Indians was heard. Even the dogs were seldom noisy. The passing of the Indians was seen, but seldom heard. Elk or deer sometimes stood watching, and then bounded into the trees. In the quiet air, the chirping or singing of birds, the honking of a few flights of geese passing over, sometimes the howl of a coyote, or maybe the bugling of an elk was heard and enjoyed by the people.

Through the wide, shallow canyon and the valley of the Clark Fork River, the tree leaves and bushes were turning yellow.

As the trappers rode along in the column of Flatheads, Dan asked, "What kind of trees are the ones that have needles instead of leaves, but that turn yellow like the aspen and cottonwood do?"

John answered, "They sure show up against the green pines. I asked John Owen what they are, and he said they're tamaracks. They'll drop their needles in a few weeks. They're sure different."

When they reached the mouth of the Little Blackfoot River, the party wound its way eastward along the valley and hills to a pass over the Continental Divide. At the top of the pass, the Indians and trappers smiled as they looked eastward with anticipation beyond a beautiful scene of tree and meadow-splotched mountain slopes, into a twenty-mile wide valley along the Missouri River. That was their destination, the land of the buffalo.

When they reached the valley, they encamped near the Missouri River, and Dan said, "Well, here's the Missouri, the same river that runs near where we came from. It was sure a long ways to this end of it. Looks a lot smaller here, too."

"Looks a lot bluer, too," John answered.

For the next week, the trappers watched Chief Grizzly Standing organize his buffalo hunt. He used a method that had been successful for generations. Strict rules were observed to avoid alarming the buffalo in the area. No buffalo hunting, gunfire, or barking dogs were allowed. Only hunting of game with bow and arrow near camp was allowed.

A place was chosen where it would be the best to trap many buffalo.

The trap could only be used once because buffalo would not enter it again if it had the smell of blood.

Two miles away, a narrow part of a long, dry gulch was found with sides too deep and steep for a buffalo to climb. The part chosen for the trap was under two hundred feet wide and was about four hundred feet long, with a more narrow place at each end of the trap. Across each end a strong barrier was built of logs, rocks, and poles. At one end a forty-foot opening was left in the barrier. Everyone helped bring poles and rocks. Fallen trees were dragged from as far as the river. Logs and poles for closing the opening were laid against the barrier fence.

One warm day Jake wiped his brow and exclaimed, "We've pulled a hell of a lot of logs from the river bottoms with our horses."

"Well, they're makin' a hell of a big trap," John answered.

Dan asked, "Wouldn't it be better if they'd just go shoot the buffalo?"

John answered, "I don't think the Indians could get as many that way. Maybe they don't have enough gunpowder or arrows."

Ahead of the trap, one-half mile of a more wide, shallow part of the gulch was fenced along both sides for three hundred yards, and then on just one side for a ways farther. The long fence was not as strong as the barrier at the trap because it was only used to guide the buffalo into the trap, and not to hold them.

After the trap was completed, the trappers watched the medicine man plant a small mast in the far end of the trap with charms on it to lure the buffalo into the trap. His special charms were a streamer of buffalo hide, a buffalo skull, and the tails of two buffalo. Each morning at dawn, the medicine man beat his tom-tom and intoned his songs of incantations to conjure the spirit of the buffalo.

The chief had runners to go out for ten miles or more and report to him daily where buffalo were grazing and which direction they were moving. From beyond the herd they allowed the buffalo to see them at times to slowly turn the buffalo toward the trap.

Finally, all was ready. Many buffalo were within five to ten miles from the trap, and the northwest breeze was blowing the scent of the Indians away from the buffalo. The cool breeze would dry the buffalo meat.

Chief Grizzly Standing gave the order, the horsemen mounted their ponies, and the footmen armed with bows, lances, and guns took their positions strung at intervals beyond the end of the fences. The horsemen were spaced even farther out, and the two slanting lines formed a wide funnel two miles long that reached to the barriers at the trap.

All men, women, and children who were capable of the task were used to form the lines.

One single Indian man was sent on a fast horse to meet the buffalo. His horse was partly enveloped in buffalo robes. They approached the herd against the breeze with great precaution, and the Indian wrapped a buffalo robe around himself. At a hundred paces from the buffalo, the Indian made the plaintive sounds of a buffalo calf. As if by enchantment, the sounds of a calf attracted the buffalo herd. The Indian repeated the sounds at intervals as he moved toward the trap, and with raised heads the buffalo slowly started to follow. As the Indian moved farther away, the concerned buffalo began to follow at a trot. Keeping the same distance from the buffalo, the Indian continued the sounds of a calf as he rode faster. Soon a large herd of hundreds of buffalo was galloping behind the Indian toward the opening of the funnel. As the herd passed by the waiting horsemen, the horsemen closed in behind the buffalo. Their shouts and scent caused the excited buffalo to stampede toward the trap! At a full gallop, the rider in the lead veered to the side before they reached the fence, and the Indians at the sides closed in behind the buffalo! The stampeding buffalo could not turn back, and they were forced into the trap. Quickly, those who had been hiding on the top edge of the gully rushed down to close the opening of the trap. Some of the leading buffalo were crushed against the barrier at the far end of the trap as the herd stalled!

When the trap was almost completely closed, a buffalo cow turned back and charged the barrier! As the cow jumped the barrier, an Indian boy about sixteen years old was run over by the buffalo cow! He was violently knocked unconscious, but the opening was quickly closed by others before more buffalo reached the barrier.

Some Indian women cared for the injured boy, and the men started killing the trapped buffalo. From the top of the gully, they used bow and arrows, lances, and guns to kill the terrified animals as they ran and milled around in the trap. Squaws and children even killed some at the edge with large rocks. Some of the smaller buffalo were trampled down by the larger ones.

Buffalo do not bellow as cattle do, but grunt an *aah* sound, and make a terrific noise when they blow air through their nostrils from a huge set of lungs. With the firing of guns, the excited shouts of the Indians, and the barking of dogs, it was a noisy, terrible pandemonium as the buffalo were slaughtered.

The trappers used their muzzle-loaders to kill all of the buffalo they could as quickly as possible. They did not like the pitiful slaughter, and they were relieved when the agony of the buffalo was finished.

John declared, "I wouldn't want to join a hunt like this again. It's such a big, violent, bloody slaughter, that I just don't like to watch it."

Jake commented, "This is the old way that the Indians have always had to use, but when they get more horses maybe they won't have to do it this way."

Dan added, "I suppose this is the best way they have to kill a lot of buffalo."

When the excitement of the slaughter was over, the Indians worked hard to slice and dry the meat. Over two hundred buffalo, counting their big calves, had been killed, but the tribe would use every bit of the meat, the marrow from the bones, some of the insides, and the hides. Their dogs would clean up the rest. In a few days, nothing was left as waste.

While the buffalo meat dried for a week, the trappers rode with a band of Flathead braves each day to hunt buffalo for camp meat. Only a few miles from camp, the dark splotches of many small, wandering herds of about a hundred buffalo could be seen across the wide prairie between the small mountain ranges.

"This is the kind of hunting I'd rather do," Dan commented.

The hunters could spot a few choice buffalo, and then carefully slip up a draw or ride around a small hill to within gun-firing distance, where each man shot one buffalo before the herd ran away.

For more excitement, they sometimes rode into a scattered herd, and with horses and buffalo at a full gallop, they shot the buffalo as they rode a short distance from the sides of the galloping buffalo. The trappers could only shoot one buffalo on each chase with their muzzle-loader muskets. It was the same for the Indians who had muzzle-loaders, but those who used a bow and arrow sometimes killed another one.

"A man can enjoy hunting a few buffalo this way," Dan commented.

"It's the best way, and we get better meat and hides," John agreed. "We'll use some of these hides for robes."

Dan praised his horse, "Sonny is sure a good horse for hunting buffalo. He's fast enough to stay right with any of 'em."

Jake added, "Some pretty good horses can't keep up with a fast buffalo."

After a week, the Indians and trappers started back to the Bitterroot. They all felt their hunting trip had been a good one, and they had a good supply of meat and hides.

32

While riding beside the trappers, Chief Grizzly Standing said, "Now you see how we get many buffalo to take back for winter meat. Because of the Blackfoot, we can not live here and get buffalo every day. We take many buffalo back in one trip. It is the best way."

Except for Grizzly Standing and forty warriors, each Indian's horse had to carry a load of buffalo meat and hides, or pull a loaded travois.

Jake said, "They can't use all the horses to carry buffalo meat. Some of the warriors gotta be able to fight Blackfoot with their horses, and some gotta be scouts."

John replied, "I hope they have enough horses to use against the Blackfoot if they see us."

They followed the same trail home, and the weather stayed dry and became a little cooler.

Just a short distance down the west side of the divide, the trail passed through a long meadow and into the pine trees again. One hundred and fifty yards into the trees, the leaders came upon their two scouts who had been riding only one-eighth of a mile ahead. Both had been killed with Blackfoot arrows and scalped! Their horses were missing.

At the front of the column of Flatheads, the chief and over a dozen warriors stopped where the bodies were lying. Quickly, the chief said, "Turn back to the others, this is a trap! The Blackfoot will come!"

At that instant, many screaming Blackfoot warriors attacked the rear of the Flathead column! Nearly all of them were in the meadow. The Blackfoot rode along the column of Flatheads, shouting war whoops and shooting with guns and arrows in a blazing attack.

To Dan there looked to be more than a hundred war-painted Blackfoot warriors on horses. The Flathead horsemen attacked the Blackfoot with arrows, then lances, war clubs, and tomahawks. The footmen used one shot from their muskets, then many were not able to reload, and used lances or tomahawks. Much of the fighting was hand-to-hand combat.

Standing on the ground, Dan and his pardners were shooting, then reloading their muskets while fighting off Blackfoot with pistols. Dan watched as a dozen or more Blackfoot charged toward the white trappers. The hideously painted warriors rode straight at the trappers with guns pointing or bows ready.

Dan said loudly, "They seem to want to get us more than they do the Flatheads!"

33

Charging thirty feet from Dan, a war-painted Blackfoot leaned to his right, pointing his musket past his running pony's neck as he aimed at Dan with intense purpose in his eyes. Their eyes met as they both drew aim, but Dan's musket shot was a split-second faster and blazed through the right side of the Indian's chest.

As the Indian fell, his horse veered away in front of Dan, but three more Blackfoot were only a few feet behind in their charge. Dan reached for his pistol, but he could see the lead Indian's lance would get him first! John's shot brought him down just in time! Dan's pistol shot killed the second one, and Jake's musket hit the third one. All four Indians were piled in front of Dan. The others had turned toward the nearby Flatheads.

That was the last charge in a deadly battle that had lasted only a few minutes. After that second sweep along the Flathead column, the Blackfoot rode away.

Angrily Dan said, as he nodded toward the nearby dead Blackfoot, "Damn them! They were all tryin' to kill me at the same time!"

"They wanted that wavy-haired scalp of a white man to hang on their scalp pole," advised Jake. "They were afraid to take mine."

"Yeah, they probably were afraid they couldn't cut through that tough old grizzled scalp of yours!" Dan answered, but then he cooled down and laughed.

John said, "We've let your hair get too long, and they saw it."

"Then you better cut it again," Dan said.

Jake exclaimed, "Keeps a fella pretty busy this morning, just tryin' to stay alive, don't it?"

"Some didn't," John replied.

The Blackfoot left a bloody scene on that green mountain meadow. Many Indians lay sprawled as they had fallen, and would never rise again.

There were fourteen dead Flathead Indians, and fifteen dead Blackfoot. Some of the wounded Blackfoot who rode away would surely die, and some of The Flathead's wounded would probably die.

"Looks like the Flatheads paid a terrible price for buffalo meat on this trip," John stated.

"An' the Blackfoot paid a big price tryin' to stop 'em," Jake said.

Chief Grizzly Standing rode by the trappers holding a fresh scalp, and said, "I see you killed some Blackfoot. That is good. They took four horses. You still have your horses."

John answered, "Our horses didn't go away. Some good boys helped hold our horses."

In spite of their grief, the Flatheads soon caught their horses that were loose, straightened up their loads, and were ready to leave. Because of his bruised legs and some broken ribs, the Indian boy who had been run over by the buffalo cow had ridden this far on a travois loaded with hides. Now, he insisted that he would walk, so that the ones who were badly wounded by the Blackfoot could ride. The Flatheads carried their dead almost to the Clark Fork River before they placed them on burial platforms. There were no more incidents as the Flatheads traveled home.

When the trappers reached Fort Owen, John told Owen, "The Flatheads had a bad battle on the pass with the Blackfoot. We counted fourteen dead Flatheads and fifteen Blackfoot."

Owen replied, "That's too bad. The Flatheads need the buffalo, but they always get some of their people killed."

In November and early December, the trappers worked throughout much of the Bitterroot Valley trapping mink, marten, weasel, and muskrat, but no beaver. They trapped along the Bitterroot and its tributary creeks.

One day John said, "We didn't catch much yet. Let's go talk to John Owen about what's north of here."

Jake agreed, "Yup, let's do. The early trappers have cleaned out most of the beaver here. I'm sure there'd be a few at the head of the creeks, but we really should leave 'em for seed."

At the fort, when John asked about trapping farther north, Owen answered, "There may be more beaver on past Flathead Lake, but you'll get along trapping for smaller pelts. Beaver price is low since the city fellas back east started wearin' silk hats. Country people still wear beaver hats, but the price is low."

Jake said, "Well pardners, we might as well have a look up at the Flathead after we sell Owen these pelts."

"I'll pay all I can for 'em. Jim Bridger comes up about May or June with a pack train and buys pelts from me. He comes from Fort Bridger or sends some men."

Dan asked, "Can they get through the Indians all right?"

"Half a dozen men come up. Some just for a look. They're well armed, and don't usually have much trouble. From his fort, Bridger sends the pelts down the Oregon Trail to market."

The trappers sold their pelts to John Owen, then rode north over a low pass into a wide basin bordered on the east by the white peaks of the Mission Mountains. Three days from Fort Owen, they came to Flathead Lake.

The smoothly pointed peaks of the high, snow clad Mission Mountains, and the Swan Range, rose abruptly behind the immense blue lake that was still unfrozen.

As they gazed at the scene, Dan said, "We've seen a lot of pretty places, but I'll be surprised if we ever see any place prettier than this one."

That winter, they trapped on the Little Bitterroot, west of Flathead Lake, and then in the area north of the lake. They found that the weather on the west side of the divide brought them quite a lot of gray skies, wet snow, and little wind. A few storms brought the temperature below zero.

When they returned to Fort Owen in the spring, they had enough furs to buy the supplies they needed and still get a little cash.

John said, "We didn't make a lot of money trappin', but we bought all the supplies we needed, so how could we want more? If we had more, we'd just have to pack it around with us."

In the summer, as they visited with the Flathead Indians, they learned a lot about the geography of the surrounding areas, and even more distant areas to the east and west. They learned where many of the mountain passes were located.

In August, the three men were in an area about thirty miles northwest of Flathead Lake prospecting for gold. There had not been a general rain in these western mountains since early June. The small mountains in this region were densely covered with pine, fir, and spruce trees. The underbrush, cones, and pine needles had become extremely dry. For several weeks the oppressive heat and haze had settled down over the area. The haze was from forest fires in the western territories and Canada.

Just the small amount of exercise from scratching around a little with shovels and picks examining rocks made the men too hot to continue working.

One day, Dan said, "Down in these tree-covered, small valleys there's not a stir of air to help cool us. I sure didn't expect it to ever get this hot and dry in these western mountains."

John answered, "If it don't cool down and rain good, this creek will soon be dry. There's barely enough to water the horses now. Looks like

36

this is usually a pretty good little creek, but this heat has been terrible. I never saw anything like it before."

For several days, a few light afternoon thundershowers had been passing over with a few minutes of rain and several bolts of lightning. One night, there was a red glow along the northern sky. The next morning, Jake exclaimed, "The smoke's gettin' thicker all the time."

That afternoon, great billowing thunderheads passed over all through the sky. A few clouds poured rain for a short time and some only sprinkled, but there were dozens of lightning flashes in every direction. Smoke appeared thicker in the northern sky again, and that night there was a great ominous red glow in the western sky.

Jake said, "We could be in a lot of trouble. I think that fire's comin' our way!"

John answered, "I guess we should've left here yesterday, after all of the thunderstorms and lightning."

"I don't know how we can possibly go now in the dark of night," Dan said. "There's no moon and the smoke's so thick, there's no light at all."

Before dawn, boiling clouds of smoke were rolling over them from the west. They were packed and ready to go at the first faint light.

John said, "We better head south for that lake we passed coming here. It's nearly four miles back. Sure hope we can make it."

"Can't think of a worse fate if we don't," Jake said. "We better not make any more mistakes now. We'll have to lead our horses down this game trail until it gets lighter. Can't take a chance of breakin' a leg."

As Dan led the way, the suspense of walking along in the dark was bad. He was anxious to gallop away from the fire. While leading the horses, they were apt to step on a man's heels. It was a strain on the men's patience when they could faintly hear the roar of flames and still had to walk along carefully down the rough, uneven trail. Occasionally, small fallen trees had to be crossed in the dark, and it slowed them down.

After fifteen more minutes, when it was just about unbearable to go slow any longer, John said, "It's light enough, let's mount and ride slow."

Soon, the trail was less steep as it neared the floor of the narrow valley. They were now able to break into a trot, but they were only halfway to the lake. It seemed they were losing the race as dense smoke swirled over them!

John said, "We've got to go faster."

Soon after they reached the narrow valley floor, sparks and fire

37

brands were falling on them, but they were able to gallop across the narrow meadows and only had to slow down a little on the trail through the small groves of trees.

Ahead of them now stood a half-mile-long grove of thick pines and aspen on flat ground, and cut by a fifty-foot-wide swath of meadow. A wall of orange flame was nearing the grove as they entered it!

John shouted, "Race for it!"

In a high run they raced for their lives through the narrow meadow as the wall of flame raced toward them across the grove of trees! Just as they broke out of the grove into the edge of a wide slough by the lake, the heat blast and flame crossed the trail behind them with a terrific roar! It was a fire storm that barely missed them as it arched across the narrow meadow and ignited more trees.

Jake said, "If we'd been a minute later, we'd be dead!"

As they trotted around the mile long lake, the air became better. Near the lake were hundreds of wild animals that had avoided the fire. The men watched as the fire burned away from them in a northeasterly direction.

John said, "If we'd waited 'til daylight to leave, we'd never have made it." The country's all burning north of here!"

Dan exclaimed, "It was awful goin' so slow in the dark, but it kept us from having an accident and gettin' caught in the fire. I hope we'll never get close to a forest fire again. This was a bad summer to be in this forest."

"Hope that's the closest I ever get to Hell," exclaimed Jake. "I said a prayer comin' down here."

"Amen," said Dan and John.

Then Dan said, "It's a good thing we tied our packs on extra good; we didn't lose any of them."

When their horses fast breathing had subsided and the men were dismounted, Dan patted Sonny's neck, and while rubbing him down, said, "Sonny, you saved my life again. You're the best horse a man ever had. I'll always take good care of you. Yes sir, I sure think a lot of this horse.

"I think it'll be all right to water and feed our horses, have some breakfast and rest for a while down at the end of the lake," suggested John. "I don't see any more fire coming this way, but it's gonna keep burning real bad northeast of here. I doubt it if any of these wild animals will bother us. A lot of them need a rest, too. They'll leave in a little while, after they drink. I'm afraid a lot of animals got caught in that fire, the poor things."

After resting, the men started to Fort Owen.

At Fort Owen that fall, the trappers told John Owen they'd like to try trapping in the Gallatin Basin.

John Owen told them, "The Blackfoot often hunt there. Their home is farther north, from the Sun River clear into Canada, but they like to hunt, steal horses, take scalps, and try to control the Gallatin Basin. They're a dangerous tribe. I'd like for you to stay in the Bitterroot. It's safer here."

John said, "We can try it in the Gallatin. If we have to, we can go on to the Yellowstone."

"Yes, it's safer there with the Crow. They're friendly to white men. There's a basin north of the Yellowstone and the Musselshell Rivers. You might want to try it sometime. North of the Musselshell is a range called the Big Snowy Mountains. I've heard the basin on the north side may be a pretty good place. Some of the Indians are friendly, but the Blackfoot go there sometimes."

"Well, a fella's always gotta be careful wherever he is," John answered. "We'll just have to stay out of sight of the Blackfoot."

Just before the first little snow, the trappers left for the Gallatin country. They followed directions the Flatheads had given them. From the Bitterroot, they rode eastward up Skalkaho Creek.

Near Skalkaho Pass, Dan said, "There's that high waterfall the Flatheads told us about. Must be close to a hundred feet high. Sure a pretty one."

"Yup, its purty all right," Jake agreed.

"Sun sure makes it bright," John mentioned.

From Skalkaho Pass, the three pardners continued eastward through mountainous country for two days until they came to a wide prairie.

"It's just the way the Flatheads told us, all right. Now we'll head south for that other pass," John said.

When they crossed Deer Lodge Pass, Dan said, "We've crossed the Continental Divide again, like John Owen said we would. That divide must be crooked as a snake. We're on the east side again."

In two more days they reached the lower Big Hole River.

"Well, we sure did a lot of wandering around through mountains, along creeks, and over mountain passes to get here," exclaimed John. "It's a good thing the Flatheads told us how to get through there, or we could've wandered around, finding a harder way through, probably over some higher mountains."

"It was a pretty mountain country, though. It had lots of meadows with deer and moose, and big herds of elk. I see some higher mountains east of here," Dan offered.

They crossed the Big Hole River, and rode on eastward to the wide Beaverhead River Valley.

"Were in Bannock Indian country again," Jake advised. "I'm glad they're friendly, 'cause it looks like the edge of a village there in the cottonwoods along the river, and I see some braves on their horses just startin' this way. I hope some of 'em know a little English, 'cause what few Indian words I know, usually seem to be for a different kind o' Indians."

The ten braves that met them were dressed only in breech clout and moccasins. Their leader and Jake both raised a hand in a friendly greeting.

The Bannock spoke broken English, "Why you come to Bannock country?"

"We come to the Bannocks in peace. We go to Crow country from Bitterroot. We want to trap in the Gallatin country, and then find the Crow Indians," Jake spoke, and already, John and Dan were approaching the Bannocks with small offerings of beads. The beads were accepted by the braves with friendly nods.

Their leader spoke, "Watch out for Blackfoot. Crow our friends. Come, time to eat moose," and the leader led them to camp.

There were over a hundred tepees in the village, where the white trappers were met with friendly looks from the curious Bannocks. They were taken to the lodge of Chief Four Bears.

After they met the chief, John handed him a small sack of tobacco and said, "This tobacco is present for Chief Four Bears."

They could see the chief was happy with the tobacco, and he said, "We smoke peace pipe."

They sat in a circle in front of the chief's lodge, and passed the pipe around the circle with a dozen braves, the trappers and the chief. They used the new sack of tobacco, and passed the pipe around the circle twice with much fanfare.

John thought, this tobacco is really appreciated, and he was rather amused.

These Bannocks also spoke some broken English. The trappers explained how they had come from the Bitterroot, then some of the braves spoke of mountains and elk in that area. A few stories of moose hunting incidents were also told. The trappers were then treated to a feast on moose meat, flavored with what seemed to be some kind of berries. Huckleberries and wild plums were also a tasty part of the meal.

The trappers stayed in the village that night. Before they left the next morning, Chief Four Bears cautioned them, "Be careful in Gallatin country. Blackfoot make raids there. They want to take the land. When you see Crow, tell them where we are. We live close to Crow long time ago."

He pointed southwest, "Follow creek two days to pass. After pass, follow river north to end of high mountain. What white man call Gallatin is there."

The trappers traveled up the Ruby River, then crossed a pass and found the Madison River between the Tobacco Root Mountains and the high Madison range. They found the Madison-Gallatin Basin at the north end of the Madison range. To them, it looked to be fifty miles wide and was surrounded by seven high mountain ranges.

"I didn't know there were so many mountain ranges in the West," Dan said. "Everywhere we go we find range after range of mountains. Before we came here, I just couldn't picture how these mountains looked."

"We've traveled a long ways to find this high, wild basin," John said. "For a long time, I've heard what a fabulous place it is. They say this is the area where the Louis and Clark expedition found the Three Forks of the Missouri River. All three rivers meet somewhere in the basin, where they form the Missouri River. That would be real interesting to see, but we don't dare cross this wide basin. The Blackfoot would be sure to discover us. We'll have to stay near the mountains along the south edge of the basin, and look for places to trap."

"With so many creeks that run out of these mountain canyons, there should be some good trapping left here," Jake surmised. "Prob'ly, the Blackfoot kept the trappers from getting enough time to catch all the beaver."

"This would be a good place to stay a few years, if we could keep the Blackfoot from finding us," Dan said. "There's a lot of good grass and buffalo here, and it looks like a great place for beaver."

Beginning in October, the trappers spent a month carefully staying away from the Blackfoot Indians by trapping in the most remote, small mountain creeks. Dozens of small creeks ran from the Gallatin and Madison Mountain ranges, and joined the Gallatin and Madison Rivers. In the creeks, they found dozens of beaver dams and ponds. The tracks in the snow showed there were also many other fur-bearing animals.

The trappers did not travel across the wide basin where their tracks were sure to be found by the Blackfoot. They did not travel any more than was necessary. Snares were used to take wild game instead of a musket because the sound of a shot would carry so far. Very dry wood without any pitch was burned so there was very little smoke from their campfires. Campfires were only used when there was a breeze to scatter the smoke. Some days, the men had to do without a fire and get by with eating dry jerky. In a week, the men had taken some pelts, but they were uneasy and always vigilant.

One day, beside a small tree-lined creek above a beaver pond in the Madison Valley, John was preparing to set a trap. While chopping a stick to anchor the trap, John heard quick steps behind him. He turned and met a surprise attack by a lone Indian with a raised tomahawk! John blocked the striking tomahawk with his own ax. Both drew knives, but John was the quickest. With one deep thrust of John's knife into the Indian's chest, the Indian lay dead!

John was thankful there had been no gunfire to alert other Indians who must be in this area. With rawhide strings, John tied rocks to the body of the young Indian brave, and sunk it in a very brushy part of the creek. He hoped this would slow down a pursuit by the Indians the brave must have been with. He thought the Indian was a Blackfoot. It could be a few days or a long time before the dead Indian's fate would be known to his companions, but they could soon track him to where the fight took place. The Blackfoot would start tracking the young Indian when they decided he was too long overdue.

John took his horses and traps and soon found Jake and Dan. After telling them what had happened, Jake told them, "It counts more coups for a brave to kill an enemy without any help, so that must be why he was hunting alone. Your scalp would've made him a great warrior. Now we'd better sneak out of here the best way we can."

John stated, "When they find that dead Indian, they'll sure start hunting us. When he never comes back, they're goin' to be damn suspicious."

Jake answered, "They're gonna be watching this country real close for a long time. We'd better get a snow to cover our tracks, or we may not get away."

The trappers packed up and rode down the valley along the edge of the Madison Mountains. They camped that night, well hidden near the base of a mountain. Although the clouds were threatening, it failed to snow by the next morning.

42

Jake looked at the clouds, "Without a snow, I don't know of any way we can be sure to escape the Blackfoot. When they find the dead one, they'll follow the faintest tracks until they catch us. We can't reload these muzzle-loaders fast enough to kill more than two each if they're far away, and they'll sneak up on us so close we wouldn't get over one each."

"The Blackfoot are just as cunning as the Sioux were when they jumped us," said Dan, "We may not have a chance to kill even one."

"I wish that young Blackfoot warrior hadn't been so anxious to get my scalp," remarked John.

"Maybe we better cut your hair shorter," Dan laughed.

As they hurried north, they saw several bunches of buffalo grazing on the wide prairies between the mountain ranges. "These big herds of buffalo are the reason so many tribes come here to hunt," Jake said.

On the prairie half-a-mile away, a small bunch of buffalo suddenly started running. Some wolves were after them. The men could see the wolves soon had one buffalo down, and the rest of the small herd continued to run for a mile.

"Hey," exclaimed John, "that bunch of wolves just gave me an idea when they stampeded that little bunch of buffalo. I wonder if we could ride in the middle of a buffalo stampede without gettin' killed? They'd sure trample out our tracks."

"Damn likely trample us out, too!" expressed Jake.

"What a hell of an awful idea!" Dan swore, "But it just might work. Could be better than gettin' caught by a bunch of Blackfoot."

"Well, Hell, if you want to ride in a buffalo stampede, I'm willing to try it too," agreed Jake.

"When I mentioned it, I thought it was a crazy idea, but I'm glad both of you like it so well," John smiled. "We're goin' to have to have a lot of luck though. Let's ride on and find a big herd."

Jake grinned and shook his head, "This sounds like an exciting day. It's a good thing we've got some real fast horses."

Dan suggested, "We'd better tighten the packs on the horses."

John nodded, "We can't fire our guns for the Blackfoot to hear, but I'll bet we can start a stampede all right. Maybe we should keep two of the pack horses between us, and let Dan lead with Sonny and his pack horse."

After a while John pointed ahead, "Well, there's our big herd of buffalo; must be five hundred of 'em. We're lucky; there's miles of smooth prairie here, so maybe we won't fall."

"Get a big herd like that started and they'll run a long time," Jake advised.

"Let's hope they don't notice us too close when we get in the middle of 'em," Dan added.

As they rode up to the herd, John said, "Better hope they run pretty loose, and don't bunch up too tight. Now, lets go!"

The men started whooping, screaming and waving their hats as they galloped toward the buffalo herd. The herd turned tail and started running. As the horses ran into the herd, the whole herd stampeded.

From then on, it was even a worse ride than Dan had expected. The horses had to run at nearly full speed to hold their places. There was a rumbling roar of hooves. For miles, bobbing backs and heads of buffalo were all that Dan could see as the herd ran on and on through the dust and stench. Sharp buffalo horns bobbed menacingly only inches from Dan's legs and Sonny's sides. Soon, buffalo and horses were breathing very hard. Sonny was sweating and buffalo were slobbering, but still the herd pounded on! Dan wondered how many more buffalo had been swept into the stampede. His mouth was dirt-caked, his throat dry and his eyes watering. Dan prayed that no horse or buffalo would fall, or dozens would die in the pileup! He hoped his pardners following him were all right, and wondered if this stampede was a mistake.

After what seemed forever, the herd slowed and soon stopped. The buffalo paid slight attention as the men rode their horses quietly to the front of the herd. The horses' and buffalo's dust-covered sides were heaving, but all of the horses were still together. The buffalo had never crowded the horses enough to cause a fall.

After the men had walked their horses a quarter of a mile beyond the herd, John said, "Before we stopped, I had begun to wonder if we should've chose to fight the Blackfoot."

Jake answered, "To fall in that stampede would've been a fast death. To fall fightin' Blackfoot may not be so quick a death."

Dan said, "It would be worse to be captured and tortured."

The men rode slowly a half-mile down to the Madison River where they cooled and rubbed down their horses before they let them drink. The horses' breathing had become normal, so the men did not think they had wind-broken them.

Dan patted Sonny and told him, "I'm sorry I had to treat you like that, Sonny, but it's a good thing you're strong enough to stand it. Now you've saved my life again."

John commented, "It seemed like an hour that we ran with the buffalo herd, but it was prob'ly fifteen or twenty minutes, and about five miles. There must be over two thousand buffalo in that herd now! We could rest awhile, and then move on to the edge of the mountains. This big herd will rest and drink longer than we will, then they'll leave in every direction and trample out the tracks that we leave now."

Jake agreed, "Blackfoot won't find our tracks for a long time. We oughta be safe for quite awhile."

That evening they rode far and camped near the north end of the Madison Mountains.

At dawn the next morning, where the high peaks of the Madison Range trailed down to low mountains and hills at the north end of the range, the men wove their way over a low pass and dropped down to the Gallatin Canyon. They followed the river several miles northward, and then left the river and rode eastward. They carefully chose a route along the north base of the Gallatin Mountain Range where they crossed several creeks as they rode around the south edge of the Gallatin Basin. From high ridges, the trappers watched their back trail and could not see any signs of being followed by the Blackfoot.

Finally, where a small creek ran from the mountain foothills at the east side of the basin, Jake said, "We just might be safe here for awhile. We must be fifty miles from where you left the dead Indian."

They trapped here for over a week, but they spent more time watching from the groves of trees on the hillsides for approaching Indians than they wanted to. Someone always had to be on guard, and all of them had to be constantly alert. They did not want to be surprised.

John commented, "No amount of pelts could be worth this risk. The reputation of the Blackfoot is the reason this country still has quite a few beaver in it. We'd better head for Crow country."

Dan agreed, "We'd enjoy living in this place more if we didn't have to be watchin' over our shoulders all the time. We've heard the Crow Indians are friendly, and live in a real good country. I think we'd like it there."

They gathered their traps, and early the next morning they were leaving the area. From a high hill they saw about twenty-five Blackfoot coming their way. They'd soon find the trappers tracks.

John declared, "When they reach the upper end of the valley, they'll find our tracks all over the place where we've been trappin'. They'll be after us like a swarm of hornets. They've been lookin' all over the basin for us. Since they must have found the dead one, it will be gruesome if they catch us. We've got to hurry."

Jake replied, "The clouds are hiding the east pass, so it's startin' to snow up there. We're far enough ahead so we can lead 'em into the east pass, and as the snow covers our tracks, we'll give 'em the slip by ridin' southward over the low mountains to the other pass that leads to the Yellowstone."

They rode into the pass that led eastward from the Gallatin Basin. As they gained altitude, they found it was snowing there.

Jake smiled and exclaimed, "Our trick is workin'. The snow's coverin' our tracks." So they rode out of the pass and over a low mountain to the other pass that leads to the Yellowstone River.

The pass they followed was not terribly high, but this north end of the Gallatin Range was an area of heavy snowfall. They reached the summit in a half day, and the new snow was already six inches deep.

Jake grinned and said, "The Blackfoot will get no scalps today."

As they rode down the pass, the snow nearly stopped. When they reached Paradise Valley on the Yellowstone, there was only an inch of snow. They were in Crow country now and had probably lost the Blackfoot.

The following day, they found the tracks of some Indian ponies leading south up the Yellowstone River in Paradise Valley. They followed the tracks, and in two hours came upon the tepees of the Crow village. The Crow were camped near the west base of the Absaroka Mountains beside a big, turbulent creek that came rushing down a canyon into the Yellowstone Valley. The Crow tepees complemented an incredibly beautiful scene of a forty-mile-long string of snow-tipped peaks, one down each side of the valley. The Absaroka Range stood on the east side of the valley, and the Gallatin Range on the west. The tranquil scene was a welcome sight to the trappers, who were weary of hiding.

John said, "If the Crow like us, this will be a good place for us."

Some Crow braves on horses met the trappers near the village. Each wore a buckskin clout, leggings, moccasins, and shirt. Jake gestured to them and said, "We come in peace. We would like to talk to your Chief."

One of the braves spoke good English. "I am Striking Hawk, a Crow warrior. We will take you to our chief, Red Bear."

When they met Chief Red Bear in his tepee, Jake said again, "We come in peace. We would like to be friends of the Crow."

The trappers then took a few presents from their packs; tobacco, a knife, beads, and a mirror. They gave them to Chief Red Bear. Chief Red Bear thanked them. As they talked, he appeared to be an intelligent, quiet, well-mannered chief.

He wore a buckskin suit very colorfully decorated with beads, quills, and elk teeth. He wore an eagle feather thrust horizontally at one side of his head. On the other side he wore white pelican feathers. Several articles, such as those used by medicine men, were apparent in his tepee. Jake continued, "We came on the Oregon Trail. We trapped on the Bitterroot. Not many beaver there now. Still mink and other pelts."

Dan said, "We saw Chief Four Bears on the Beaverhead."

Chief Red Bear answered, "The Bannocks are friends. They live too far away now. The Blackfoot between us cause much trouble."

John explained, "We learned how bad they are. We fought them with the Flatheads. We wanted to see the Yellowstone country of the Crow. The Blackfoot nearly caught us in the Pass from the Gallatin. While it snowed, we rode to the other pass. The snow covered our tracks."

Chief Red Bear nodded, "Winter is coming. When the Blackfoot lost you, they would start for their home in the Sun River land. That is where they should stay."

While they talked, he seemed friendly, and looked at Dan often. Dan said, "It looks like the Crow live in a good land. It has pretty mountains and rivers."

Chief Red Bear agreed, "Crow live in best land. We are Mountain Crow. We have many buffalo. Not as much beaver now, since the first trappers came. Enough beaver and other pelts for Crow. You are Crow's friend. You can trap in Crow country. It is time for Crow to move to Stillwater soon. Come with us."

That made the trappers smile. John thought there was a sense of power about this medicine man chief.

Striking Hawk then took the trappers to meet his parents, who were living in the Crow village. Along the way, he said to Dan, "That's a real good stud you're ridin'. He would be a good one to use in my herd."

As they were riding along, Dan took notice of Striking Hawk's handsome face, and his quick-moving, six-foot, athletic body. He was friendly, but looked to be a courageous warrior. They arrived at a large tepee. Striking Hawk said, "My white man name is Leo LaFountain. The man coming is my father, a French trader."

As the French trader arrived, he heartily greeted the trappers. Each person gave his own name.

The traders name was Louis LaFountain. Dan could see that he was about fifty years old, with dark hair graying at the edges. He was medium height, friendly to visit, and probably a sharp trader.

Soon he went to his tepee and brought out two women. He said, "This one is my wife. She is a Crow woman. Her name is Pretty Feather, and she is a pretty one."

"Yes, she is," John agreed.

Louis gestured, "And this one is our daughter. Her name is Lily. She is named for the wood lily, and they are both beautiful. Lily is seventeen years old."

The trappers again each gave their names.

Dan was surprised how pretty the two women were. Although Pretty Feather had to be somewhere in her forties, she was still a very attractive woman with medium-dark skin, black braided hair, black eyelashes, dark brown eyes, well-shaped features, and even white teeth.

Dan was amazed at the shocking beauty of the young woman, Lily. She was medium height, and had a well-blended, curvaceous body. Long, black braids of hair fell down in front of each shoulder to the curve of her breasts. Sunlight and shadows accentuated the delicately molded cheekbones, a very slightly arched nose, broad forehead and strong jaws. Dark, shining eyes and a glittering smile matched the ivory elk teeth that decorated her doeskin blouse. Her features were very Indian, smoothed into great beauty.

Dan was so struck by her beauty that he could hardly stop watching her, even though he felt embarrassed to stare. Once she looked directly at Dan and smiled. It thrilled his whole soul.

They learned that Louis LaFountain had an arrangement with the American Fur Company to buy furs for their trading post. Louis LaFountain was a French Canadian who had worked for the American Fur Company for twelve years in the northwest. When he wanted to leave, the company had semi-retired him as an agent with the Crow.

These things Louis explained to the trappers during their conversation. He also commented, "When you are selling your furs, I can help you get top price. Just tell the buyer at the trading post that you are selling your furs with Louis LaFountain as your agent."

Soon, Striking Hawk left for his own tepee. Then Louis explained, "My son's given name is Leo, but his Crow name is Striking Hawk. He was named that by the Crow because he strikes an enemy or an animal he is hunting with the speed of a striking hawk. He has a Crow wife and two children. He is one of the Crow's greatest warriors."

"I'm sure he's a very strong man and a great warrior," John agreed. "I'm glad he's our friend."

"And I'm glad that you have come to Crow country," exclaimed Louis. "I'm sure you'll like it here."

"Before the deep cold of winter comes, we'd like to go to the basin that John Owen told us about, then we'll return," Jake promised. "It's north of the Big Snowy Mountains."

The next day, the Crow and the trappers followed the bend of the Yellowstone River, and for a few days traveled slowly eastward along the north side of the pretty Absaroka Mountains. A trail was then followed southeast over a ridge of hills toward the Stillwater River. At the crest of the ridge, the Crow and trappers were then looking at a mighty range of peaks that continued on eastward from the Absaroka Range. They were seeing the great snow-capped peaks of the nearby Beartooth Mountains. The top of the huge peaks stood white with snow, far above timberline. Great canyons separated the peaks. It was a tremendous and majestic range of mountains.

From this high hill, the sharp-pointed Crazy Mountains were seen across the Yellowstone River, thirty miles northwest. A long, level, blue ridge of mountains was also visible one hundred miles north.

Louis pointed to the those mountains and said, "Big Snowy Mountains."

John asked, "Is that pretty good country?"

"Yes, I worked there buying furs a few years. The Big Snowy Mountains are not as high and don't have big peaks like the mountains here, but they are what they are called, big and snowy. North of them is a wide basin that is surrounded by more mountain ranges farther north and more ranges farther west. It is known to the Indians as Snow Hole, but white men call it Judith Basin. It has snow there when many other places are bare. It is pretty country, much like the Gallatin Basin. It has lots of moisture, high grass, and good creeks. Fifteen miles north of the Snowy Mountains is a big spring that forms a good creek. It would be interesting for you to see it, but you won't stay long. Several different bands of Indians live or pass through there. The Cree and Assiniboin are there the most, but they're not bad. Sometimes there are Blackfoot from the west or Sioux from the east. They seldom go there, but you'll need to be cautious. Like other places, there's still some beaver there."

49

Louis continued, "There's a big white trapper there who lives on Spring Creek. He's a little crazy. Other trappers call him 'Bonehead Ben'. Be careful of him."

John grinned and said, "Sounds like an interesting place, all right."

The Crow and trappers rode on for a day, and then reached the Stillwater River below the mouth of the huge Stillwater Canyon.

The Trappers had traveled close to the LaFountains on the way to the Stillwater River, so Dan and Lily had a chance to get better acquainted. To John and Jake it was plain to see that the young couple was strongly attracted to each other. They were shy, but after a few days, Dan and Lily managed to talk together several times. Dan thought Lily was the prettiest girl he had ever see, and it made him happy any time she smiled at him.

It was evident to the trappers that the Stillwater country where they camped with the Crow was abundant with elk, buffalo, and deer. For several days the trappers hunted with the Crow along the Stillwater and some of its tributaries.

One evening John said, "This looks like real good country to be living in, anywhere along the north side of these big mountains."

Jake answered, "It's full of game, and it looks like trappin' would be good."

Dan agreed, "It's really pretty here. I think I like it better here than anywhere we've been."

Jake grinned and said, "Yup, I'll bet you do," and John smiled at them and said, "I think we should have a look at that 'Snow Hole' country pretty soon, though."

Dan was not eager to leave, although he did want to see that country. He spent any time he could in the vicinity of the LaFountains, and used any excuse to say hello, or talk to Lily. Before they left, Dan made sure to say good-bye to Lily.

The trappers started for the area north of the Snowy Mountains early in November. From the Yellowstone River, they rode across the plains and on north through the low, pine-covered hills known as the Bull Mountains. They camped on the Musselshell River, and then rode over more shortgrass prairie with many bands of antelope and herds of buffalo. Near the east end of the Big Snowy Mountains, they led their pack horses over the high, tree-covered ridge between the Snowy Mountains and the Judith Mountains farther north. This twenty-mile-long ridge was the divide between the Judith Basin (Snow Hole) and the plains to the east. It had been very warm riding across the plains. Although these mountains were not high enough to hold much of last winter's snowbanks, it was noticeably cooler when they crossed the divide.

The men were riding down a trail along East Fork Creek that came down from a canyon in the Snowy Mountains. They came upon two white trappers camped near the creek.

Jake raised his hand in a gesture of peace and so did the strangers. As they stopped at the camp, Jake said, "Howdy, friends," and so did John and Dan. "Howdy," was the reply. "Get down and visit awhile. Haven't seen another white man for a long time, except for a strange one that lives down on Spring Creek.

"We've heard of him," said John.

The two trappers were young men, probably about thirty.

One said, "I'm Ned Green and this is Pete Miller."

"I'm Jake," he gestured, "And this is John and Dan," and they all shook hands.

"Did you come up the Missouri to Fort Union like we did?" Pete asked.

"No, we came up the Oregon Trail to the Bitterroot, and then came back this way to the Yellowstone," answered John.

Pete shrugged, "Sounds like a heck of a long way around, but on horses it's gotta be easier than what we did. We came up the Missouri on a flat-boat to Fort Union with a tough bunch. Seemed like we had to pull the damn thing with ropes from shore about half the time," and he raised his palms. " I still got calluses from it."

Ned offered, "If you're not in a hurry, stay around awhile and we'll do some visitin'."

John agreed, "We didn't come West to be in a big hurry."

Ned smiled, "It's only once in a blue moon that we even see a white man. Sometimes we see a half-breed we can talk to, or maybe an Assiniboin."

The young men seemed honest and friendly, so after visiting awhile the trappers pitched camp close by.

While they visited the next day, Ned said, "We had fair luck trapping along the Big Snowy Mountains, the Moccasin Mountains, and the Judith Mountains. There's still a few beaver along these creeks, but a trapper's got to get other pelts, too."

"We didn't go farther west to the Little Belt Mountains, " said Pete. "More chance there of meetin' Blackfoot, we've been told."

The five men spent the day swapping stories about where they had been. They were interested in learning all they could.

John told of the big mountains farther south, and of making friends with the Crow Indians. "It's easier for a man to keep his scalp where he's with friendly Indians."

Pete agreed, "We don't feel too safe here. Some of the Indians are friendly and some are not. A few half-breeds from Canada that are living here are friendly, and the Assiniboins are, but other Indians come through here on war parties, and we can only hide from them."

Ned said, "Big ole Bonehead Ben lives alone down below the Big Springs, a few miles above where the creeks meet. Sometimes he's friendly, and sometimes he's real sullen. We never trap closer than six or seven miles from him. He seems to act like this is all his land. No one knows where he's from, but I heard he's been here a long time. The Indians leave him alone 'cause he's kinda crazy. You oughta go see the Big Springs, though."

Next day, the three pardners left for the Big Springs. After they rode away, Jake said, "We'll look along the north side of the Big Snowy Mountains first. After we trap a month or two and start back to the Yellowstone, we can prob'ly find Ned and Pete over the divide on Flat Willow where they said they might be."

"They sure were fine fellas," John said.

They turned up Spring Creek, and soon saw Bonehead Ben's cabin. It was nice fall weather, and Ben was outside barbecuing some venison. They rode over and greeted Ben.

Ben seemed rather friendly, but suspicious. He was a great hulk of a man, about six-foot-three and 270 pounds. Ben was a little fat, and no doubt very strong. He had very homely, big features, and a low, flat skull above a thick, fat neck. The two sides of his head did not match, and somehow looked bent out of shape. He had a short beard, and thick, black, stringy hair about five inches long that must have been cut with his knife. His buckskin clothing was slick with grease, smoke, and dirt.

"Step down and have some venison," offered Ben. He took a big oversized hunting knife from his scabbard, cut off a chunk, and offered it to John.

John felt a little apprehensive as he took the piece of meat from Ben's huge, dirty hand, and with Ben's other hand holding such a wicked looking, long, sharp, knife, but he did not know how to refuse.

Jake grinned as John accepted the meat and thanked Ben, even though he sure hated to have his food handled with such a dirty hand.

It was Jake's and Dan's turn next, and they also accepted with reluctance as John partly suppressed a grin.

52

As they answered some questions of Ben's, Ben continued cutting off pieces of meat with his big knife and chewing them down as he talked. He offered more to the men, but John said, "Thanks, but we just ate down the creek a little ways."

Ben said, "This is good whitetail dry doe," and then, "Where ya goin'?"

"We just came by to see the Big Springs," replied Jake.

"It's purty, all right," and Ben paused, "You look like trappers. Where ya gonna trap?"

"We're just passin' through," answered Jake. "We haven't been here before, but we'll find someplace."

"Well, don't trap around here. This is mine," declared Ben. "You can get all the fish ya want, though. There's lots of big trout here."

John noticed that Ben had lots of beaver traps piled here and there, and hanging from tree limbs. He wondered why Ben had bought so many more than he could use. Ben also wore three rings on his fingers, and it was inconceivable that he would own such things. He was a very strange person, and John thought maybe even a bit sinister.

After a little talk about the weather, the men started to leave.

"You sure don't eat much," Ben said as they rode away.

When out of hearing, John said, "Well, damn, he's sure something."

Jake offered, "The poor devil didn't get a fair deal when it came to brains. By his looks, maybe he was hurt at birth. Wonder where he came from? Looks like about a quarter Indian."

"He lives about like a bear, and he smells about like one, too," suggested Dan. "Let's not stop there anymore for dinner," he laughed.

A little farther along they came to the Big Springs. It was a beautiful spring rising from several places. Two of the largest ponds, one higher than the other, were about sixty feet across and six or eight feet deep. The bubbling water rose from blue ponds with rock and sand bottoms. In some places, bright green patches of watercress reached to the surface of breaking bubbles. Along some edges, thick, dark-green mint leaves waft a clean, spicy aroma into the air. The green, grassy banks were nibbled short by deer, and the surrounding short meadow was nearly clear of brush. Dan was enchanted by the singing of the bubbling, rippling water at the outlet of the spring as they caught a few big glistening rainbow trout for lunch.

As they ate the trout, John said, "That big pine on the hillside by the upper spring is the biggest one I ever saw; must be a hundred feet high. Looks strange standin' above all the others; like something left over from another age."

The men and their horses relaxed at the spring for a few hours, then Jake said, "I expect we'd better move on. It's plain to see the Indians camp here a lot. Some of 'em might come and take our scalps."

They rode south toward the Snowy Mountains up the narrow Castle Creek Valley a few miles and camped by a small spring. John drank from the spring and said, "that's the best tastin' cold water I ever drank."

"There are lots of arrow heads and other Indian signs here, too," cautioned Jake, "But we'll take a chance and stay here tonight."

The next morning the men traveled about two miles to the end of the valley at the bottom of a big hill. They passed by two beaver ponds, and Dan remarked, "Maybe we'd better leave these beaver for Ben."

They climbed around patches of thorny brush to the top of a big mountain foothill that was near the Big Snowy Mountains. From there they could see most of the Judith Basin.

They looked into a basin reaching fifty miles from east to west, and over thirty miles north and south. Along the south side was the thirty-mile-long ridge of the Big Snowy Mountains. Big, rolling mountain foothills filled the land northward twenty miles to the pretty, rounded Judith and Moccasin Mountains along the north side of the basin. Another long, level, purple ridge of mountains, the Little Belt Mountains, crossed the western horizon. Sixty miles northwest, they could see the big square tip of the Highwood Mountains through the clear air. The western three-fourths of the basin was wide-sweeping, thick-grassed prairie.

The men gazed across the wide vista, and John exclaimed, "What a prairie. It has to be some of the best buffalo land on earth."

The next day they rode west near the Snowy Mountains, over big rounded foothills. Much of the hills had open meadows and much was covered with dark green pine, fir, and spruce trees. Because it was late Fall, the area was splotched with great patches of still-red thorn brush, mountain maple, chokecherry, and buckbrush. Some remaining yellow aspen leaves added to the splash of color. Dan exclaimed, "There's still lots of pretty color here."

A few days later as they were riding along, Jake was leading his pack horse around some thick patches of thorn brush, chokecherry brush, and aspen, followed closely by John and then Dan, each leading his pack horse. Suddenly, all hell broke loose! An unbelievably huge black bear raised up onto his hind legs at the edge of the brush just twenty feet from Jake's horse! The cross wind had prevented both from knowing of the other's presence. The bear looked seven feet tall. With terrified snorts, the horses reacted to the bear's growl.

Jake's horse reared to turn away as his pack horse jerked back against his lead rope. It jerked Jake's horse onto his side as the lead rope broke, and the pack horse fell back onto his rump against John's horse. Jake's horse missed landing directly on Jake, but his head struck Jake on the side of his face, which kept Jake down momentarily. Nearly the same thing happened to John and his two horses.

John held onto a rein as his horse fell and nearly rolled over him. Amid the snorting, squealing, and flying hooves, John's horse got up and started away, dragging John holding a rein. The horse was so scared that he paid no attention to John's repeated "Whoa! Whoa!" He dragged John over a low thorn bush, grass, and rocks for over a hundred feet before John could stop him and get on him!

Sonny had whirled away so fast with Dan, that he broke the pack horses' lead rope. Dan could not stop Sonny before he had run a hundred yards.

When Dan turned back, the bear was leaving at a high lope. All that noise, thrashing hooves, hollering, and confusion was just too much for a poor old hungry black bear. In spite of their troubles, the men were amused at the frightened bear's retreat.

Jake was standing when Dan returned on Sonny and said with a smile, "Maybe Sonny didn't exactly panic, but thought he'd better run to save me."

"What a bear," exclaimed Jake, "he could've got me while I was down."

John rode over and Jake climbed up on John's horse behind John; then they rode away to catch their horses.

"They're plum out of sight," complained Jake.

"We came west for excitement, and that cute little bear sure gave it to us," laughed John.

"Cute hell," replied Jake, "I'm gonna have a damn awful black eye 'cause of him."

"An' I'm gonna need you to pull a couple thorns out of my butt before I can ride any farther, 'cause I can't reach 'em."

They got off of the horse, and Jake pulled the thorns out, "Next time you'd better not fall off your horse in the thorns." They all chuckled and rode on.

It was over two miles before they found, and were able to catch, their spooked horses. Dan was relieved, "Looks like we had the diamond hitches on our pack horses tight enough to hold. They stayed out of the trees and didn't scrape any packs off."

John pointed, "We have a broken rein and broken lead ropes. The packs are a little crooked and shook up, but we came out of that scrape smellin' like a rose."

They rested at camp a day while they healed up and the horses settled down. While the men were sitting on the ground and leaning back against trees, John mused, "It's kinda strange, here by the Big Snowy Mountains. We saw big Bonehead Ben and his big bay horse he had there to ride, then, there was the great big pine tree beside the Big Springs, and next, we met the biggest black bear we've ever seen. Hope we don't find any grizzly like that, cause I'm sure he'd be big."

Dan smiled, "That's a lot of big things all right, but I sure like it a lot better down by the big Beartooth Mountains with the Crow."

"Yeah, I think you should, all right," Jake pondered. "I could see by the way that purty little half-Crow girl looked at you that she thinks you're just all right."

"I stopped by the LaFountains a few times, and I didn't notice it that much," Dan replied.

"It'll get so that even you can notice it before long," John smiled.

"Well, I hope so," Dan declared.

"What about that girl friend back in Missouri?" John queried.

"She's a good friend, but I've never made any promises to anyone."

"We thought you'd go back, though."

"Yes, but I never said I'd stay. I'll figure out a way to get back here."

"Yes, I do believe you like this girl here a lot."

For a few weeks, the men trapped from several creeks along the north side of the Snowy Mountains. It snowed four to ten inches of snow about once a week, but the warm chinook winds soon melted part of it off. It did not get colder than ten above zero, and sometimes warmed to fifty degrees. The trappers enjoyed those pleasant weeks of trapping.

The men camped in their tepee at night. After breakfast, and before sunup, each man went out to follow his trapline along a creek near where they camped. Their trap lines were only a few miles long, but they moved to a new area each week.

One day, Jake surmised, "We've been gettin' more pelts than we expected to find here. Do you suppose Bonehead Ben has been able to keep most of the trappers away from here for several years?"

John answered, "I don't know, but maybe he's made some trappers uneasy since he seems to be goofy enough to be unpredictable."

"Well, anyhow, we're gettin' quite a few pelts," Dan agreed.

One nice morning, John returned to camp earlier than usual. Just for pleasure, he decided to ride down along the creek to where Dan was trapping. He would soon find him by following the tracks of Dan's horse in the snow. For a little while, John rode through clumps of pine and aspen trees on the sides of the hills, and then dropped down to the creek bottom where he soon found Sonny's tracks.

By the tracks in the snow, he saw where Dan had set a trap in the edge of the creek. Just a quarter of a mile farther along the creek, John was surprised to see the tracks of another mounted rider join Sonny's tracks. Because the new tracks had fallen on top of Sonny's, John could see that Dan was being followed. This caused John to be very concerned for Dan's safety because he did not know of any other trappers in the area.

John urged his horse to a trot as he followed the tracks through trees and meadows near the creek. He could not tell if the rider was an Indian or a white trapper, but the tracks were of a big unshod horse.

Soon, John came to another place where Dan had set a trap. He said, "What the Hell?!" when he immediately saw that the man tracking Dan had pulled Dan's trap up and had taken it. John rode faster, and as he hurried past the next spot where another trap had been taken, he exclaimed, "Damn him!" Now he knew the thief had to be Bonehead Ben because of the piles of traps he had seen at Bonehead's cabin. Bonehead had stolen them from other trappers, but worse than that, he was wearing three rings that he should not be wearing. John was sure that Bonehead had killed the trappers to get their traps and rings, and said to himself, "Oh my God, Dan was wearing a ruby ring. The crazy fool will kill Dan!"

John had never been so excited and scared in his life as he loped, trotted, and dodged his horse through the trees and brush while following the tracks. He expected to see someone any second, and prayed it would be Dan.

Suddenly, he broke out of the trees into an opening. In a flash, with every detail seemingly posed before him, he saw Ben standing in the trees and brush, with a big bow and arrow raised and ready to draw the bow! Unaware of Ben, Dan was setting a beaver trap just fifty yards ahead of him.

57

John's horse slid to a stop as he jumped to the ground. At the sound, both men looked toward him as he fired his musket at Ben, but by the hard splat of the lead ball on wood, instead of a plunk into flesh, he knew the ball had been blocked by a limb!

Just as quickly as it had happened, the shadowy figure that John thought was Ben, disappeared with the scraping of brush through the trees.

From a hundred yards away, Dan shouted to John, "Did you shoot a bear?"

"I think ole Bonehead was tryin' to kill you, but I hit a limb."

"Well, I'll be damned! I didn't even know anyone was around, but I'm glad you showed up when you did. I was busy settin' this trap. He must be sneakier than a cat, 'cause I didn't hear a thing."

"I followed his tracks, but I never did get a clear look at him. It had to be Bonehead though, 'cause of the big hoof tracks."

"He better not come back again."

"I doubt if he will. He must be smart enough to know that we suspect him. That shot hit right by his head, so only a limb saved him. He sure panicked and got out of here. I'll bet an antelope couldn't catch him. If he ever comes back, we'll have to kill him even though he is crazy. We'll watch out for him."

As they were returning to camp, they met Jake loping toward them. As they met, he exclaimed, "I saw the tracks, and wondered what was goin' on. When I heard the shot, I got worried." They told him what happened as they returned to camp.

In another week the trappers were ready to leave for Crow country. The snow was not too deep yet, but they were anxious to leave this place that was so famous for snow. Each man had a small bundle of furs that could be traded at Fort Sarpy, near the mouth of the Rosebud, on the lower Yellowstone. They started toward the Big Springs again, with Dan in the lead.

After they left the Big Springs, the men rode by Bonehead Ben's place. They did not see Ben, but his big bay horse was there with his smaller pack horses near his old tepee. They went on and turned up East Fork Valley. They had ridden two miles when they saw Ben coming behind them. His big bay horse was coming at a fast trot, but the men kept going. When Ben got closer, he held his musket above his head and yelled, "Come back here!"

Jake said, "I think he's mad at us for trappin' here. We'll just keep goin'."

Ben stopped, aimed his musket and fired at them. John exclaimed, "That's too damn close!" when the shot whistled by. He dismounted, aimed his muzzle-loader that he had loaded while riding, then fired and killed Ben's horse. "Sure hated to kill that good horse, but it was the horse or Ben."

Ben got up from his fall and waved his musket, screaming, "I'll kill you!"

John said, "He's really slobberin' mad now. I'd hate for him to have a hold of me. Let's go."

They started their horses into a run and were out of range when Ben had reloaded and fired again. After a mile, they slowed their horses and rode on up the East Fork to beyond where they had met their new friends. Ned and Pete were not there, so the trappers crossed over the divide and rode down Flat Willow Creek where they found them.

After a friendly greeting, and some visiting, the trappers told Ned and Pete what had happened with Ben. Pete said, "We left East Fork a little sooner than we planned to because of being too near Bonehead Ben, but if he comes here we'll shoot him."

The men visited overnight, and then the trappers said, "Good-bye," and started for Fort Sarpy, a hundred miles southeast on the Yellowstone. The trip was across a quite dry sagebrush and shortgrass prairie, where only a few small creeks were flowing in December. All of the mountain ranges were a hundred or more miles away and only visible from the tops of hills on clear days. The men were seldom out of sight of buffalo and antelope. It was easy country to cross, as there were few natural obstacles and only a few inches of snow.

The third day, they arrived at Fort Sarpy, near the confluence of the Rosebud and Yellowstone Rivers. The trappers sold their furs as Louis LaFountain had advised them to, by naming Louis as their agent, and the fur buyer paid them top market price. The men stayed at the fort for two days, and then left with new supplies.

During the next three days, the trappers rode up the Yellowstone Valley where they encountered a village of friendly River Crow Indians. After a friendly, short visit, the trappers continued on to the mouth of the Stillwater River. Twenty-five miles up the Stillwater Valley, they found the Mountain Crow village of Chief Red Bear, and the trappers figured it was nearly Christmas. They were glad to be back, and the

Indians and LaFountains were happy to see them again. Chief Red Bear seemed to be unusually friendly to these white men.

The men had brought some presents from Fort Sarpy for Chief Red Bear and some of their friends. Dan gave Lily some beads to decorate her clothing, and a steel pan. With a little hug, Lily said, "Oh thanks, Dan, for these good presents. I'm happy that you remembered me, and brought me these presents, and I'm really glad that you're back."

"I'm really glad to be back, where we can visit together again." Some friendly conversation, a smile, and a squeeze of Lily's hand was enough to make Dan very happy. He was happy just to be near her. Through the winter, they became better acquainted, and everyone knew they were in love.

The trappers and Indians found enough beaver and other animals that winter to be able to trade pelts for the supplies they needed at Fort Sarpy.

In spring and early summer, the trappers camped with the Crow along the East Rosebud and West Rosebud Rivers. These rivers rushed from huge canyons in the Beartooth Mountains.

One time the three trappers and Striking Hawk rode far up East Rosebud Canyon where the melting snow formed tumbling cataracts down the canyon sides and joined the roaring stream in the bottom of the canyon. Every few miles, like a jewel, a blue lake lay nestled at the bottom of thousand foot cliffs, and a series of great peaks scraped the white, fluffy clouds floating by. A few times, white mountain goats were seen balanced on sheer canyon walls so far above that they were difficult to spot. Dan told his pardners, "This canyon is the greatest sight I ever hope to see. I could never be this happy living away from Crow Country."

During June and July, the hillsides were carpeted with green grass and wildflowers. Soon, chokecherries and buffalo berries hung in bright red clusters. Dan was completely happy here as he walked hand in hand with Lily along a mountain stream.

3

▼▼▼▼▼▼▼▼▼▼▼▼

THE VISION

▲▲▲▲▲▲▲▲▲▲▲▲▲

One August day in 1854, Jake and Dan were sitting in the shade of a clump of aspen trees at the edge of the Crow village on the West Rosebud River as John walked over to inform them, "I just learned the village is goin' to visit the River Crow on the Little Bighorn River in a few days. We could go that far with 'em, and then go on to Missouri from there. It's a lot closer from there than from the way we came, so far west on the Bitterroot." Then he looked at Dan, "It's over two years since we left, and I promised your dad and mother that we'd return in two years."

"I'm not ready to go back, but I suppose we'd better. I'd sure rather stay here, but I'll soon come back."

Jake looked eastward, "It'll only be half as far, but it'll be twice as dangerous tryin' to sneak through Sioux country. If a good sized bunch of Sioux jump us, we can't hold 'em off with our muskets, but maybe we can go through places where they're not as likely to be camped or huntin'."

John agreed, "There's a lot of big, empty country out there all right. I guess we oughta try it."

Soon the whole camp packed up their travois and horses with everything they owned: tepees, utensils, tools, and apparel, and headed one hundred and twenty-five miles eastward, across the creeks, hills, and prairies close along the north edge of the Pryor Mountains, and finally reached the camp of the River Crow on the Little Bighorn River, several miles north of the Bighorn Mountains. It was a happy and exciting reunion.

The River and Mountain Crow tepees were pitched together in a fresh camp, in the cool shade of the scattered cottonwood trees along the Little Bighorn River. The trappers saw that it was a very colorful village. This was a good time for them to take a close look at Indian life, so they did pay closer attention than they ever had before. They could see that the conical buffalo hide tepees of the Crow were generally higher than other tribes and the longer poles projected farther above the coverings. Twenty-five foot poles of light, thin fir or lodgepole pine were used, and various pennants were attached. Depending on the desired size, ten to twenty buffalo hides, scraped and dressed to a white color, and decorated with quills and paint were used. A new tepee was smoke cured to turn rain by building a smoking fire inside.

The trappers saw that the lodges were arranged in a circle or ellipse, but not with any arrangement of the clans. A shade was erected near the lodge. It was made of a frame of vertical posts and a pole roof, usually flat, and was covered with green foliage.

Dan could see the Crow village was very picturesque here along the river with the Bighorn Mountains in view.

At this gathering of the Mountain Crow and River Crow, the trappers were invited to a feast each day by an Indian friend's family or group of several families. A variety of cuts from venison, elk, antelope, and buffalo was served. It was cooked in metal containers, but in cases where more was needed, stone boiling with the use of hot rocks in a rawhide container or stone kettle was used. Roasting by the fire was a very common method the trappers and Indians used, especially for ribs.

The trappers always told their hosts that the meal was delicious, very good, as they patted their stomach and smiled. Some did not understand the words, but they understood the tone and gesture. By their smiles, the trappers knew their hosts appreciated the comments, and they were invited to many feasts.

The men knew the Crow never tilled the soil, but they were fed corn meal the Crow had traded for with the Hidatsa on the Missouri River. Corn cakes were very good with their meat. The Crow women used a digging stick to dig up wild turnips, bitterroot, camas, and other roots that were edible. They knew which to gather, and many times the trappers watched them. Wild rhubarb, strawberries, sarvisberries, wild plums, chokecherries, and wild grapes were eaten fresh, and also made into pudding, or made into pastry and dried in the sun. Pemmican was an important part of the diet. To make it, dried, roasted meat was pounded with stone hammers, chokecherry juice in water was used to boil bones, grease was skimmed from the bone marrow, and the marrow was mixed with the pounded, dried meat. It was then poured into buffalo heart skins and allowed to dry. This was fine food, and often used as a treat. The trappers had even learned to make it, but they had a better variety of food when they ate with the Crow than when they cooked their own food. They were glad that mice, snakes, frogs, turtles, muskrats, dogs, and other such inferior food was not eaten in this land of abundant buffalo. Actually the Crow and trappers fared very well for food. They were fond of a diet of a variety of meat and berries.

The three men circulated through the village and enjoyed seeing the colorful clothing worn at the gatherings where spectators watched the games, story telling, and races that were held.

Men's clothing included the G-string, breechclout, leggings extending to the hips, a buckskin shirt or jacket, and moccasins. Their dress clothing was decorated with fringed buckskin, broad decorative bands of colorful quills, beads, and white bones fashioned into small cylindrical and disc-shaped adornments. Bear claw necklaces were worn with pride. The usual plains-type war-bonnet was often used, or there were other arrangements of eagle feathers in the hair. The old hair style was to divide the hair into halves and let it fall loosely down the sides of the face and back. Now, due to the Nez Perce influence, the hair was fashioned into two braids.

Women's clothing included a long buckskin or mountain goat skin dress and belt, leggings extending to the knee, and moccasins. The dress was sleeveless with cape-like shoulder pieces. It was adorned with many elk teeth, and intricate, geometric designs of colorfully dyed porcupine quills, and beads. Necklaces and bracelets, made of colorful beads were worn. The women's hair was divided and fashioned into two long, black braids falling ahead of the shoulders to the breast. The line of parting was often painted red. Both men and women's dress clothing were beautifully decorated.

"I'm surprised at the beauty of the Indian's clothing," John commented.

Dan replied, "They sure do some colorful beadwork and quillwork."

Much of the time, Dan and Lily strolled together through the village and watched a variety of unscheduled games that were played, some among men, some among women, and some among children. When Dan and Lily strolled hand in hand, they were noticed by the Crow because that was not their custom.

They came upon a game being played by some men. There were seven men on each side. Lily explained to Dan, "This is a hand game called *Hiding Making*. An elk tooth is hid under a buffalo robe, where it is changed from one hand to the other by two men. The guesser from the other side tells which hand is holding the elk tooth. When he is wrong, he loses a tally stick from his side. They have ten tally sticks, and when one side has taken all of the sticks, the game is over. They bet all kinds of things on who wins, and sometimes it is bad because they lose things they need. They play Hiding Making a lot, though. Let's look for some more games."

Dan could see that the players had many beads, tools, knives, and other possessions ready to bet. He shrugged his shoulders as they left.

As they passed by another shade, a group of women was intent on a game. Lily said, "Even the women bet. They play dice with a pair of bone buttons, a pair of disc shaped bones, and one elk tooth. The dice are put on a stretched buffalo robe, then the robe is hit with a bowl to make the dice bounce. The score is counted by which side of each dice lands up. The women use ten tally sticks. They play the game fast, and the men don't understand how the women count the dice," and Lily smiled, "I don't either."

Lily continued, "The women play a stick version of the game of dice, too. They throw four different marked sticks on a flat stone in the middle of a piece of round, tanned hide, marked with a white circle. Each one that lands in the circle counts what the stick is marked. The sticks have burnt decorations on them. Some are grooved, and some are colored red or blue. They have different patterns and marks on them. Some count nine and some count ten. Each woman has her own special sticks. Sometimes, a great warrior has made marks on them for her," and she smiled at Dan. The women had dresses, robes, elk teeth, and other articles ready to bet.

One morning, before it became too hot, Dan and Lily found a group of young men and boys playing several hoop and pole games in the open space at the center of the village. "Sometimes the game is called *Shooting The Buffalo*, or *Mock Hunting*," Lily explained to Dan.

Some players used a knee-high, bark-wrapped, green willow ring for their target. Others used a netted hoop with a hand-sized, bark wrapped, open circle in the center.

Dan could see that many different types of darts or javelins were used. They were often made of straight, dry, finger-sized willow, three to five feet long, and wrapped at intervals with rawhide or sinew. Heavier wrappings were used near the center to balance the pole. It was tipped with the point of a deer or elk horn, and a double plume of buffalo hair or buffalo tail was used at the back end.

The game was played on level ground, and two score keepers used small sticks for counters. The hoop was thrown to roll across the ground, and two players hurled their darts at it. The one whose dart came nearest to the hoop, scored. Sometimes, an expert player could put the dart through the net or even through the open circle. Dan and Lily did not see any betting in this game.

One day, Lily took Dan to where many of the people were watching some Crow women play a game called *Shinny*, (ball hitting). A large hand-sized stuffed ball was used. The shinny sticks were three-foot pieces of unpainted sapling, curved at the lower end. For the goal, each side had a robe at the same end of the field. At the start, the ball was tossed into the air at the far end of the field, then each side raced for the ball and drove it toward their goal with the shinny sticks. In the excitement, they sometimes hit someone with a shinny stick. Heads were sometimes bloodied, and the men had to stop a few fights among the players. Dan said to Lily, "Gol-dang, they really get excited playin' this game."

"Sometimes they have to stop playing," Lily answered.

Boys and men had contests of archery, with many variations of targets, moving and stationary. To Dan, these were the most interesting contests.

Top spinning was another attraction. Many different models of wooden tops were made from every kind of wood available. They were cylindrical, with round or flat tops and a conical bottom. The tops were colored to show different hues as they spun. A buckskin lash, sometimes attached to a stick, was used to wrap around the top, and then to throw the top on the ground as the lash unwound. It could be spun very fast this way. Dan and Lily watched both boys and girls spin tops. Sometimes they tried to see whose top could upset the other.

There were horse racing events for boys, girls, and men. Dan did not enter Sonny in any of the races. From curiosity, he had occasionally raced Sonny against individual opponents, but Sonny had always been the winner, so Dan felt that with such an advantage and the fact that Dan was not a Crow, he should not race Sonny.

Dan noticed this gathering was an opportunity for the children to get acquainted as they played together. Sometimes, the young boys would go rabbit hunting, and the girls would then cook the rabbits for them, in imitation of their elders. Much of the children's play was an imitation of their elders actions, but as they grew a little older, they became more shy. A boy may then try to meet a girl he liked as she was returning to her lodge with water or wood she had gathered. Sometimes, the boys joined the girls while they were picking berries or digging roots, and this gave them a chance to tell the girl things he hoped she would like to hear.

Sometimes a young woman led a young brave's best horse as they looked for buffalo close by. When she saw a buffalo of her choice, he mounted his horse and killed the buffalo for her.

A few times, Dan saw a young brave dressed in his best wardrobe go near a young woman's lodge in the evening, where he played the flute for her to hear. Sometimes the brave found her as she followed the trail to get water for the evening, and there he played the flute for her.

Young people were sure to find ways of courting, and a meeting such as this one between many clans provided them with their best opportunities for courting.

Dan and his pardners spent most of a week watching the festivities of their Crow friends and joining in some of the events, especially the feasting with friends. It was a great experience for them, as they learned much about the Crow's dress clothing, and many of the Crow customs. Dan said to John and Jake, "These are some of the things I was interested in seeing in the West."

Of the many events the Crow engaged in, the trappers thought the dancing was the most colorful and spectacular. Each evening, Dan and Lily attended the dance together as spectators.

At dusk, among the circle of spectators, Dan and Lily sat close together on a log and watched the fast, nimble footwork, and colorful buckskin garments of the young braves as they danced individually around a large circle to the penetrating beat of tom-toms and the high pitched voices of the singers.

The dancers wore colorful garments with bold designs of beads, porcupine quills, and elk teeth. Necklaces and bracelets of bear's teeth decorated some bodies with bare arms, legs, and chests. Long eagle feathers were formed into headdresses, or worn singly. Sometimes, a fan made of an eagle wing was held in the hand.

In a column, several braves thick, dozens of dancers moved counterclockwise in the circle. To the steady beat of tom-toms, dancers feet alternated with two small, quick hops on each fast bouncing foot. Dusky braves stooped down and up, turned left and right, whirled and bobbed with arms pumping. With great agility and speed, but never colliding, many leaped and whirled gracefully in patterns of individual variation, as feathers quivered on leggings, vest, fan bustles and headdresses.

As some danced, they sang continuous short monotones with quavering voices that varied throughout the scale of music, remindful of the plaintive wail of a coyote and the lonesome cry of the loon. Perhaps the music was composed from ages of wandering across the wide, lonely prairies. It seemed to be a cry to the Great Spirit.

The circle of spectators watched as different groups performed. When a mixed age group danced, a little three-year-old boy dressed in a small but beautifully decorated and fringed buckskin suit stomped his feet and whirled with very serious attention to the cadence of the tom-toms.

Dan remarked to Lily, "That just has to be the cutest thing I've ever seen."

The Indian women joined in some of the dances with more sedate steps, but dressed with as much or more of the exquisite, colorful, primitive decorations. Their neat, black braids of hair that reached down in front of their shoulders swayed with the rhythm. The graceful women dancers added the final touch of finesse to the spectacle.

After watching for a few hours, Lily asked, "Do you like the Indian dances, Dan?"

"It's great, I'm surprised at the graceful patterns and quick steps timed to the steady beat of the drummers, and the wild, strange songs of the singers. It's really exciting, and it seems strange for me to be so far out here watching people whose ways are so much different, so unusual compared to what I'm used to. Sometimes it seems like a dream for me to be here watching such strange things, but I'm really enjoying it. I like to sit here with you while we watch." He looked at Lily as she blinked those long, black eyelashes, and her smile was a string of pearls. "Lily, you're beautiful; I just don't want to leave here."

"Please don't leave, Dan."

"I'll come back just as soon as I can, Lily."

"I'll be sad all the time you're gone, Dan," and his arm pulled her closer.

Dan turned to Lily and talked softly, "Maybe sometime I'll whittle a flute, and learn to play it for you."

"Oh Dan, you won't need to do that, I love you already. Soon you'll be leaving, and there's not time for you to learn to play the flute now."

The night air quickly cooled down from the very warm daytime temperature of August. By the light of large campfires, the dance continued for several hours into the night. When it was over, Dan walked with Lily to her parents' lodge. They met in a light embrace, and after a goodnight kiss, Dan walked to the trappers' tepee.

The Crow had a very sociable meeting as the time drew near for the trappers to leave. One morning, Dan said to John and Jake, "I've enjoyed living here with the Crow even more than I thought I would. I think they have the best way to live, here in this place where there's never a shortage of buffalo and other game for food. The Crow do a lot of things to make life enjoyable. They've been having a real good time at this meeting. I know we have to go back to Missouri, but I sure want to come back here."

John answered, "I can see a lot of reasons why you like it here. I know Lily must be the best reason you have. I like it here too, and I'll be comin' back. You can come back with us next spring if your folks can't get you to stay and farm."

"I'm about as likely to start farmin' as you are," Dan answered.

In the afternoon, while others were celebrating, Chief Red Bear rested in the shade of a large cottonwood tree in deep thought. He had an uneasy feeling about changes that had been happening. More white men were coming, and he had heard that many buffalo were being killed far to the south.

That evening, the trappers and some of the villagers watched Chief Red Bear as he sat alone near his tepee on a small rise at the edge of the village. Facing the setting sun, wearing full headdress, moccasins, and his most decorated buckskin suit, Chief Red Bear sat cross-legged, with a small buffalo robe draped over his left leg. On his legs he held a very old buffalo bull's skull. At times he rubbed the skull with his hands, and at other times he tapped it lightly in cadence as he would a tom-tom, and intoned his songs of incantations to the spirit of the buffalo. He then laid the skull and buffalo robe aside and danced alone around them for a short time, beating time with an all-white medicine arrow as he continued his high-pitched singing and wailing to the Great Spirit. He then retired to his tepee for an hour, returning later in the evening to join the festivities of the tribe, where bright campfires lit the dancers in their colorful buckskin clothing.

The following morning, facing the rising sun, Chief Red Bear performed the same ritual.

Later on that hot, hazy day, Chief Red Bear left the powwow remarking that he would ride alone to the top of the long hill, east of the village on the Little Bighorn. He was quiet, and there seemed to be a serious, distant look in his eyes. Slowly walking his horse, he reached the crest of the hill, watching the high, strangely swirling clouds to the east. On a wide, dusty buffalo wallow, he sat quietly for a long time on his pinto horse and gazed eastward while shimmering heat waves danced across the distant high hills. He did not hear the song of the nearby meadowlark or see the coyote's furtive glance as it trotted by.

After some time, his attention was drawn to a golden eagle soaring in graceful circles high in the sky before it disappeared in the haze. Where the eagle had been, a white soldier then appeared with long, wavy hair, and riding a great black horse. Many buffalo and Indians fled on foot ahead of them, but the buffalo and Indians were only skeletons! Following far behind them was an older Dan than now, with a buffalo calf closely trailing him, as the calf would follow its mother. Soon, the figures faded into the hazy clouds. After a time, when no more had appeared, Chief Red Bear solemnly rode back to the village.

When the trappers were ready to leave the next morning, as Dan kissed Lily good-bye, she said, "Dan, please come back some day. I'll be sad as long as you are gone."

Dan replied, "Somehow I will, Lily, just as soon as I can."

69

As the white trappers started to leave, Chief Red Bear said to them, "Come with me; I show you best way home."

From their village, with several braves accompanying him, Chief Red Bear led the trappers to the top of the hill where the chief had been the day before.

There on the wide, dry buffalo wallow, he told them of the vision he had seen the day before.

"What does the vision tell you?" Jake asked.

"I am not sure," spoke Chief Red Bear. "I think after white soldier with long hair come, all buffalo die and Indians starve."

"But there is grass everywhere, and too many buffalo to count!" Dan exclaimed.

Chief Red Bear shook his head, "Don't know how it can be."

The Indians all stared at the hazy hills; they saw only hazy hills.

Dan pondered, "How strange and weird."

"Maybe something happen long, long time from now," spoke Chief Red Bear. "Watch, but do not speak of this to the people; they would be afraid."

"I will watch for the long-haired white man who kills all the buffalo," declared Striking Hawk.

"One man can't kill all the buffalo," John commented.

"Maybe he is the leader of many buffalo killers," exclaimed Striking Hawk.

Chief Red Bear turned to the white trappers and lifted his arm toward the east, "Now I show you best way home." In the dirt of the dry buffalo wallow, he used an arrow to draw a map. He drew the long range of the nearby Bighorn Mountains running to the south and the shorter range of the Black Hills over a hundred miles farther east. Below the south end of the Bighorns, he then drew the curve of the North Platte River and the Oregon Trail running southeastward. He continued, "The Sioux and Cheyenne will be camped along the east side of the Bighorns and in the Black Hills where there is much grass. From here to Black Hills, other Sioux tribes will be along creeks that run north to Missouri River. Watch close for Sioux near creeks." And then, "On wide prairie not much water; only enough to go across. Maybe no Sioux on hot prairie; maybe hunting party somewhere along west side of Black Hills and down to Platte River."

Chief Red Bear then laid an all-white arrow on the ground pointing southeastward. "Go where the arrow points. Near Black Hills you will see strange rock tower higher than the hills. So high you will see it two days before you get there. At tower go south along edge of Black Hills. Do not go into Black Hills; too many Sioux there. From end of Black Hills, cross prairie to Platte River. Do not go close to rock tower. Maybe some Sioux tribe there at river."

John laid his compass on top of the arrow that Chief Red Bear had laid on the ground, pointing the direction they should follow to the tower. The arrow pointed to 120 degrees on the compass. With the compass, they could sight to landmarks on the horizon and follow them to the tower. Because it was visible from so far away, they were sure to find it.

John spoke, "We thank Chief Red Bear for lettin' us live with the Crow. We were happy here. It is good you point the way for us to go," and the chief replied, "We want you to come back."

Dan said, "I want to come back."

Chief Red Bear answered, "We want you to come back to live here with us. Some day you can help the Crow people when it is a bad time and I am gone. You will come back. The Indian girl, Lily, you will not forget. She bring you back."

Dan smiled and shrugged.

The trappers then slowly turned their horses and rode away. Soon they looked back and waved. The Crow watched until their white friends were out of sight, and then turned and rode slowly down the hill to their village on the Little Bighorn River.

When they were out of sight, Dan felt very sad about leaving, and he was worried about Chief Red Bear's vision, even though he doubted that it could ever happen.

There was a little haze in the air, so in two days the trappers gradually rode out of sight of the Bighorn Mountains. Antelope were within sight most of the time, and dark bunches of buffalo dotted the plain. They camped the first night on upper Rosebud Creek. There was no sign of any Indians there.

During the next four days, they followed their compass heading from horizon to far horizon across the rolling prairie. By riding southeast, they did not follow the north flowing creeks, but crossed the prairie from creek to creek. By not following the creeks they would avoid most of the Indian villages, as the villages were always located where there was a creek.

The creeks were evident from a distance by a shallow valley with a line of trees wandering northward across the prairie. Very few trees were

71

found while crossing the wide prairie, except cottonwood trees in the valleys or pines on the bordering hills.

As the men approached any valley to be crossed, they watched very closely for tracks of Indian horses, smoke from a village, or any sign of movement. From a high spot with a telescope they studied the entire area very carefully before proceeding.

When the trappers approached the Tongue River, with the use of the telescope they sighted an Indian village eight miles away along the river. The village was close to the route they were following. With the compass, John sighted to the farthest point on the horizon, far beyond the Indian village, to a high, dark hill twenty miles straight ahead. John said, "We'll have to stay eight or ten miles away from the village as we circle around it. Then we can ride to that high dark hill and follow our compass again."

When the trappers crossed through the trees in the Tongue River Valley, eight miles south of the Indian village, they found fresh tracks of Indian horses left by about fifteen Indians of a hunting party returning northward to the village.

Because of grass and other plants that had not yet sprung back to their original vertical positions after being trodden down, the trappers knew that the Indians were only a little more than just out of sight beyond the clumps of trees.

"We better wait real quiet-like and watch for a few minutes before we go on," Jake spoke softly.

"I sure hope there's not a straggler from their party following behind," John quietly cautioned, "or we'll have the same trouble we had when I killed the Blackfoot Indian." Then to Dan he quietly warned, "Don't let Sonny whinny if he sees or hears something. He sure looks alert, like maybe something is passing by out of sight in the trees!"

Dan dismounted and closely held Sonny's bridle while he laid one hand on Sonny's nose. Sonny sensed the danger and stood quietly, but his head slowly turned as he watched with ears cocked forward. Something was passing by just out of the men's hearing! The quiet suspense made Dan's mouth turn dry!

Pretty soon John quietly said, "I think some more Sioux just passed by ahead of us. Good thing they all passed before we did, so they didn't have our tracks to find."

"We're always needing some good luck," Jake replied softly. "Now let's ride to the far edge of the valley."

They crossed the small Tongue River, and at the edge of the trees, while Dan held John's horses, John slipped a short distance through some brush up the bottom of the hill. He watched for a little while, then returned and said, "I watched two small bands of Indians ride through the bend. They did pass by us. We can go up through this draw between the hills now and get the hell out of here. That was a close one!"

The men rode eastward to the high hill they had used as a landmark on the horizon, and then followed the 120-degree course southeastward on their compass. They rode forty miles across the prairie and over pine splotched hills until they were on a high hill where they could look down on the Powder River Valley. From this hill, they gazed ahead in search of the rock tower. The smoky haze of forest fires had cleared from the air, but they did not expect to see the tower from this far away.

After a few minutes of searching the far distance, Dan pointed and said, "There, just below the horizon, at the left end of the dark strip on the horizon, that must be it! It looks like a tiny twig, less than a quarter of an inch long, standing on end. Can you find it? It's standing on a little dark place."

"Oh, there I see it," exclaimed John. "Gosh, it's small."

"Oh yeah, now I see it," exclaimed Jake. "No wonder it was hard to find. It's really little. You sure have to look close to find it."

"Now that I know how it looks, it's easier to find again," said John. "See the compass reading; the tower is right straight where Chief Red Bear's arrow pointed!"

"He sure knew," Jake nodded, "Said he'd been there twice with a war party to raid the Sioux."

John commented, "We still have a good two days ride to it, all right."

"Well that's something to see, that little thing in all this space," mused Dan. "What a landmark."

During the next two days, the men rode across the slow flowing Powder River, then on over the wide, dry prairie, across the Little Powder River, and crossed the upper end of the Little Missouri River. The tower gradually appeared closer as the miles passed by. No more Indians were seen, although occasional Indian signs and tracks were found.

As the men drew within a few miles of the high rock tower, they could see it was a great, lone stump a thousand feet high, sitting on top of a pine-covered hill. The vertically grooved sides gave it the appearance of the core of a very ancient volcano.

John said, "That's really somethin' strange, never saw a rock anything like it before. I'd like to ride closer to it, even right to the base of it, but there's too much chance of finding some Sioux camped there. If we come by here again, we'll try to get closer to it."

Dan commented, "It stands up so high above everything around it, that there's no wonder we could see it from so far away. It's sure a good land mark for finding directions. It must look huge from closer to it. The sides are so straight up that no one could ever climb it."

Jake frowned, "We've been seein' more tracks an' Indian signs. I'll bet some Sioux are camped along that river on the other side of it. My scalp's beginnin' to tingle already. Let's turn south an' get the hell outta here!"

For the next two days the men rode southward along the west base of the high, pine-covered Black Hills. They could only imagine what nice meadows, streams, and valleys the round-topped, pine-covered small mountains held in the interior. These were the sacred mountains of the Sioux tribes, and white men dared not enter them, but they were near enough to the base of the mountains to enjoy some of the cool air from them.

The last evening the trappers were near the Black Hills, they started riding over the crest of a hill and discovered a hunting party of ten Sioux Indians. They were one-fourth of a mile below them, heading for the mouth of a valley leading into the mountains. The Indians were returning from the prairie with antelope they had killed and loaded on six pack horses they were leading.

The Indians and the trappers discovered each other at about the same time. Both parties stopped and watched each other for a minute. Dan said, "It seems the Indians may be deciding a strategy for an attack."

"If they try it, three Indians are gonna die," answered John, "and I think they know it."

"They're figuring some trick," pondered Jake.

Then the action started. Four Indians, riding their horses and leading the six pack horses, started on a slow trot toward the mountain valley. The other six Indians started a charge toward the trappers, riding between the trappers and the retreating pack horses. The Indians were coming toward the trappers at a slow gallop and were making a lot of war whoops. They made a pass just out of musket range and started back on another pass just a little closer.

Jake smiled and said, "Hold your fire a minute; they're putting on a big show to keep us away from the antelope and the boys leading the pack horses."

"You're right," John agreed. "They don't want to get three Indians killed. They're just tryin' to protect the ones leavin' with the pack horses."

The trappers sat on their horses with their muskets ready, and waited.

The Indians waited until the four Indians were a half-mile farther away, and then they slowly followed them toward the mountains.

"Well now, that was the smart thing for them to do," Jake said.

"Yes, and we'd better do the smart thing and get a lot of miles from here before they come back with about fifty more braves," John urged.

They rode far that evening and left early the next morning. They watched the trail behind them but never saw any Indians following them.

As they rode a hundred miles south across the hot, dry prairie toward Fort Laramie, they and their horses were thirsty much of the time. Because this was August and the dry time of the year, the small creeks had little water in them. They were getting mighty dry before they crossed the Cheyenne River and several of its tributaries.

There were a few buffalo and many antelope on the wide, dry prairie for the men to use. When they were beyond the tributaries of the Cheyenne River, they had most of a day without water until they found a creek that was flowing south toward the North Platte River.

"Dang glad to find this little stream," Dan commented as he watered Sonny, and each man dipped up some to drink. "That's why we didn't see any Indians out here. It's just too dry."

John nodded, "Plenty dry, but we made it past the Sioux." In another day, the three pardners reached Fort Laramie.

The commanding officer at Fort Laramie was a little surprised the three trappers had seen so few Indians on their trip from the Yellowstone. He did say they would have seen many Indians along the east side of the Bighorn Mountains and the east side of the Black Hills. Crossing the more dry, desolate prairies had been the best way to avoid Indians.

The officer said there hadn't been very much trouble with the Indians when the settlers didn't try to take their land. The settlers were avoiding the more warlike Indians to the north and going farther west on the Oregon Trail.

The trappers stayed two days at the fort. They rested their horses and bought a few supplies. The rest of the trail home would be easy.

On a nice morning, they started east on the Oregon Trail. Dan kept looking back until the last of the mountains slowly faded from sight. When they were gone, it seemed they had been swallowed by time and distance. They seemed to have faded away as Chief Red Bear's vision of the buffalo had faded from sight. It made him sad, and he felt very lonely for Lily and his Indian friends. Days passed as they rode farther and farther eastward on the trail across the flat green prairie. Dan's memories almost seemed to have been a dream when he would think of the far away mountains where they had been, and he sometimes wondered if he would really ever get there again.

John said to him, "Cheer up, Dan; the mountains we left will always be there, and that pretty girl you left was real sad to see you go. I'm sure she'll wait a long time for you to come back."

"I hope I get back," Dan replied.

Compared to the dangers and excitement where the trappers had been, their return trip on the Oregon Trail was very dull. The men met wagon trains of settlers heading west nearly every day. Most of them were going to California or Oregon. People on the wagon trains they met had so many questions to ask that it actually slowed their progress. The settlers did not know much about the West, but they were anxious to learn.

It was a long trip of about six hundred miles from Fort Laramie to St. Joseph. Sometimes as they jogged along, when Dan's thoughts were not on the mountain country or the people he had left there, he thought of his family he would see when he reached his home in Missouri. He knew they would all be extremely happy when he returned, and the closer he got to home, the more excited he became about seeing them. A few times he even became curious about the girl friend he once knew. Her name was Elaine Elliot. She was quite a pretty girl, with blue eyes and light brown, wavy hair. Maybe just an inch taller than most girls her age, and beginning to have a pretty figure. Most of the boys were attracted to her good looks. She had a pretty good personality, even though she had been the center of attention so much. Dan may have been the boy she liked the most when he had left St. Joseph. Now he wondered if she had completely forgotten him.

While riding along the Oregon Trail toward Missouri, Dan spent about half of his time daydreaming about the places he had been in the

West, and he never had Lily out of his thoughts for very long. He did not pay close attention to the changing landscape as he jogged along, but mile after mile it steadily passed by.

It took the three trappers nearly three weeks to reach the Big Blue River on the Oregon Trail. From there the Oregon Trail angled southeast to Independence, so the trappers left the trail and rode due east one hundred miles to St. Joseph.

4

▼▼▼▼▼▼▼▼▼▼▼▼

WELCOME HOME

▲▲▲▲▲▲▲▲▲▲▲▲▲

In October, 1854, the three men reached St. Joseph, Missouri. They soon went to see John's daughters there, and were welcomed with great affection. John's daughter, Ann, cooked them a dinner such as they had not tasted since they left Missouri.

After dinner, Dan bid Jake good-bye and said he would try to go west again when Jake and John were ready to go. Dan went to visit his parents three miles out of town.

The next morning Jake started for the Ozarks of Missouri to visit his relatives. John planned to visit with his daughters for much of the winter.

When Dan reached home, he was welcomed by his mother and father with outstretched arms, his mother's tears and his father's firm handshake. Dan's sister hugged him, and his young brother welcomed him with a hearty hand shake and stated, "I'm sure glad you didn't get killed by Indians, Dan. We've all been worried about you."

For several days, Dan's family questioned him about his life in the West. He told them much about the great beauty of the mountainous land and some about the Indians. He was careful not to tell the most dangerous experiences the trappers had.

In following days, Dan looked over the farm and the farm animals with his father and brother. He enjoyed helping them with some work occasionally.

Dan's horse, Sonny, realized he was home and was unusually calm. He was in a good pasture and always whinnied to Dan when he saw him.

After a week, Dan started visiting friends and went to church on Sunday, where he met his friend Elaine.

When they met outside of the church before the service, Elaine greeted Dan with a pretty smile and a coy "Hello, Dan."

Dan said, "It's good to see you, Elaine. It's been a long time."

"Oh Dan," exclaimed Elaine, "I've wondered about you so much. I hope we can visit soon and you will tell me all about your experiences in the wilderness. It must be a very hard life there. It seems to have made you so much more mature."

"We'll soon find a time to visit," promised Dan.

A few days later, Elaine invited Dan to her parents' home for dinner one evening. They had a very cordial visit, and when Dan left he kissed Elaine once, very casually. The second time Dan went to dinner at Elaine's parents' home he was very courteous and friendly, but again, one little goodnight kiss was all there was.

It was obvious that Dan's mother was happy Dan and Elaine visited a few times, and within a few weeks she seemed to expect that Dan would have a romance with Elaine.

Elaine was so friendly to Dan that he knew she also expected him to fall in love with her. She had every reason to expect it. She was a very pretty, charming and vivacious young lady who could have her pick of the available men.

Dan, however, remembered Lily every day. Her full name was Lily Marie LaFountain, and each time Dan said her name it sounded to him like the music of the rippling mountain streams where he first saw her. The quiet smile on her face, the calm trust in her eyes, and the sincerity of her love were qualities that Dan admired so much in Lily. In the eyes of Dan, her wonderful beauty was unmatched by any woman he had ever seen. Some men may choose the fancy beauty of Elaine, but Dan could really love only Lily.

As the winter was passing by, Dan's father could see that Dan just was not falling in love as Dan's mother had hoped. Sometimes Dan told his father of some of his exciting and dangerous experiences in the West, the beauty of the western mountain lands, living among the Crow Indians and the LaFountain family, and Lily. Dan's father immediately understood the situation when Dan told him just a little about Lily. He accepted it, and even encouraged Dan to live where he would be happy. He understood why Dan preferred to live in the West.

Dan was happy that his father understood his feelings, and he hoped that his mother also could some day. It was now easier for Dan to think of returning to the Yellowstone country.

One day while visiting Elaine, Dan told Elaine of the trip he soon expected to make with John and Jake to St. Louis for supplies for another trip west next spring. Elaine was very disappointed, and told Dan of the opportunity that was possible for Dan to become a merchant in St. Joseph with the help of her father.

Dan told Elaine, "I just can't be interested in such a quiet life when there's so much excitement in the West and so many beautiful places to see."

"But this is an opportunity of a lifetime," replied Elaine, "and if we would someday get married, just think of the nice home and good life we could have. It would make us a wonderful living. Oh, Dan, don't miss a chance like this."

"I do appreciate your concern and your feelings for me, Elaine, and you are a very fine friend of mine, but that great, wild, free, beautiful land out west just keeps calling me back. I could never forget it," and Dan was looking past Elaine, not in her eyes.

With a flash of temper, Elaine exclaimed, "Then you'll have to forget me, Dan! I don't understand what's wrong with you. You must be crazy. You can go now. Go on back to your mountains and Indians!"

As Dan walked out the door, he turned and said, "Only for you am I sorry, Elaine. If I had never seen the West, it would've been different, but someday, some man here will make you happy, I'm sure. Good-bye, Elaine."

She never answered as Dan left.

Dan felt bad because he had hurt Elaine's feelings. He wondered if it would have been better if he had never gone to see her at all after he returned from the West, but that would have hurt her, too. Although they had been very close friends and almost considered lovers, he had never made any plans for the future with Elaine, and although she did have other boy friends, it looked now as though he had been the one she liked the most. She could choose any of them now, and that boy would be happy to live in any manner she would like. Her wounded heart and pride would heal, and she would soon be happy again. Dan certainly was not invited there for dinner again.

Soon Dan was occupied with plans for the return trip to the Yellowstone. Everyone was resigned to the fact that he had chosen to live there.

Planning for the trip was exciting. The men had plenty of time to make their plans and get their supplies ready. In the spring John and Dan made a trip by passenger boat on the Missouri River to St. Louis to get supplies. It had been arranged for Jake to meet them there.

They bought some clothing even though they would eventually have to make their own buckskin clothing in the West. They bought all the supplies they should need. For trade and gifts to Indians, they found buttons, beads, needles, thread, awls for punching holes in leather, knives, small mirrors, tobacco, and other small articles.

"Our beaver traps will be safe where we cached them by the West Rosebud," John advised. "When we need more, Louis LaFountain always has traps for trade. We'll sure get the new guns we saw, though."

Dan agreed, "I'm surprised they make such good guns now. That new Sharps breechloader will really help us."

All three men bought the latest model Sharps breechloader carbines to replace their muzzle-loaders. They were the latest successful development in rifles. They fired a new .52 caliber shell made of heavy paper holding the large bullet. The cartridge was fired by the use of percussion caps or primer. The Sharps was a single shot rifle that, in tests, had been reloaded and fired ten times a minute. One man armed with the new Sharps breechloader was equal to ten or fifteen men armed with muzzle-loaders. The men also bought new Colt Revolvers. These arms were the most outstanding weapons on the American frontier in the 1850s. With the accurate and hard-hitting Sharps carbine, game had been killed at 450 yards. The men bought all the ammunition they would have room to carry. When they needed more, they could get it at Fort Union on the confluence of the Yellowstone and Missouri Rivers.

The three men returned to St. Joseph and continued making plans for their trip to the land of the Crow Indians on the Yellowstone.

Their trip would not be by river boat up the Missouri as so many frontiersmen traveled. They would ride saddle horses and lead pack horses as they had on their trip to the Bitterroot and Yellowstone. Each man would ride a horse and lead one pack horse. To be able to carry more supplies, they would take one extra pack horse and take turns leading it. Dan would ride Sonny again.

One day John said to Dan, "Striking Hawk will be glad you're bringing your stallion, Sonny, again. He knows you won't sell him, but he'll make you a deal to use him with his mares part of the time. He has about two dozen mares now, or he did when we left. The way Indians steal horses from each other, they never know how many they'll have the next day," he laughed.

"We should be able to arrange some kind of a deal," Dan answered.

5

▼ ▼ ▼ ▼ ▼ ▼ ▼ ▼ ▼ ▼ ▼ ▼

TRAIL TO
THE YELLOWSTONE

▲ ▲ ▲ ▲ ▲ ▲ ▲ ▲ ▲ ▲ ▲ ▲ ▲

On a morning in early May, 1855, John, Jake, and Dan had their saddle horses and pack horses all tied to the hitching rack in front of Hogan's General Store in St. Joseph. The pack horses had packs tied down and ready to leave. The men had stopped to buy a few small articles and bid good-bye to their families and a few friends.

While they were in front of the store, Elaine walked up and spoke in a friendly manner, "Good morning, gentlemen; I see you're leaving this morning for the wilderness. I'm glad I met you, Dan, before you were gone. I want to say good-bye and tell you I'm sorry I lost my temper that day. Maybe some day I'll be able to understand why you must live in the West, but right now I am only sad."

She kissed Dan and said, "Good-bye, Dan," then started to turn away with tears in her eyes.

Dan held her hand a moment and said, "I've always liked you very much, Elaine. I hope we can always be friends. I give you my best wishes for the future. Good-bye, Elaine," and their fingers slid apart as she left.

Tearful farewells were spoken by members of Dan's and John's families.

Dan's mother said, "I'm always afraid for you, Dan, when you're in such a wild and savage place. Please be as careful as you possibly can."

His father shook his hand and said, "I'd like to be goin' with you three men. I hope you find a good life in that land you like so well, Son. Good-bye now," and their hands parted. The three men then rode away to the ferry on the nearby Missouri River.

After the men crossed the river on the ferry, and were finally riding at a brisk walk along a wide trail with their pack horses being led behind, John said, "Well, after all of the sadness this morning, we're finally on our way. We have a pretty morning and a cool breeze in our faces to cheer us up as we head for what are really our unknown destinies. The one thing we know for sure is that it will be interesting."

Dan remarked, "Even the horses are anxious to be headin' back. Look how they're stepping along, with bright eyes and their ears cocked ahead, even the pack horses," and Dan was smiling.

Jake mused, "I guess you found the only way you could go back to the Yellowstone was to just break away, Dan. I'm sure glad you did."

This was the first day of a long ride. However, this time they would follow a route that would be about half as long as when they went to the Bitterroot, and then came eastward to the Yellowstone. It would be shorter than if they rode a boat up the Missouri and the Yellowstone.

Their route would be even shorter than their last trip home along the west side of the Black Hills. While in St. Louis, they had bought some of the latest maps of the West. Most of the West was not surveyed, and that which was, was inaccurately mapped, but there was enough information from expeditions for maps to be reasonably close in some areas.

Father DeSmet had made sketches of the Yellowstone, Powder River, and western edge of the Black Hills from his 1851 trip. Dr. Ferdinand Hayden's trip to the White River Badlands in 1853 helped in mapping the area on the east side of the Black Hills. The White River Badlands were fifty to seventy-five miles east of the Black Hills. St. Joseph was southeast of the Black Hills.

With a map of what was known of the area, and the three men's knowledge of their own trip, they had a fairly close idea of the direction and distance from St. Joseph, Missouri to their last camp with Chief Red Bear on the Little Bighorn River.

While looking at the maps, they found something very strange. They had returned from Crow country a year before by going to the great rock tower by the Black Hills, then south to Fort Laramie, and then east to St. Joseph, Missouri. The same direction that Chief Red Bear had laid his arrow on the ground pointing their way to the great rock tower, now, on the new map also pointed to St. Joseph! Therefore, by following the compass in the opposite direction, the men could go straight from St. Joseph, through the White River Badlands, the north edge of the Black Hills, the great rock tower there, and continue on to their former camp on the Little Bighorn River where they had left Chief Red Bear a year ago! They only needed to reverse the direction they had followed the compass to the great rock tower before, from 120 degrees to 300 degrees, in order to return. This was uncanny! Now they remembered Chief Red Bear's reputation among the Crow. Not only was he a powerful medicine man, once turning day into total darkness for hours, but he was also a great prophet.[1]

It was a pleasant time of the year. They could travel twenty to thirty miles a day and still graze their horses. They headed northwest at 300 degrees on the compass, directly toward the north end of the Black Hills. If they could follow near this direction, it would take them to the north side of the Bighorn Mountains. Somewhere between the Absaroka Mountains and the Yellowstone River they would find the Crow Indians in a land of many buffalo and beaver. Dan was very eager.

In two days time they were well away from the broad valley of the Missouri River and were riding through the smooth, tallgrass prairie of eastern Nebraska Territory. Here in early summer, water was plentiful as streams were numerous in the area of the Big Blue River. On the seventh day they crossed the North Platte River where they first got wet in water flowing from the western mountains.

The Oregon Trail was along the North Platte. This time they did not follow it west, but stayed on their 300 degree heading on the compass to the northwest. After leaving the Oregon Trail, they were very much alone except for Indians they may meet, friendly or hostile.

As they journeyed northwest near the Loup and Calamus Rivers, the land changed from tallgrass prairie to shortgrass prairie. They could see the change to a dryer climate and knew they were at the edge of the great western plains.

One morning in some rolling sandhills, not far from the Calamus River, a dozen mounted Indians were sighted a mile to the west. The

Indians were riding at an angle toward them. Jake said, "Just keep goin' like we are, but keep your rifles handy, and in sight."

As the Indians came close, they looked to be some Pawnee braves. Probably a hunting party. The trappers and the Indians stopped and faced each other a hundred feet apart.

Jake raised his hand in a gesture of peace, and the Indians approached. Jake greeted them, "We travel in peace."

Their leader replied, "You cross Pawnee land. You have tobacco?"

Jake handed a flat can to him. "We have can of tobacco for you."

The Indians were staring at the rifles now held low across the trappers' saddles. "You got new kind gun."

"We got new guns. Shoot many time quick," said Jake.

"We go, you no shoot too much buffalo," and the Indians turned to leave.

After they left, John said, "I know they wanted to see under the tarps on the pack saddles, but they knew they couldn't out-fight these new guns. We better be careful tonight, though."

At night camp the trappers always kept their rifles handy. Each took a few hours on guard duty watching from a well-hidden place.

They crossed many miles of good grass land each day. Buffalo and antelope were plentiful across the rolling prairies and ridges. Some lakes were seen that were alive with many kinds of waterfowl.

Eight days from the North Platte River they reached the Niobrara River. They had traveled for fifteen days and were more than one-third of the way on their journey. It was June fourth.

Their horses were in good shape, although they had lost some weight. The weather clouded up, and it rained for three days. This was a good time and place to take a break from traveling and rest their horses while it rained. It was fortunate they had reached the river where there were some trees to camp in to break the wind. They camped six days until it stopped raining and the river receded.

On June 11th, they left the Niobrara River and rode to the Little White River. They crossed Bear In The Lodge Creek, and the fifth night from the Niobrara they camped on a small creek near the Big White River. Here they rested a day and a night, for now they were facing the mysterious White River Badlands.

Dr. Ferdinand Hayden had led his exploration party through the grotesque area two years before, so the trappers thought it must be possible to survive crossing it. Jake Barn's years of frontier experience helped them now. At one time, he had been in some very dry and remote areas of the Green River. That experience had taught him to devise a way to carry water in dry areas. They had several large canvas water bags, one for each horse and each man. They soaked the water bags in the small creek where they rested a day. The Big White River carried a fine, white silt that made it nearly unusable. When the trappers were ready to leave, they filled the water bags from the small creek and tied them on the horses. The soaking had swelled the canvas material so the bags held the water very well. Evaporation even kept the water cool.

June 16, they started across the treeless badlands. They found it to be a land of fantastically eroded colorful peaks of soft rock. In places, level, flat land a few miles across was cut by deep gullies where small sharp buttes and cones were left standing. Rivulets of rain had cut vertical grooves down their sides. The flatlands were edged by ridge after ridge of high jagged buttes and extremely eroded hills and canyons, all cut down the sides with deep wrinkles and creases. They were shaped from many layers of gray, white, yellow, brown, and pink sedimentary rock. Some of the round-topped cones looked like fancy pastry with pink or yellow frosting. The high ridges and buttes were tipped with sharp-toothed points. In some places, numbers of pointed buttes stood, each alone, on a flat plain of shimmering heat waves where the buttes seemed to dance as glassy mirages, but were real. It was a place unique in its own form of strangely eroded colorful buttes. At evening time, dark shadows marked the edges of sharply cut patterns as the lowering sun enriched the colors. It was a stark landscape of timeless beauty.

The men and their horses wound their way westward through the strange sights until evening. Their night camp was on a flat, shortgrass meadow they had found. The water bags allowed the horses and men to be comfortable at a dry camp. Dan said, "What a terrible place this would be on this hot, blazing day, if we didn't have these water bags. We'd probably die." The next day they found their way out of the badlands and crossed the prairie to the Cheyenne River by late evening. They camped by the Cheyenne River. That night, Dan said, "The badlands were interestin' to see, but I'm glad we're out of 'em."

From the Cheyenne River, the trappers again rode northwest. They happened on to Rapid Creek and rode near it toward the Black Hills for a time. They seldom followed creeks because of the danger of meeting Indians, but the creeks all ran in the direction they were going toward the Black Hills.

They had to camp one night in the Rapid Creek Valley, but they camped a half mile from the creek and had a guard all night. They were close to the Sioux here.

As they neared the Black Hills the next day, they found a beautiful sight. This side of the Black Hills was covered by a healthy growth of dark green pines that grew on the sides and over the tops of the long ridge of rounded peaks. Lighter green oak trees were scattered in splotches among the pines at the base of the peaks. Creeks of clear cold water flowed from the mouths of pretty canyons. John said, "No wonder the Sioux love this land."

Dan exclaimed, "I sure would like to follow one of these shallow canyons back into those dark tree-covered mountains. There must be some beautiful places there for the Sioux to live."

Jake answered, "I'm sure if we rode just a few miles up one of these pretty canyons, only to have a look, we'd never return. We'll just be lucky if we can get past the Black Hills, even riding around the outside."

The direction they were riding would take them into the high peaks of the Black Hills. They would have to ride around the mountains. They turned to a more northerly direction and rode alongside of the mountains that were about four miles away. The trappers watered their horses in a clear, cold creek they crossed, and filled part of the water bags for night camp. They camped a half mile from the creek to be less likely to be found. They were very uneasy because of the danger of being found by the Sioux, but they were not bothered that night.

The next day, after they had ridden about fifteen miles alongside of the mountains, a band of about forty Indians approached them from the direction of the mountains. The Indians trotted their horses rapidly toward the trappers.

Jake said, "We can't get away if we run. They'll kill us if we try. We can't outfight that many, but keep your guns ready when we meet them."

The trappers stopped as the Indians approached. Jake raised his hand in peace.

The Indians rode up fast and stopped in front of them. Their chief said, "I'm Chief Bear Rib. We are Hunkpapa Sioux. Few white men come here. Not many leave. Why are you here?"

Jake said, "We are on our way to Yellowstone country. This is our shortest way. We would like to see the high stone tower."

Chief Bear Rib said, "This is the land of many Sioux tribes. We want to be left alone. We do not want to be spied on so more white men will come to take our beautiful land that you call the Black Hills. We call this land 'Paka Sapa.' We will keep it forever."

Jake said, "We are not settlers who want land. We are trappers who trap on the Bitterroot and Yellowstone. We have presents with us to give to Indians whose lands we cross."

John had taken some of the presents from a pack. He offered them to Chief Bear Rib. There were two one-pound cans of tobacco, a six-inch rectangular mirror, a pound sack of beads and large red buttons, a very fancy hunting knife, and a two-pound sack of salt.

Chief Bear Rib accepted the presents and said, "I believe you speak the truth. You do not seek our land or search for gold. Go to the Yellowstone and take the beaver and buffalo of our enemies, the Crow. Soon the Crow will not need as many buffalo. My warriors need some practice and some fun. They will go kill many Crow and take their horses."

Chief Bear Rib said, "Your guns look new and different. What are they?"

Jake said, "They are new Sharps rifles. They are easy to shoot." Jake did not offer more information.

Chief Bear Rib said, "When we go to Fort Laramie, I will get one."

Then Chief Bear Rib continued, "We don't want you to pass through these high peaks. They are sacred to the Sioux. Go a little farther north until you have gone by them, then go west through the low hills for two days' ride to the tower we call 'Mateo Tepee.' It means grizzly bear's lodge. You will see how the grizzly bear has scratched it. You may find other Sioux who will kill you. That is the chance you take. Now go, while my heart is good."

After the trappers had gone a half mile, John said, "Chief Bear Rib must have some beautiful valleys in those mountains that he doesn't want white men to see."

As they started around the north side of the high peaks, they rode into partly pine-covered hills with valleys of knee-high grass. The air was cooler as they rode into the hills. Whitetail and mule deer were scattered throughout the area. Buffalo were nearly always in sight. Ice-cold water flowed from big, beautiful Spearfish Canyon. This was a low mountain paradise few white men were able to see.

They rode west for two days and camped that evening a half mile from a small creek. The hills were not as high in this area. Sometimes they could see the open plains to the west.

The next morning they rode over small hillsides and creek valleys partly covered by trees and partly open meadows. Finally they rode over a hill and saw the tower, two miles west.

They crossed along the upper side of a grass-covered open slope and stayed just in the edge of the trees, where they stopped and watched the strange sight ahead.

On the top of a pine-covered ridge stood the lone, huge, stump-like rock tower. It was over eight hundred feet across the top, and its pleated-looking, vertically fluted sides reached twelve hundred feet above the surrounding area. It was the magma of the center of a very ancient volcano. As the molten rock slowly cooled, it shrunk and solidified into polygonal-shaped columns that remained standing as the softer sedimentary cover was slowly worn away.

This was the tower Chief Bear Rib called, "Mateo Tepee," meaning grizzly bear's lodge. The high towering sides with their deep vertical grooves did look as though a huge grizzly had scratched it. The tower dominated the entire area. It was a tremendous sight. No other lone pillar of rock such as this was known to the world. It was a spectacular and very distinct landmark.

At the bottom of the ridge a small, brown river flowed slowly to the northeast past some low, bare, red buttes. This was the Belle Fourche River, which flowed around the north side of the Black Hills and then onto the east to join the Cheyenne River and on to the Missouri River.

Several dozen Indian tepees could be seen in the open spaces among the oak and cottonwood trees along the river. The trappers were out of sight as they peered from the edge of the trees across the open spaces to the strange sight before them.

A quarter mile ahead, a band of twenty mounted Indians started across the opening toward the tepees. The trappers were standing in front of their horses. Dan's stallion, Sonny, noticed the Indian horses. He pricked up his ears and started to whinny. Dan quickly pulled his bridle reins and clamped a hand across Sonny's nostrils before he made very much sound. The Indians did not notice.

John said, "That was the thing that bothered me most about having a stallion with us, but if we're careful, we'll make it yet. We'd better slip back through the trees and get out of here before our luck runs out."

They rode north for over five miles and stayed out of sight of the Belle Fourche River to avoid meeting Indians. When they finally crossed the river, they were not seen. Now they started on their same old 300 degree heading on the compass.

John said, "This compass direction that we took from Chief Red Bear's arrow has worked real good for a trail to Crow county. We only needed to bend a little through the Badlands and around the Black Hills. It was close to the general direction. We're a little north of our trail now, but we can work our way back."

They were nearing the upper Little Missouri River in late afternoon. From over a ridge, a small band of about two dozen warriors rode toward them at a gallop as they gave their war whoops.

The trappers dismounted quickly and Jake held the horses. He said, "Now you can try fighting Indians with your new Sharps Rifles."

The Indians were under two hundred yards away when John knocked one off of his horse. Dan quickly killed another one, but the Indians kept coming, firing a few guns. The Indians did not all have guns, but would soon be in range to use bow and arrows. The trappers would be goners if that many Indians reached them. At one hundred yards, John and Dan each killed another Indian.

The Indians had not expected the trappers to reload before they reached them. Because too many had been shot so fast, they turned away. When the Indians were out of range, they stopped and held a powwow. Soon they tried another attack. John and Dan each killed another Indian at two hundred yards. The Indians quickly turned and rode out of sight.

Jake said, "They couldn't figure out what was happening when we reloaded so fast. A fourth of them is a real bad loss. I don't think they'll come back."

Dan exclaimed, "A little practice killing game with these Sharps Carbines sure made us dead shots!"

John remarked with eyebrows raised, "I would hate to face these guns in enemies' hands. They're really deadly weapons."

They mounted and then rode past each Indian to see if they were all dead; they were.

Jake said, "I think they're Brule Sioux. This is the south side of where I've heard they live."

For a few days they traveled a little north of where the three men had traveled a year ago on their way to Missouri.

Making a new trail gave the trappers a chance to see a variation in their scenery. They rode from creek to creek across rough, sharp waves of gray sagebrush prairie and past distant pine ridges. Rimrocks sprouting short pines bordered shallow, narrow valleys. It was an enchanting land of ever-changing panoramas as they rode across the wide area of the Little Powder River, the Powder, and the Tongue Rivers.

On a warm day, the squeak of saddle leather and the dull, steady clop-clopping of their horses' hooves could make the men drowsy. The startling whir of a prairie chicken's wings from underfoot could nearly unseat one as his horse jumped sideways. Clear, sharp notes of a meadowlark's song helped nudge them to an awareness of possible tall feathers thrust into black hair slipping through shadows or protruding above a rock.

Many bands of antelope were seen. Some raced by, wheeled, stopped, stared and raced by again as if to challenge the horses to a race. Scattered herds of dark buffalo with tan calves grazed slowly across the shortgrass prairie. Curious little black-tailed prairie dogs sat on their haunches and barked from their mounds at the new intruders. Coyotes and jack rabbits played their game of chase. Low, squat badgers waddled along, looking for a prairie dog or rattlesnake to dig out and have for dinner. What was thought of as lonely, desolate prairie, was teeming with wildlife.

The men crossed the Tongue River a mile farther south than they had on the trip to Missouri, and then returned to their original compass heading. This time they did not encounter any Sioux Indians here. As they traveled on, the north end of the Bighorn Mountains came into view. High, snow-capped peaks towered behind the front range of peaks.

Dan gestured toward them, "There's our first view of the high mountains. It won't be long now until we'll be in Crow county."

John smiled, "I think you're getting anxious to see Lily."

They rode over many miles of grass-covered hills toward the Little Bighorn River, and finally reached the top of the same hill where Chief Red Bear had seen his vision. As they crossed the same buffalo wallow, they saw Chief Red Bear's white arrow still lying pointed toward the great tower, Mateo Tepee. The buffalo had shied away from the arrow as from a snake.

"I'm surprised the buffalo haven't trampled the arrow," John mused.

"Yes," Dan agreed, "It is strange. There's something about this hill that gives me an eerie feeling, ever since Chief Red Bear told us of the vision he saw here."

The men started down toward some tepees along the river and were met by some River Crow who rode with them to the village of Chief Twines His Horse's Tail.

There they smoked his peace pipe, and the chief asked the white trappers to camp for a time with the River Crow. He said their friends, the Mountain Crow, were along the north side of the Beartooth Mountains now.

The trappers gave presents to the Chief and also the sub-chief who had brought them to camp. Jake said that they would continue their journey the next day, as they would like to finish their trip and unpack their supplies.

The next morning the trappers left the River Crow's camp. In the next two days they crossed the Bighorn River and rode by the north side of the Pryor Mountains. They were safe in Crow country now. The Yellowstone River angled twenty miles to the north of them. Along the east side of the Bighorns, and on along the north side of the Pryors, Beartooths and Absaroka Mountains was probably the greatest buffalo range on earth. This was the land for which many Indians were willing to make their last stand against the white people.

It was a wide sea of lush grass, with herds of huge buffalo always in sight. Antelope raced across shimmering waves of prairie grass. Prairie chickens and sage grouse strutted among the silvery sage brush. This was a wildlife paradise.

Farther west, they rode to the top of a high grass-covered divide and looked down across the deep and wide Clarks Fork Valley. On the western horizon a great long arc of snow-capped mountains flared into the blue sky through crystal clear air. At the center of the arc were the huge peaks of the Beartooth Mountains with shoulders of great white plateaus. The Beartooths were flanked on the south by an unbroken series of peaks that faded from sight a hundred miles away beyond the Shoshone River. Bending west from the Beartooths were the Absaroka Mountains, that faded into endless sharp, miniature white peaks.

Range after range of high mysterious mountains, each separated by fifty or a hundred miles of wide open spaces, faded to infinity in the northwest.

From the top of the divide, the men sat and gazed in wonder.

Dan was ecstatic and declared, "This is the sight I was longing for; everything I'll ever need is here before me, even Lily Marie LaFountain is somewhere out there."

"Yes," John agreed, "I suspect this is where we'll spend the rest of our lives. This must be where our destiny lies."

"It's the best place I've ever known," agreed Jake.

The trappers rode twelve miles down the long slope of the high hill to the Clarks Fork River. This river rushed from a canyon on the east side of the Beartooth Mountains and flowed north for seventy miles down a wide valley to the Yellowstone River. Along the lower part, they crossed the 150-foot-wide river where it ran a foot deep over a riffle. The mosquitoes were bothersome along the river because of nearby sloughs, so the trappers rode farther west eight miles and camped by Rock Creek.

The trappers did not search for the Crow village along the creeks down here. It was July now, and the weather was hot. The Mountain Crow would be camped near the high, cool mountains.

The next morning, the trappers continued on west toward the Beartooth Mountains that ran in a northwest direction. They left Rock Creek Valley and rode to the top of another high ridge of hills between Rock Creek and the East Rosebud River. It was twenty miles across the ridge. The pine-covered top broke steeply down the north side to the Yellowstone. The grass-covered south slope reached to the base of the tremendous Beartooth peaks, twenty miles to the southwest.

As they rode west on this high ridge, they saw the most incredible close-up, panoramic view of the range of snow-capped Beartooth peaks. The lower half of the great peaks were covered by dense pine forest. Sheer walls of rock on the sides of gaping canyons were rimmed along the top by sharp pinnacles. Above the canyon walls, wide, snow-covered plateaus reached to immense cliffs and steep glaciers on the sides of high, cloud-scraping peaks.

The trappers crossed the hills of lush grass, crossed East Rosebud Creek, and over another hill to the edge of the West Rosebud Valley. From the side of the hill, they saw the Crow village below them. The tepees stood among cottonwood and aspen trees that bordered the rushing blue waters of West Rosebud Creek. Along the small valley, grass-covered hills sloped up to the base of the nearby great peaks.

Moose and deer browsed along the creek, and scattered herds of buffalo and elk grazed across the hills. Gentle, cool breezes rustled aspen leaves, and pine-scented smoke of campfires in the Crow village drifted lazily through the white-barked trees.

A dusky band of hunters rode into camp leading their ponies loaded with a fresh supply of buffalo and elk. They were met by inquisitive children and their dogs. The squaws were ready to quickly dress the meat. It was a peaceful scene in a primitive paradise.

"Pardners, there's a scene we'll never forget," John exclaimed.

6

▼ ▼ ▼ ▼ ▼ ▼ ▼ ▼ ▼ ▼ ▼

HAPPINESS WITH
THE CROW INDIANS

▲ ▲ ▲ ▲ ▲ ▲ ▲ ▲ ▲ ▲ ▲ ▲

On the side of the hill, the white trappers were met by a dozen Crow braves on horses. When the big, strong Indian in the lead met the trappers, they saw it was Striking Hawk. He was a proud and handsome warrior in his colorfully beaded buckskin breeches, brass armbands, and bear-claw necklace.

"Hello, my long lost friends. We have been watching for your return each day. I see the Sioux and Cheyenne were not able to take your hair."

"We slipped through real careful," Jake explained. "Only a few tried."

"I see you have the new guns that I have heard are so fast to load."

"Sure have, and they are dandies," John answered. "Ten times better than the old ones."

Striking Hawk nodded to Dan, "Lily's been waiting, waiting for you. Sometimes she's been quiet and sad. I want to see her face light up when you meet."

As they rode on, Sonny started prancing, and Dan had to control him firmly. Striking Hawk nodded his head toward Sonny, "The first thing I could see as you came down the hill was Sonny. Sure glad you brought him."

"Sure wouldn't leave him," Dan answered. Just then, with head held high and nostrils flared, Sonny gave a loud, wild, whinny as only a stallion can. "That's all right, Sonny, for a stud I guess you've been quiet long enough. Just don't forget I'm here," Dan cautioned.

"He knows my mares are over past the village, watching and listening," gestured Striking Hawk. "I have three good colts of his from last year. I would give you my best two horses just to use him with my mares each summer. My two best horses are almost as fast as Sonny."

"When we get to the village, you just use him right away. He'll be a real bother to ride until things quiet down. I wouldn't take your best horse, though; it could cost you your life. You're on the warpath too often. I'd need you're second best horse, though."

"You might need to save your own scalp sometime," Striking Hawk suggested.

"This new gun will help with that, and I'll be using Sonny most of the year."

"You can take my third horse, too, any time you want him; I have others," and then Striking Hawk stopped the men where they had arrived, at Louis LaFountain's lodge. From in front of the lodge, Lily came, reaching her arms to Dan as he dismounted to meet her.

"Dan! Oh, Dan, you've come back!" and they embraced.

"Lily! This is the happiest I've ever been."

"I was sad and lonely while you were gone, Dan. I felt something was making it hard for you to come back, but I always thought you would sometime. My spirit would just die if you hadn't."

"I was always longing for you, too, Lily. When we left, the farther we rode away, the worse I felt. I couldn't wait to get back to you."

"I'm so happy now, Dan."

"Honey, I know this is where I should always be, here by these mountains with you. We'll always be happy here together now. I'll never leave you to go to Missouri again," and they stood with an arm around each other.

Louis and Pretty Feather came out of their lodge and met the trappers. "We're glad you've finally come back, my friends." Louis spoke each man's name as they clasped hands. "Did you come back through Fort Laramie?"

"No, we came along by the north end of the Black Hills," John answered.

"That must have been plenty risky," Louis suggested.

"Risky enough, all right," Jake agreed, "but these new guns helped," and they discussed the new guns.

After a short visit, John said, "We'd better go on to meet Chief Red Bear," and they parted after Dan had pledged to come to see Lily tomorrow.

Striking Hawk held Sonny again for Dan when the men dismounted and greeted Chief Red Bear, who was standing in front of his lodge.

"Ho," they each spoke and raised a hand.

"We have returned from our people, far away in Missouri, to be with your people again," Jake spoke. "The arrow you pointed took us straight to the great rock tower. From there, we rode south to the Oregon Trail along the North Platte, and then far east to our home. On our return, we rode straight back all of the way on the path of the arrow you pointed. We found where you had left the arrow on the hill by the Little Bighorn! It was still there! The buffalo didn't trample it."

"I believe Chief Red Bear's medicine is very strong. It guided us safely through the Sioux Nations," John declared.

"It was a medicine arrow," Chief Red Bear informed them, and the men recalled that the arrow was made with a white granite arrowhead, a white wooden shaft, and trimmed with shaped, white tail feathers of a Bald Eagle.

"I see the young man, Dan, has returned with you as I expected him to. The beautiful girl and the beautiful land of the Crow brought him back. He will need to have strong medicine after the man in my vision, the long-white-haired soldier on the black horse, has been here," he prophesied.

"All of the way from the Black Hills we rode through strong grass, crossed many creeks, and saw endless herds of buffalo," Dan explained. "As they have always been, the buffalo are strong and there are many. I don't understand how this could not always be so."

"In my vision, I saw their end, but for one calf. This I do not understand, but when the time comes, you will know what to do, Dan. The time is far away. Now we will smoke the peace pipe," and then Chief Red Bear gestured for them to sit and smoke the pipe.

101

As they passed the pipe, Chief Red Bear told them, "We still have many buffalo, elk and beaver for our people. There is enough for our good white friends. We want you here with us. The Sioux from the east, and the Blackfoot from the north we must always fight off. Our Blackfoot enemy, Sinopah and his warriors, come each summer to steal our horses and take Crow scalps. He always leaves some of his dead warriors behind."

The trappers went to their pack horses and brought presents for the chief. They brought him tobacco, a knife, a new Sharps carbine and bullets. For his squaw, Fast Deer, they brought beads, two steel needles with an awl, and a hand mirror.

The chief and his squaw were very pleased with such fine presents.

As the trappers left to go set up their tepee at the edge of camp, Chief Red Bear told them, "You are always welcome among the Crow."

The trappers settled down into camp over the next several days. They were welcomed as old friends by all of the Crow of this Mountain Crow Village of Chief Red Bear. The trappers gave a small bunch of beads to each clan and a few other presents to some of those living close by.

The men found there were about two hundred tepees and seven to eight hundred people in this village. This varied, because there were usually some clans that had gone to visit or live for a while at another village, or some people of other villages were in Chief Red Bear's village. The Crow were very free and congenial.

This village had several large bands of horses that were guarded and cared for by their owners and many younger Indian boys. Striking Hawk was using Sonny with his band of over twenty mares. Dan was riding the horse named Stepper, that he had taken in trade from Striking Hawk for the use of Sonny. Stepper was a blaze-faced, medium-sized bay horse. He was a fast walker, and well trained. He was trained to stand where his reins were dropped; he would never leave. Stepper was an easy rider and a good horse for hunting elk. Dan was very pleased with the horse.

The summer and fall were spent in hunting and exploring the area along the Beartooth and Absaroka Mountains. Sometimes the trappers went alone, but most times they hunted with the Crow. It was the kind of life that was the most enjoyable for the men from Missouri.

Dan went to visit Lily every few days. They were both very happy now. Together they visited her parents and other families. Sometimes they strolled hand in hand along the edge of the village or along the creek and had pleasant conversations together. This was the part of their lives they enjoyed the most. The whole village was pleased with this love affair.

The Indian camp was moved every few weeks to a fresh area along one of the creeks that ran from the mountains. There was another big swift creek every four to eight miles along the north edge of the mountains. The wonderfully clear, cold water came plunging over cataracts, bouncing and turning through big boulders and cascades in huge canyons, then flowed swiftly into the valleys. There were stretches in the creeks where the water ran smooth and slow before rushing through the next riffles and rapids.

Dan was the happiest while he walked and fished with Lily in the creeks where the water took the blue color of the sky. It was so clear that the small, smooth rocks could be seen to the bottom of the deepest holes, where speckled trout wriggled leisurely along the rocky bottoms.

Here in the fall, among yellow-leaved aspen, the Indians pitched their tepees by the creek. Mornings were a little frosty, but most of the days were sunny and warm. The braves brought in many smooth coated elk from the base of the mountains, and the squaws dried and stretched their hides for making clothing and many other uses. Sometimes one could just lie back in pleasant idleness and watch the fluffy, white cumulus clouds drift slowly across the wide blue sky. It was what is known as Indian summer, and the men felt as they had in the carefree days of their youth.

The trappers gave several dozen awls and steel needles to some of the squaws. The squaws helped them build new, warm tepees made of buffalo hides for the coming winter. The trappers canvas tepees were all right for summer use and for traveling on long trips, but they would need much warmer tepees for cold winter weather.

In late October it rained nearly two inches. The clouds hung low for a few days. The sky cleared in the night, and the next morning at sunup the people in the village looked up at the dazzling, white range of snow-covered mountain peaks nearby. While it had rained in the village near the mountains, it snowed over two feet in the top half of the peaks. The brilliant, jagged, white peaks shone above timberline and looked twice as high as they had before the new snow came.

For the trappers, the new snow and the very cool northwest breeze were a harbinger of the approaching trapping season. There was an invigorating excitement in the changing of the seasons that added a

103

dash of spice to the routine of everyday living. Although the sky was blue again, the warm, pleasant idleness of Indian summer had vanished with the coolness borne on the breeze whipped down from its intimacy with the arctic.

During the next week, the three trappers gathered their traps from the places where they had cached them the year before and took the traps to their tepee where they repaired them. Some were replaced with new traps purchased from Louis LaFountain.

For the trappers it had been an easy summer and fall while living among the Crow Indians. No major battles had been fought against their traditional enemies, the Sioux and the Blackfoot, although there had been many small skirmishes. Dan had visited with Lily many times during the summer. It had been the kind of living he had longed for while he was in Missouri.

In September, Dan had returned Stepper to be cared for with Striking Hawk's band of horses and was again riding Sonny. Dan liked for his horses to be with Striking Hawk's horses because they were well guarded.

7

▼▼▼▼▼▼▼▼▼▼▼▼

LO WAUK AHO
TU COM TU

▲▲▲▲▲▲▲▲▲▲▲▲

He was an Indian brave belonging to a hunting party of over two hundred Bannock Indians who were from a large Bannock village in the area of the upper Beaverhead River. Although there were many moose, elk, and deer in the Bannock's land, buffalo in that area were not as plentiful as they were in the land farther east. It was far away, but the Bannocks had sometimes gone to the upper Yellowstone to hunt and dry buffalo meat on the Crow's land because they were friends of the Crow. Usually they did not go farther than the Gallatin.

The Bannocks traveled to the area in large hunting parties for protection against the fierce Blackfoot warriors who also sometimes hunted there, but usually in smaller bands of two or three dozen braves.

One day in late fall, the Bannocks were drying many racks of buffalo meat east of the Three Forks of the Missouri after having several successful buffalo hunts. They had not seen any Blackfoot Indians, so one day twenty Bannock hunters rode three miles eastward up the Gallatin Valley, where they killed three more buffalo. Suddenly, they were attacked by about thirty Blackfoot warriors who rode out of their hiding place in the trees along the river. They attacked with war clubs and lances and were met by desperately fighting Bannock braves. The vicious Blackfoot, Chief Sinopah, quickly struck down six of the Bannocks with his tomahawk and war club. Eight more were clubbed and killed by his warriors. Only six Bannocks managed to escape after killing two Blackfoot.

Lo Wauk Aho Tu Com Tu had been knocked unconscious with a war club and taken prisoner. When he awoke, he found himself tied to his horse and being led over the pass eastward to the Yellowstone River. Another fifteen miles down the Yellowstone River, the Blackfoot camped one evening among the cottonwood trees. Lo Wauk Aho Tu Com Tu was thin and slightly taller than most men. He was about thirty years old, had quite homely features, and black loose hair that had been cut at the top of his slightly stooped shoulders. Most of his clothing was taken by the Blackfoot for the few ornaments on them, and he was fed only a small amount of meat.

During the night, he managed to chew through two of the rawhide strings around his wrists and ankles that held him to a tree, and then quietly escaped. For a while, Lo Wauk Aho Tu Com Tu did not know why he was able to get loose, but then he realized that it was a game they were playing with him as a contest among the Blackfoot warriors. They had intentionally allowed him to escape so that they could then hunt him down. The winner would take his life and his scalp.

Lo Wauk Aho Tu Com Tu knew the sport of the game would be in tracking him the following morning, so he went to the Yellowstone River. The Blackfoot could not track him in the water, so by dawn he had waded and swam two miles down the river which was not deep or very swift in the fall of the year. He passed by log debris along the edge which would be the obvious place to hide, and he stayed in the water on past a long tree-and-brush-covered island that they were sure to search. Finally, along a rocky shore, he came out of the water and crossed the rocks to where the trees grew to the edge of the rocky shore. There were endless cottonwood trees all of the way down to the shore, growing continuously in a wide belt all along the river.

When he left the water, he was careful not to leave even one track. Lo Wauk Aho Tu Com Tu was more desperate than his trackers would be, so he was also more careful. Beside the river bottom he found a tree small enough to climb. It was beside a tree too big around to climb from the ground. He climbed from the small tree into the branches of the big

106

tree, and in a crotch out of sight high in the big tree, he found a good place to hide. The Blackfoot could not look in all of the thousands of trees along the river that were still holding half of their leaves, even if they had a week to waste.

The Blackfoot looked for the Bannock for a few hours and even passed close by, far beneath him. Lo Wauk Aho Tu Com Tu had lain very still for a long time so that even the birds and squirrels were not aware of his presence and would not give him away with their scolding and chattering.

The Blackfoot searched very carefully all along the area, but they were unable to find their quarry. A few times he even heard them calling to each other. Sometimes he felt like an animal cornered in its den.

After the Blackfoot had passed on down the river, Lo Wauk Aho Tu Com Tu stayed hidden in the tree for half of the day. He then stood on a very high, big limb, peered eastward down the river where the Blackfoot had gone, and laughed quite strangely before he climbed down to the ground.

Lo Wauk Aho wanted to go back to his people, but it was threatening to storm, and it would probably snow in the high mountain passes. He was very hungry and a little cold because he had almost no clothing. He knew that he was now in friendly Crow territory. Now, he should be able to avoid the Blackfoot, and find a Crow village where he would be safe. He started up a creek that led toward the base of the Absaroka Mountains.

8

▼▼▼▼▼▼▼▼▼▼▼▼

WINTER TRAPPING
1855-1856

▲▲▲▲▲▲▲▲▲▲▲▲

As the weather became colder, the animals' pelts turned to prime condition. It was now time to start setting traps for beaver, mink, weasel, marten, and other fur bearing animals.

The trappers packed their traps and all of their supplies for the winter. They told the Crow Indians they would return in early spring. Dan said a special good-bye to Lily. She told him she would be lonesome while he was gone. So they would not bother the Crow trappers, they left the Crow camp on the Stillwater River and moved seventy miles west, along the north side of the Absaroka Mountains. All of the creeks from the Absaroka and Beartooth Mountains flowed north into the Yellowstone River, which ran northeast to the Missouri River.

Their camp on Mission Creek was ten miles east of where the Yellowstone River, flowing north down Paradise Valley, turned to the east. They were still in friendly Crow land.

After they had trapped from one camp for a week, Dan moved alone to a small creek four miles west at the base of a big peak. There were several good beaver ponds along two small creeks where the brush, trees and high grass furnished the beaver a good living. He set his camp in a deep draw protected from the wind by pine-covered slopes. In a few days, he had six mink and two beaver, but these two tiny creeks were a good place for only one trapper.

One day, Dan rode in the open area toward the west side of the mountain. From the tree line at the base of a big peak, the grass-covered land sloped several miles down to the great bend of the Yellowstone River. Dan rode around to the west side of the peak and gazed into Paradise Valley.

From the south, the river flowed down forty-mile long Paradise Valley, through a great gap between mountain ranges, and around the great bend of the river where it started eastward. Paradise Valley was bordered on the west by the Gallatin Range, and on the east by a series of pointed peaks of the Absaroka Mountains. For as far as Dan could see, many thousands of elk and buffalo grazed in scattered herds in the wide valley. Dan had been in this valley when he first came to Crow Country, but from the high slope where he watched, he thought a more beautiful valley he had never seen.

The wind gathered strength down the mountain slopes, and gained speed to seventy miles an hour, with stronger gusts. Sometimes it was difficult to breath while facing into the wind. It was as though one had been grasped by giant hands that would nearly drag horse and man along with them. Clothing rippled and slapped, while the nose and eyes watered. The temperature was above forty degrees, and the shallow snow had been blown away. It would have been impossible to live long in this wind if it was really cold. In the winter, one would have to stay in the areas that were partly protected because the southwest wind seemed to blow most of the time here. It was an uncomfortable ride that day, so he was glad to get back to his sheltered camp on the north side of the mountain that evening.

Dan had most of the hindquarters of an elk suspended with a rope from a high tree limb. His other supplies were also suspended out of reach of bears. When he started to cut some steak from an elk quarter, he wondered if the quarter looked cut in the same way as he had left it. Surely Jake or John had not been here, or he would have found extra tracks. When he began to start his fire, he could feel a slight warmth still in the rocks of the fire circle. The rocks could not have stayed warm that long after his morning fire.

Now he did feel spooky! Could someone be watching from the dark shadows of the pines? It made the hair on the back of his neck tingle. Carrying his Sharps carbine and his pistol, Dan walked a circle around the camp a hundred feet out, but did not find any sign or tracks of man or animal. As he prepared his supper, he never left his back turned one way very long. This was the bad thing about being alone, but if someone or something had wanted to ambush him, they already should have as he rode into camp.

Dan had tied Sonny and his pack horse at the edge of his camp instead of picketing them out on the nearby meadow. Finally, near dark, Dan decided since he had found no tracks of anything around camp, that maybe he was letting his imagination run wild. He could have forgotten about how the elk quarter had looked, but the rocks had been a little warm; that was still questionable.

About that time, Sonny jerked his head up high; with bowed neck, blazing eyes, and nostrils flared, he gave a rolling snort. That panicked Dan; he nearly jumped out of his moccasins! In two quick jumps, he had reached his Sharps carbine leaning against a tree and in a split second had pointed it toward the outside edge of the light of his campfire where Sonny was looking. Nothing moved there, but if it had, Dan would have instantly blown it away. That Sharps would have blown away just about anything except possibly a grizzly bear. Maybe that was what was lurking out there in the dusk now, or maybe a wolverine, or maybe some strange trapper. Damn it, Dan did not like being watched by something! Maybe Dan had too much imagination, but he knew Sonny did not. Sonny was somehow aware of something out there beyond the light of the campfire.

Dan gradually calmed down, but he kept a campfire going all night. If a grizzly came, he would at least like to be able to see him when he fired his gun.

Dan did not sleep in his small tepee, but rested in the dark shadow of it. Sonny settled down and seemed to be nearly asleep while standing there. They were not bothered again by anything that night. Dan was guarding the camp, but he must have dozed off for awhile. At bright dawn, Dan's eyes flashed open. Quickly he looked all around, but everything was all right.

After breakfast, Dan planned to pack up and return to where John and Jake were. He was frying breakfast when the horses raised their heads to look toward the opening in the trees.

111

Dan looked. There stood a lone Indian with his hand raised, and he spoke, "Ho."

Calmly now, Dan scrutinized the Indian. So, this was the phantom that had spooked Dan and his horses so badly. Dan was relieved to see that it was not an apparition or a deadly enemy; it was simply a near-naked, half-starved, lone Indian who did not even carry a weapon! He did not look dangerous; in fact, he only looked pathetic.

The Indian continued to stand there with one hand raised as Dan studied him and then quickly glanced around the area to see if there were any others. There were no others, so Dan motioned for the nearly naked Indian to come into camp. Dan noticed that the two horses watched the Indian with their ears standing forward as if interested, but not frightened. They saw no spooks in bright sunlight.

The Indian came in and squatted down about twenty feet away, where he remained silent. Dan saw that he had only two rabbit skins for clothing, although the air was very cool. He had a red ring around both wrists that indicated he had been held captive recently. Dan observed the poor, homely looks of this man. He did not look fierce or dangerous, but Dan could not guess what tribe he was from. Dan was careful not to give the Indian a chance to attack him, but he felt that the Indian was friendly.

Of the half dozen elk steaks that Dan fried, the Indian ate four of them, and each man had a piece of fry bread. Dan was satisfied that this was the person who had taken just a small steak from the elk meat yesterday. The Indian spoke some words of what Dan regarded as thanks for his breakfast.

After breakfast, the Indian watched as Dan broke camp. While loading his pack horse, Dan found some clean, winter buckskin leggings, moccasins, and a jacket he could spare. He measured them against the tall Indian, handed them to him and remarked with a smile, "About all you'll frost now is your shins."

After dressing, the Indian pointed to his ankles, spoke "Ha," gave a low, funny laugh and smiled. What had been a spook was beginning to be a friend.

After loading, Dan stepped into Sonny's saddle, and motioned for the smiling Indian to follow. The Indian could have left at any time, but for an hour he closely followed Dan four miles back to home camp, where Jake met them.

As Dan rode up with the Indian following him, Jake said, "Well, what in the devil did you bring in?"

"Well, for a while I thought a devil's about what it was. He sure had me spooked for a while." Then Dan told Jake what had happened, and Jake talked with the Indian for a while.

John came in while they talked and Dan quietly and briefly explained the situation to him.

After a while, Jake told them what he had learned from the Indian. He was a Bannock Indian from the area of the Big Hole River. His name was Lo Wauk Aho Tu Com Tu. Jake related to them the Bannock's capture and escape from the Blackfoot Indians. Before he could return to his people, it had snowed too much on the high mountain passes for him to be able to return afoot in his naked condition. He had come up closer to the base of the mountains to avoid the river valley where the Blackfoot or other Indians were more likely to travel.

He had found Dan and was afraid of him. Then he decided Dan could be as friendly as a few other white men, who did not fire their guns at him. He used a small piece of Dan's elk meat and his fire ring when he saw Dan leave for the day. For a while, he could not find a way to approach Dan's camp without spooking Dan and the horses. But in the bright morning sun he took the risk and came into Dan's camp.

The trappers decided to let the Indian stay with them. The Bannocks and the Crow were friendly to each other, so the trappers felt that the Crow would accept the Bannock in their village. It would be a dangerous trip in the winter for him to try to return to the Big Hole country. There would be many high mountain passes too deep with snow to cross.

John said the Bannock's name was too long and hard to say. Since he had walked into camp alone and had no horse to ride, they could name him Lone Walker.

The trappers continued to trap in their usual way as Lone Walker stayed with them and learned what he could do to help. He was very friendly and made himself useful with camp chores and many other tasks.

After a few more days of trapping on Mission Creek, they packed their horses and followed a small stream over a low mountain pass to the southeast for about twelve miles. Here they found a good, tree-lined creek in another pretty valley. The creek came from a big canyon several miles to the south in the Absaroka Mountains. It was the West Boulder. Extending a few miles beyond the canyon mouth were huge, lone boulders as high as a horse, that were thinly scattered across the valley floor. Dan noticed the boulders looked strange sitting out there alone. They surely had not rolled that far from the base of the mountains. Only an ice age glacier could have carried them so far.

All along the valley, and for the few miles they traveled in the canyon, they found many beaver ponds along with all the other animals they wanted to trap. This was one of the best creeks they had ever trapped. In the mouth of the canyon, the creek ran slowly through a flat, swampy area less than a mile long. A maze of small streams also wound their way through the swamp. Dozens of beavers and other fur-bearing animals lived there. Many moose browsed on the willows and reached under water for moss and water cress. This was a trapper's paradise, but they had to be careful of the moose, so they camped a mile from the swamp. They dared not go into the swamp to trap too early in the morning or too late in the evening. Most of the moose left the swamp through the middle of the day and went up into the edge of the canyon in the pines.

Camp was located in a wind-protected place in the trees a mile down the creek from the swamp. Near their camp was a hundred-acre grassy meadow on the slope at the base of a mountain. A half mile farther down, a cliff reached almost to a gorge the creek passed through beside the trail. They blocked the trail with poles to keep their horses from leaving. The hard wind always blew the snow off of the steep part of the meadow. It was a perfect winter pasture for their horses. Bighorn sheep passed above them a few times, and Rocky Mountain goats were sighted farther above on the steep mountainside. This was a perfect winter trapping area. The wildlife and horses could not go more than three miles up the canyon because the snow was too deep up there. The wildlife easily jumped the poles and went down to the valley as they wished. The horses never left their pasture, but they had room to avoid the moose.

Lone Walker cheerfully helped with any task he was offered. There was skinning and stretching of hides, and always much wood to gather. He soon learned enough of the English language to be able to talk some. One day he gave Dan a buckskin jacket that he had made.

Dan tried the jacket on and exclaimed, "Wow, that's nice! You can really make good clothes, Lone Walker. Thank you! Now I know the Blackfoot took your clothes 'cause you make 'em so good. They didn't want to spoil 'em when they killed you, cause they wanted 'em."

It was evident that Lone Walker was grateful to be allowed to live with the trappers, and had even become a friend. They were not concerned with any possibility that he would take a horse and leave. Even if he wanted to return to his people, it would be a very bad winter trip. There were three high mountain passes from the Yellowstone to the Big Hole River where his tribe should be. Not even with a horse would he be able to get through the mountains now. They learned that Lone Walker did not have a squaw or children that he needed to return to, so that was why he was not unhappy. He really was a lone walker.

For all of the men, trapping here was an interesting adventure. The bears were not bothersome now because they were hibernating in their dens, but the moose really kept them alert. Very often the men were challenged by a moose that stood its ground and shook its head so the men had to yield. It would be senseless to kill the moose except for food. They did not ride their horses to trap in the canyon because they could not avoid moose on the trail through the trees. In their open pasture the horses could avoid the moose.

The trappers never went close to a moose in the willows because it was impossible to get away from a moose there. The men did not set long trap lines, so they walked in pairs for added safety. Even though the trappers were careful, they still had some dangerous moments when they unexpectedly met moose.

By late December the trappers had nearly all the pelts they wanted. They had taken less than half of what were there, but there was another winter for trapping next year. There had not been really heavy snowfall, but the snow had built up and had not melted. There was nearly two feet of snow in the canyon now, so they packed up and made their way out of the canyon and down the valley about ten miles. Here they could trap during the winter.

This was very windy country so they found some good trees and willows to camp in. The snow was not deep here and more than half of the ground was blown bare. This was why the buffalo and other wild animals could live in this land in the winter. It was also why horses could live here.

In a week it snowed over eight inches in the valley. When it cleared, Dan said, "It's a good thing we got out of that canyon; I'll bet the snow's belly-deep on a moose up there now."

The moose and other wildlife came down from the mountains to the hills and valleys. Even the goats came down to wind-blown canyons at the lower edge of the mountains.

In late January, a sky full of solid, slate-gray clouds moved in from the north. A steady wind blew from the northeast, and the temperature dropped down near zero. It snowed four inches. The sky stayed solid gray and the temperature continued to drop, then snowed a few more inches. The temperature was from zero to thirty below for two weeks. Living in a buffalo hide tepee was not as warm as a log cabin, but it was reasonably comfortable. A small fire was kept in the center of the tepee. Buffalo robes covered the floor except for fire space. The amount of air entering and leaving was controlled by the tepee flaps. There were plenty of furs for clothing and coverings.

The temperature in the tepee was usually above freezing. Food was plentiful. Elk and buffalo were always near. The animals were still in good condition with some fat on them. The trappers shortened their trap lines because of the cold, and as it grew colder they quit trapping.

One day the sky cleared to bright blue. There was not a cloud in the sky and not even a slight breeze. The temperature dropped fast after sunset. Wild animals sought shelter among the trees along the creek. The arctic air grew colder all night long, and by morning it was forty-five degrees below zero. It remained below zero all day and another night.

John mused, "This is part of the great life of being a trapper in the western mountains. If you don't like it cold and still, just wait a while and it'll get cold and windy!"

At sunrise the next morning, there was a faint stir of breeze from the southwest. That was the most common direction of the wind along the east side of the continental divide. As the wind became stronger, the temperature climbed to thirty degrees above zero. The snow was wiped from the ridgetops and hillsides. The horses had been pawing through snow for feed. Now the horses and wildlife could graze on the snow-free places.

Even when there were no places free of snow, the buffalo did not starve. They pushed the snow aside with their massive heads to uncover grass. Other wildlife pawed through the snow for grass or nibbled on the brush. The hardy buffalo and other wildlife seldom starve or die of the cold; they are adapted to this severe climate. The buffalo were the most abundant and dependable food supply for the Indians and also for the trappers.

The men quit trapping early in February. They had enough furs and that was all they wanted to pack on their horses. They moved their camp down to the Yellowstone River during some good weather.

116

9

▼▼▼▼▼▼▼▼▼▼▼

TRAIL TO
FORT SARPY

▲▲▲▲▲▲▲▲▲▲▲▲

In March 1856, the trappers rode around the north end of the mountains to the Stillwater River. Lone Walker did not have a horse. Each trapper had his riding horse and with the pelts their four pack horses were loaded. They traveled slowly enough for Lone Walker to keep up with them. Dan had left his extra horse with Striking Hawk.

The pardners and Lone Walker did not find the Crow until they met some Crow scouts near the mouth of the Stillwater. They learned that Chief Red Bear's village was near the mouth of the Clarks Fork, and rode there with the scouts.

Everyone was glad to see the white trappers again. Lily gave Dan a big hug, exclaiming, "Dan! Oh, Dan, I'm glad your back! You just don't know how glad I am to see you."

"Oh, thank you, Lily, honey. I've sure been lonely for you too," and they held each other and kissed. They were inseparable the rest of the day.

The trappers put up their tepees in the Indian village again. Lone Walker was welcomed as a friend by the Crow. One night when Lone Walker told the story of his escape from the Blackfoot, he was praised by Chief Red Bear with the simple statement, "Bannocks are friends of the Crow. Lone Walker will be good warrior with Crow warriors."

One day, soon after their arrival, Dan got his extra riding horse from the Indian herd and loaned it to Lone Walker, with the expression, "You can use him as long as you need him. Someday, you'll steal a Blackfoot or Sioux horse from them."

Although Lone Walker did not have to walk now, he was always known as Lone Walker.

During the last week in March, Chief Red Bear and the Mountain Crow traveled down the Yellowstone Valley to Fort Sarpy, below the mouth of the Rosebud. The white trappers and Lone Walker accompanied them. Lone Walker had made several friends among the Crow, and seemed content to stay with them rather than to try to return to the Bannock Indians.

The journey was a joyous occasion. The squaws anticipated seeing the wonderful articles to trade for. The braves were equally excited, as there would be many new articles for them.

The 120 mile journey to Fort Sarpy was made in six easy days. The weather was warm and showed signs of spring. Tree buds were swollen and the short spring grass had turned green at this lower elevation along the Yellowstone River. Even the clouds had changed from the slate-gray stratus of winter to white cotton puffs floating slowly across the deep blue sky. There was a wide, flat carpet of grass across the Yellowstone River Valley, bordered on one side by a band of cottonwood trees and the bending river. Light-colored sandstone cliffs formed miles of rimrocks at the edge of the valley. Rounded hills and great, long, grass-covered slopes rose wave upon wave to the base of distant purple mountains. As the Indians strung along the valley, it was a charmingly idyllic scene of a large band of colorful horses and Indians moving peacefully along their way.

When the Crow and trappers reached Fort Sarpy they found a forty-five foot mackinaw boat tied at the edge of the Yellowstone near the Fort. The ice had gone out of the river and the boat had brought supplies from Fort Union at the mouth of the Yellowstone.

James Kipp was the factor for the American Fur Company trading post at Fort Union. It was the headquarters for all of the company's trading posts. Each spring James Kipp sent boats up the Yellowstone to supply Fort Sarpy. Fort Sarpy was about two hundred miles closer for the Crow to trade than Fort Union.

The Crow camped near the fort, and the next day they had the pleasure and excitement of trading their furs for the many articles available to them. Salt, tobacco, steel needles, thread, beads, buttons, various trinkets, metal pots, knives, traps, ammunition, a few guns, hatchets, and other articles were traded. No whiskey was traded as that was against company rules.

A day later, Chief Red Bear and the Mountain Crow were joined at the fort by Chief Twines His Horse's Tail and the River Crow. The River Crow had come from the Bighorn River. A happy week was spent in the excitement of trading furs for new supplies and playing many of their games again. There was much story telling, and visiting with friends.

After Dan and his pardners finished trading, Dan and Lily spent much of their time together watching games and dances again. Sometimes the trappers hunted buffalo or elk with Crow hunting parties. Jake had cautioned, "The Sioux trade at this fort too. They're sure to have scouts watchin' all the time. I'm sure the Sioux would jump a small huntin' party."

The trading of pelts was not hurried. The Indians enjoyed bargaining and getting all they could for their furs. Both sides seemed satisfied with the results.

After a week, the trading was finished, so the chiefs, the medicine men, many warriors, and the trappers held a big powwow. They had a problem without a clear solution. An English Baronet, Sir St. George Gore, had come to America for a hunting expedition in the west. He had left Fort Laramie on the Platte River in 1855 and traveled down the Powder River. He then journeyed up the Yellowstone and turned up the Tongue River several miles. There he had a fort built to winter in.

This aristocrat had unlimited funds for his trip. He had twenty-eight Red River Carts, 110 horses, twenty yoke of oxen, fifty hounds, and forty frontiersmen led by the legendary explorer and mountain man, Jim Bridger. Gore paid very high wages to these men, or they would not have stayed with him. He rode in a yellow carriage and had all the conveniences for extravagant living as he was cared for by his servants. The likes of this expedition had never been seen before.

Gore hunted from a magnificent gray Kentucky Thoroughbred named Steel Trap. He had a collection of seventy-five custom made, variously gauged pistols, rifles, and shotguns. The rifles were highly decorated percussion cap muzzle-loaders made by the best English gunsmiths. Gore loped across the plains and killed scores of buffalo, elk, bear, and wolves. None could escape his hounds. He was here for the chase and kill. Seldom did they use the meat. He occasionally took a trophy head or hide. He left a trail of thousands of dead, rotting animals on Crow Land!

The Crow were furious, and a delegation from the tribes had gone to talk to the government Indian agent at Fort Union, Alfred Vaughan. Vaughan was reluctant to act because Gore's trip had been authorized by the Superintendent of Indian Affairs, Alfred Cumming, in St. Louis. Vaughan had relayed the message to St. Louis, but there had not been any answer yet.

The Crow did not know how to handle the situation. They had good relations with the whites and did not want the army on them for killing Gore.

Chief Red Bear wondered if Gore could be the destroyer of buffalo and Indians in his vision. The council did not believe this was the man in the vision because this man was not a soldier as the one in the vision had been. However, he was such a destroyer of buffalo that a plan must be made to force him to leave.

Striking Hawk and John Daily offered to take the responsibility of George Gore's death if he was killed. They both hated this insane, sadistic killer of buffalo who seemed to be a menace similar to the long-haired soldier in Red Bear's vision.

John Daily told the council, "If I kill Gore, the Indians will not be responsible, and no army will come. Neither will it come to get one trapper in this land where there is so much wilderness to hide in."

Striking Hawk contended, "I should be the one to kill Gore. I am part Crow, and he is killing Crow buffalo."

The chiefs decided a large war party would force Gore out of their land, but if he refused to leave, they would kill him. The chiefs organized the force to carry out the plan for dealing with George Gore. They intended to get rid of him one way or another. Their scouts were keeping track of him as he moved up the Tongue River, and the reports of his killing was even worse now.

The next morning, the big war party started east. In two days the Crow and the trappers had crossed Rosebud Creek and reached the

Tongue River. For part of a day they followed the trail of destruction left by the Gore party. They were appalled by what they found. Hundreds of dead buffalo were found scattered along the area. Gore evidently returned to the dead buffalo, where, with his horse and hounds, he ran down scores of wolves, coyotes, bob cats, and bears that were feeding on the carcasses. Using dozens of hounds in the chase, no animal could escape. Evidence of all the animals' hopeless last stand was pathetic. Gore was the devil on a horse.

The Indians and trappers had seen enough. Out of sight, they circled ahead of Gore who was riding his horse over a mile ahead of the caravan. Gore was accompanied by three riders. The big Crow war party was just out of sight over the hill as Chief Red Bear, four of his sub-chiefs, Striking Hawk with three other warriors, and the three trappers at the back of the small war party rode through a shallow ravine and approached the Gore hunting party.

They gave no hint of their intentions, but when they stopped in front of Gore, they aimed their weapons at him and the others.

Chief Red Bear said, "We've had too much of your waste and killing of Crow Buffalo. It is bad. Leave now, or we will kill you."

Gore's face showed rage. Striking Hawk warned, "Make a move with your gun, and you'll get a bullet through your chest!"

Dan knew that Striking Hawk preferred to kill Gore and only wanted an excuse to shoot him.

Just then, with excellent timing, two hundred Crow Indian braves rode slowly over the low, close hills from three directions toward George Gore.

Shock showed on the hunters' faces. Even Jim Bridger showed surprise and concern.

Gore blurted, "This trip was authorized by the U.S. State Department."

Jim Bridger stated, "The American Fur Company and the Indian Agency in St. Louis agreed to this expedition."

Chief Red Bear spoke, "The Indian Agency and the army are far from here. Our Crow warriors are here," and he gestured toward them as they were getting close. "You will die. They will burn your wagons unless you leave now."

The warriors were close enough now that Gore could see their war paint. "Damn you," he exclaimed, but he turned his horse back toward the wagons and they trotted away.

Dan said to Striking Hawk and John, "I could see both of you were hoping for a chance to kill Gore, but it could have caused you trouble. Now everything has worked out just as planned and they'll be gone."

John answered, "Yes, after following Gore's trail of death, I did want to kill him. It's the only time I've wanted to kill a man except in self defense, but I guess it's better this way."

Striking Hawk said, "We will not let them kill our buffalo."

Dan knew that only the presence of Chief Red Bear had prevented Striking Hawk from killing Gore. Striking Hawk was determined that buffalo should not be wasted ever since Chief Red Bear's vision.

The chiefs were relieved, but solemn because they were having a little trouble holding their authority with some of the braves who were wanting to massacre the Gore party.

The Indians and trappers followed a few miles behind the Gore caravan when it left. The second day, they passed Gore's fort that he had built on the Tongue River, and he had burned it when he left. They followed Gore thirty miles down the Yellowstone, sometimes within his sight. After that they turned toward home, while Gore proceeded on to Fort Union at the mouth of the Yellowstone.

It was later learned, after a heated disagreement with Fort Union factor, James Kipp, that over the purchase of Gore's surplus goods, Gore burned nearly all of his outfit in a fit of rage. Kipp then refused to build the large mackinaw boats for Gore's trip down the Missouri. This was the route originally determined at St. Louis. Gore sent half of his men down the Missouri in two ten-by-twenty-four foot flatboats with his trophies and most of the remaining supplies, but he decided on an alternative route for himself because it would be more adventurous. It turned out to be more adventurous than he desired. He, Bridger, sixteen remaining men, sixty-five horses and fifty dogs would explore the uncharted Black Hills and then reunite with the boats at the mouth of the Cheyenne River near Fort Pierre on the Missouri.

After the boats left, the remaining Bridger and Gore party traveled up the Little Missouri into hostile Teton Sioux country where travelers usually disappeared. Gore no longer had his grand luxuries and had to live as a frontiersman. He still had the opportunity to kill many buffalo, elk, deer, antelope, and bear. Despite the warnings, they had not seen any Indians, so they crossed the Belle Fourche River and rode into the Black Hills. Suddenly, they were surrounded by a hundred-fifty Sioux warriors under Chief Bear Rib.

It was Bear Rib's practice to slay whites who entered the sacred Black Hills, but he relented and allowed the whites to leave the way they came in, only without any weapons, horses, equipment, or even clothes.

They traveled naked three hundred miles back down to the mouth of the Missouri! They traveled at night to avoid any hostile Indians, and survived on roots, berries, and a few rabbits taken from the hounds. Near the Missouri River, they were rescued by friendly Hidatsa Indians, and they finally returned to St. Louis on an opposition fur company's boat.

Because of Gore's insane slaughter of the plains animals, and the animosity he created among the Indians, the American Fur Company and Gore's hired frontiersmen were completely disgusted with him. He was ranked among the most infamous men of the West.

After the Gore incident, the River Crow moved to the Bighorn River. The Mountain Crow moved to Pryor Creek.

10

▼ ▼ ▼ ▼ ▼ ▼ ▼ ▼ ▼ ▼ ▼ ▼

CLARKS FORK GOLD
1856

▲ ▲ ▲ ▲ ▲ ▲ ▲ ▲ ▲ ▲ ▲ ▲

Chief Red Bear and the Mountain Crow moved west from Pryor Creek and camped for three weeks at the forks of Rock Creek and the Clarks Fork River. As the weather became warmer in the spring, they slowly moved their campsites up along Rock Creek.

One day in July, Dan and Striking Hawk went to inspect the Crow horse herd on some big grass-covered hills by Rock Creek, north of the mountains. The Indian horse herd was scattered along a hillside. Over 450 horses were grazing where there were no trees for mountain lions to hide in, as lions were very fond of eating young colts. Some were horses for riding that were not being used at the time, and some were mares with young colts. Many of the horses were hobbled, some were picketed, and some were loose. The loose horses were not likely to leave the herd, as several young men and boys watched over them.

Twenty of the young colts were definitely sired by Sonny as a result of the agreement for the use of Sonny in Striking Hawk's herd. Both men were very well pleased with the quality of the colts.

Striking Hawk told Dan, "When the colts are two-year-olds, pick the best one for yourself. They'll look real good by then."

"That'll be good," Dan replied. "I hope none are lost by then. One of these colts could be the horse I'll be ridin' when Sonny gets a little too old for hard riding. I don't like to think of that time."

Sonny was near the top of the hill when Dan and Striking Hawk rode up two hundred yards from him. Dan whistled to Sonny as he usually did.

Sonny recognized Dan's whistle, threw his head up and nickered. He had not forgotten Dan. Dan whistled again, and Sonny came galloping to him. He playfully ran by the men several times, stopped, whinnied loudly and ran around them again. He stopped near Dan, bowed his neck and nickered a greeting to his old friend. He reared, turned, jumped, bucked and farted, then galloped up the hill, turned again, and in a majestic stance, whinnied loudly.

Dan laughed and hollered, "Sonny!" He was glad to see Sonny feeling so good, but it was what he expected, and Dan was glad he had brought Sonny to this high, wild, and beautiful land. Dan said, "This place is enough to make anyone feel good."

Striking Hawk laughed and said, "Yeah, but I'll bet you can't jump and fart like that!"

"Well I sure as hell don't intend to try, but I'm just as glad to be here. Living in this land is even better than I expected, if that is possible. I enjoy this kind of living and the friendly people." Then Dan and Striking Hawk rode back to camp.

It was summertime now, so no trapping could be done. Some of the Crow hunters had told the white trappers of the big Clarks Fork Canyon in the Beartooth Mountains. The river came from many miles far back in the mountains. At the mouth of the canyon, the Clarks Fork River entered the valley from between two high, rugged peaks.

From the Crow hunters' description of the canyon, the trappers thought it would be an interesting place to pan for gold.

Soon the Crow were ready to move west along the foot of the Beartooth Mountains. The trappers were ready to move south to the Clarks Fork Canyon at that time.

When the trappers said good-bye to their friends, Lily said, "It seems like you're always goin' away, Dan."

"Yes, but I'll always come back, Lily."

Lone Walker was ready to go sheep hunting with some Crow friends.

126

The trappers traveled forty miles south up the Clarks Fork Valley along the east side of the Beartooth Mountains. The Clarks Fork River flowed north through a thirty-mile wide gap between the Pryor Mountains and the Beartooth Mountains. Long, sloping hills of semi-arid desert rose to the mountains on each side of the river. Sage brush, prickly pear, and short grass grew on the dry, rocky flats. Some areas were completely barren. There were places where many acres were flat, windswept rock. A few bands of antelope roamed across the area.

The Clarks Fork River flowed from the Beartooth Mountains through a wide canyon mouth that was formed by a huge, barren mountain peak on each side. Saw-toothed rock palisades sloped up the inner canyon walls. Trees grew along the river, but the canyon walls were nearly barren.

The upper portion of the mountain peaks farther ahead were capped with snow and pine trees. This was an immense and lonely area. It was uninhabited, and only rarely did a few Indians pass through the gap between the mountain ranges. This was the north edge of Shoshone country where Crow and Shoshone land met.

The trappers rode a few miles up the wide canyon to where it narrowed and the river flowed between high, vertical rock walls. Beyond here it was impassable.

They camped among the trees along the river. Although it was hot on the dry prairie, it was pleasant here where the cool breezes from the snowbanks and glaciers floated down the canyon from the great mountain region to the west.

They had come here to try their luck at panning for gold. This seemed to be the type of stream that would work well for panning gold. The river alternately flowed over rapids and boulders, then slowed to smooth water in places. The river banks and river bottom were usually gravel. There were many gravel bars and some sandbars.

They dug up gravel and washed it with their gold pans in many places in the edge of the river and some ponds close to the river. A small amount of gold dust and flakes were found nearly every day. They were not getting much reward for their hard work, so they usually quit early in the evening and went trout fishing or hunting.

There were several water ouzels busily working along the river. The trappers enjoyed watching them as they would come within fifty feet. A water ouzel, or dipper, is a robin-sized, slate gray bird. It is a dull, dumpy, homely looking little short-winged bird, but it is fascinating to watch its expert performance. It has strong yellow legs and special oil glands that allow it to enter the swift water and swim a little or walk on the bottom, even without webbed feet. It walks right over slick water-washed boulders. Their downy undercoat protects them from icy water temperatures. Their strong, black-tipped yellow bill is used to pry around stones and break hard water beetles. The ouzel bobs up and down on a rock a few times, then plunges into the swirling waters and comes out a minute later from a different place. Although one expects it to be washed away, it always comes out again. It works along the edge of the stream and all the way across the boulder strewn rushing water. Any evening the men went fishing, they always saw two or three water ouzels that busily worked along the stream almost unmindful of the fishermen.

The men worked along the canyon sides and never found a trace of gold. They returned to the river gravel where they found enough flakes to slowly fill a few small bags. After two weeks it did not seem very interesting anymore.

One morning they were working near the mouth of the canyon where the river made a big bend. A small gravel bank was along the edge of the river, and wide flat layers of rock sloped all the way across the river bed. It was August and the river was low. The water ran shallow and slow over the flat, wide layers of rock shelves, dropping from one shelf to the next as over stair steps. The shelves completely crossed the river and were irregular shaped from three to twenty feet wide. There were a few cracks in each shelf, an inch to several inches wide and a foot or more deep. They ran crosswise to the flow of water. John was digging gravel and sand out of one of the cracks and washing it when he gave a whoop and holler, "Whoowee, I think we've found it! Look!" He was holding a nugget bigger than a walnut in his hand.

Jake and Dan splashed over to where John was holding out the nugget, and Dan exclaimed, "Wow, what a chunk of gold! I'll bet there's more!"

Jake laughed and shouted, "Man, oh man, a nugget big as a moose turd. I'll bet there's a lot more. Just watch me dig now!"

Now their interest caught fire. They scraped the mud, gravel, and sand out of the cracks and washed it with their pans. There were flakes of gold in nearly every pan full. They sometimes found nuggets from the size of grains of sand to nearly fingernail size. They found a few almost as large as John's first big one.

The rock steps ran down the river for over two hundred yards. After the first day of excitement, they worked out a method so they would not rework the same cracks in the bottom of the river. They built a small sluice box and cleaned out the cracks farthest down the stream. Then they worked their way upstream. This way the waste sand and gravel was swept down stream from where they were working. The cracks filled in again minus the gold. Before long, no one would be able to see where they had worked.

John said, "Pardners, I think we've got a good system worked out now. Thousands of years ago, the heavier pebbles and gold washed along the bottom of the stream and caught in the cracks. The rock slabs have worked like a giant sluice box to catch the gold. It must be coming from way back in the mountains at the headwaters of the river. Far up this huge canyon, into these rugged mountains, would be a hard area to explore, but someday, someone will find the source and dig a mine. For now, we're getting rich fast right here."

The men picketed their horses to graze in open meadows in the morning and evenings. During the hot part of the day they tied them in the shade of trees along the river.

One day, John walked out of the shallow water and climbed onto the river bank to get a pick. Dan and Jake were still washing gravel through the sluice box. There were no trees on the north side of the river where it flowed from the canyon into the prairie. John saw a band of over fifty Indians riding their horses across the river from the south. He softly called to his pardners, "Indians coming! They're down around the bend about a mile! Big bunch, must be over fifty. Stay down out of sight while you drag the sluice box over here by the south bank and lay it on its side, so they won't know what it is. I'll put a couple small logs against it to help it look like driftwood. Drop your tools in the edge of the brush."

They quickly did as he said, and with their rifles, they hid across the stream near the river bank, in brush, trees, and a few big rocks. Their horses were out of sight in the trees two hundred yards up the river. Jake said, "We've got a little cross wind, I don't think the horses will hear 'em and nicker."

"Damn, I hope not," John answered.

The trappers were hiding and watching from the tree-lined south bank of the river. The Indians rode up the river on the bare north side.

Because the Indians had been riding north, there seemed to be no reason for them to follow the river into the impassable canyon, but they were coming!

129

The trappers lay watching from their hiding place with rifles ready to sight down the barrel. They dared not let so many Indians get too close. Jake whispered, "They're not Crow; they look more like Shoshone Indians, and they sure don't like gold prospectors."

At two hundred yards the Indian warriors were still coming! As they got closer the men could see they were not wearing war paint, but Dan knew they would fight in an instant anyway. At 150 yards it was time for the trappers to start shooting! In breathless tension the trappers still waited as the Indians slowly rode another thirty yards! Now the Indians stopped, and some of them spoke a few words. The leader pointed, but it seemed he may be pointing high up on the mountain to something of interest. As a few more words were spoken, one brave farther back rode closer to the river and stared at the sluice box! If the brave recognized it as something built by men he would give an alarm!

The trappers aimed their guns at the Indians as the brave stared at the sluice box, but he failed to figure it out. He lost interest in it, and then watched the mountain with the other Indians. "Whew," Dan softly blew in relief.

None of the trappers' horses nickered. No sounds of movement came from the trees for the Indians to hear while the trappers quietly watched. Finally, the Indian leader turned his horse north, and the band of Indians rode away. When the Indians were a quarter of a mile northeast, Jake exclaimed, "That was awful damn close. They're probably Shoshonean, I'm not sure, but this is their land. If they'd found us, they'dve been on us like a bunch of hornets! I don't think they'll be back, but we'd better stay outta sight in these trees for an hour or two."

John said, "They probably saw some goats up high on the mountains. Too high to go after, but I think that's what they were lookin' for. There was too many of 'em. Sure glad we didn't have to shoot. We'd better not work any more today, and just keep a careful watch."

"Hope they don't go on north to raid the Crow," exclaimed Dan, with some concern.

"Don't worry, Dan. Old Louis LaFountain and Striking Hawk will kill any of them that come close to Lily, you can be sure of that. They've always taken real good care of her," John advised and smiled.

In the following days they worked hard getting the gold, but they looked more often for anyone approaching or traveling past the mouth of the canyon.

They had to make leather bags from deer and antelope hides for carrying the gold. These animals were also the main part of their diet. There were deer farther along the base of the mountain. Antelope were able to graze on the dry flats and drink at the river or at other unknown sources. They never saw any buffalo on the dry, nearly barren flats east of the mountains.

The trappers stored the gold in holes in several rock cliffs where rats and other varmints could not get to it. It was well hidden and would not be found by anyone else. By working quite steadily, in a few weeks they had taken all the gold they could find and were ready to return to the Indian village by late September.

When they left the canyon, the pack horses were loaded very heavily with their equipment for living, a few tools, and many sacks of gold. They traveled slowly through the gap along the east side of the Beartooth Mountains. No Indians or whites were sighted while they traveled northeast down the Clarks Fork Valley.

Twenty miles from the confluence of the Clarks Fork River with the Yellowstone, they turned straight north and crossed Rock Creek. A series of three eighty-foot cliffs rose eight hundred feet along the edge of the valley. The cliffs were eroded with hundreds of holes and caves. In the second layer of cliffs, the trappers cached one-third of their gold in a small cave twelve feet above ground. They covered the gold with sand and rock, and then destroyed the ladder they had used. As they left, they brushed away their tracks in the sand with a pine bough. They rode on to the Yellowstone River, between the mouths of the Clarks Fork and Stillwater Rivers. There were many high cliffs and caves in the rimrocks along the Yellowstone where they cached most of the remaining gold in two separate holes high up in the series of cliffs.

With leather thongs, they tied short poles into a ladder and hid the gold in small caves ten feet above ground level. These two caves were a mile apart. They took the ladder apart and threw it over the cliff. Again they brushed away their tracks near the cache with a pine bough as they backed away. Then John said, "With the gold hid in a few small caves where there's hundreds of holes and caves, I don't know why anyone would ever find it."

Dan agreed, "There's no reason for anyone to come up in these cliffs, and they sure wouldn't look in all these holes the wind and rain made."

As they were bringing the gold from where they found it, the men had discussed how to sell it. Their plan was to ship one-third of the gold each year to St. Louis to sell it. They planned to have the American Fur Company at Fort Union transport the gold and deposit the proceeds in a St. Louis bank in each of their names.

The trappers had a spell of gold fever while they were finding the gold. Probably no one ever looked for gold or found it without experiencing some gold fever. It was a very exciting adventure to discover gold. Actually, it was more exciting to find gold than to own it. However, it was a great satisfaction to know they had been successful and would have the wealth to do some things they may want to do some day.

Right now, they were just anxious to find Chief Red Bear's camp, relax and enjoy themselves. Dan, of course, was the most anxious because of Lily. They found the Crow camped on the Boulder River where Chief Red Bear had said they would be at this time.

The trappers were again happily welcomed to the village. Lily had a warm and loving welcome for Dan. They were so happy to be near each other again.

Lone Walker had stayed with the Crow and was still with them as he had not found an opportunity to return to the Bannocks. Louis LaFountain said, "We think Lone Walker is happy to stay with the Crow. Maybe he will never go back to the Bannocks."

Striking Hawk and many Crow warriors had defended the horses and village from an attack of Cheyenne and another from the Sioux. Two Sioux, one Cheyenne, and two Crow warriors were killed. Only seven horses were lost. One had belonged to Striking Hawk, but Sonny was still all right. Striking Hawk had been the most deadly fighter. He was becoming one of the greatest Crow warriors.

John said, "Maybe that was Cheyenne that nearly found us. We thought they were Shoshonean." Jake told Louis, "We found a little gold and cached it." He did not say what a big amount it was. No one would have guessed it.

Dan only told Lily they had found some gold, and that someday, after they were married it would be a lot of help to them.

October and November were spent in hunting game and gathering food for winter. It was really a good time of the year and the whole camp was happy.

In late November the Crow moved to the lower end of the Clarks Fork River. They wintered there and along the nearby Rock Creek.

The trappers spent December and January trapping the small tributary creeks of the Clarks Fork and Rock Creek.

In the spring the trappers had only half as many furs as they had the winter before when they trapped the West Boulder, but it was all they needed, as they planned to sell some gold. The trappers went to their first gold cache near Rock Creek and took half of the gold that was cached there.

In March, 1857, they went with the Crow to Fort Sarpy where they would all sell their furs. Again they all traveled together down the Yellowstone Valley, past the mouth of the Bighorn River and five miles past the mouth of Rosebud Creek to Fort Sarpy.

The supply boat, "The Cottonwood," had reached the fort with new supplies of trading goods several days before the Crow arrived. It was another happy rendezvous. Several days of fur trading were accomplished in friendly fashion. All steel articles were eagerly traded for. The usual articles were available. It had been a good year for the Crow. They were able to trade for many things they needed.

Captain Reynolds agreed to transport the trappers' gold to Fort Union on the boat. He would deliver it to James Kipp, the factor for the American Fur Company at Fort Union. For a commission, the company would transport the gold on one of their river boats to St. Louis. The company would sell the gold and deposit the proceeds in a St. Louis bank for the trappers.

The usual games and dances were held at the rendezvous. Many old friends were able to meet again. One evening as campfires flickered among the many tepees scattered along the river, a meeting was held in a big circle around a fire at the center of the camp. It was a social meeting for the purpose of recounting deeds and happenings of the past year. Stories of bygone days were also told for entertainment and as learning and history for the young people. War and hunting were the exciting stories, but many others of travel, meetings, and various happenings were related with much interest. Some told of the great places they had seen.

The Crow traditionally have a great fondness for their land. Standing before the gathering, and gesturing toward the four directions, Arapooish gave the following eloquent description of Crow country:

The Crow country is a good country. The Great Spirit has put it exactly in the right place; while you are in it you fare well; whenever you go out of it, whichever way you may travel, you fare worse. If you go to the south, you have to wander

133

over great barren plains; the water is warm and bad and you meet with fever and ague.

To the north it is cold; the winters are long and bitter and there is no grass; you cannot keep horses there but must travel with dogs. What is a country without horses?

On the Columbia they are poor and dirty, paddle about in canoes and eat fish. Their teeth are worn out; they are always taking fish bones out of their mouths; fish is poor food.

To the east they dwell in villages; they live well, but they drink the muddy waters of the Missouri—that is bad. A Crow's dog would not drink such water.

About the forks of the Missouri is a fine country; good water, good grass, plenty of buffalo. In summer it is almost as good as the Crow coutry, but in winter it is cold; the grass is gone and there is no salt weed for the horses.

The Crow country is exactly in the right place. It has snowy mountains and sunny plains, all kinds of climates and good things for every season. When the summer heats scorch the prairies, you can draw up under the mountains, where the air is sweet and cool, the grass fresh, and the bright streams come tumbling out of the snow banks. There you can hunt the elk, the deer and antelope when their skins are fit for dressing; there you will find plenty of white bears and mountain sheep.

In the autumn when your horses are fat and strong from the mountain pastures, you can go down into the plains and hunt the buffalo, or even trap beaver on the streams. And when winter comes on, you can take the shelter in the woody bottoms along the rivers; there you will find buffalo meat for yourselves and cottonwood bark for your horses, or you may winter in the Wind River Valley, where there is salt weed in abundance.

The Crow country is exactly in the right place. Everything good is to be found there. There is no country like the Crow County.[1]

When Chief Arapooish finished speaking, many nods of agreement could be seen in the light of the campfire. Dan was sitting beside Lily, and remarked, "Chief Arapooish knows all the good things about Crow country. This really is the best place, and best of all, Lily, I found you here."

When the rendevous ended, Chief Red Bear, the Mountain Crow, the LaFountains, and the three white trappers slowly worked their way back up the Yellowstone and Clarks Fork Rivers. This was a good area for camping in early springtime. The grass grew earlier at this lower elevation and not so close to the mountains. In a few weeks, the Crow moved to Rock Creek.

[1] From the Arapooish Crow Tribal Treaty in the Centennial Issue of *Absaroka*, ed. Eloise Whitebear Pease, 1968, 2.

11

▼▼▼▼▼▼▼▼▼▼▼

SINOPAH AND
JOHN DAILY, 1857

▲▲▲▲▲▲▲▲▲▲▲▲▲

The Blackfoot Indians were located along the east base of the
Rocky Mountains in Canada and the United States. The Piegan
Blackfoot roamed from the Three Forks of the Missouri to Waterton
Lakes in Canada. Their tepee villages were set anywhere from the Sun
River to the Milk River, and into Canada, along the Rocky Mountain
Front, where long, rolling prairies meet the rows of great saw-toothed
peaks that form the backbone of the continent. A more beautiful
range of magnificent, glacier-draped peaks does not exist. From azure
blue lakes, dark evergreen forests slope up the base of triangular-
shaped peaks that stand in series before rolls of white cumulus clouds.
This land of the Blackfoot is the home of the grizzly bear and Rocky
Mountain goat.

In wintertime, icy winds sweep in from the arctic, and are later
blown away by steady, warm Chinook winds. It is both a beautiful and a
harsh land. It bred a strong and fierce race of people. The Blackfoot
were a proud, warlike, self-confident people.

One of the clans of Blackfoot was led by Sinopah, a Piegan warrior chief. Sinopah was over six feet tall, lean, strong, very active, and a fierce warrior, twenty-seven years old. His black, piercing eyes were set above a full, straight nose, even, white teeth, and square jaw. His long, black hair fell loosely around his neck, and a long, narrow lock on his forehead was cut square at the bridge of his nose. Two eagle feathers were thrust at a slant above the back of his head. His swarthy complexion was painted with curved stripes of red and yellow ocher.

He did not wear a breechclout; however, his long buckskin leggins tied to a belt crossed at the front and left his buttocks bare. He wore fringed moccasins with bead and quill decorations. He did not wear his buckskin shirt in battle, but he wore his necklace of grizzly bear claws.

Sinopah was a great hunter. He was able to bring down any of the mountain animals with bow and arrow or with a muzzle-loader. Elk, moose, buffalo, and even grizzly bear were the prizes of his ability. A mountain peak by Two Medicine Lake was his favored goat and bear hunting ground. It was also one of his particularly beautiful places for summer camping.

The Blackfoot had never been able to build their horse herd to the numbers they needed, so they raided the Flathead and Crow herds each summer at different times. It was never known when they would come to raid.

In mid-June 1857, thirty Piegan warriors, with Sinopah as chief, rode around the lower end of the Scapegoat Mountains to the west side, and raided the Flathead Indian horses from the south. The year before they had raided the Flatheads from the north. This year they raided during a rain storm, and met only a little resistance. With his tomahawk, Sinopah surprised and quickly killed one of the horse herd guards while his Blackfoot warriors killed the other two. They took twenty horses and traveled fast back around the mountains until they were well into Blackfoot country. Here, five warriors parted from the band and rode north toward home with the captured horses. The other twenty-five started southeast toward Crow country.

They crossed the Missouri River near the Dearborn River, and rode southeast between the long ridges of the Big Belt and Little Belt Mountains. The Piegan warriors continued nearly straight to the southeast, between the Bridger Range and the sharp-peaked Crazy Mountains. They rode down the Shields River Valley to the north side of the Yellowstone Valley at the edge of Crow land. This was a very direct route from the home of the Blackfoot to Crow country. It was only 170 miles from the home of the Blackfoot on the Teton River to the Yellowstone. The trip could be made in five days. With seven days of travel, it was a leisurely hunting trip for the Blackfoot through long, wide, beautiful valleys and low passes. Most of the mountains along both sides were not high jagged peaks, but lower, tree covered, rounded peaks, except for the Crazy Mountains. The Crazy Mountains were very pretty, pointed, snow tipped peaks. It was a land of moderate rainfall, with wonderful grass and water. Herd after herd of buffalo, elk, antelope, and deer wandered over the land. It was part of the western paradise.

At the Yellowstone, the Blackfoot watched carefully, and stayed out of sight as they rode eastward down the Yellowstone Valley. They were looking for Crow, whites, or just any Indians to raid. Their faces were decorated with war paint, and they were eager for battle. However, their first concern was to steal Crow horses.

The Crow village of Chief Red Bear was camped near the forks of Rock Creek, about nine miles up from its mouth at the Clarks Fork River. Lone Walker and three young Crow men, Bird Hat, Flat Rocks, and Gets The Weasel, were scouting along the Yellowstone, twelve miles north of the Crow village. One morning, Bird Hat and Flat Rocks had a fire for roasting venison under trees near the river. Lone Walker and Gets The Weasel were nearing camp from down the river when they heard shouts and war whoops from the direction of their camp. They left their horses and sneaked within view of their camp. The Blackfoot had surprised the two Crow and killed them without gunfire. Lone Walker and Gets The Weasel sneaked back to their horses and stayed out of sight by riding up a deep coulee as they headed for the Crow village. They rode along at a fast gait, and traveled through low areas so as not to be seen along the crest of hills. They reached the village and alerted Chief Red Bear. The Chief quickly organized a defense for the village. The horses were brought into the village. Half of the braves guarded the village, and half started northeast down Rock Creek Valley. They were in two bands of over fifty in each band and rode at a fast trot. Scouts fanned out just a little ahead as they looked for the Blackfoot. It was a wide, grassy valley with trees bordering the creek. They had gone only about three miles when they heard gunfire from the north.

The three white trappers had been hunting to the northeast, and had checked on their cached gold to see if it had been disturbed. Near the mouth of a canyon, they were returning on a long, wide slope from the high hills and rimrocks to the Rock Creek Valley. A Blackfoot scout had seen them, so Sinopah and his band of twenty-five warriors were hiding in wait. They were in a thin row of trees in a shallow gully, but would be seen when the trappers were within three hundred yards. The trappers were riding along near the edge of the gully.

Sinopah had hoped that by this time of year, the Crow would be camped close to the mountains, far enough away not to hear gunfire. He wanted to kill the trappers because they may discover the Blackfoot or their tracks and alert the Crow.

The trappers were leading two pack horses, each with a deer on it. When the trappers were about three hundred yards away, the Blackfoot burst from the gully firing. They fanned out to the left and forced the trappers toward the canyon walls.

The trappers dropped their pack horses, turned and galloped away, pursued by whooping Blackfoot with some firing guns at them. They were being forced toward the big canyon. As they rode, they turned in their saddles and fired with their rifles. It was hard to hit anyone while riding at a gallop, and difficult to reload, but Dan killed one Blackfoot. Jake was leading. Below the rimrocks in the big canyon, steep, tree-covered slopes came down to the deep gully in the bottom. It could only be ridden through slowly. Near the mouth of the big canyon, Jake led them into a shorter, rimrocked, flat-bottomed box canyon.

One of John's shots killed Sinopah's horse at the mouth of the short canyon. Right after that, John was shot in the side of his back above the hip. It could have been Sinopah's shot. It was an awful blow that nearly knocked him from his horse. He dropped his rifle and held to his saddle horn with both hands. "Oh, God," how the pain stabbed with each bounce of his horse as he bent forward and held on. Through his swimming vision, he could see the huge scattered rocks higher than his horse at the end of the box canyon, then Jake lifted him from his horse and laid him on the grass behind a big rock.

From the protection of the rocks, Dan and Jake killed seven Blackfoot in one minute with their fast loading Sharps rifles. The Blackfoot, stunned by the rapid fire, turned back.

Striking Hawk was riding fast two hundred yards ahead of the rest of the Crow warriors as they neared the battle. He saw Sinopah afoot ahead of him. Striking Hawk was trying to reload. With empty guns they clashed. From his horse, Striking Hawk clubbed at Sinopah, but

140

was quickly knocked from his horse. He landed in a crouch on his feet and instantly grabbed his knife. Sinopah was racing at him with tomahawk raised! Like lightning, Striking Hawk threw his knife. It made one fast revolution and the blade buried at the base of Sinopah's neck, driving him to his back! Striking Hawk was over him in a flash, and buried his other knife under Sinopah's breastbone into the heart!

As the Crow warriors raced by, Striking Hawk grabbed Sinopah's loose hair, circled his scalp with his knife and jerked the scalp free. He held it up, and let out a blood-curdling war scream. Unbelievably, the great Sinopah was dead from the lightning flash of Striking Hawk's knife.

Striking Hawk wiped the blood from his knife and reloaded his rifle, but by the time he reached the battle, it was over. The Blackfoot had been caught between a hundred Crow and the accurate fire of Dan and Jake. Two Blackfoot had ridden through a notch to the top of the rimrocks along the canyon's rim. They intended to get behind Jake and Dan, but now they had escaped. If need be, they would run their horses to death to escape. It would be futile to pursue them.

The whole battle had not lasted over ten minutes, but now twenty-three Blackfoot and four more Crow warriors were dead, and John Daily lay dying.

Dan and Jake were kneeled down beside John, trying to help him. They propped him up slightly on a pillow of grass and gave him a tiny sip of water from a canteen. Jake had tied a bandage over the wound. It was not bleeding outwardly now, but it was obvious he was bleeding inside. He was steadily getting weaker. Striking Hawk, Lone Walker, and some of the other Indians were standing nearby. All were very worried.

John spoke weakly, while Dan was holding his hand as he spoke, "Think I'm about to go. Too weak."

Jake said, "It's about enough to make me wish we hadn't come out here to the West."

John replied, "No, It's just fate. Our trails all met here. No more Sinopah either." They had told him what happened during the battle.

John's eyes were staying closed for longer periods now. He opened them again. "Better marry that girl, Dan. Don't lose her." After pausing, "Give my girls . . . some of the gold . . . if you can. What a great country . . . to have . . . to leave . . ." His eyes closed. He went to sleep or fainted. In a few minutes, he stopped breathing.

141

Jake said, "He's gone."

It hurt Dan so much he could not speak. It just seemed that it could not have happened so suddenly. He was so strong and wise. Now, gone forever. It seemed to nearly paralyze Dan. Quiet tears rolled down his cheeks. There were tears in everyone's eyes.

After a while Jake asked, "Would you want us to bury him here, Dan?"

"No, let's just take him up to the head of this little canyon by us." Dan motioned to it, "Too many dead ones here."

Those who were gathered around helped. They took John up the short, little canyon. At the top of the slope, near the base of the rimrock, they dug a shallow grave and laid him in it.

Dan and Jake recited the Lord's Prayer. Then Dan said, "And now he belongs to you, O Lord. Please take him to heaven with you. Amen."

They laid a buffalo robe over John and covered him with dirt, then rocks to keep the animals out, and more dirt. Dan said, "I'll come back after a while and make a marker."

Down at the scene of the battle, the Crow had caught the trappers' horses with the deer still on them. They gave Dan the rifle John had dropped. It had been found with a dead Blackfoot.

The Blackfoot were left where they had fallen. It was not the custom of Indians to bury dead enemies. They would only place their own dead on platforms. The wolves, coyotes, and magpies would soon obliterate the Blackfoot bodies. This was part of the harsh side of life here.

The Crow had taken the Blackfoot weapons and anything they wanted. They took the four dead Crow warriors with them as they left the scene of the battle.

As the Crow and two white trappers were riding toward camp, Striking Hawk stopped beneath a big pine tree. Lone Walker held the horse for him while Striking Hawk stood on the horse's back. He tied Sinopah's scalp of long, loose hair to a limb and said, "May the spirit of Sinopah be lost in the wind forever."

That was something strange, but Striking Hawk felt very sad about John's death. He did not want to keep the scalp to constantly remind him of John's death.

When the Crow warriors reached the village, they were met by the people with great anxiety. Lily ran to Dan and hugged and kissed him. The great amount of rapid gunfire had been plainly heard from the village. They knew many warriors would surely have died. The squaws had waited in fear, knowing some of the braves would never return. Two braves had been killed that morning on the Yellowstone, and now four more were dead from the battle at the canyon. For their families, it was a terrible tragedy. Now there was the wailing of the death songs.

One-half mile from camp, platforms were made against the trees, and the dead warriors were placed on them. They were covered with hides and boughs. Their weapons were left with them for hunting in the Happy Hunting Grounds.

Everyone was saddened by the death of John Daily. Louis LaFountain told the trappers, "We were afraid of what might happen, knowing the Blackfoot were near, and you didn't know it. Sinopah was a tough and cunning warrior. We were sure he would see you. I'm thankful two of you got back. I feel bad about John. I'm glad my son killed Sinopah."

To Dan, it seemed to be such an unnecessary tragedy. Here was a land of plentiful buffalo and elk for all. Even more berries, plums, and roots than could be gathered. Yet the people found a reason to battle each other. They always had. Was it needed to preserve the vigor and strength of the race? Sioux Chief Bear Rib had said his warriors needed to fight Crow for fun and practice. Dan could see it kept the warriors strong and proud, but was it necessary? At the time, it did not seem to Dan that it was.

On the next trip to Fort Sarpy, Dan planned to mail a letter, with the news of John's death, to John's daughters in Missouri.

Jake and Lily were a comfort to Dan; Jake so calm and steady, and Lily so kind and gentle.

Soon, the Crow moved their camp four miles up the fork of Rock Creek. The valley was more narrow here. Big grass-covered hills rolled out from the valley on both sides. The willow and tree-lined creek was about thirty feet wide. Like every creek that flowed out of these big Beartooth Mountains, this one also was sparkling clear and full of trout.

Dan and Jake spent time fishing, hunting, and just scouting around taking in the scenery. Dan visited Lily very often. They walked together along the banks of the silvery, gurgling waters, past singing riffles and blue pools, hand in hand. The music of the stream, the thrill from the touch of Lily's hand, and the magic of love helped in Dan's mending over John's death.

143

After three weeks, and just before time to move camp again, Dan and Jake rode down to John's grave in the short canyon. Near the grave were fifteen-inch thick slabs of sandrock that had broken away from the rimrock cliff at some time. A two-by-three-foot piece happened to be shaped about as they wanted it. It was nearly square on one end and shaped to a point at the other end. Dan had an old knife of John's, and they used it to wear grooves in the rock to form the letters "R.I.P." for "Rest In Peace," "JOHN DAILY, BORN 1802, DEATH 1857."

They only had to roll the rock about twenty-five feet, but that was far enough for such a heavy rock. They set it straight up on end at the head of the grave, and it looked very nice. They were lucky to have such a well-shaped stone so close. They had to use what was near, and had no way to shape it.

Dan thought, this certainly is a place to rest in peace, all right. Few people will ever ride into this short, dead-end canyon which is not even in view from the valley. From the bottom of the short canyon, the stone was not noticeable up the canyon slope at the foot of the rimrock.

Dan saw that it was a very lonesome place, but it had a quiet, simple beauty. Fifty foot red-tinged cliffs rimmed the nearby grass-bottomed canyons. Patches of low brush decorated places beneath the cliffs. Far above, delicate, swirling streaks of wispy, white cirrus clouds floated in an endless blue sky. A dozen buffalo grazed slowly across the mouth of the big canyon. This day it was a picture of serenity. Dan thought it must also be quiet and peaceful wherever John's spirit was.

Dan stood beside the tombstone and looked at it carefully. The picture was deeply imprinted on his mind, just as the letters were engraved on the stone. It seemed so unreal to Dan that John was dead and gone forever, that only the engraving on the stone could cause him to realize it. The grief he felt was deeper than he had ever supposed it would be.

Dan was thankful for the strong feelings he and his uncle John had had for each other, and he was thankful they had shared so many happy or even difficult experiences together. A few of those experiences he recalled now.

John, Dan, and Jake had been great pardners, and they had always been kind and fair to each other.

Without John, it looked impossible to Dan that life could be as happy as it had been. He was sure John would have expected Dan to be sad for him, but to be strong and carry on without letting the grief overcome him.

Dan resolved to do just that, and then he turned and slowly walked to where Sonny stood calmly waiting for him.

In the evening, Dan and Jake started back to the Crow village. By the stare in Jake's eyes, Dan knew that Jake's heart was breaking for his old friend.

Although Dan had resolved to try to control his grief, he knew that he would always have a vivid memory of this place and this tragedy, but also a memory of the warm friendship and good life with John.

12

▼ ▼ ▼ ▼ ▼ ▼ ▼ ▼ ▼ ▼ ▼

THE MARRIAGE

▲ ▲ ▲ ▲ ▲ ▲ ▲ ▲ ▲ ▲ ▲ ▲

Through the summer of 1857, the Crow migrated slowly westward along the bottom of the mountains. The creeks and rivers flowed from the mountains down to the Yellowstone River. They hunted and camped in each valley they crossed. In August, they traveled south up the Yellowstone through Paradise Valley. This was the valley where they had first found the Crow. There was a long, sweeping view up the valley to the mountain peaks forty miles ahead. The valley was bordered on the east side by the pointed peaks of the Absaroka Mountains. The high shining, peaks of the Gallatin Range stood farther back in the west. It was a wide, flat valley from one to three miles across. Hundreds of buffalo and elk grazed along the base of the peaks. Moose and elk roamed far back into the mountains. When the deep snow drove them down from the high mountains, the wind-swept valley held thousands of buffalo, elk and all of the species of western animals. It was a very beautiful game-filled valley, which was an important part of the Crow homeland.

Near the upper end of the valley, Dan and Jake found a stream where they panned for gold. They found a little gold dust, but not like the find on the Clarks Fork the year before.

The Indians told Dan and Jake there was a strange place of hot water springs farther up the Yellowstone. The Indians did not like the area. Dan and Jake rode twenty miles up the Yellowstone through a canyon at the head of a valley. In the cool morning, steam rose from the mountainside ahead. They rode another few miles up a tributary from the southwest. There, a creek of hot water poured down the mountainside. Farther up the mountain there was an area of hot sulphur water springs. Over the ages, the minerals in the hot water had formed yellow and orange colored domes and terraces. Hot water carrying dissolved limestone and sulphur flowed from delicately colored rimestone pools and cascaded down a series of white, pink, yellow, and orange terraces. There were terraces of small size up the acre-sized steaming ponds. These strange formations covered nearly a mile on the side of the mountain. Many places did not look safe to walk near. They could understand why the Crow did not like the place.

Dan and Jake returned through the canyon into Paradise Valley. They found the Crow camp farther down the valley. Soon they would leave. They knew of the extremely strong, steady wind that blew down this valley in the winter. Although the wind blew quite steadily in most areas along the eastern side of the mountains, there were some areas that were not as bad.

The trappers moved with the Crow through the gap at the lower end of Paradise Valley, and then slowly moved east along the north side of the Absaroka Mountains.

As fall came they were in Mission Creek Valley. It was one of the prettiest places in Crow country. Yellow cottonwoods followed the bending creek. Large patches of red, orange, and yellow buck brush, thorn brush and vivid chokecherry brush colored the big rounded foothills and base of the mountains. Groves of light green and brilliant yellow aspen shared the mountainsides with dark green fir and pines. Early fall snow shone on the tops of the mountain peaks. Ever-changing cloud patterns floated across the blue sky.

Bears fed on fat chokecherries hanging in black bunches from red bushes. Big-eared mule deer bounced gracefully over the hills. Golden eagles soared in spiraling circles in the sky. It was a land of great beauty and enchantment. This was the most enjoyable time of the year.

Dan and Lily were walking near camp along a hillside enjoying the fall scenery when Dan said, "Sure nice to be together, walking along, enjoying this beautiful place. I would like for us to always be together, Lily. I really love you. Would you marry me? Now?" Then he embraced and kissed her. "Will you?"

"Yes, Dan, I will. It does seem to be a good time to get married." She kissed him again. "I love you, Dan. We're going to get married sometime. Let's do it now."

"I'll speak to your father about it today," said Dan, and they turned toward camp.

When they reached the LaFountain tepee, Louis and Pretty Feather were standing beside the tepee.

After a short conversation, Dan said, "Louis and Pretty Feather, I want to ask if you would give the hand of your daughter, Lily, to me in marriage? We are very much in love and would like to be together always."

"Yes Dan, You have our blessings. We ask that you will always be kind to her." Louis replied.

"Yes, I'll always be kind to Lily," Dan promised. "I wonder how we can have a wedding ceremony? Out here there is no church."

"I'll just do it myself," Louis replied. "I really don't know much about it, but we'll do it right."

Plans were made to have the marriage in three days. The Crow women made a new tepee for them and set it at the edge of the village.

Jake was happy about the marriage and told Dan he might do such a thing himself someday.

On the wedding day, the Crow gathered in the center of the camp. It was a different way for them. Dan had a gold ring for the marriage that he had bought in St. Louis. Louis read a few verses from a Bible he had. He managed a very short ceremony. He asked the Lord's blessing on the marriage, gave a prayer, and pronounced them husband and wife.

Dan kissed the bride before the smiling Crow. The Crow then had a big feast for everyone. They were all happy with the celebration.

Dan and Lily's tepee was located beside a few trees on a slight rise where there was only a little privacy. It could be unsafe to camp away from the village, but they were left to themselves that evening.

For a while at dusk, Dan and Lily sat together on a log before a small fire as they talked. At dark, the flame flickered to embers in the red coals as they sat nearby and embraced on a buffalo robe. A faint,

149

warm breeze stirred and died as they watched a new moon in the western sky. They felt it was a symbol of their new life together. In their tepee, they slipped from their clothing and were possessed by an overwhelming desire as they pressed together in intense passion. They found the zenith of love and then slept together in complete peace and happiness.

From this time, with happy hearts they lived and roamed in a carefree Indian life along the streams and mountains of the Yellowstone country. Theirs was a simple and uncomplicated love with a complete trust and faith in each other. Together their efforts gave them more satisfaction and a greater meaning to their lives.

A week after Dan and Lily were married, Jake took two wives. They were squaws who were widowed in the battle with Sinopah. Having more than one wife was allowed in the custom of the Indians in those days. It was a practical solution for survival in a way of life that was often harsh. Many braves were killed in battle, and some lost their lives in hunting accidents.

Jake did not have a Christian wedding, as two wives are not allowed in Christianity. He took his wives by making a statement to their clan and offering a gift in good faith. Jake figured the widowed squaws needed someone to hunt for them. Soon winter would be here, and they would have a much better choice of game with a good hunter, rather than depending on the charity of others.

The squaws were younger than Jake, and they made life much better for him. Besides cooking the meat, they prepared dried berries and many roots into foods that he did not even know about. They got the wood, built the fire, made the clothing, and did almost all of the work except the hunting. Besides all of that, they liked old Jake. They were happy and they were very good to him.

Jake and Dan were sitting by the campfire visiting one evening when Jake told Dan, "You know, I've traveled over a lot of the West. Through range after range of enormous mountains, across wide open spaces where snowy mountain ranges seemed to float on a far away horizon. In the southwest I've been through a maze of huge red canyons more beautiful than you can imagine, and camped on quiet, lonesome mesas seldom seen by men, not even Indians. I've lived in some real nice valleys, but of all the places I've seen, I think the valleys along the north side of the Absarokas and Beartooths down to the Yellowstone are the best places to live. There's always plenty of game here, lots of good water in creeks every few miles, and a climate that's pretty good most of the time."

Jake gazed at the campfire and then continued, "I've been married before. My first wife was a nice girl in Missouri. That was when I was a young man. In a few years she died of a sickness we didn't understand. I had a Cherokee wife for a year once, but she died too. I don't have any children.

"I'm glad I saw so many pretty places in the West while I was still young enough to do it. I did a lot of traveling, but it was sure something to see. Now I have two good squaws, and I'm just goin' to settle down here and we'll have a good living in a land that is easy to live in and as pretty as any place I've seen."

A few days later, Lone Walker must have decided since his friends all seemed to have it so good, that it should be good for him too. Another brave and Lone Walker took the last two widows. Now each recently married man had a mate to help him who would proudly make him handsome buckskin clothing and happily cook his food. It should be a good winter for everyone.

Through the fall, as Dan and Lily grew more accustomed to each other, they found that their love grew and became even stronger as they experienced life together. They were deeply and completely devoted to each other in a love that would endure for always. Dan and Lily now knew that only in love can people be completely happy.

13

▼ ▼ ▼ ▼ ▼ ▼ ▼ ▼ ▼ ▼ ▼

THE GRIZZLY BEAR

▲ ▲ ▲ ▲ ▲ ▲ ▲ ▲ ▲ ▲ ▲ ▲

From the Mission Creek Valley, the Crow with their white friends moved to the West Boulder River for a few weeks. The camp was about three miles down the creek from where John, Jake, and Dan had spent part of the winter when they had trapped in the West Boulder Canyon two years before.

Dan and Jake rode up to the slough where they had trapped to find out if there were very many beaver there now. From the tracks and other signs of activity, it looked as though there were nearly as many beaver and other fur-bearing animals now as there had been when the men started trapping there. In another year, Jake and Dan thought the animals would be back to their original number. This was because these trappers never took all of the beaver or other animals where they trapped. By the tracks in the snow, they knew when they had left about one fourth of them, so that in a few years there would be as many as there were before they trapped them. Because the Indians had always left enough to breed, there had always been an abundance of animals of all kinds in the Indian lands.

Later in the fall, the village moved to a creek near the mountains west of the Stillwater River. West of camp, a small mountain ridge trailed down to the north toward the Yellowstone from the huge Beartooth peaks. Half of the area's big hills and wide flats were grass and sagebrush covered, but without trees. Most of the big foothills were steep and rough, with big brown rock outcroppings and cliffs. In some areas there were scattered patches of buck brush, juniper, and old wind-blown gnarled pines. There were scattered, small bunches of buffalo, some elk, many deer and a few small bands of bighorn sheep. It was also an ideal area for mountain lions and grizzly bears.

One day in late fall, Dan and Jake left the village and rode about three miles northwest. Although they did not expect to get close enough to a sheep to kill one, they would try it. If they did not get a sheep, they could get an elk or one of the numerous deer.

They rode halfway up one of the small, rugged mountains where they dismounted and led their horses up over a short, steep rock ledge. The ground sloped steeply up four hundred yards to a nearly vertical rock face at the top of the mountain. Jake was fifty feet farther up the slope than Dan, and one hundred feet to the left of Dan.

A dozen sheep stood on top and peered down at the hunters as they came over the lower ledge. At an angle up the slope to the right of Dan, two hundred yards away, was a huge, lone grizzly bear. On the open slope, he was on Dan's side of a ravine full of juniper and thickly growing small pines. There were some scattered waist-high, and smaller boulders on the mountainside and a few low junipers. Some gnarled pines were to the right along the ledge. The grizzly had also heard and seen the hunters as they reached the top of the ledge. His disposition was bad. He had tried for a sheep and missed.

Dan's horse, Stepper, was a very good, strong, fast horse. He was the horse Dan got from Striking Hawk. Stepper was trained to stand where his reins were dropped on the ground. In this way a hunter could shoot from the ground while standing in front of his horse and never need to hold his horse. Stepper would never leave. It was as though he was tied there. He had always been hunted with in this manner.

The bad tempered grizzly had Dan pegged. With a growl, he started his two hundred yard dash toward Dan. Dan shot him immediately, but the big, tough grizzly only jerked slightly and did not slow down. Dan could reload, aim, and fire his single shot Sharps carbine every ten seconds. Just before Dan fired again, Jake's bullet hit the bear in the chest, and he kept coming. As Dan fired his second shot, he could see that the terrific speed of the grizzly had brought him two-thirds of the way to Dan. Dan had four or five seconds left. He grabbed for Stepper's reins, but the horse that would never leave him was gone! Dan spun back as he drew his Colt .45, and fired into the bear's mouth as the monster reached him! At a double roar of guns, Dan was knocked flat on his back, dazed, and with the grizzly partly on him. For a few seconds Dan was helpless with the breath knocked out of him. The grizzly was dead! Jake and Dan had fired their last shots together.

Quickly Jake was there, "Dan, how are you?!"

"Alive," replied Dan, "but he sure gave me a hell of a knock."

Jake said, "He was still charging as he died and fell on you!"

As Dan got to his feet, Jake said, "We couldn't seem to stop him. Damn, he came fast. Damn near as fast as a horse."

"Yeah, horse, where the hell's my horse? When did he leave?" asked Dan.

"He left when the bear was about 150 feet away. Stayed longer than most would have with a bear like that coming. He went down the mountain," replied Jake.

"Hope he stops," said Dan, as he stepped over and bent down to look at the bear. "Looks like we both got him in the head."

"Looks like he got you in the chest, too," said Jake. "He must have started to strike as he died. Reckon you're lucky you still got a head. Here, let me have a look. Ripped your buckskin shirt and left his claw marks down your left shoulder and chest. You're not bleeding much. They didn't cut deep. More bruised than anything."

"Yeah, so's my back; he knocked me into the rocks."

"Good thing he didn't get a real whack at you," Jake said. "Do you want his hide?"

"I do, if I can get it. Can't do much with this left arm," said Dan.

"Well, I tell you what," said Jake. "It would take me awhile to skin him. We'd never be able to load his hide on one of our horses. They're too spooked. If your horse is around, it won't take long to get to camp. I'll get some help. They would all like some bear meat. Judgin' from the size of him, there's enough to go around. We'll have to haul him on a travois."

Jake had walked over to the edge of the ledge and looked down. "There's Stepper. He stopped at the bottom of the mountain. We'd better go."

Jake led his horse to the bottom of the ledge and Dan walked. "Here Dan, you ride. I'll walk down. Better zigzag down so it won't be so steep for you."

"Oh, I can walk," said Dan.

"Yes, I know you could, but you're bruised up more than you think. It's not far for me to walk down. Here," and he handed Dan the reins.

Stepper was waiting for them at the bottom. He bobbed his head up and down a few times and snorted a little, but waited for them. Jake said, "Good old horse. Anyhow, let me catch him, Dan. You must have bear smell on you."

Stepper was pretty spooked, but Dan got on him. He patted Stepper's neck and said, "That's all right, Stepper, I don't blame you. I wanted to run, too."

When they got to camp, everyone got quite excited about the grizzly. They were enthused about going to get him. Lily was concerned about Dan. About thirty braves and a bunch of younger boys took a travois with them and rode hurriedly away. Jake went along and pointed up the mountain to where the bear was.

They lashed the bear on the travois and were soon back to camp. There was lots of help, and they had fun skinning and butchering the bear.

While skinning, they examined the bear for bullet holes. Dan, Jake, and their women were sitting near and watching.

Every bullet had hit the grizzly. Dan's first shot went in the front of the chest, into the lungs. The second shot was Jake's in the right chest. It took a very small piece of the bottom of the heart. The third shot was Dan's into the lower front of the neck where it did not hit a vital spot to kill quickly. The last two shots were fired at the same time. Jake's bullet hit the brain from the right side. Dan's .45 went through the back of the mouth and shattered the first vertebra at the base of the brain. Either of the last two shots would be instantly fatal.

They soon finished skinning and butchering the bear. With that much help, they could have skinned and butchered ten bears real fast. Soon they would be eating bear.

A boy brought the claws and held them out to be taken.

Jake said, "You take 'em, Dan. I've got some just like 'em. It's your bear hide. You can have the skull too, when the birds and ants have

156

cleaned it up. He was a big bear. The claws are over four inches long. He's fat and must be seven feet long. Probably weighs eight hundred pounds."

Some of the squaws said they would cure the hide for Dan. The trappers had always been generous with the Crow, and the Crow were just as generous to them.

Dan and Lily went to their tepee for Dan to rest. In the evening, Jake and his two squaws brought some of the roasted bear meat to Dan and Lily's tepee.

Jake said to Dan, "After all your trouble, I wondered if you'd want to eat bear meat?"

Dan said, "Yes, I'm sure goin' to eat some of that bear meat, unless it's as tough to chew as it was to kill."

After Dan tried some, he smiled and said, "This is a man, eating bear; I'm sure glad it wasn't a bear, eating man."

Jake said, "If the Crow didn't have all these dogs in camp, there probably would be bears eating us. Fifty dogs would give any bear trouble, though."

Dan was really stiff and sore for about a week from his encounter with the bear. After a while, he only had five narrow, small scars down his chest.

There was plenty of game in the Stillwater area where the village was. Besides the Stillwater, there were several smaller tributary creeks there. The village was located at the base of a mountain in a forest of big pine trees for protection. This was an area of terrific winds. It would not even be possible to keep a tepee standing in the open. It was a good winter grazing area for wildlife and horses because the wind kept most of the ground bare of snow. The wind was miserable for men to go out in, but there was an abundance of fur-bearing animals to trap.

They remained camped there for two months in early winter until everyone had enough pelts for trading again.

Dan and Lily were very comfortable in their new tepee. They were as happy and as much in love as two people can be.

Dan saw Sonny quite often, and he always came to Dan. Sometimes Dan rode him. The yearling colts of Sonny's and the spring colts of 1857 were very good-looking colts. Dan would get one of Sonny's two-year-old colts next spring.

Dan had John's horses and guns now. One day Dan asked Striking Hawk to come to his tepee to look at the guns. He said to Striking

Hawk, "I have my own rifle and revolver. I have John's guns, but I don't need 'em. We bought these new guns just before we came here. They're the best there is now."

He showed Striking Hawk John's rifle and revolver and how they worked, then said, "This breechloader is a lot faster and easier to load than your muzzle-loader."

"Yes, I know it is. I've seen you use it," said Striking Hawk. "The revolver is even faster."

Dan said, "Striking Hawk, you're one of the most important warriors to guard the Crow against the Sioux and Blackfoot. I want you to have John's guns. They'll make you the best warrior of the Crow. I'm sure some of the Sioux warriors will have these kinds of guns soon, so you really need them."

"I would sure like to have them," said Striking Hawk, "but I don't have anything to trade that you need. You don't need any horses now, and you must have money to buy supplies at the traders."

"That's right," Dan said. "I don't really even need to trap since we found the gold. You've been good to take care of our horses when we're not using them. If you'll give your old muzzle-loader to Lone Walker, and help us take the gold to Fort Union, I'll give you the guns now. I'll even pay you for every day you help with the gold. We should make two trips. One each year, so we'll not have to risk all of it in one trip."

"Plenty good. That's a trade," said Striking Hawk.

The next day Dan told Jake about the deal with Striking Hawk.

Jake said, "We should leave what is left of the first cache where it is for sometime in our life when there's an emergency or when we need it for something."

"Sounds like a good idea to me," Dan agreed. "There's almost no chance for anyone to ever find it where it is."

During a warm spell in December, the Crow moved the village to the lower end of the East Rosebud River a short distance above its confluence with the Stillwater River. It felt warmer there because it wasn't nearly as windy.

In January and February the weather was very cold, and it snowed several times. Dan and Lily were cozy with many furs to keep them warm, and a small fire in the center of the tepee. At one time, the new snow was a foot deep. On quiet, clear nights the arctic air settled down with intense cold. The full moon cast shadows of dark pines onto cold, glistening white snow.

Dan noticed a profound silence covered the land so that each sound was magnified. The plaintive howl of coyotes, and the mournful howl of a wolf drifted from the top of the white hills and across the wide flat. Dan listened to these distinctive sounds of wilderness that quicken one's pulse and stir one's awareness, and thought, they are etched in the memory, never to be forgotten. Truly, they are the haunting call of the wild, that forever beckons one back to the wilderness.

When Dan ventured outside, the cold, crisp snow squeaked with every step of his high moccasins. Far above him, through the clear air, millions of glittering stars were set in a black canopy of infinite depth. The thin, cloudy veil of the Milky Way floated diagonally across the sky. The vastness of the western wilderness seemed to shrink as Dan's mind tried to fathom the depth of the universe. He thought, the distant, twinkling stars are unfathomable. They are there to make us think, to humble us before our Maker, but mostly they are there for the beauty of it all.

14

▼▼▼▼▼▼▼▼▼▼▼▼

TAKING THE GOLD
TO FORT UNION

▲▲▲▲▲▲▲▲▲▲▲▲

A warm chinook wind from the west started blowing during the last week of February. The temperature was over fifty degrees. After several days of warm weather, the decision was made by the Mountain Crow to move to a place on the Yellowstone ten miles below the mouth of the Clarks Fork River. Here, the Yellowstone Valley is partly protected from wind by the high rimrocks. The elevation is lower, and on sunny days it can be pleasantly warm near the shelter of the big cottonwood trees along the river. Many thousands of buffalo wintered throughout the valley and everywhere across the hills.

In March, a few days before time to go to the trading post at Fort Sarpy, Dan and Jake took two pack horses and rode to the Yellowstone rimrocks where the gold was cached. They made sure they were not being watched when they went to the gold caches and left a wandering trail.

At the first gold cache they made a ten-foot ladder of poles and leather strings. It was used to climb to the small caves where the gold was cached. The first cache was in good shape, and they left it there for next year. While leaving, Dan brushed out their tracks in the sand with a pine bough.

The second cache was also intact, and the gold bags were still strong. As Dan examined the bags of gold and handed them down to Jake he said, "There's always a feeling of excitement about gold. Looking for it is exciting, but finding it is a real thrill. Uncovering these bags and seeing the gold in them is a little like the thrill of finding it the first time. Some time, if Chief Red Bear's vision does happen, we may need the money from selling this gold more than we know."

Jake answered "I still can't see any way that vision could happen, but you're right, if it did, I'm sure we'd need the money from this gold."

They loaded the bags of gold on the two pack horses and covered them with furs. Again, Dan backed away and brushed out their tracks. They took the ladder apart and scattered the poles. Dan commented, "There's almost no reason at all for anyone to ever ride up these steep hills and wander through trees and brush around these high ledges, but we'll make our trail confusing anyway." They left a wandering trail as they rode back to the Crow village.

Dan put half of the gold in his and Lily's tepee. Jake put the other half in his tepee with his two squaws. The gold was perfectly safe now.

Near the first of April, Chief Red Bear and the Mountain Crow started their annual journey to the trading post at Fort Sarpy.

Dan and Jake each led two pack horses. Each had one pack horse loaded with furs and the other loaded with gold and covered by a few furs.

The journey was made in six short days. The Crow usually traveled at a rate that allowed for pleasant living. They had time to hunt, make camp and enjoy the evening. The horses had time enough to graze.

Once, from the trees along the Yellowstone River, and twice, from where they waited in a coulee, a war party of thirty or more Sioux warriors rode within a mile of the columns of traveling Crow to start an attack on the flank of the Crow, but they were quickly driven away by a much larger force of Crow warriors. The Crow galloped in hot pursuit, but they were unable to get quite close enough to the Sioux warriors to battle them. The Sioux did not really expect to be able to attack the Crow columns, but they wanted to tantalize and dare the Crow warriors. The Crow and Sioux warriors both enjoyed the excitement of daring each other and tried to find a way to set traps for each other. It was interesting to Dan and Jake to watch the attempts of these warriors to count coup on their enemies. A strong guard was maintained by the Crow day and night.

The weather was warm, except for a few days when gusty clouds passed over and produced some snow flurries. The six-day trip to Fort Sarpy was pleasant in spite of the need to guard against attack. When they reached Fort Sarpy, there was another happy rendezvous with clans of the River Crow.

Many bundles of furs were traded for tools, weapons, metal pots, beads, and other articles that were very useful to the Indians. Again races, games, and dances were held. Many stories were told, and encounters with enemies were discussed.

After two days, Dan and Jake had traded their furs and made arrangements to take the gold to Fort Union with pack horses instead of sending the gold on the boat. They wanted to meet James Kipp, the factor for the American Fur Company, in order to get the bank deposit slips for the gold sent a year ago, and then arrange to send some more.

It was very possible they would be attacked by the band of Sioux they had seen or some other enemies, so they asked more Crow warriors to come with them. There were seven in the party: Dan, Jake, Striking Hawk, Lone Walker, Gets The Weasel, Bear Claws, and Gray Wolf. They were some of the best Crow warriors. Dan and Jake knew there was a risk of being attacked, but they felt sure they could repel an attack if they were careful not to get ambushed at close quarters by a large band of warriors.

Dan and Jake would each lead a pack horse loaded with gold. Lone Walker, Gets the Weasel, and Bear Claws would lead pack horses with a tepee and supplies. Lone Walker no longer had to walk, as he was now riding a good pinto he had traded for with Striking Hawk.

Chief Red Bear told Dan, "You take more warriors, then nobody bother you."

Dan said, "With these good warriors, if they try, we'll make it so bad for them they'll soon quit. We want to leave most of the warriors here to protect the village and the horses. While we're gone, a big war party could attack the village. It will take seven days to get to Fort Union and seven more to come back to Fort Sarpy. I want to be sure Lily will be safe while I'm gone."

"We will take good care of her," declared Chief Red Bear. "We go slow up Yellowstone and wait for you at Clarks Fork."

163

When they were ready to leave, Dan hugged Lily and said, "Everything will be all right."

"Be careful, Dan," Lily cautioned, "I would rather have you than all of the gold."

When they left, Lily waved good-bye and watched until they were out of sight.

When the men were a few miles away from camp, Dan motioned for a halt. After they had all gathered, Dan said, "It's time to decide how we're goin' to fight when we are attacked. We'll probably be attacked sometime by the Sioux that have been following us. They'll think our small bunch will be easy to wipe out, but they're in for a surprise. I don't like to run for cover and get shot in the back like John did. I would rather dismount and face them so we can all shoot straight. Our horses are all trained to stand while we shoot. We should be able to get eight or ten or them real fast, when they charge, and the rest will be glad to get away. If they lay out of sight on the side of their horse when they attack, then kill the horse. We can't let that many get close or they'll wipe us out."

Jake agreed, "Yup, I think you're right, Dan. Three of us have Sharps carbines that we can load fast. When they attack, if we get the ones in the lead first, that should be enough to drive them away. If there's any shelter real close we'll use it, but we better not ride away while they're shooting at us."

Striking Hawk said, "We have to be careful not to get ambushed. We will stay in the open so they'll have to come to us from a long ways. We'll kill a lot of them before they can get to us."

"We'll need a guard on both sides of camp at night," Dan advised.

While they were still near the Yellowstone River, Dan pointed to some log walls of an old fort. "Looks like there's been another fort here before they built Fort Sarpy. Most of the logs are not rotten but a lot of 'em are fallin' down, and a lot of 'em are gone."

Jake noted, "Part of the old fort's been burned. Do ya suppose they got 'er on fire?"

"They could've, or maybe the Sioux did it?"

Not far away, they found a few remains of another old fort. "Well that's gotta be part of another old fort," Dan exclaimed, as they rode past it.

Striking Hawk was riding near Dan, and added, "There's a few logs of another old fort back up the river by the mouth of the Bighorn.

Dan wondered aloud, "I wonder why they left all of 'em?"

"They probably know down at Fort Union."

As they traveled on, Striking Hawk rode two or three hundred yards in the lead when they rode over the top of a hill or any place where they could not see a quarter of a mile ahead. They stayed a half a mile to two miles away from the trees along the Yellowstone River bottom. There was seldom a tree anywhere else. They avoided deep coulees and high rock outcroppings where any enemy could hide and wait. When they had to go to the river or cross a creek for water, they always picked a place with few trees for the Sioux to hide in. It was a pleasant and interesting trip riding over the grass-covered prairies. They were not worried about being attacked, they were just cautious.

The first night they made their camp on a low rise a half mile from the trees along the river. The camp was near a small stream that ran from the hills bordering the Yellowstone Valley. There was only a thin row of brush and a few trees along the stream, but their camp was three hundred yards from the small creek and trees. It was an ideal place for a safe camp. They liked to make camp about three hours before dark. They had to picket the horses and allow them to graze for a few hours each evening. At dark they were brought in close to camp. A few poles were cut and the tepee was set up. The tepee was for use in bad weather. The men slept under robes in scattered places outside when the weather was no colder than this day. This was so they would not be surprised in their tepee by the enemy who might think they were sleeping in the tepee. Dan and Jake each kept their load of gold near them. Each man's weapons were within reach. With a guard sitting near the camp, it was impossible for them to be surprised. The guards took three hour shifts.

On the second day, they followed a route that would be safe from an ambush. No Sioux or other Indians were seen. However, everyone thought that Sioux scouts must be watching them all the time. Striking Hawk confirmed it that evening when he returned to camp and advised, "I found tracks. Sioux scouts didn't think I would notice."

"I expected them to be watchin' us, alright," Dan stated.

They camped in another good place the second night and were still not attacked.

In late afternoon of the third day, they were riding on the north side of the river. They were approaching a place where the river made a bend to the left across the valley and ran for nearly a half mile rather close to a rimrock at the edge of the valley. There was a strip of bare land between the trees along the river and the rimrock that was two hundred to three hundred yards wide. Dan, Jake, and Striking Hawk were riding close together at the front of the column. When they were just over a quarter of a mile from the narrow strip, they all stopped.

Striking Hawk said, "There's seven deer standin' at the bottom of the rimrock that are looking back toward the river along the narrow strip. This is a little too early in the evening for them to come out to graze. I think they left the trees because someone scared them out."

Jake said, "There's two hawks circling and screaming high above the trees. That's what Red Tailed hawks do when someone's near their nest. I think you're right, Striking Hawk; a lot of Sioux are hidin' in them trees."

Dan said, "The deer are starting up through that narrow opening in the rocks. They've set a trap for us. If we ride through there, not one of us will get out."

"We better see if we can fool 'em," Jake said. "This is a pretty good spot. Let's make camp. If they come at us now, we'll make it so hot for 'em they can't stand it. We'll sneak away when it's dark. The skeeters and deer flies can chew on the damn Sioux while they wait down there in the trees and brush.

One hundred yards ahead was a small stream where they watered their horses. Then they returned to the high spot and made camp. They picketed the horses closer to camp than usual and on the side of the camp away from the Sioux. They could defend themselves very well here. They could lie behind their packs and shoot at the approaching Sioux.

As they were feasting on roasted buffalo, Jake said, "Now is when I'd like for the Sioux to come." He grinned. "We'd give 'em a lot of lead for supper."

Dan said, "If thirty or forty Sioux come crawling into camp tonight, it could get bad."

"We'll sneak away before they come," Jake advised.

The Red Tailed hawks had never landed in the big trees where the Sioux were hiding, but circled on down the river. At dusk a coyote howled from the rimrocks. More coyotes howled from far across the river. No sounds came from the place where the Sioux were hiding.

As soon as it was dark enough, the trappers and Crow very quietly loaded their pack horses and left. They left a small campfire burning. They rode back up the river valley along the base of the rimrock. They heard a faint whinny of a horse once after they left. Now they were even more sure the Sioux were where they thought they were. Dan smiled, "I hope the skeeters are bitin' good tonight down there."

A mile up the river valley from camp they found a wide opening in the rimrock and rode up onto the rolling prairie where they headed northeast again.

There were only a few clouds, and a light, warm breeze was blowing. A half moon lighted their way until it set about midnight. They camped again a little while before the moon set. They had angled farther away from the valley and had ridden over eight miles from their evening camp. It seemed impossible that they could have been followed, but they kept one man on guard that night.

They rode along the prairie for nearly three hours the fourth morning until they came to a small stream between two hills. They unpacked their horses, watered them, and picketed them to graze. There was a light breeze, so the smoke from their camp fire did not show above the hills. The dry wood did not make a lot of smoke to attract more enemies. The buffalo steaks for breakfast were good.

As they were eating the steaks, Jake said, "The Sioux are real curious. They're dying to see what's in these packs, and some of them will die tryin'."

Dan said, "They know it's not furs because we would've left them at Fort Sarpy."

After breakfast the men packed up and were soon on their way again. They angled down to the Yellowstone Valley. That afternoon they passed along the north side of a big area of white and gray colored, weirdly-eroded, badland buttes. The badlands were across the Yellowstone along the southeast side of the river. Dan gestured toward them. "Some of these buttes look as bad as the badlands east of the Black Hills. Glad we don't have to go through 'em."

In the late afternoon, the men found a place to camp that was easy to defend. It was on the top of a low knoll that had a few pine trees and some waist-high rocks. There was a small stream along one side of the knoll at the foot of a steep cut bank. Dan said, "This place is better than a fort."

From the top of the knoll they spotted a small streak of riders nearly four miles up the Yellowstone Valley. With their telescope they could see it was the band of Sioux coming down the valley toward them. They followed the trappers' trail until they were only a half mile away where they stopped and held a parlay. They knew by the direction of the trail the trappers were on the knoll.

The trappers watched the Indians with the telescope. They were the band of Sioux they had seen on the trip to Fort Sarpy. There were over fifty in the band of Sioux warriors. The Crow thought they were the war-like Brule Sioux. After five minutes, the Sioux rode on down the valley and out of sight.

As they disappeared around a bend, Jake said, "You can be sure we haven't seen the last of them."

The trappers and Crow spent a relaxed and enjoyable evening. They were in such a protected place they only posted one guard, but each took his turn that night.

They led their horses down the knoll and picketed them in some good grass for an hour the fifth morning. When they had finished breakfast, they packed up and were on their way again.

Striking Hawk and Gray Wolf rode out over a half mile and killed a two-year-old buffalo that morning. They used bow and arrows again. Two or three days was as long as they kept fresh meat, even in sixty-degree weather.

They followed the tracks of the band of Sioux for five miles, but then their tracks led north out of the valley and into the prairie hills to the east. Jake said, "We're supposed to think they left."

The trappers and Crow rode down the valley all day until about two hours before sunset. They were watching for a place to camp for the night. They were one-fourth of a mile from the river trees, and only a fourth of a mile from the north edge of the valley. It looked like they would have to go farther to find a good place to camp.

Suddenly, over forty of the Sioux came galloping toward them from a coulee a quarter of a mile behind. Another eight were coming down the hill to their left. When they looked at the Sioux behind them, they were looking into the sun, and it would be difficult to shoot straight.

Dan shouted, "We have time to ride halfway to the hill so we won't have to look straight into the sun. Damn them!" In a minute they were halfway, and off of their horses. The men were trapped in a furious attack from two sides! The speed and fury of the whooping Sioux was a surprise to Dan, and he knew his men would have to shoot straight or go under the raging Sioux. "Better shoot straight now!" he shouted.

They looped their horse's reins over one arm, took careful, deliberate aim, and fired at the eight Sioux who were racing toward them from the bottom of the nearby hill. Three of the Sioux fell to the ground. The five Sioux fled toward the other Sioux that were now coming within range of the Crow's gunfire. The Crow and trappers killed another three Sioux that were in the lead. The Sioux kept coming, but Striking Hawk, Jake and Dan quickly reloaded their Sharps as bullets whistled by. Striking Hawk reloaded first, and killed one more Sioux. The Sioux were close as they fired from their galloping horses and killed two of the Crow's horses. The trappers and Crow had time to fire again, and killed three more Sioux. That was more than most of the Sioux could stand, and only two kept coming. They were seventy-five feet away when Jake and Dan wounded them with their pistols, but they were able to ride away.

The men had killed ten of the Sioux really fast. That was too tough for the Sioux and they were leaving.

Jake said, "If they have any sense, we'll never see 'em again."

Striking Hawk gave a war whoop and exclaimed, "If they come again we'll kill another ten!"

Dan said, "Some of 'em didn't even have guns, only bows and arrows. We were sure able to hit a lot more by standing on the ground than the Sioux could riding horses."

Striking Hawk said, "They killed two of our horses. We better see if we can catch two of theirs that have no rider now."

Dan said, "Bear Claws, Gets the Weasel, and Gray Wolf, stay here with our pack horses, and the rest of us will see if we can catch any Sioux horses."

Three of the Sioux horses were not far away. The Sioux had caught three, and the other two were following the Sioux.

The men slowly approached the three Sioux horses. They were able to catch two, and the third galloped away.

The battle had taken fewer than five minutes, although so much had happened it seemed longer.

The men brought the two Sioux horses back and gave them to Bear Claws and Gets the Weasel.

Striking Hawk said, "They're a little older than your horses were, but when we get back to the village I'll see you get some better ones."

That evening in camp Jake said, "Without these new Sharps rifles, the Sioux just might've wiped us out. It's a good thing we had time enough to ride a little ways to where the sun wasn't straight in our eyes."

Dan said, "They kept trying, and they almost found a plan that worked. I'm sure they thought it would, but they didn't figure on these Sharps rifles."

It took them two more days to reach Fort Union. They did not meet any more hostile Indians on the way. At the fort the men could see that Fort Union was a big fort here where the Yellowstone meets the Missouri River.

When Jake, Dan, and the Crow were identified at the gate, James Kipp, the factor for the American Fur Company, ordered that they should be brought to him.

They were escorted to his office where James Kipp met them with a friendly hand shake. "Well, we finally have a chance to meet. Welcome to Fort Union." He shook hands with each of them, including the Crow. James Kipp was a friendly person who did not try to act superior to his guests.

"Did you have a good trip down the valley?"

"We had to fight off some Sioux, but we had a good trip," answered Dan.

"I see you have Sharps rifles. You can hold off a lot of Sioux with them."

An aide helped unload the gold, and their horses were taken to the stables and cared for by the Crow. A guide then showed the Crow around the buildings.

Tea was served as Kipp and the two trappers visited. Kipp said,"The news reached me that John Daily was killed in a battle with Sinopah and his Piegan Blackfoot. I'm very sorry about that. That was a fateful meeting with Sinopah. Fateful for both of them."

"Jim Bridger told me of meeting Daily and the Crow, and of being forced by Chief Red Bear to leave Crow country, while he guided Sir George Gore. The meeting was kind of a relief to Bridger. He didn't like guiding Gore on his killing frenzy, but he had a contract with Gore that would have lost him and his men a lot of money if they had broken the contract. We found we couldn't get along with Gore. We couldn't agree on a price for his outfit when he was ready to go down the river on a couple small boats, so in a fit of rage he burned most of it."

Kipp then continued, "Well men, I shipped the gold that you sent down on the boat with Captain Reynolds last year. The assay in St. Louis was high. The total amount for the gold was $25,000. The company charged a twenty-five percent commission for shipping and

170

other services. Here is a $5,000 deposit slip for each of you from the Bank of St Louis, and here is another $1,250 each in cash. With four of us to divide the $25,000, we each received $6,250."

"That's better than I hoped for," and Dan smiled.

"That's really great," Jake agreed, and we sure thank you for getting it to St. Louis for us."

"Yes, we sure thank you," Dan added. "The commission is fair enough. Dividing the money into fourths makes it real simple. Now we have the gold we brought today for you to send, and some more for next year."

Dan continued, "John wanted us to give his share to his daughters. I'll write them a letter tomorrow and send John's share to them. Can you get the letter to them in St Joseph?"

"Yes, I'll have a boat stop there and have the captain deliver the letter in person," Kipp promised. "Do you want me to handle the rest of his share of gold the same way?"

"I'd appreciate it if you would," Dan answered. "Could you have the captain leave a letter to my parents with one of John's daughters?"

"I'll be glad to do that, Dan," Kipp agreed. "Now let's go to dinner in the guests' dining room. Your friends are eating in the mess hall. The servants will take good care of them."

Near the end of dinner, Dan remarked, "I'm amazed that you have such good food here: canned vegetables and fruit, bread and pastry, fresh milk and eggs, coffee, tea, wine, just about anything they have in St. Louis!"

"Yes we do. We ship it up on our boats. We haul hides and pelts down, and supplies back. We even keep a few milk cows, and have some chickens here. Having good food is part of our compensation for staying here at the fort. We don't get to travel in a lot of good places like you do. Even good food can't make up for that. Some very important guests have stopped here, and they're just as surprised as you are."

"We haven't tasted this kind of food since we left Missouri in 1855," Jake exclaimed. "Sure tastes good. We've had a diet of almost straight meat and a few berries and roots. It's a wonder we don't get the scurvy, but we eat all the plants we can get."

Kipp offered, "We have a lot of dried fruit, vegetables, and berries in the storehouse. Take all you can back with you. Next year, bring all the pack horses you want to for supplies. We always have plenty for the trade. In a few more years, the trade in food and supplies will be big

171

business out here. You and I won't like it, but I'm afraid too many people are goin' to come here. I hear there are a lot of people on the trail to California and Oregon. We'll see the time when the fur business will be real small."

"Maybe you're right," Dan replied, "but I hope not."

"I suppose you could find more gold?" Kipp questioned. "I'm not askin' where you found it, but it looks like gold panned from a river. Maybe you can find a place to mine above there."

"It was gold from a river, all right," Dan agreed, "but we worked the place out. It's not likely a person could ever find a place like that again. Probably someone will find where it washed down from someday, but I don't intend to look for it."

"It looks like you fellas have enough to get by all your lives. People don't need a lot of money the way they live out here. Well, it's been a long day. I'll show you a place to sleep." He took them to a large guest cabin, big enough for all of Dan's group to lay their sleeping robes on the floor.

When Kipp showed them around the fort the next day, and explained it to them, they saw that it covered more area than they had first thought. It was like a small town. There were all the buildings, supplies, craftsmen, and various workers they needed to operate a large trading post in the wilderness.

Fort Union was a very large and well-defended fort on the bank of the Missouri, a short distance above the mouth of the Yellowstone. All trees, stumps, and brush had been cleared from the land for a quarter of a mile around the fort to prevent an enemy from shooting at the fort from protective cover. Boats could land, unload, and load in safety where the fort met the river. The living quarters, storehouses, mess hall, barns, blacksmith shop, gunsmith, and other supporting buildings were all in the main part of the enclosure. Only a few strangers or Indians were ever allowed into the main part of the fort at one time.

The staff and the common workers ate in separate parts of the mess hall and were fed different menus. Expensive food items were shipped up on boats from St. Louis. After meals, extra food from the tables was given to some of the local Indians on the outside. They were anxious to get any of this food they could. Anything was an unusual treat for them.

Dan and his friends enjoyed their tour of the fort and thanked Kipp for it.

That evening, Dan wrote letters to John's daughters and his own parents. He told them of the great distances in the western wilderness, about trapping, his marriage to Lily, the warring Indian tribes, and the circumstances of John's death. He also explained about the gold, and sent John's daughters the check for their share. He said that they would receive more as it was sold. He gave the letters to Kipp.

Next morning, the men looked around the fort some more. The Crow were astonished at the many things the white men were using in their living.

Dan and Jake happened to meet Kipp near his office. Dan said to him, "This is a lot bigger fort than any of the others. We even saw a couple old fallin' down forts near Fort Sarpy. Probably you must know all about whose forts they were."

Kipp answered, "Oh, yes, we have the records of all the forts on the Yellowstone. Come in, and I'll tell you about them."

In his office he explained, "Manual Lisa built the first trading post on the Yellowstone in 1807 at the mouth of the Bighorn River. After only two years he abandoned it.

"The American Fur Company, that I work for here at Fort Union, built Fort Cass near the mouth of the Bighorn in 1832. The help just didn't like stayin' in the fort all the time to keep from gettin' killed by Indians, so it was abandoned in 1838.

"We operated little Fort Tullock near the Rosebud in 1838 and 1839. Then we built Fort Alexander near it and operated it a while longer, from 1839 to 1850. You saw the remains of Fort Tullock and Fort Alexander.

"We built Fort Sarpy in 1850. It's bigger than the other forts were. Maybe it'll last a little longer if we can get the help to stay there."

He continued, "Fort Union is our main fort in the northwest. We supply our smaller forts on the Yellowstone and Missouri from here. This is a big fort. We have everything we need, and a lot of people work here. Boats come and go real often. There's a good social life here, so we're able to keep help. I won't trade with any tribe that gives us trouble, so that helps keep them peaceable at the fort."

Dan remarked, "Looks like the abandoned forts soon disappear."

Kipp replied, "We reused some of the logs, and some of the logs have been used for firewood on our boats. Hostile Indians have burned parts of the old forts, too."

"Well thanks for tellin' us about the old forts, Mr. Kipp. I didn't know there had been so many. Fort Union should last a long time."

173

"I think it will."

In the afternoon, the men chose the articles they would buy to take with them the following day. For their pay in helping to bring the gold to the fort, Lone Walker, Gets the Weasel, Bear Claws, and Gray Wolf each requested a Sharps rifle and ammunition, two blankets, a skillet, and thirty pounds of dried food. Dan and Striking Hawk each bought ammunition, a skillet and thirty pounds of dried food. Dan and Striking Hawk each bought two blankets, but Jake needed three because he had two squaws. Striking Hawk added steel rings, buckles, and various other articles for making gear for use with horses. He already had John's Sharps rifle.

The Crow were happy with these articles for their pay. Dan and Jake were very well satisfied. Dan bought a Sharps rifle and ammunition to give to his father-in-law, Louis LaFountain, when they reached the village. Five more Sharps rifles would be very helpful in protecting the Crow tribe. The four pack horses would not be overloaded on the return trip to their village.

On the morning of April 11th, Dan and Jake and their party packed their horses to leave. They stopped as they passed by the company office. James Kipp came out and shook the hand of each one of them and bid them good-bye. Hand shaking was not a custom with Indians, but it was the custom of James Kipp. "Come again," he told them. "I'll expect you in a year. We'll take good care of your gold."

"We thank you very much for your hospitality," Dan answered. "Just hold the pay for the gold 'til next year. We'll bring some more gold then. Good-bye, sir."

They rode out through the big gates of the fort. The Crow were pleased with the visit and the articles from the trading post. Dan knew they were anxious to try out their new guns.

Soon, they were riding up the Yellowstone on their way home. They used the same precautions for safety while traveling and camping as they had when they traveled down the river to Fort Union. The first procedure for safety was to avoid places of possible ambush.

In the afternoon, when they were far enough from the fort so their gunfire would not be heard, the men with the new guns practiced firing at targets and getting familiar with their action. The new Sharps breechloading rifles were so much easier and faster for them to load and fire than their old muzzle-loaders. They were soon shooting very well with them. The party was about as well armed as it could be.

Lone Walker raised his new rifle above his head, smiled and remarked, "Soon Blackfoot know Crow are best warriors."

After traveling up the valley for awhile, Gray Wolf and Bear Claws rode nearly a mile ahead and killed a young buffalo for camp meat.

The party did not meet any bands of Indians as they rode up the Yellowstone Valley toward home. They did not find any fresh signs or tracks of anyone that looked threatening. Each day was uneventful except for the abundant wildlife they saw. It was now the middle of April, and the grass was green, but still short. The days were warm and spring-like until they were only one day's ride from the mouth of the Clarks Fork River. They had not caught up to the Crow village yet, but by the tracks, they could see they were only a few days behind.

On that day, early in the afternoon, the whole northern sky turned very dark gray. Soon the wind turned and blew hard from the northwest as the low clouds approached. These were not spring thunderclouds. It was an ominous, long, dark front that soon engulfed them in a snowstorm of intense fury. Big wet, wind-driven snowflakes cut visibility to fifty feet. This was the worst storm Dan had ever been in. The cottonwood trees in the river-bottom lands were only a quarter of a mile away, so the men soon rode far into a thick grove of big cottonwood trees that gave them a great deal of protection. Compared to being out in the wind, it was almost comfortable. A man would not survive long out in that wind. The trees they camped under were good, solid trees, so that limbs would not break off and fall on them as they became heavy with snow. They cut poles for their tepee and set it up right away. They covered their packs and supplies with robes. With their horses, they dragged in a big pile of dry limbs for firewood. Already the snow was six inches deep. They tied their horses at the bases of big cottonwood trees where they had good protection, some grass, and a few leaves of bushes to eat until the snow became too deep.

By the time the work was all done, the men were soaking wet from the big, wet snow flakes. As their clothing slowly dried by the fire inside of the tepee, the men were soon warm. There were enough robes and pelts to be comfortable. They had a front quarter and two hindquarters of a buffalo, so there was plenty of food. There was barely room enough for all of the men to live in the tepee, though.

All through the night, the men could hear the hard wind blowing in the tops of the trees. At daybreak, it was still storming just as hard as it had been. There was a foot of wet snow. Once during the day, they tied the horses to different trees so they could paw out more grass and nibble a few leaves from some of the low bushes. Even that little job was disagreeable as it continued to snow.

It stormed all night again the second night, and by the next morning there was over two feet of snow. Now it was really getting monotonous. It was a dangerous storm for the wildlife. All day long, there was no let up in the storm. The men used limbs and pushed some of the snow away so the tepee would not collapse. The horses had only a few mouthfuls of leaves, and they gave them just a little inner bark of cottonwood trees. The men had plenty of buffalo to eat, but they had trouble getting wood that would burn. It stormed all night the third night, but it did not snow quite as hard. When the men looked out the third morning, it was almost unbelievable. There was an incredible three and a half feet of snow, but the storm stopped one hour after daylight, and the sky turned completely blue. None of the men had ever seen a storm like this before on the prairie. Some had seen it snow two and a half feet near the mountains a few times in their lives, but never three and a half feet on the prairie.

The temperature stayed in the thirties all day and dropped below twenty that night. The next day it warmed very fast, and the snow started settling and melting.

They tied the horses in new places, and they were able to get just a little to eat. The sun was so bright on the snow that they made leather covers with a slit in them to look through for both men and horses so the glare would not damage their eyes.

Because the wind had drifted the snow so much, some places were nearly bare and some places had five-foot drifts. They tied each horse on a bare spot where it could get a little grass. They moved their tepee to a bare place close by. Gray Wolf shot a deer, so they had fresh venison.

After two warm days, half of the ground was bare and the rest was covered by two to eight-foot drifts. The sky was mostly covered by high clouds so that the snow was no longer so bright. The horses were getting enough grass to eat now, so the next morning the men decided to continue their journey home.

The tracks showed that most of the wildlife in the valley had found shelter from the storm among the cottonwood trees. The men saw a few places in the edge of coulees and near the crest of a few steep hills where some of the wildlife did not reach the trees. They had taken refuge over the side of a hill from the direct wind, and had been covered over with the drifting snow where they had suffocated. More of the small animals, such as deer and antelope, had died than buffalo and elk, but in a few drifts even they had died.

Dan said to the men, "This was such a terrible storm that I wondered if it was goin' to kill all of the buffalo and maybe even us."

Jake answered, "We must've been in the middle of the storm. It can't snow that much all over the West. Buffalo are really tough. They face the storm with that big hairy head and cape over the front of 'em. It helps keep 'em warm. There'll be dang few buffalo dead."

Dan gestured to the route ahead, "We'll thread our way through these drifts and try to get to the village. We're all anxious to see if there's been any loss of people or horses there."

Dan led the men toward the Clarks Fork of the Yellowstone, where Chief Red Bear had told them he would wait. In some places, Sonny had to lunge through the edge of deep drifts, but they were able to travel. A place was found to cross the rising Yellowstone.

In late afternoon, the men found Chief Red Bear's village on the Clarks Fork River a few miles above its confluence with the Yellowstone. The village looked to be in good shape because it was located in a well-protected place where there were many big cottonwood trees. The people were very happy to see that no one was missing in the returning party. Lily rushed from the tepee to Dan and gave him a big hug and kiss, then said, "Dan, oh I'm glad to see you. I'm glad you got back and all the men are all right. Wasn't that an awful storm? I thought you'd get in the trees along the river and be safe, but I never know if you've been killed when you're gone so long."

"Lily, it's good to get back and see that you're all right. I've been lonesome for you," and they continued to hug. "Did you keep warm and have enough to eat while it was stormin'?"

"Yes, Dad and Mom helped me push the snow away from the tepee. This is a good place here in the trees when it storms. Stepper didn't get much to eat while it was storming, but he's all right now."

When they were unpacked and the horses cared for, Dan and Lily went into their tepee. After eating, Dan gave Lily the blanket he had brought from the fort. It was brown, rust, and eggshell white, with a pretty design.

"Oh, Dan, that's the prettiest blanket I ever saw," and she gave Dan another kiss.

177

When Dan unpacked the skillet and dried food, Lily just could not be happier and said, "More nice presents. Dan, you're so good to me."

"I'll always love you and be good to you," Dan promised.

15

▼▼▼▼▼▼▼▼▼▼▼▼

CHEYENNE RAID

1858

▲▲▲▲▲▲▲▲▲▲▲▲▲

Chief Red Bear and the clan leaders held a powwow the next day. They said with so much melting snow, the streams from the Beartooth and Absaroka Mountains would be very high and hard to cross for a while. The Pryor Mountains were not as high or snowy, and there were not as many streams that ran from them. They knew that north of the Pryor Mountains was a rolling prairie of luxuriant grass that continued from ridge to ridge and out of view beyond the horizon. There, within one's sight, were uncounted thousands of buffalo, many elk, and antelope all roaming across the prairie. The elevation was a little lower and spring was a little warmer than near the Beartooth Mountains.

It was decided to cross the Clarks Fork the next day and move to the area north of the Pryors. They would be a little closer to the Sioux there, but with eight Sharps rifles they would be more able to defend their people. Chief Red Bear was very glad that Dan and Jake had bought the rifles for the Crow.

They found a wide, shallow place and crossed the Clarks Fork the next day. There was a high, twelve-mile-long slope they climbed that was the divide between the Clarks Fork Valley and Pryor Creek. From the top was a view of the endless prairie stretching eastward. They made it down to Pryor Creek and camped that night.

From this time until the first of June, Chief Red Bear's Crow slowly moved eastward across the prairie until they reached the Bighorn River. The game was so plentiful that it was not necessary to move as much as they did, but they were a wandering people who enjoyed new scenery often. This also kept their enemies guessing where they were.

The horse herd was in fine shape. There were enough new colts to increase the herd more than what was lost in the last year. The grass was so good that the horses were all too fat. Dan frequently saw his stallion, Sonny, although Striking Hawk was using him again for a couple of months. Dan could see that many of the colts were sired by Sonny. Sonny always knew Dan and nickered to him, although he did not act up quite so much anymore. He was a little older, a little too fat, and more calm. Sonny was living in a horses' heaven, and all of the Indian tribes were living a wonderful life during this great time. In the marvelous prairie lands east of the northern Rocky Mountains, millions of buffalo still roamed freely in herds scattered across the vast land.

At the Bighorn River, Chief Red Bear's Crow met the River Crow with Chief Twines His Horse's Tail. Again they held the usual social celebrations and dances. Some of the young braves of each tribe took squaws from the other tribe.

After the celebrations, the Mountain Crow killed enough buffalo to make jerky. It was early June, and the weather would soon be hot here. The jerky would be useful as the Mountain Crow traveled back to their land where it was cool along the north side of the Beartooth and Absaroka Mountains. Soon the Mountain Crow would start west toward Pryor Creek.

Three hundred miles to the southeast of where the Crow were making jerky, a band of thirty-five Cheyenne Indian warriors were leaving their village beside the Little Medicine Bow River. This is south of the North Platte River, along the west side of the Laramie Mountains. From the cool shadows of the Laramie Mountains, many miles of high, lonely plains stretch westward to the sharp peaks of the Wind River mountains. North of there, the great, long ridge of the

Bighorn Mountains divide the wide plains between the east side and west side. It is a land of great contrasts. Some prairies are well covered with thick buffalo grass, and other plains are almost arid desert. There are seldom any trees except along the few streams and in the mountains. Long, sloping prairie ridges rise from crest to crest to the far away mountain ranges. South of the Bighorn Mountains is a wide depression of arid, grotesque erosion that sinks into the plain. It is a terrible area of badlands.

The wide, semi-arid areas are inhabited by prairie dogs, badgers, coyotes, rattlesnakes, hawks and prairie falcons. The many bands of antelope prefer these wide open spaces where their great vision and speed protect them from all predators. Migrating herds of buffalo, shadowed by wolves, cross the prairies toward the mountain foothills.

Only widely separated Indian tribes lived in all the area from the North Platte River to the Missouri River. It is an immense land of far away, quiet, lonely places.

The thirty-five warriors were led by Feathered Leggins, one of the great Cheyenne warrior chiefs. They were mounted on good horses that were used to much riding. The Cheyenne warriors were well armed, each had a muzzle-loader. They also had the other usual Indian weapons. They were starting on a summer raiding trip to steal horses from the River Crow and some of the Sioux tribes. Their trip would take them in a big circle around the Bighorn and Pryor Mountains. They were a tough and adventuresome band of warriors. Each summer they made a trip in some direction to fight and raid. They had even raided as far away as the Navajo Indian lands.

The Cheyenne camped the first night on a small creek near the south side of the North Platte River. The next morning they crossed the North Platte and were soon on the Oregon Trail. It was the wagon road of white settlers going to the west coast. This was where they would like to raid and loot a wagon train, but the treaty made in 1851 forbade them from raiding settlers traveling the Oregon Trail. If they were to kill any of the settlers along the trail, the troops at Fort Laramie would surely raid the Cheyenne village. Fort Laramie was only a little more then one hundred miles down the North Platte River. Just for plain devilment, the warriors followed the trail for three hours until they saw a train of twenty-five wagons ahead. Whooping and waving rifles, they loped alongside the wagon train, just out of rifle range. The train quickly formed a circle and prepared to fight, but the Cheyenne warriors rode on past and out of sight. They came as near to laughing as a Cheyenne could.

The Cheyenne left the trail and turned north through a pass in the low, bleak Rattlesnake Mountains south of the terrible badlands. They followed Deer Creek and Poison Creek northwest down to the mouth of the Wind River Canyon, where they camped only four days after leaving their village.

The next day, for excitement, they hunted Rocky Mountain bighorn rams along the high rim of the Wind River Canyon. The horses were left with guards and they hunted afoot. The challenge was to get the ram without losing him or themselves over the canyon wall. This was the wild nature of these Cheyenne warriors. One warrior killed a young ram with bow and arrow. Two older rams were killed with muskets, but one fell down the canyon wall where they could not get it. They returned to the mouth of the canyon and feasted on ram that evening.

From there, they could see the long ridge of snow-capped, saw-toothed peaks of the Wind River Mountains. This is an extremely rough, jagged string of great sky piercing peaks, fractured into huge pointed columns and tremendous cliffs. The ridge of mountains sits in a northwest direction. From the north end, creeks drain into the Snake River. From the west side of the Wind River Mountains, the Green River flows south to the Colorado River. From the east side of these mountains, the snow water drains to the Wind River. It flows southeast, then loops north and passes through the Wind River Canyon. From there it is called the Bighorn as it runs north to the Yellowstone.

Along the east side of the Wind River Mountains, and other mountain ranges to the north, lived the Shoshone Indians. They were led by the grand old chief, Washakie. Washakie was born in 1804 and lived until 1900.

The Shoshone Indians were not particularly enemies of the Cheyenne Indians, but if the Cheyenne found a good opportunity, they would certainly relieve the Shoshonean of some horses. This was a game all of the Indians played.

The Cheyenne left the Wind River Canyon one morning and in a long day rode up around the long bend of the Wind River to near the base of the Wind River Mountains. Then they rode northwest between the mountains and the Wind River. Across forty miles of prairie to the northeast was another ridge of mountains.

Somewhere along the base of the Wind River Mountains, or the other mountains farther north, the Cheyenne expected to find some sign of the Shoshone Indians. They may find the tracks of horses of a hunting party or see a small plume of smoke from a campfire some quiet morning. Perhaps they would catch a glimpse of distant riders. This is a land of magnificent vistas, where a band of horsemen can be an insignificant speck in the distance. They could even fail to find a trace of the Shoshone tribe in this immense land.

The Cheyenne rode up the Wind River Valley, between the Wind River and the high, jagged Wind River Mountains for three days. They found an abundance of all kinds of game and really enjoyed the trip through such a scenic land. Every few miles a cold, clear, mountain stream ran from a mountain canyon and made its way through the hills to the river.

Where the valley became narrow at the upper end, the Cheyenne warriors rode for ten miles alongside of high, beautiful red buttes and cliffs. They looked from the south side of the river to the colorful buttes standing along the north side. Miles of brilliant red, pink, and white cliffs were designed by intricate patterns of erosion. Each red cliff was etched with a new design of sharply cut grooves, ledges, and spires. Every new sight brought a scene of natural artistic wonder.

Chief Feathered Leggins said to his warriors, "I get as much pleasure while riding through this beautiful land looking for horses as I do in finding the horses."

When the Cheyenne came to the upper end of the valley and it began to be a narrow canyon leading into the mountains, they turned back to the northeast.

They now rode along the north edge of the prairie, at the south base of the Carter Mountains. As they rode on, the distance across the prairie widened between the Carter Mountains and the Wind River Mountains. The Cheyenne could look forty miles back across the prairie to the peaks of the Wind River Mountains that stretched for one hundred miles along the southwest horizon.

Thirty miles north of the Wind River the Cheyenne started into the mouth of a pass between the Carter Mountains and the Owl Creek Mountains. Although they had watched carefully for tracks of the Shoshone horses, none had been seen. As they were riding into the shallow canyon at the mouth of the pass, they rode around a bend and saw a large band of warriors three hundred yards ahead! They had to be Shoshonean that were coming out of the pass from the north. The Cheyenne warriors looked back and saw another large band of Shoshone warriors coming up the shallow canyon behind them! The Shoshone chief had sent scouts ahead and had been alerted to the Cheyenne warriors who were starting through the pass.

It looked bad for the Cheyenne. If they rode hard, some of them might get away by forcing their horses over the steep hill at the side of the canyon, but most of them would not make it. The Shoshonean could shoot them before they got out of the canyon.

The chief in the lead of the Shoshonean raised a hand in the peace signal, then came slowly on to meet the Cheyenne.

It seemed the Cheyenne's lives may possibly be spared! They watched with caution and slowly rode forward to meet the Shoshonean. Both sides had their weapons ready as they stopped and faced each other. The Cheyenne were far outnumbered.

In the lead was Chief Washakie. He raised his hand again and said in Shoshone language, "Peace."

Feathered Leggins raised his hand and said, "Peace."

"I see you are Cheyenne. Where do you travel to?" said Chief Washakie.

Feathered Leggins said, "We go to Crow land for horses."

"It is good that you did not try to take the Shoshone horses," said Chief Washakie. "We have many scalps of warriors who tried to take Shoshone horses."

"We would take Shoshone horses if you sleep too much," said Feathered Leggins, "but we are the ones who sleep too much and get caught in the pass."

"Chief Washakie is old and has been through too many canyons to let his people get caught there," said Chief Washakie. "Our scouts are very brave. They ride far ahead. We will smoke the peace pipe. After our people go by, you go through the pass."

After they puffed the pipe and were ready to go, Chief Washakie said, "Be careful in the passes, or the Crow and Sioux will take your scalps."

"I was ready to send my scouts ahead when we got to the canyon," said Feathered Leggins.

"Old chiefs are careful chiefs," said Chief Washakie, "Now go."

This conversation was all carried on in Indian language. They each raised their hand and parted.

The Shoshone Indians traveled on to the upper part of the Wind River Valley where they often spent the hot months of summer. The Cheyenne warriors had missed finding them there by one day. Their meeting would likely have been violent if the Cheyenne warriors had found them there and tried stealing the Shoshone horses.

The Cheyenne warriors rode through the ten-mile-long pass and camped that night on the North Fork of Owl Creek. They were in sight of the spires of the 12,495-foot Washakie Needle to the west.

Because they had no dogs with them, when it was nearly dark a big grizzly bear tried to get to the horses. They were alerted by the snorting and squealing of the horses. The bear was shot over a dozen times by the warriors. He was very hard to kill. It would have been a disaster with just two or three men firing muzzle-loaders. His hide was shot full of holes, but they could not take it with them on the horses anyway. They did take the grizzly's teeth and claws.

In the next few days, the Cheyenne rode through the green hills around the outside edge of the barren Bighorn Basin. There were many elk here. They passed by hundreds of buffalo. Hundreds of antelope roamed at the edge of the hills and far out into the basin. They camped one evening on the Greybull River. Above the haze of the hot Bighorn Basin, the high peaks of the Bighorn Mountains were visible one hundred miles east.

The next evening they camped near the mountains on the Shoshone River. The river came out of the mountains through a very narrow, deep canyon above them. They were now in the north end of Shoshone country. They had not seen anymore Shoshonean since their meeting with Chief Washakie, but there could be some across the Bighorn Basin at the base of the Bighorn Mountains. They could even be farther up in the mountains where they often hunted the Rocky Mountain bighorn sheep.

The next day, the Cheyenne rode north through shortgrass antelope country until they met the Clarks Fork River two miles from the mouth of the Clarks Fork Canyon. They were now only ten miles from where the trappers had found the gold. As they rode down the Clarks Fork Valley, the Cheyenne kept scouts fanned out several miles ahead because they had been here several times to raid the Crow.

185

After camping a night in the Clarks Fork Valley, the Cheyenne rode northeast out of the valley. They crossed a wide flat between the Little Pryor Mountains and Big Pryor Mountains. That night the Cheyenne camped on Sage Creek near the south end of Pryor Gap. Pryor Gap is a six-mile-long canyon running north that passes all the way through the Little Pryor Mountains. At the north end of the gap there is a view down on the north-flowing Pryor Creek. There are some trees and many willows growing along the creek.

Since the Cheyenne had been in Crow country, they had not fired a gun, but killed their game with bows and arrows. When the air is still, the noise of a rifle shot may carry fifteen miles in this big, quiet land.

That evening the Cheyenne scouts reported back to their camp on Sage Creek. They had ridden through the gap and found the Crow village four miles down Pryor Creek. Many horses were grazing outside of the village. There might be three or more guards with the horses.

The Cheyenne had expected to find the River Crow farther northeast, but finding the village here would be just as good. They did not know it was the Mountain Crow who were readying to leave for the foothills of the Beartooth Mountains.

The Crow horse herd and the Crow village were a quarter of a mile west of Pryor Creek. The horse herd was a quarter of a mile south of the village that night. There were over five hundred horses in the herd. Most of the Crow warriors also had a horse near their tepee.

Before daybreak, the thirty-five Cheyenne warriors rode very quietly down Pryor Creek. Five scouts rode a little ways ahead. Thirty warriors rode in the cover of the high willows growing in the creek bottom lands in the early dawn light. The five scouts who had gone ahead in the near dark, tied their horses in the willows and crawled toward the three guards. The three guards were each in a different place around the horse herd. When there was enough light, the scouts quietly killed two of the guards with arrows. They were unable to sneak up on the third guard. When he saw them, he killed one of the scouts with his rifle, jumped on his horse and loped for the village.

All of the Cheyenne rode out of the willows, quickly roped fifteen hobbled horses and cut their hobbles. They surrounded some more loose horses and roped ten of them. The stallion, Sonny, was one of the horses they took. He was a real prize for them. They drove fifteen more loose horses ahead of them as they loped east across Pryor Creek. There were also four two-month-old colts with their mothers in the loose horses that were being driven ahead of the Cheyenne. They only took what horses they could take quickly.

The shot fired by the escaping Crow guard had badly spoiled the Cheyenne's plans. If they could have had more time, they would have taken a hundred horses.

At the sound of the shot, the Crow warriors and the trappers sprang to action. Some of them were up, but most were not. They grabbed their breech clouts and weapons, quickly bridled and mounted their horses and raced away. Dan and Striking Hawk were slightly in the lead because their tepees were on the close side of the village. Some of the Cheyenne in the lead were already across Pryor Creek, driving the loose horses ahead. The last of the Cheyenne crossed as the leading Crow and Dan came within rifle range. They dismounted, carefully aimed, and fired. With seven shooting, they killed three Cheyenne warriors. Those at the back of the Cheyenne warriors laid over to the far side of their horses so that only an arm and leg was all there was to shoot at. The loose horses were ahead of the Cheyenne. They were whipping them to their top speed. Other Cheyenne were whipping the horses that were being led. They were all going their top speed across the prairie to the east. Dan saw Sonny being led away.

"Damn the Cheyenne," Dan swore.

"Come on, let's kill some more of the crazy devils," Striking Hawk yelled.

They reloaded their rifles, jumped on their horses and galloped after the Cheyenne. They were nearly out of rifle range now. There was no use firing from a galloping horse; they might hit their own horses.

The four colts could not keep up, so they fell behind the Cheyenne. Their loose mothers dropped back with them. Even with whips, the Cheyenne could not hold them.

There were over a hundred Crow chasing the Cheyenne now. By the time they had gone a mile and a half, the Crow were gradually falling behind. The Cheyenne horses were no better than the Crow's, but they were leaner and tougher from having been ridden so much. The Crow's horses were a little soft. Their hunting trips had not been long ones.

After another fast half mile, the Crow slowed their horses to a trot. They were even farther behind. There was no use wind-breaking their horses. They trotted along for another mile. The Cheyenne also slowed, but they were still slowly pulling away from the Crow.

187

The Crow slowed their horses to a fast walk. The horses soon breathed slower and cooled down. After a little while, they stopped. They formed a circle for a pow-wow.

Dan said, "They've got Sonny. Someway I've got to get him back, if I have to follow them all the way home."

"I'll go with you," said Striking Hawk, "Looked like they have one or two more of mine. I'd like to take a scalp for each horse."

Jake said, "We can never catch them. With a hundred Crow after them they have the most to lose: their lives. As long as we follow them, they'll get farther away. If they have to, they'll ride their horses to death."

Dan said, "I feel like going alone to their village and sneaking up and stealing Sonny."

Striking Hawk said, "If just the ones who went to Fort Union would go with us, maybe we could get some horses back."

Chief Red Bear had helped chase the Cheyenne. He had been listening and now spoke. "The Cheyenne came a long ways to steal Crow horses. They like to steal horses. Crow warriors like to steal horses. The Cheyenne only took a small herd of Crow horses. They killed two young Crow men. The Crow killed four Cheyenne warriors. Not a good trade for the Cheyenne. Thirty or forty horses for four dead warriors. Now there will be sad Cheyenne squaws and children when they return. Even the Cheyenne warriors already feel bad. Dan and Striking Hawk have two good stud colts from the big stallion. They will make you happy again. It is a long ways to go to Cheyenne land. Maybe what happened to them happen to you, if you go to the land of the Cheyenne. Wait and see how you feel. It would take many thoughts and big medicine before such a long trip. It is far away to Cheyenne land. We go back to village now. Maybe some loose horses get away and come home."

There was no happiness in the Crow village that day. There was mourning for the two young braves who were killed.

Lily hugged Dan and tried to make him feel better. Dan knew it was not a tragedy such as losing a member of a family, but he was sorry to lose Sonny. He was an old friend from the days of his youth. He was more than a horse to ride, he was a pet. Dan usually saw Sonny every few days when he went out to see about his other horses. Now Dan wondered what Sonny's new owner would be like. Would he be good to Sonny?

Through the next day, Dan continued to consider the possibilities of going after Sonny. With the problems involved and the risk to other people, it really was not the logical thing to do. If it had been Lily they took, he would not hesitate a minute to go after her. Maybe in a few days, when the Cheyenne would no longer expect to be followed, he and Striking Hawk would go after Sonny.

Chief Red Bear said because of the trouble the Cheyenne had brought, the tribe would wait a few days to move to the Beartooth country.

At evening time, a day after the raid, all the campfires were burning for people to prepare their food. Dan was sitting on a log not far from the fire, and Lily was preparing the food. When Dan looked beyond the willows along Pryor Creek he saw two horses coming. They had no riders. The horses were trotting at a good gait. As they came closer, Dan was astonished. Without a doubt one of the horses was Sonny, and the other was a gelding that had been with the loose horses. The two horses were heading in the direction to take them two hundred yards south of the village on their way to the horse herd.

Dan's tepee was at the edge of the village. He quickly walked out and whistled to Sonny as he came by. Sonny stopped and looked at Dan. Dan called him, "Sonny, come on." Sonny nickered and started toward Dan. "Come on, Sonny," Dan called. Sonny trotted up to Dan with the gelding following. Dan reached out his hand and patted Sonny's neck. Sonny had a rope looped around his neck with about three feet hanging down where it had broken off. He had a bad injury three inches under the corner of his left eye. There was a big, swelled bump with a short, deep gash on it. There were dried sweat marks on both horses.

Many of the people had gathered at the edge of the village, and one brave, Red Arrow, slowly walked up to the gelding while coaxing him to come. The gelding stood quietly as Red Arrow put his hackamore on. He was a tall, long-legged pinto that looked to be a really fast runner. "The Cheyenne never got him roped," said Red Arrow.

Striking Hawk joined Dan and said, "That's really something. Your horse broke loose and came back to you."

"Now I feel good; I'm really happy. I didn't think they would ever let him get away from them," Dan said smiling broadly.

"He hated them and wanted to come back to you enough to fight and break his rope," Striking Hawk declared.

As they looked the horses over good, Dan said, "I think they're all right, except the bump below Sonny's eye."

Striking Hawk observed, "He's not lame, and his feet and legs are not swelled or cut, but he has dried blood at the top of his right front hoof."

Dan pondered aloud, "The broken rope, the bruised face, blood on his hoof—someone clubbed him. I'll bet he bit the hell out of some Cheyenne. A stud can really bite a chunk out of a man, you know. I think he just got mean and they couldn't handle him. He probably struck and killed the Cheyenne."

Jake mused, "Yup, it's strange how fate works. Sometimes it ain't purty; it's usually violent. I'll bet you couldn't *give* that stud to the Cheyenne now. Their long trip was a disaster. If it wasn't for bad luck, they wouldn't have no luck at all."

Striking Hawk said, "Hold Sonny here and I'll get something to put on that cut."

When he returned, he said, "Here's some medicine I got down at Fort Sarpy. It's real good for cuts and sore spots. It'll keep the flies off too. If we can keep from getting our heads stomped on, we better put some of it on that cut. Here's a hackamore. If you'll put it on him, Dan, we'll lead him over to the trees and tie him."

Dan took the hackamore and put it on Sonny without any trouble. It did not touch the cut. Dan said, "I think I can put the medicine on if you'll hold him."

Striking Hawk said, "I've seen horses strike so fast you can't see what's happening. The medicine might sting him a little, and he may strike before he can think. We'll do it in a way that we'll be safe. Tie him short to that tree. Here's a rope to pull up a hind leg."

Dan tied Sonny to the tree with the hackamore. With the rope he put a loop around Sonny's neck and tied it with a bowline knot so it would not tighten. He then ran the rope around the back of Sonny's hind foot, just above the hoof, and then through the loop on Sonny's neck. He pulled the rope tight, so that it pulled Sonny's back foot off of the ground. He tied the rope so it would not slip. This left Sonny standing on three legs. Now, he could not strike with a front hoof while a hind foot was off of the ground.

Striking Hawk handed Dan the can of medicine. Dan softly said, "Whoa, Sonny," then gently put the medicine on the cut. Sonny never moved. Dan then let the foot down and took the rope off.

Striking Hawk said, "If we use the medicine on him for a week or more, he'll heal up good. He knows you're an old friend he can trust, Dan. He didn't even snort."

Dan said, "I'll doctor him until he's healed."

Dan and Red Arrow curried and rubbed down their horses. With the sweat marks gone, they looked all right. The horses were a little gaunt from the long trip, but they would soon have time to graze.

Red Arrow led his pinto and Dan led Sonny over near the horse herd. They turned them loose. Their horses nickered and trotted away to the herd. They were happy to be back.

Dan and Red Arrow had not expected to see their horses again. As they watched them, Dan said, "I'm sure glad we got 'em back."

The men went back to their tepees. It was nearly twilight on a warm summer evening. The men were a little late for their meal. The buffalo roast was very well done. Now, Dan did not need to consider a way to get Sonny back any longer.

Lily put an arm around Dan, "I'm happy for you, Dan. It hurt me to see you so sad, but now we'll both be happy again."

16

▼ ▼ ▼ ▼ ▼ ▼ ▼ ▼ ▼ ▼ ▼

CROW TRAIL TO
FORT UNION

▲ ▲ ▲ ▲ ▲ ▲ ▲ ▲ ▲ ▲ ▲ ▲

The first week in July, 1858, the Mountain Crow left Pryor Creek and moved to the East Rosebud River. Game was plentiful as usual, and the Crow led a very happy and easy life. They kept a constant vigil against enemy raids, but there were none.

Dan and Lily were very happy together. Sometimes they would go riding together along a hillside or trail where flaming Indian paintbrush bloomed. They may take a leisurely walk hand in hand along a creek where the big reddish-orange wood lilies bloomed among the white-barked aspen. These were the lilies that Lily was named after. She was born in July when the wood lilies were blooming along the base of the mountains. Dan and Lily were sitting together on a log by a grove of aspen near the village one evening. The sunset lit up bright gold and red waves of clouds above the big, long peak at the end of the Beartooth Mountains, and the wood lilies glowed in the reflected light. With his arm around her shoulder, Dan told Lily, "Lily, you're as pretty as these beautiful wood lilies. When the glaciers have worn that big mountain away, I'll still love you."

"And I'll love you forever, too, Dan."

In faithful love, Dan and Lily lived pure and simple lives in a clean, primitive wilderness.

Through the summer, the Crow slowly moved their village west along the area near the Beartooth and Absaroka Mountains, just as they had for longer than they could remember. There was plenty of the natural foods they used, and now they even had some of the white man's tools to help them. These years were some of the happiest of the Crow's history. They were located in the center of a vast area where there was still no pressure of white settlers taking their land. Although in most years they occasionally had to fight the other Indian tribes that surrounded them, many of the battles took few lives or none, and usually few horses. Actually, they were protected by the fierce tribes surrounding them because they kept the white settlers out for a long time after most other areas had been lost. The Sioux east of them, the Cheyenne and Shoshone in the south, the Blackfoot to their north, the Nez Perce and other tribes west of the Crow all had many battles with the whites in the 1860s and 1870s while the Crow lived a comparatively peaceful life.

In early winter, the Crow, Dan, and Jake trapped along the West Boulder and the Boulder Rivers. Then through January to almost March, 1859, they lived and trapped along the Stillwater and West Rosebud Rivers. Dan and Jake only trapped a little because they would have plenty of money from their gold. The Crow trappers had a good supply of furs by the first of March.

The Crow who had helped deliver the gold to Fort Union told their people of the many more articles for trade at Fort Union as compared to Fort Sarpy, and what a large fort it was. Now the Crow had decided to travel to Fort Union to trade their furs.

In early March, the Mountain Crow village was near the mouth of the Stillwater River. It was only about twelve miles to the other cache in the rimrocks along the Yellowstone River. One day, Dan and Jake rode to the rimrocks with their pack horses to get the gold. They were very careful again. Striking Hawk and Lone Walker went with them. They left a misleading trail to the cache. They made a ladder and Dan climbed to the small cave that held the gold. When he looked into the small, shaded cave, something jumped at him! He ducked and threw his arm up, and the arm got clawed as his head got pounded!

"Watch out!" Jake shouted, as Dan held to the ladder and the big gray thing flew away. A great horned owl had built a nest in the cave, and had three young owls in it.

"Gosh Dang, I didn't expect that," Dan exclaimed.

"You all right? Hope she didn't get you in the eye!"

"No, she just bruised me. Sure scared me though."

The three young owls stood against the wall at the back of the nest while Dan took the bags of gold from the edge of the nest and handed them down to the men. When they were finished, they threw the ladder over the cliff and left.

They arrived back at the village safely. There were just no people in the area to see them.

Before the middle of March, the Crow and whites started to Fort Union to trade their furs. Dan and Jake took their gold. Even with good weather it would take more than two weeks to get there. They could only travel short days because the horses needed time to graze.

When the Crow village moved, it was always a great sight. For a short move, the village did not always move altogether, but may string along several hours apart. This would be a far longer trip than they usually made, and into land where other tribes roamed. It was more than three hundred miles down the Yellowstone to Fort Union.

A long trip such as this was well organized. The whole village had to move. None could be left behind because of the danger of enemy raids. There were about 750 people with nearly two hundred tepees, a tepee for each family. These were good times for the Crow, so they owned almost enough horses. One horse pulled a travois for each family. Yearling colts were even lightly loaded as pack horses. Some dogs, led by children, still pulled a small travois as in the days of long ago before the Indians had horses. In those days, many dogs were used and most Indians carried a pack on their back. Now they could even own modern cooking pans and use larger tepees.

Another two hundred horses were ridden by the braves. There was over another hundred horses for the squaws and other family members. Even with over five hundred horses, some had to walk or take turns riding. Some horses carried two or three people. There were also quite a few colts that followed alongside their mothers and raced back and forth.

The Indians did not form a long line, but fanned out into many short lines across the prairie. They were better protected from attack this way, and it was more sociable.

Scouts watched miles ahead, and warriors guarded around the perimeter. Hunters brought in fresh game each day. There was a very loose command in organizing the journey, but it was congenial and it worked well.

The Crow were enthused with the long journey where there was a new scene around each bend of the river. They were nomadic in nature, as had been their practice through their known history. They were excited with the anticipation of seeing the big trading post.

It was a dramatic sight as the loosely formed lines moved down the wide valley or sometimes cut across low rolling hills. Buds were starting to swell on the cottonwood trees, and there was a bit of green tinge of grass in places. Some days, white puffs of cumulus clouds drifted across the valley to accentuate the bright blue sky. Sometimes swirling streaks and waves of high, thin cirrus clouds formed intricate patterns in the blue. Wide ribbons of buffalo and antelope moved aside ahead of the advancing Indians.

In the evening, among rows of light-colored tepees, flickering campfires gleamed in the twilight. The mournful wail of a coyote and the long, weary howl of wolves split the silence across the darkening shadows. Sometimes the throb of tom-toms and the shimmering songs of red warriors echoed their call. It was a vibrant pageant of life in harmony with the wild creation.

The Crow rode past Fort Sarpy without stopping. They saw the remains of the two old abandoned forts. Dan knew the Crow would be astonished at what they would see at Fort Union.

When the Crow Indians were camped near the mouth of the Powder River, a blustery March snowstorm developed that kept them in camp two days. An inch of snow on the ground soon melted in the warm morning when they resumed their journey.

Lily and Dan rode side by side. Dan led two pack horses, and Lily led one. One of Dan's pack horses carried gold.

Jake and his two squaws rode close by. Jake also had one pack horse carrying gold. His other two carried their equipment. Each of Jake's squaws led a pack horse.

A few times small bands of Indians were seen in the distance, but none approached the traveling Crow. This was a pleasant and safe trip for Dan and Jake to take their gold to Fort Union. They would not need to bring any more. They had agreed to leave the small cache in the high cliffs near Rock Creek indefinitely. They would leave it until they needed it.

Eighteen days after leaving the mouth of the Stillwater, the Crow Indians arrived at Fort Union. There was already a small village of Assiniboin there. Their homeland was in the area of the fort, so they were at the fort often. Many times they were given handouts of leftover food from the fort. Tribes of Chippewa and Cree were there, but were ready to leave. Almost any kind of Indians could show up here, but they were peaceable near the fort.

The Crow Indians took no chances, and kept their camp well guarded and their horses protected. They went to the fort in guarded groups. They took turns going to the fort, and in the next week everyone had a chance to see the great variety of trading goods and select what they wished to trade for. The Crow were allowed to tour the inside of the fort in small groups, as they had never been hostile to white people.

It was a great experience for the Crow. They were shown many things that greatly amazed them. The tools, weapons, white man's food, cooking utensils, blankets, and clothing were some of the most desired things. There were others that were less important.

Dan, Jake, and the LaFountains entered the fort with their horses and wives. James Kipp had a friendly greeting for them. He put their gold in a vault and had their horses cared for.

"I'll send your gold to St. Louis this summer," Kipp said. "The last gold you sent was just as rich as the first load. There was just a little more than twice as much. The total amount for the gold was $52,000. The company's twenty-five percent commission and your three equal parts makes it $13,000 each. We have already delivered the proper shares, as you instructed, to John Daily's daughters. Here are your deposit slips from the Bank of St. Louis. You each have a savings deposit receipt for $10,000 and a checking deposit receipt for $3,000.

You can buy all the supplies you want here with a bank check. The gold you just brought weighed a little more than your last pile. You are a couple of pretty wealthy fellows."

"We really don't use much money," Dan advised. "The only place to spend it is here, to get our supplies each year."

Jake agreed, "With no place to spend it, we have more money than we'll ever need. We don't even trap much anymore."

Kipp smiled, "If you keep bringing a load of gold each year, you'll soon have more money than you could spend in St. Louis."

Jake explained, "This is the last load of gold that we'll be bringing. Next year all we need to do is collect the money for the gold we brought today."

Kipp said, "Your money will be here before November. It's uncertain how long Fort Union will operate. The fur business is falling off each year, but there should still be plenty of business selling supplies."

After the business was finished, Kipp treated Dan, Jake, and their friends with them to dinner in the company mess hall. Some of the Crow ate there too. They had tasted very little of white men's food before, so this was a strange experience for them. They enjoyed most of the food, and were amazed how it was cooked and served. They really liked the bread, but of course Indians had no way to bake bread, so they showed them how to make fry bread. The next day a company cook even came out to the Crow camp and showed them how to make fry bread. For the next several days, groups of Crow were busy taking turns going to the fort to trade.

Dan, Jake, and the LaFountains showed their wives the many buildings in the fort, and particularly the kitchen. For them, the kitchen was a magical place.

During the next few days, Dan and Jake traded their small lot of furs and also used some of their cash from last year to buy supplies. They bought ammunition, a few blankets and clothing, some skillets, pots and pans, and a few other articles, and enough various foods to finish loading their pack horses.

Dan and Jake helped buy supplies for a few Indian families who did not have many furs to trade. Most of them were old people. Dan and Jake had the protection of traveling with the Crow to Fort Union and felt they owed something. They were also living on Crow land, and wanted to help in ways that they could.

After the Crow had been at the fort a week, they finished trading and sight-seeing. They were happy with the supplies they bought. Besides ammunition, pans, axes, saws, blankets, beads, and many other articles, they had all bought what they could of the food and blankets. Most of them even bought flour for fry bread.

After bidding farewell, Jake and Dan and the Crow started up the Yellowstone Valley toward home. It was now the last week in March. The weather was good, with daytime temperatures well above thawing. There was still very little green grass, but there was plenty of last year's grass for the horses.

The second day from the fort, Chief Red Bear's Mountain Crow met Chief Twines His Horse's Tail and a large band of River Crow. They camped by each other and visited part of a day. They did not hold any celebrations because the River Crow were anxious to get to Fort Union. When they parted, the Mountain Crow continued on up the Yellowstone.

After a pleasant trip up the Yellowstone, they turned up Pryor Creek and camped along it in two places. The first camp was only a few miles up the creek, and the next camp was five miles below Pryor Gap. They watched closely, but were not raided by the Cheyenne.

After the first of June, the Mountain Crow moved along north of the Beartooth and Absaroka Mountains again. The usual great numbers of buffalo and other wildlife roamed across the area. There was normal rainfall, so there was a good berry crop, along with other plants the Crow used. There was another crop of colts big enough to increase the horse herd. Many colts had the mark of Sonny.

The bushes in Mission Creek Valley were brilliant again that fall. Dan and Lily enjoyed the fall scenery together again.

The Crow trapped the Boulder River, the West Fork of the Stillwater, and its tributaries that winter. Dan and Jake trapped very little. Crow scouts saw four white trappers that were strangers in Paradise Valley in early winter.

In March of 1860, Chief Red Bear and the Mountain Crow made the trip to Fort Union again. Fort Sarpy no longer was operating.

The same guests received the hospitality of James Kipp. When he handed the deposit slips to Dan and Jake he said, "You hit a high gold price this year. It weighed a little more, too. The total for it was $64,000. Each twenty-five per cent share is $16,000. That's real fortunate to find gold like you did. The total for all the gold from the three sales is $141,000. Each of us received $35,250. Of course, these are just rounded-off figures. I can understand why you are not trapping much when you don't need to. Have you heard there was a gold-strike in Colorado in 1858? Last year, in 1859, there was a big gold rush. If we get a big gold strike in this area, you can be sure thousands of miners will come."

"I sure wouldn't like that," Dan stated.

The Crow traded their furs for all the items they could buy. After they had bought all the essential supplies, they bought what they could of white man's food. Most families took two or three sacks of flour to make fry bread. That was about all they could carry with them.

On the return trip up the Yellowstone Valley, when the Crow were nearing the mouth of the Rosebud River, Chief Red Bear led Dan, Jake, and twenty-two Crow braves in a specially arranged hunting party about three miles ahead of the moving Crow. Each brave in the hunting party wanted to kill a buffalo for the camp of several hundred people.

Six of the braves were young men about eighteen years old who were anxious to prove that they could be great hunters and warriors. They were very courageous and were proud of their weapons, their horses, and themselves. They were armed with excellent bows and arrows that each one had skillfully made, and were dressed in elkskin leggings, beaded jackets and moccasins beautifully fashioned by expert seamstresses of their clan. This was a traditional hunt for the young men of their age.

Each of the young braves had a father in the group who had taught him the many skills of hunting. He was also armed with an excellent bow and arrows, and would kill a buffalo bull after his son had killed one.

There were another six good Crow hunters armed with muzzle-loaders. Dan, Jake, and four great hunters, Striking Hawk, Bear Claws, Gray Wolf, and Red Arrow, all armed with Sharps breechloaders were included in the group.

The hunting party had been well planned. It would be divided into three equal groups that would attack the herd from three different directions at the same time.

In each group were two of the young braves armed with their bows and arrows, each of their fathers were also armed with bows and arrows, two more Crow hunters were armed with muzzle-loaders, and two more hunters were armed with Sharps breechloaders.

A herd of three hundred buffalo were sighted grazing in the low, rolling hills a mile from the Yellowstone River. Every brave would have a chance to kill one.

Chief Red Bear directed each one of the three groups of hunters to a different place out of sight of the herd, and at equal distances from the nearby herd. Chief Red Bear rode alone to the crest of the hill, and at his signal each group of hunters approached the herd from a different direction. It had been decided that the hunters with the superior breechloaders should allow the bow and arrow hunters to kill their buffalo bulls first, and those with the muzzle-loaders were second. The hunters with guns were not a part of the traditional hunt. They were along for protection from enemies, for courtesy, and because the buffalo were needed for the camp.

With the bow and arrow hunters in the lead, each group quietly trotted slowly to the edge of the herd. When they were near, the buffalo raised their heads to look at what was coming. When the hunters were 100 to 150 feet from the herd, the buffalo turned and started running. Dan was in the middle group of hunters. He followed two hundred feet behind the young hunter, Little Elk, and the two other hunters with him.

At full speed a buffalo can run as fast or faster than many horses, but because the hunters had approached quietly and slowly, the buffalo were not greatly alarmed and did not immediately run at full speed. This allowed Little Elk, on his fast pinto horse, to overtake the herd.

Dan was horrified as he watched Little Elk speed to the side of a magnificent dominant herd bull. The bull's light brown cape over huge shoulders sloped down to a dark brown back and small hindquarters. He had a great, broad, heavy, black head, with a black shiny nose and black shining eyes. Strong, sharp pointed, eighteen-inch, light black horns curved from both sides of his head, straight upward.

The great bull was running at a rolling gallop as Little Elk rode within seven feet of his right shoulder. Dan prayed that Little Elk would know better that to fire an arrow into such a monster, but he did not. With his strong bow bent until the arrowhead was at the string, Little Elk fired.

In a flash, the great bull whirled and hooked Little Elk's horse in the belly, throwing him twenty feet, where he rolled over with much of his entrails torn from the long gash in his side!

Galloping two hundred feet behind on Sonny, Dan raised his Sharps carbine, but before he could aim and fire, the bull was onto Little Elk! Dan was aghast as, with one horn, the bull flipped Little Elk high into the air with his entrails gushing out! Dan had never seen such a horrible thing happen before. He fired his Sharps. It hit behind the bull's shoulders, and the bullet broke his back. The bull was down on his hind legs, but still up on his front feet, swinging his huge head. Little Elk's father fired his muzzle-loader into the bull's lungs. The other Crow hunter fired his muzzle-loader into the bull's chest and still did not hit the heart. The bull could not get up. Dan reloaded and fired a bullet as big around as a man's middle finger into the base of the bull's brain. He dropped like a rock. Little Elk was dead.

201

Little Elk's father exclaimed, "I called him, but he didn't stop. He should know ten arrows couldn't kill that bull. He wanted to be a great warrior too soon. What a bad day this is."

In a few more seconds, Striking Hawk arrived. He rode over to the wounded horse that was barely alive and shot it in the head.

More Crow men arrived, and they wrapped Little Elk in some blankets.

It had been a short hunt, but three of the other young men had each killed a small yearling bull.

Soon the rest of the tribe arrived, and Little Elk's people cleaned Little Elk, put new clothing on him, wrapped him in blankets and robes, then sadly took him down to the trees along the Yellowstone and put him on a burial platform with his bow and arrows. There was much wailing and death songs that day and night.

All of the Crow tribe was sad, and Dan was exceptionally sad. It was several days before Dan could stop thinking constantly of Little Elk's violent death, which he had witnessed. Dan felt that most of this way of life here was wonderful, but he also knew that all of life anywhere held danger, grief, sickness and sadness. Even in this land he loved so much, all things could not be happiness and beauty. The shock of the tragedy slowly faded as each day was lived.

In a few days of traveling along the area of the Yellowstone Valley, the Crow reached the mouth of Pryor Creek, and in several weeks time they gradually moved camp along the creek until they were near the Pryor Mountains. There were great herds of buffalo roaming these abundant prairies as there had always been.

One day, while Dan and Jake were hunting with some of the braves who had been present when Chief Red Bear told of his vision, Dan suggested to the group, "We should remember the great numbers of buffalo here, and in time to come, we will know if there are any less."

"Yes," agreed Striking Hawk, "We will watch our buffalo and not let people like Sir Gore destroy them. We are still hoping the vision will never happen."

From Pryor Creek, the Crow moved their village over the hills to where two large springs bubbled from the ground near the west end of the Pryor Mountains. Many deer and antelope grazed and played here, as well as some buffalo.

While they were here, Striking Hawk brought a three-year-old colt and gave it to Dan. It was a colt of Sonny's that Striking Hawk had promised to Dan for the use of Sonny as a stallion. Striking Hawk had kept the colt an extra year as a favor to Dan. As agreed, the colt had been gelded to make a quieter riding horse of him. Striking Hawk had broken and trained the colt very well. He would be a very good horse for Lily to ride and also another very good horse for Dan to use.

After looking the young gelding over closely, Dan commented to Striking Hawk, "Well thank you, Striking Hawk. This is a good looking three-year-old from your best mare. I appreciate it that you even broke him for us too. He must be the best colt you had. I sure like his looks and everything about him. He's nearly a perfect image of Sonny. I was just trying to think of a name for him. I wouldn't like such a name as Image or Junior for him; he needs a good name."

Lily was standing close by and had been looking at the horse with them. "He is a real image of Sonny all right, so I just thought of the name, Shadow. I think he would fit Sonny's shadow just about right. Do you like that name?"

Dan put an arm around Lily's shoulders, "Why, I think that's a wonderful name, Lily, and I hope you are just as good at naming babies. Looks like we're gonna need another name one of these times," and Dan smiled broadly.

Through the summer months, the Mountain Crow moved along the north side of the Beartooth and Absaroka Mountains. This year they moved up Paradise Valley again as far as the great cone-shaped Emigrant Peak. Dan and the Crow saw a few white prospectors pass through Paradise Valley in the summer, and a few more came up the Yellowstone Valley and traveled over the pass to the Gallatin Valley. The Mountain Crow returned to the Mission Creek Valley in September.

It was in late September, 1860, when the valley was ablaze with color that Lily gave birth to a fine baby boy. He was a perfect baby, and Lily was in good health after the birth. This was one of the greatest events for the people of the Crow tribe, and they were happy about it.

Dan and Lily were as happy and pleased with the pretty little brown-eyed baby as proud parents can be. They decided to call him James Louis after his two grandfathers. Children were often named in this manner.

The winter was spent on the Boulder and Stillwater Rivers. March of 1861 found them on the lower East Rosebud again. The Mountain Crow made their yearly trip to Fort Union and back without any unusual trouble. Through the summer and winter of 1861 they followed their usual migration routes. Sometimes a few horses were quietly stolen from the Crow, but the new colts more than replaced the lost ones.

Dan and Lily, with their dandy little baby boy, were living a very happy life together. Jake and his two squaws were doing fine. The LaFountain families were happy too. The Crow people were living a good life. The most serious problem was the health of Chief Red Bear. Although he was born in 1807, and was not really old, by the spring of 1862 when the Crow made their trip to Fort Union, he was getting quite thin. White Temple, the chief scout, was a protege of Chief Red Bear. He helped with some of the duties of Chief Red Bear.

Fort Sarpy was no longer operating, and it was another enjoyable trip to Fort Union in 1862. The Crow were anxious to trade their furs for articles they needed. They liked to see what new articles were available. Besides the usual articles traded for, flour and other food articles were very popular items. Fry bread was greatly enjoyed with their buffalo meat.

The white trappers also traded some furs. While trading at Fort Union, James Kipp told Dan and Jake of the start of the Civil War in 1861 between the North and South. He did not know who was winning, but knew it was a terrible war. Dan and Jake were concerned that it may cause trouble in Missouri. Anyhow, it was a long ways from the Yellowstone.

When the Mountain Crow were returning from Fort Union in April 1862, they were near the mouth of the Bighorn River when about fifty Sioux warriors started dogging the Crow. Chief Red Bear led a charge at the Sioux. Of the Crow, only Chief Red Bear was killed. One Sioux warrior was killed before the Sioux retreated from a force of over one hundred Crow warriors. In the charge, Chief Red Bear had ridden farther in the lead than usual. The Crow wondered if he had intentionally taken a greater risk of being killed by the Sioux because of his failing health. Probably he would rather die in battle than to be a lingering burden.

While Dan, Jake, Striking Hawk, and some other braves were discussing the death of Chief Red Bear, Striking Hawk suggested, "Some of the people think Chief Red Bear might have let the Sioux kill him because he was not as healthy as he should be, but I wonder if he just didn't want to live long enough to see the vision that he had years ago near the Little Bighorn come true."

Dan answered, "We have to realize that he could've been just a little too anxious to fight the Sioux and made a mistake, just like Little Elk made a mistake trying to kill such a big buffalo bull. We sure have lost a great chief, though."

Jake nodded agreement.

The Crow Indians took Chief Red Bear to Pryor Gap, so he could be buried in the mountains. The Beartooth Mountains were too far away to wait to bury him there. On a high point in the mouth of Pryor Gap, overlooking Pryor Creek, Chief Red Bear was placed on a high platform. He was wrapped and covered with robes. His weapons and medicine pouch were placed beside him for use in the Happy Hunting Grounds. Chief Red Bear had been a wise leader and a great prophet.

After Chief Red Bear was gone, White Temple became the leading chief of the Mountain Crow. White Temple and the Mountain Crow followed their usual migrations along the Absaroka Mountains and Yellowstone River. They were always alert against raids by their enemies. There were many skirmishes with the Sioux and Blackfoot, but both sides seemed to avoid major battles.

In June, 1863, while camped on the West Rosebud, Lily gave birth to a baby girl. Dan and Lily were very happy. She was just what they wanted. She was a beautiful brown-eyed, dark-haired baby. They named her Lillian.

In late summer of 1864, Chief White Temple and the Mountain Crow were shocked to find a settlement of over a dozen white families living at the base of Emigrant peak in Paradise Valley of the Yellowstone. It was evident why they were there. This was the gulch where Dan and Jake had panned a small amount of gold in 1857. Probably there was more gold on up the steep canyon. For Dan, Jake, and the Crow it was an ominous feeling of things to come. Chief Red Bear had told them of his foreboding. The other Indian tribes that surrounded the Crow were being encroached upon by the white miners and settlers. The treaties of 1851, that set the boundaries of each tribe's land, were being broken. The Sioux, Blackfoot, Cheyenne, and other tribes were fighting back. The Crow had chosen a policy of friendship toward the whites, partly because they somehow sensed that it was impossible to win against them.

When Dan and Jake talked to the new settlers, they found that they had traveled with a wagon train and soldiers over a new trail called the

Bozeman Trail. Some of the settlers had gone to the Gallatin Valley, and a few had stopped in Paradise Valley. The Bozeman Trail came from the Oregon Trail near Fort Laramie, along the east side of the Bighorn Mountains on to the Yellowstone, and then over the pass to the Gallatin Valley. Dan and the Crow heard that there were several thousand miners farther west at a place named Bannock, and more miners were on the Beaverhead and Ruby Rivers. They had come up a road from the Oregon Trail and the Snake River.

When Dan and Jake learned from the new settlers about the thousands of people along the Beaverhead and other rivers there, Dan said to Jake, "Well, we sure know how easy it was for them to come up from the Oregon Trail to the rivers west of here. That's the way we came in 1852, when the land was almost untouched by the whites except for a few trappers. I wish it was still the same now."

Jake replied, "I wonder how long the Bannock and Flathead Indians can survive. The future sure looks bad for them because so many miners are goin' there, but I don't see any reason for lots of people to come here. There's not much gold here, and I don't know why anyone would want to farm here. This is a place for buffalo, not corn fields."

There were only a few poor and hungry settlers here in Paradise Valley. There was plenty of buffalo and elk for them to eat, but they were very low on other food. The Crow hoped there would not be a great gold strike that would bring thousands of miners. As it turned out, they found a little gold, but not enough for a gold rush. The Crow would be safe awhile longer.

Because there were so many miners in the area to the west, Montana Territory was created in 1864. Montana was a Spanish name for mountains, and to some it seemed a fitting title for a land of so many beautiful mountains. The western border generally followed the summits of the Bitterroot Mountains to the Canadian border. On the east were the Dakotas. The Absaroka, Beartooth, and Pryor Mountains were along the southern edge. The Bighorn Mountains were just south of the Montana border. Crow country was in Montana Territory.

When the Crow, Dan, and Jake learned of this development, they were very shocked. Striking Hawk declared, "This is not Montana, this is still the land of the Crow. This is Crow Country."

Dan complained, "I don't like what's happening. Too many white people have come to the valleys west of here. There's only a few white people in Crow country now; not enough to ruin the way of life we have, but more are sure to come and we don't know how to stop them. I came here because the country was wild and beautiful, the people were happy, and friendly, and I didn't think it would change in my lifetime. Our future looks like it could get real crowded."

In the next three years, Dan, Jake, and the Crow could see that the size of the buffalo herds were getting a little smaller all through the Crow country. The Civil War had ended and more people were coming west. They heard that great herds of buffalo to the south of the Bighorn Mountains and in Colorado were nearly exterminated. Along the Missouri River in the Dakotas, the buffalo were very scarce. Too many buffalo had been killed just for their hides. This put more pressure on the buffalo herds on the edge of Crow country and the tribes there had to hunt in Crow country more. Therefore, although there were still millions of buffalo, the herds were slowly getting smaller in the great buffalo land of the Crow.

17

▼▼▼▼▼▼▼▼▼▼▼

THE HIDE HUNTERS
1867

▲▲▲▲▲▲▲▲▲▲▲▲

In June 1867, Bill Brown and Joe Taylor left Fort Laramie and drove their wagons west on the Oregon Trail. Each man drove a covered wagon pulled by a big, strong, bay team. A saddle horse was led at the back of each wagon. The wagons were well supplied with food, clothing, guns, ammunition, and salt. They had all the other supplies that buffalo hide hunters would need. Bill and Joe were single men, both near forty years old.

They had been hide hunters in Texas and Colorado. They were in the 1859 Colorado gold rush, and although they had not struck it rich, they had made high wages.

Both men had spent a lot of money in the saloons and gambling in the wild mining towns of Colorado. Towns like Central City. The men were not outlaws. They were hardworking, rough, carefree fellows, and occasionally a bit tough and mean. Sometimes they gambled and drank too much, but they did not spend all of their money foolishly. They had made and spent a lot of money, but they always saved enough to buy the things they needed. Thousands of other men on the frontier lived wild, careless lives in the same manner.

When they had tired of working in the dark mines in Colorado, they wanted to work in the daylight again. Bill and Joe went hide hunting north and south of the Platte River and by the Laramie Mountains, but by this time the buffalo herds there were small and scattered. There were only a few small bunches to be found. They did not get many buffalo hides, so they returned to the new town of Cheyenne on the Union Pacific Railroad.

In Cheyenne, Bill and Joe learned of the conditions farther north. There were still millions of buffalo roaming there. They were in the Black Hills, along the east and north sides of the Bighorn Mountains, east of the Wind River Mountains in Shoshone country, in Crow country on the Yellowstone, and in Blackfoot country near Canada.

The Sioux had been warring with the army and kept all hunters and settlers out of their land in the area of the Black Hills, and east and north of the Bighorn Mountains. They had even closed the Bozeman Trail along the east side of the Bighorns. In April, John Bozeman had been killed on the Bozeman Trail along the Yellowstone. It was thought he was killed by Blackfoot even though it was in Crow country. Chief Washakie would not allow hide hunters on Shoshone land along the Wind River Mountains and on north. However, he did allow some whites to pass through on the Bridger Trail through the Bighorn Basin west of the Bighorn Mountains. It was absolutely impossible to hunt in the Blackfoot country in the north.

Bill and Joe knew the Crow were not at war with the whites. It may be possible to hunt up there in the Yellowstone country and haul the hides west to Bozeman and to the Oregon Trail in southern Idaho.

Bill said to Joe, "Do you want to go back to the mines or take some of the Crow's buffalo?"

Joe replied, "Looks like a hell of a gamble, but sunshine sure looks better in the summertime than a black hole in a mountain." So now they were rolling west on the Oregon Trail. They had a sketchy map that showed they were nearing the turn off of the Bridger Trail.

At the northwest side of the Laramie Mountains, they turned away from the North Platte River and the Oregon Trail and headed northwest toward the south end of the Bighorn Mountains. They felt very lonely on this seldom traveled, dim wagon trail. As they passed around the southwest side of the weird area of what the pioneers called

Hell's Half Acre, it did not raise their spirits a bit. The strange and grotesque-shaped pillars and buttes of light and dark gray streaked colors were depressing to the lonely men. At another time, perhaps, they may have enjoyed the strange sight. Looking across the endless miles of prairie to the glittering, miniature peaks of the Wind River Mountains over one hundred miles west almost disheartened them enough to turn back.

In this year of 1867, there were no white settlements or forts for five hundred miles between Fort Laramie on the North Platte River and Fort Union, near the mouth of the Yellowstone on the Missouri River. There were no white settlements in six hundred miles from Ft. Pierre on the Missouri, in Nebraska Territory to Bozeman, on the Gallatin River. A few hundred white trappers, traders, prospectors, and adventurers lived in this huge area by their wits and the good will of some of the Indian tribes.

That evening they camped by a little creek where there was good grass for the horses. They fixed some of their best food and drank a few cups of coffee. At dark, a big friendly looking moon came up in the east and shone brightly all night. The moonlight revealed the dark pines on the slopes of the nearby low mountains. After a nice evening, a good night's sleep, and a hot breakfast, the men's spirits rose to where they were actually happy. It must have been the shock of leaving the well-traveled Oregon Trail that had depressed them, but now they were enthused about traveling on to places they had never seen.

By evening they came to a place where the trail followed a small creek through a pass over the low mountains. It was Bridger Creek, twenty-five miles east of the Wind River Canyon. The trail went through this pass because the Wind River Canyon was impassable for wagons. They camped at the bottom of the pass. The next day, they traveled through the pass to the Bighorn River, below the mouth of the Wind River Canyon. On this side of the Wind River Canyon, they were in the Bighorn Basin, and the Wind River was now named the Bighorn River. At this place, there was a great mineral hot springs. They spent a day there while they relaxed in the hot water.

For two days, the men drove their wagons down the Bridger Trail along the Bighorn River. The wagons were covered with brown canvas. Even their horses were bay colored. The color blended in with the landscape. They would not be noticed from far away.

Bill said, "I think the brown colors of our outfit are helping to keep the Indians from seeing us, or maybe there's not many Indians in this part of the country. We've only seen one set of tracks of a few Indians headed for the Bighorn Mountains."

After two days along the Bighorn River, the trail started out into the barren land toward the northwest across the Bighorn Basin. They filled their water barrels before they started across. It was hot all day while they drove through the nearly barren, dry plain. The trail passed around the edges or sometimes crossed a small area of barren, rough badlands. By evening, out in the middle of the dry plain, they came to a good creek that was running from the mountains twenty-five miles to the west and crossing the desert eastward toward the Bighorn River. This was the Greybull River, and it was a mighty welcome sight. It was a place where there was a little more grass for their horses. Each man had some sacks of oats for emergency use such as this. They used a little of the grain.

While camped that evening, Joe said, "I was wondering why Bridger made the trail out in this Godforsaken, dry place until we came to the Creek. This must be the flattest place to cross the basin and get around the mountains."

Bill replied, "I've heard of a place called Bighorn Canyon. They say it's deep and narrow with walls a thousand feet high, and no place to cross it. The river was headed for the low place between the mountains. That must be where it is, but we're headed west of there. Bridger's map and trail hasn't led us wrong yet, as near as we can guess."

The next day they followed the trail a little northwest through terribly barren land. They started with full water barrels, so they had no trouble except for the heat. Joe said, "If we meet any Indians here I'll be surprised, 'cause there's nothin' here." By evening, they came to a big Creek again that was called the Shoshone on their map. They were still doing very well, and they could see that they were nearing the edge of the Bighorn Basin. They had a good camp that evening on the Shoshone.

With full barrels of water, they followed the trail north the next day. They were pulling up a long, gentle slope for over a day. It led them through a twenty-mile-wide pass between the Pryor Mountains to the east and the immense snow-capped peaks of the Beartooth Mountains twenty miles west. According to their map, the Clarks Fork River was somewhere this side of the Beartooth Mountains. From the top of the

212

wide pass, the land gradually sloped down to the north. The Yellowstone River was somewhere down there. They thought this must be in the edge of Crow country.

There was another small creek west of the Pryor Mountains for them to camp beside that night. It was still a dry area of sage brush and short grass. There were antelope in this area, so they killed one because they were out of meat.

That evening Bill remarked, "The Bridger Trail has been a good trail. At least the Sioux and Shoshone didn't find us out in that dry country. Sometimes, there wasn't enough grass for the horses, but we carried enough water to get by. It took us over three weeks to get here, and the horses have lost a little weight. We need to find some good grass and give 'em a rest."

After camping another day on Sage Creek, near the Pryor Mountains, the men drove their wagons west down to the Clarks Fork River. They camped for two days in the shade of cottonwood trees near the river. There was enough grass for the horses to get by on, but the nearby hills were still quite dry.

One evening Bill said, "I think there would be a lot of good grassland north of those big Beartooth Mountains. Must be a lot of buffalo there."

"Must be a lot of Indians there, too," Joe answered. "I hope they don't find our wagon tracks until after we get our buffalo hides and leave."

"We should be able to fill our wagons with hides and follow the Bozeman Trail to Bozeman. Our horses need more rest and good grass now, so we better go west to a good place and camp."

The men drove their wagons west across the hills. The farther west they went, the better the grass became. From the top of the hills, just before dropping down into Rock Creek Valley, they got a close-up view of the Beartooth Mountains only a dozen miles away. Farther away, due to their snow-capped brilliance, other mountain ranges to the south and far to the northwest were in view. As the men studied the landscape, Bill remarked, "There's another one of those views that makes me wonder if a man could ever cross it. It's so far. Some of the mountain ranges must be two hundred miles away!"

They had seen some scattered small bunches of buffalo as they crossed the hills. Now, as they looked across Rock Creek Valley and the hills beyond, they could see several hundred buffalo. With the telescope, they could see more herds of fifty, and some with over several hundred buffalo in each herd.

Joe pointed toward them, "There must be herds of buffalo and elk across the prairies to all those mountains, and even beyond them. There must still be millions of buffalo in this big, wild land. I think we came to the right place."

Bill suggested, "Maybe we should camp on this creek for a couple weeks. It'd give the horses a chance to get rested and strong on this good grass. Some of the buffalo are a little shaggy yet, anyhow. In two or three weeks, a lot of 'em should be smooth and shiny enough to make robes that are worth more than leather."

Joe advised, "A little fishin' and restin' would be good for us, too. We don't know where the Crow are. There might be less risk to go on northwest, closer to the Bozeman Trail and the Yellowstone, before we start shootin' buffalo. We'd be closer to the west edge of Crow country. Maybe we could get the hides and get out in a week."

"Sounds like the best way to me."

They drove their wagons down to Rock Creek and camped. One day, two weeks later, Bill said, "This is a real paradise. It's full of buffalo, elk, and deer. The creek is clear and cold running down from these big snow-tipped mountains. The trout are over a foot long. This would be a good place to live."

"It sure would, but I think it's time for us to head west and find a place where we can load up with buffalo hides."

Three days later, Bill and Joe crossed the Stillwater River about five miles west of where it meets the East Rosebud River. Above their crossing, the river came through a canyon for a few miles, and above there it widened into a valley again near the mountains. The Crow were camped there after coming from the upper West Rosebud River.

Bill and Joe's luck was still holding. They had not seen any Indians yet, not even any fresh tracks. It was because they traveled west ten miles north of where the Crow traveled west.

Bill and Joe drove their wagons northward up the hill and out of the Stillwater Valley. A rolling prairie of thick grass stretched five miles northward to the Yellowstone River. There were herds of buffalo as far as they could see to the Yellowstone River breaks.

They unhitched their teams and tied them to the sides of the wagons. They saddled their riding horses, took their guns, lots of ammunition, and rode toward a herd of buffalo just over a quarter of a mile away.

Bill exclaimed, "We sure stumbled onto the right place. Our wagons will be full of hides as fast as we can skin buffalo. When we sell the hides, we'll hire some men and come back here with a lot of wagons."

They rode slowly to within rifle range of a small herd of about one hundred buffalo. They dismounted and fired carefully. By killing the buffalo that tried to break away, they killed twenty before the herd ran. They mounted their horses and rode toward another herd farther west.

Striking Hawk and Dan had left the Crow camp, up the river from the canyon, the same morning Bill and Joe were killing buffalo north of the Stillwater below the canyon.

Striking Hawk and Dan rode out to check on the horse herd and bring a couple back to the village. Dan was riding Shadow, the horse that was one of Sonny's colts. He was proving to be a very good horse to ride. Dan rode past Sonny. Sonny nickered to Dan, so Dan stopped and petted him and talked to him. Sonny was seventeen years old now, but he still looked really good. Dan thought he should live a long time yet. Dan knew Sonny enjoyed being free with the Crow Horses, and Dan was happy that he still had Sonny.

Striking Hawk found that six of the loose horses had left the herd during the night. Striking Hawk and Dan tracked the horses down through the canyon and saw them grazing in the valley. Before they reached the horses, they heard the steady firing of Bill and Joe up on the prairie north of them. Bill and Joe were killing buffalo in the second herd. Because the wind was blowing down the canyon, their firing had not been heard near camp the first time.

Striking Hawk and Dan wondered if there was some kind of a small battle or some stray Indians hunting. They rode up the hill and looked over the crest. The two wagons were in view. So were the two hide hunters and many dead buffalo. It was plain to see that they were hide hunters.

Dan was disgusted with them, but Striking Hawk was furious. He exclaimed, "We can't let them do this, or hundreds of hunters will come." He started toward the hunters, and Dan rode beside him.

Dan warned, "Be careful."

As they approached the hide hunters, the hunters were standing together with their rifles across their chests, held in the crook of their left arm. Striking Hawk raised his hand to show he wanted to talk.

When they were fifteen feet apart, Striking Hawk said, "You are hide hunters killing the Crow's buffalo. Now get off of the Crow's land!"

The hunters started to turn their rifles toward Striking Hawk and Dan as Bill said, "Two damn Injuns can't run us off!" On Bill's last word, Striking Hawk's thrown knife buried in the center of Bill's chest and instantly a slug from Dan's Colt .45 tore through Joe's heart!

The hide hunters' luck had just run out! Maybe it was fate, or maybe it was destiny, but it was the end of Bill and Joe's trail.

Dan exclaimed, "Damn it, I hated to do that."

Striking Hawk replied, "I never heard you complain about killing Indians."

"I never had any choice about killing Indians. I always had to."

"You never had any choice now, except to let them kill us, but they could have left."

"What'll we do with them now?" Dan asked.

"Same as we do with the Blackfoot and Sioux, leave 'em for the coyotes and bears. They'll soon be gone."

They took the hide hunters' knives, guns, and shells. They took their saddle horses too, and rode to the wagons. There were a lot of things in the wagons, but they would come back with helpers.

"Those are really big work horses," Dan said. "They're real good ones too. They might be worth a lot to some people."

"They're too big for Crow to use, but I'll bet the miners in Paradise Valley would pay a good price for 'em."

"They would think we killed some settlers for their horses," Dan warned.

"They'd be wrong. We killed the hide hunters because they tried to kill us. Let's take all the horses to camp."

They led the hide hunter's horses away. When they came to their own horses in the valley, they drove them up the canyon ahead of them.

Along the way, Dan said to Striking Hawk, "You're really deadly at throwing knives and tomahawks. Why don't you use John's .45?"

"Sometimes it misfires. I practice throwing my knife and tomahawk about every day. They don't misfire."

"Sometime we'd better take that Colt .45 to a gunsmith at Fort Union and see if he can fix it."

"We'd better. A knife or tomahawk are only good when I'm close."

They took the horses through the village and explained what had happened. The big horses were a very interesting thing to the Crow.

Chief White Temple and the council questioned Striking Hawk and Dan very closely. They did not want to kill any white people, but they could understand that Striking Hawk and Dan's only choice was to kill the white hunters or be killed.

The chief and clan leaders decided to go get everything with travois and leave the empty wagons. For now, that seemed the safest thing to do. Half of the Crow left for the place where the buffalo had been killed.

The Crow skinned the buffalo. They all had good pelts. The hide hunters had chosen the ones with the best pelts. They cut the thirty-eight buffalo into quarters and hauled them and the hides back to camp on their travois. They brought everything out of the wagons. At camp, they divided everything among the people. The guns were given to some of the warriors.

In early September, while the Crow were camped in Paradise Valley, the council decided to have Striking Hawk and Dan take the big work horses to the settlers at Emigrant Gulch to see if they could sell or trade them.

Dan and Striking Hawk found more families there now. Some of them lived in the gulch at the base of Emigrant Peak where they were working the gold ore that was brought down from the canyon.

The miners liked the horses very well. One of their leaders, named Gene Cunningham, asked, "Where'd you get these horses?"

"We found them," Striking Hawk answered.

"Yes, I'll just bet you did," said a man called Strickland, "but I'd hate to be with the guys who lost 'em. These are dandy big Belgian draft horses. It would be dang strange if they let them run away."

Cunningham said, "We'd like to have these two big teams. We have a long, steep road up the canyon to the mines, and they'd be a lot of help. We sure don't have any horses this good. I wouldn't want to buy these horses and have the previous owners come looking for them, though."

"I'll guarantee you they'll never come," Dan promised.

"I believe that!" Strickland exclaimed.

Dan replied, "I better tell you exactly what happened," and he did.

Then Strickland said, "Well, I guess you had to kill them all right. They were crazy to try what they did. They knew they were on Crow land. They tried to kill you instead of leaving."

Cunningham said, "I believe your story. We want the horses all right. The hide hunters sure don't need 'em anymore. There's no other place for 'em near here. They'll be all right here. We cut some hay and raise a little oats for horses now. These big horses will need a lot of feed. They must've been pulling a couple good wagons. Do you know where they are? I hope you didn't burn 'em."

Striking Hawk said, "After you deal for the horses, we'll lead you to the wagons. They're good ones. The big horses will take four days to get there."

Cunningham said, "If the wagons are all right, I'd pay you two hundred dollars for each team and wagon."

"Should be worth more to you than that," Dan countered.

"Well, I guess I could stretch it to two-fifty if the wagons are good ones when we get 'em."

"We want fifty dollars for each set of harnesses, too," Striking Hawk added.

"That's a pretty big price for the outfit, but I'll take 'em."

So the miners took the big Belgian horses and paid Striking Hawk five hundred dollars. Cunningham said, "We'll come by the Crow camp in two days with lighter, faster teams to go after the wagons. If they're in good shape, I'll pay you the other hundred then."

Before Striking Hawk and Dan left, Strickland told them of some of the hardships the settlers had their first winter in the valley in 1864 and 1865. "We only had enough flour for the women and children, except on Sunday when the men could have some bread. The price of flour had gone up to one hundred dollars a sack in the western mining towns. We had almost a straight meat diet. Before spring, the flour was all gone, and everyone got the scurvy. We found a place with a lot of watercress in the edge of the Yellowstone River. Eating the watercress cured our scurvy. Now we have vegetable gardens. We dry berries, dig roots, use watercress an' we don't get scurvy anymore."

Strickland continued, "We have a lot of trouble in the village with black bears and quite a few grizzlies. I've killed some black bears and a few grizzlies, but the people never know when a bear is liable to come in."

Striking Hawk offered, "Come to the Crow village and get some dogs to keep the bears out of your village. Our dogs are good bear dogs. If the settlers will take bitches with pups, they'll stay with their pups at your village. If you treat 'em good, they'll soon feel at home. The Crow always have more dogs than they need."

Two days after Striking Hawk and Dan returned to the Crow village, two miners with teams came to the village. Striking Hawk, Dan,

218

Jake, and nine other braves went with the miners to get the wagons. The miners rode saddle horses, and they all took turns leading the teams as single horses. The teams were not the big Belgian horses. They were smaller, faster horses.

It was one hundred miles down the Yellowstone and across the hills to the wagons. Fifty miles of the usual route was along the Bozeman Trail, but they did not follow that route. They traveled a route fifteen miles shorter near the base of the mountains, partly along the Boulder River and West Boulder. It also avoided any curious whites or Indians. When they arrived on the prairie north of the Stillwater, the wagons were still there, just as they had been left.

Dan remarked, "The wagons are in good shape. They probably would've set here 'til they rotted without being found. Everyone travels along the Yellowstone."

Buffalo, elk, and a lot of moose were seen on this trip. On the sixth day they returned to the Crow village.

The Crow gave the miners some dogs. The miners put two good bitches, with four pups each, in each wagon. The families of dogs rode on buffalo hides and were separated by hides stretched across and over the tops of the wagons. They were at the settlers village before evening. Cunningham paid Striking Hawk, and the Crow returned to the Crow village.

At a council meeting a few days later, the Crow gave Striking Hawk and Dan each fifty dollars. They kept the rest for the Crow tribe. They did not want anyone to get rich for killing whites. Dan gave his part to Striking Hawk because he already had a lot of money from his part of the gold.

18

▼▼▼▼▼▼▼▼▼▼▼▼

CONQUEST OF
THE HOSTILE TRIBES

▲▲▲▲▲▲▲▲▲▲▲▲▲

In 1868, the Crow and their white friends continued to go to Fort Union to trade. The Crow liked to trade at Fort Union because of the great variety of trade goods. They still brought bundles of muskrat, beaver, ermine, marten, mink, fox, and even skunk.

There was new ammunition for the breechloading guns. Instead of shells being made of heavy paper, they were now made of brass. The new shells were easier to use, and easier to carry and store.

While at Fort Union, Striking Hawk had the Colt .45 fixed so that it no longer misfired. Dan doubted that Striking Hawk would ever depend on the .45, or be as quick with it as he was with that sharp, handy knife he carried.

After a trip to Fort Union the Crow camped for a time along the Bighorn River. While the Crow were camped near the mouth of the Bighorn Canyon in May, they were raided again by the Cheyenne. The Cheyenne slipped in at dawn again and quietly killed the two Crow guards with arrows. They quietly and quickly left with thirty-five horses.

Their luck was better this time, as there was no gunfire to alert the Crow village. As the Cheyenne left with the horses, they felt their pride would soon be restored when they were able to outrun the Crow, who were sure to pursue them very soon.

The Crow knew it was the Cheyenne who were to blame when they found the dead guards at sunup. They had been killed with Cheyenne arrows.

The alarm was quickly spread, and the Crow warriors hurriedly left.

Eighty Crow warriors followed the Cheyenne all day and crossed the Little Bighorn River, but they did not catch sight of the hard riding Cheyenne. Although Dan had not lost a horse in this raid, he helped pursue the Cheyenne. He was partly responsible for the horse herd and protection of the Crow village.

The next morning, they rode another three hours and seemed to be still farther behind the Cheyenne. The Crow were along the Bighorn Mountains now and getting close to the Tongue River in Sioux country. The Crow scouts found a Sioux village of about two hundred tepees on the Tongue River close to the base of the Bighorn Mountains. Chief White Temple sent three Crow warriors back to the Crow village to tell the Crow to move to the Stillwater River so they would be safer from the Sioux.

White Temple said, "We can't catch the Cheyenne. We'll take some Sioux horses."

The following morning, Chief White Temple led the Crow in a quick raid on the Sioux horse herd. There were no guards with the Sioux horses, and the herd seemed small. Some of the Sioux warriors must have been gone. The Crow quickly cut twenty-five horses from the herd and galloped away. They kept a steady trot for hours toward Crow country, and when some of the older Sioux horses began to slow, they left them behind.

Chief White Temple and thirty of the warriors with the fastest horses and best guns slowly dropped back. The rest of the Crow hurried on with the Sioux horses toward the Stillwater. The next day, the thirty Crow stopped at a place for an ambush of the Sioux that must be following them. There were few places across the big prairie for an ambush, so it was not a close ambush, but it was good enough to give the Crow a good advantage.

The place was a narrow strip of high, barren buttes on the prairie north of the Pryor Mountains. The buttes were picturesque badlands of gray eroded rock and soil. They stood in a long ridge north and south, with the distance too long to go around them. There was a place to pass through some smaller buttes. With their horses hidden behind two barren buttes, the Crow waited in deeply eroded ravines and the backsides of low buttes to ambush the Sioux.

When the Sioux came, there were only forty of them. The Crow fired at them when they were in good rifle range, but not close. Four Sioux were killed, and they soon retreated. They tried a charge around one side of the Crow, but were forced to retreat again after losing three more.

When the Sioux were gone, the Crow left, but soon the Sioux were following the Crow again. They followed for a few hours on the open prairie and then were not seen again. The Crow rode just fast enough to know the Sioux would not pass around them out of sight. They were now the rear guard for the Crow, with the Sioux horses, that were headed for the Crow village on the Stillwater River.

The Crow warriors in the rear guard reached the Crow village on the Stillwater six days after they had taken the Sioux horses.

Lily and the two children were relieved and happy when Dan and all of the Crow warriors returned. It was always a worry to those left in the village when the men were likely to get into a battle with their enemies.

The day after the Crow warriors reached their village on the Stillwater, they moved on to Paradise Valley, which was farther up the Yellowstone. The Sioux seldom came that far to raid.

The passing of time could be judged by taking notice of the growth of Dan and Lily's children. The little boy was already eight years old, and the little girl, Lillian, was nearly three.

The settlers in Paradise Valley were farming a little more land in order to raise more grain, hay, potatoes, and other food. They had to chase buffalo, elk, and other animals out of their fields about every day.

Strickland, the miner, came to the Crow village. He told them that the dogs, which the Crow had given them, were keeping the bears away from the settlement, and they were sure glad to have them. He still hunted grizzlies in the area. The Belgian horses were working real well, and the settlers had plenty of hay and grain for the horses and a few milk cows. In the fall, Strickland and Cunningham brought two wagons with potatoes and vegetables to the Crow. Jake, Dan, and all of them were very happy to get the vegetables.

During the 1860s and 1870s the U.S. Army fought many battles with the Sioux and Cheyenne Indians. Dan and the Crow always heard about them. Many treaties were made and broken with all of the Indian tribes as the white men pressed the Indians on to smaller and smaller reservations.

From their first encounter with the white men, the Crow Indians somehow made the right decision not to fight them. Although most of their land was unfairly taken from them and they had many hardships of reservation life, they were spared the terrible tragedy of a massacre.

Chief Twines His Horse's Tail, chief of the River Crow, died in 1867. He was succeeded by Chief Sits In the Middle of the Land, who in 1868, with other Crow chiefs, represented the Crow in the Fort Laramie Treaty negotiations. The negotiations succeeded in establishing a 38 million acre country for the Crow. It was from south of the Yellowstone to the Montana territorial border. The east side was the divide between the Bighorn and Rosebud Rivers.

E.M. Camp was appointed Indian agent to the Crow in 1869, and an agency post was built in Mission Creek Valley that year. There were few skirmishes between the Crow and Blackfoot after the agency post was built and after the massacre of the Blackfoot in 1870.

The fierce Blackfoot were subjected to an unjust massacre in 1870, for the slaying of Malcolm Clark near Helena by some renegade Blackfoot. Major Eugene Baker led a force against an unsuspecting Blackfoot village on the Marias River. On a terribly cold dawn January 23, 173 Blackfoot, including fifty-three women and children, lost their lives. Then it was discovered Baker had attacked the wrong village. When it was discovered some of the captive women and children had smallpox, Baker abandoned them to shift for themselves in the cold and snow.

The corridor through which the Blackfoot used to hunt and travel to raid the Crow, between the Big Belt and Little Belt Mountains and between the Crazy and Bridger Mountains, was lost to white cattlemen. In 1874, the southern boundary of the Blackfoot territory was moved from the Sun River northward to Birch Creek. To their dismay, this deprived the Blackfoot of some of their best hunting ground.

As the Sioux and Northern Cheyenne lost more land to white men in the early 1870s, they were continually forced west into Crow land. This caused more fights between them and the Crow as the great buffalo herds continued to shrink. The Sioux tribes far outnumbered the Crow and were better armed due to their close contact with white traders. The Crow were unable to get the guns, ammunition and supplies they needed from their Indian agent. The promised treaty annuities were always short. For protection, the Crow allied themselves a little closer to the white men, and some even worked for the army as scouts.

In 1871, Dan's son, James Louis, was twelve years old, and Dan was teaching him horsemanship, hunting, and fighting skills, trapping, and much other useful knowledge. Dan also taught him about the white people's country. He explained that they lived in houses and many things about their tools and farming. He said the white people always wanted more land.

Dan and his son spent a lot of time together. They heard about many of the battles between Indians and U.S. soldiers, but as time passed, they managed to avoid battles with the soldiers. Dan and James were involved in a few skirmishes with the Sioux.

Lillian was four years younger then her brother. While helping her mother, Lily, she was learning the many skills needed by women in those days. Lily also taught her what she could about the English language, and other knowledge. Dan and Lily were good parents.

After much pressure by cattlemen and miners, the government gave the west end of the Crow Reservation to white people in 1875. The Crow Indian Agency was moved from Mission Creek to the East Rosebud River.

Colonel George Custer led a surveying expedition through the Black Hills in 1874 and discovered an area rich in gold and potential farm land. The Black Hills clearly belonged to the Sioux as it was agreed to in their 1868 Laramie Treaty. Regardless of the treaty, in 1875 hordes of miners came to the Black Hills, and the Sioux were again forced out.

When the Sioux were driven out of the Black Hills, they joined other Sioux and Cheyenne who were off of their reservations and on land from the Powder River to the Bighorn River. There were still many buffalo to hunt in that area. The Indian Bureau ordered the Indians to return to their reservations by the end of January 1876. When they refused, they were labeled hostiles, and the U.S. Army organized to defeat them.

The Indians decided to fight, and through the spring of 1876, many bands of Sioux and Cheyenne left their reservation and joined the hostile villages on the Rosebud and Little Bighorn Rivers in southeastern Montana. There were over fifteen thousand Indians, including four thousand warriors, gathered in that area.

In early June, the Montana military forces from Forts Shaw and Ellis, under Colonel John Gibbon, met the larger forces from Dakota under General Terry. They camped on the Yellowstone between the mouths of Rosebud Creek and the Tongue River.

General Crook came north from Fort Fetterman, Wyoming Territory, with one thousand soldiers. He was attacked and defeated June 17, 1876 on the upper Rosebud by Chief Crazy Horse and a very large band of Sioux and Cheyenne warriors. He had almost been caught in a canyon by Crazy Horse, where his troops would have been annihilated. General Crook moved back to the Tongue River and missed the rest of the campaign. Crazy Horse withdrew to the gathering on the Little Bighorn.

At the army's camp on the Yellowstone, General Terry correctly figured the hostile Indians were gathered on the Little Bighorn.

His strategy was to move up the Bighorn and on up the Little Bighorn River to strike the camps of the hostiles from the north. Meanwhile, Colonel George Custer would take the smaller, faster Seventh Cavalry and ride down it from the south. General Terry and Colonel George Custer were to strike the hostile forces from each side on June 26, 1876. Terry gave Custer the discretion to change the strategy if the Indians seemed likely to escape.

Custer led the seven hundred soldiers of the Seventh Cavalry up the Rosebud and across the hills toward the Little Bighorn. To some of the soldiers, it seemed a desolate and forlorn wilderness as they rode across endless miles of rolling grass and sagebrush prairie toward their tragic destiny. To Custer it seemed to be his great chance to ride into glory.

Custer did not follow the Rosebud as far as ordered so that he could cross and come down the Little Bighorn. Instead, he turned off before reaching the upper Rosebud and followed a big Indian trail straight toward the Little Bighorn. This was probably the trail of Chief Crazy Horse and his Sioux and Cheyenne warriors. At dawn, June 25th, one day earlier than was planned for the attack, Custer looked down on an enormous encampment of at least fifteen thousand hostile Sioux, Cheyenne, and other Indians on the Little Bighorn. There must have been over four thousand warriors and most of their chiefs among them. Probably a thousand tepees and twenty thousand horses were strung along the Little Bighorn for miles, partially obscured by large cottonwood trees.

Custer thought the seven hundred men of the seventh Cavalry, under his leadership were invincible. Against the advice of his terrified Crow and Shoshone scouts, Custer decided to attack.

Custer divided his force into three units. Captain Frederick Benteen was to hold the Indians from escaping to the west. Major Reno was also ordered to cross the Little Bighorn and strike the village from the south. Custer would ride around the bluffs to the right and attack the village at the center.

When Reno attacked, he was quickly overwhelmed by hundreds of warriors led by Chief Gall. Reno retreated back across the river to the bluffs and dug in with his surviving soldiers. Benteen also retreated and soon joined Reno with his remaining soldiers. They managed to hold off the Indians from their dug-in positions.

Custer was unaware of Reno's and Benteen's plight. He emerged from the bluffs east of the village and attempted to cross the river and attack. Chief Gall, Chief Crazy Horse, Sitting Bull, other chiefs, and thousands of warriors attacked Custer. He tried to retreat back up the ridge, but it was too late. Surrounded by thousands of excited Indians, Custer's troops fought desperately, but within half an hour, they were overrun and all lay dead!

The Indians held a wild victory celebration while they kept Reno and Benteen under siege until the following evening. As Terry and Gibbon's forces approached up the Little Bighorn, the Indians withdrew and scattered across eastern Montana.

Terry and Gibbon arrived to a shocking sight on the battlefield June 27th. They buried over 260 dead, and prepared to remove Reno and Benteen's wounded to Dakota.

The Mountain Crow village was on the West Rosebud when, soon after the battle, Dan, Jake, and the Crow heard of the battle on the Little Bighorn and the Custer massacre.

All of the Indian tribes now knew of the Custer massacre and were apprehensive of the consequences of the battle. In the past, the white soldiers had massacred whole Indian villages for less reason than that. Soon, the army troops were being reinforced, and it looked very serious for the Indian tribes.

When Dan and the Crow leaders heard of the Custer massacre, it was thought that this must be the beginning of Chief Red Bear's vision. The description of General Custer with his long-flowing, light-colored hair, had to be the soldier in the vision.

Chief White Temple, the few Crow who were present when Chief Red Bear told of his vision, and the Crow council held a meeting. Chief White Temple had been with Chief Red Bear when he told of his vision. The problem was discussed by the council, and the decision was made to inform the Crow tribe of Chief Red Bear's vision. It was believed many already knew.

The council did not want to frighten the people, but they believed the people should be informed so they could try to understand what was happening and maybe be better able to cope with whatever situation developed.

At a following meeting for everyone, the vision of Chief Red Bear was related just as it had first been told by Chief Red Bear. When the hill where Chief Red Bear had seen the vision was noted, it was realized that this was the same hill where the Custer Battle occurred. This convinced everyone that the vision was real.

Everyone believed Custer was the soldier riding the black horse of death with the skeletons of buffalo and Indians fleeing before him. Did this mean the death of all the buffalo and Indians? Could such a terrible thing happen? But how could Custer destroy the buffalo and Indians when he was already dead? The puzzle left them dismayed and frightened.

At the meeting, Chief White Temple asked Dan, "Why do you and a buffalo calf follow behind Custer and the skeletons in the vision?"

Dan replied, "Even now, I don't understand that, but then, this was not my vision, it was Chief Red Bear's vision, and I still don't understand his interest in me."

Later, with the children away, Lily expressed her feelings to Dan. "It's just as well that I didn't know about the vision. We've been happy until now, but now we don't know what terrible things will happen. It scares me."

Dan replied, "Honey, I believed I should spare you the worry as long as I could. We still don't know what will happen, but if there's goin' to be some kind of a disaster, I think the white people will cause it. They're the ones who are changing things here, but have faith, Lily; we'll find a way to survive."

"Dan, I do have faith in you. Maybe there will be bad times ahead, but we won't despair. We'll always go on together, helping each other and our children. I worry about the Indians losing their land, though."

"I do too, Lily."

The nation was shocked by the news of the Custer Massacre. They reinforced the armies of Generals Terry and Crook. After an unrewarding pursuit of the scattered Indians through summer and fall, they disbanded most of their troops and returned to their bases. With good weather and enough buffalo for food, the Indians were able to elude the armies in the great, wide open spaces of eastern Montana.

Only tough, shrewd, vain, and ruthless Colonel Nelson Miles, with his Fifth Infantry, was left to guard eastern Montana through the winter. With five hundred well-trained, tough, well-fed, well-armed, and well-clothed soldiers, Miles attacked Sitting Bull's Sioux north of the Yellowstone in October and December. With artillery he scattered them and destroyed irreplaceable food, shelter, and horses. Some returned to the reservation, but Sitting Bull and the rest retreated to Canada.

Due to the shortage of food and clothing, the Indians suffered terribly during winter fighting.

General Crook rebuilt his forces in Wyoming, and brought a large force up the old Bozeman Trail. During the cold, snowy winter, Crook's troops attacked and decimated the big Cheyenne village of Dull Knife and Little Wolf on the Powder River. The Cheyenne fled with terrible suffering.

South of the Yellowstone, in January's bitter cold, with 350 men, Miles fought a stand-off battle with Crazy Horse. Due to bad weather and shortage of supplies, both sides had to withdraw.

Through the winter, Miles and Crook attacked the cold, hungry, hostile bands of Sioux and Cheyenne. Demoralized bands of Sioux and Northern Cheyenne straggled in to their reservations and surrendered through the spring of 1877. Even the great Crazy Horse surrendered.

Lame Deer's band of Sioux held out, so Miles attacked them. Lame Deer was killed, and Miles narrowly escaped death. Through the summer, the army rounded up the scattered remnants of this band, and by the fall of 1877, the conquest of the Sioux and Northern Cheyenne was complete.

The year of 1877 was also the year that Chief Joseph and the gallant Nez Perce Indians of Idaho made their famous retreat from the United States Army. In a dispute over Nez Perce land, fighting broke out and the Nez Perce defeated a column of General Oliver Howard's in the battle of White Bird Canyon. With great skill they fought another pitched battle with Howard's troops on the Clearwater River, and then started their great retreat eastward over the Lolo Trail into Montana.

They brought all of their eight hundred people, their horse herds, and their belongings.

The Nez Perce crossed over the Continental Divide and camped in the Big Hole Basin. Here they were surprised at daybreak by Colonel Gibbon and over two hundred men. With uncanny accuracy, the Nez Perce killed thirty officers and men, but they left eighty-nine dead, many of them women and children.

They then retreated with their families and horses across Yellowstone Park, along the Clarks Fork River and the high Beartooth Wilderness.

On the Montana prairie at Canyon Creek, just north of the Yellowstone, The Nez Perce fought a battle with units of the Seventh Cavalry led by Colonel Sturgis. The Nez Perce escaped again and hurried north toward Canada.

Chief Joseph and the Nez Perce had outrun and outfought three United States Army units in an incredible 1500-mile chase. They had suffered great hardships.

Knowing that Howard's army was far behind, but not knowing Miles had joined the chase and crossed the Missouri on a river boat and was close behind, the exhausted Nez Perce stopped to rest on the north edge of the Bear Paw Mountains, north of the Missouri River.

It was cold in September, just forty miles from Canada. They were caught here and fought several days with Miles and finally Howard. A few of the Nez Perce escaped and reached Canada. Chief Joseph stayed with his people and finally surrendered.

This, it is said, were his words. "I am tired of fighting. Our chiefs are killed. The old men are all dead. It is the young men who say yes and no. He who led the young men, Alokut, is dead. It is cold, and we have no blankets. The little children are freezing to death. I want to have time to look for my children and see how many I can find. Maybe I shall find them among the dead.

"Hear me, my chiefs. I am tired. My heart is sick and sad. From where the sun now stands, I will fight no more forever!"

It had been promised if Joseph would surrender, the Nez Perce would be returned to Idaho. As usual, the promise was broken. The Nez Perce were taken to Kansas and then to Oklahoma. They longed for their homeland. Finally, they were taken to the state of Washington, but not to their home in Idaho.

In 1878, a year after Chief Joseph's surrender, due to a food shortage on their southeastern Idaho reservation, a group of Bannock Indians under Tendoy came to their old hunting grounds in Montana to hunt buffalo. Tendoy agreed to a military escort of their hunt, and caused no problem.

There were skirmishes with other groups of Bannocks seeking buffalo. One group crossed Yellowstone Park to the Clarks Fork of the Yellowstone on one of their old hunting trails. Due to an amazing coincidence, they met Colonel Miles and some of his soldiers heading for Yellowstone Park for a vacation. Miles turned the Bannocks back to their Idaho reservation.

This was the last of any organized Indian resistance in Montana Territory. Now the white men were able to wander across the great prairies at will.

Dan and Lily heard about each of these events soon after they happened. They were very sad for all of the Indians, and they knew that even their own lives could never be as happy and carefree again.

Most Indian tribes suffered a terrible injustice of suffering and sadness inflicted on them by misunderstanding, uncaring, and sometimes cruel army officers. There was the slaughter of the helpless Southern Cheyenne village at Sand Creek, Colorado in 1864, and a tragedy of misunderstanding and incompetence that led to the massacre of many Sioux at Wounded Knee, South Dakota in December 1890. There was the sad incident of the famous retreat and massacre of the Nez Perce with Chief Joseph in 1877, and the Trail of Tears in 1878, when the Northern Cheyenne were nearly annihilated while fleeing toward home in winter cold and hunger from a hopeless reservation in Oklahoma.

Many attacks were made on Indian villages where the object was to punish or annihilate the Indians. No clear and sensible policy was ever established by the United States Government for the white people to settle on the land and still leave enough for the Indians to live in a method they understood.

During all the time of the Indian wars, the Crow managed to live without resorting to war with the U.S. Army. In spite of this, the Crow lost the greatest portion of their land, as they were ordered to give up land to the white settlers. They were ordered to move to a smaller and smaller reservation. All of the Indian tribes were now losing the great herds of buffalo that were absolutely essential to their livelihood.

Dan, Jake, and the LaFountains were thankful that the Crow had made the right decision to live in peace with the army and the white people, even though their treaties were broken and agreements for annuities were not kept as agreed upon.

Dan said to Lily, "Anyhow, the Crow have avoided being attacked and massacred by the army as most of the other Indian tribes that we heard about were. It was a cause they couldn't win."

"I know that's right, Dan."

19

▼▼▼▼▼▼▼▼▼▼▼▼

END OF AN ERA

1882

▲▲▲▲▲▲▲▲▲▲▲▲▲

In September 1878, the village of the Mountain Crow was on the West Rosebud. This was near the west side of the reservation, since the old west end had been lost in 1875. Although the reservation had been reduced in size, it was still about fifty miles wide and 150 miles long. This was part of the abundant grass lands along the eastern side of the Rocky Mountains. It was at the center of the shrinking buffalo herds.

Dan and Lily, along with their two children, were living happily in a big tepee in the Crow village along the West Rosebud. Their girl, Lillian, was fifteen years old now and the son, James, was eighteen.

Dan rode out to the nearby horse herd one morning. Sonny was standing near the top of a small hill. As Dan rode up toward Sonny, Sonny nickered, bobbed his head and nickered again to Dan. He walked over to Dan and stopped. Dan got down and stood there petting Sonny for a while. As he talked to Sonny, Dan curried him. Sonny always enjoyed being curried.

Dan knew for a horse twenty-eight years old, Sonny sure looked good. He was a little thin, moved slower than when he was young, and did not lift his feet as well. He seemed to feel good, though, as he rubbed his head against Dan.

Finally Dan mounted his saddle horse. He reached over and patted Sonny again and rode away. Sonny stood there and watched Dan ride down the hill. When Dan reached the bottom of the hill, he turned and watched Sonny standing proudly as the sound of his long whinny floated across the valley.

It was early the next morning when Dan rode out to the horse herd again. Sonny was near the top of the hill, close to where he had been the day before. He was lying down resting, with his side against a low rock outcropping. The old fella was asleep. As Dan rode closer he became concerned. When he rode near, he could see Sonny's eyes were shut, but it was more than sleep. Sonny was dead. He had shut his eyes and gone to sleep forever.

Dan was sad to lose such a loyal friend. He had never failed to greet Dan with a display of affection. For such a strong and active horse, Sonny had always been gentle, even when he had needed to be doctored. He was Dan's horse from the day of his birth and always had complete trust and love for Dan.

Sonny looked so peaceful lying there with his eyes closed, as in sleep, and his side resting against the rock. That is how Dan preferred to remember Sonny, so he went down and got a group of Indian boys to help. They covered him over with rocks, just as he was lying. As Dan rode away, he was thankful Sonny had lived such a free and happy life in a very beautiful land. He was thankful they had been such great friends.

In 1878 and 1879 the Crow's income from furs was less than it had been, so they were unable to buy the articles they needed. There were many less beaver to trap. Other small, fur-bearing animals were not plentiful, but they trapped some. They caught marten, mink, weasels, otter, muskrat, fox, wolves, and sometimes bobcat, lynx and mountain lion. There was usually a good market for these furs. The hides from the buffalo, elk, deer, antelope, and bear that the Crow killed for food were used by the Crow for clothing and shelter.

The Indian Agency was providing only a small amount of treaty annuities of food and clothing, but the Crow were still able to find enough buffalo in the year of 1880.

That year the Utah Northern Railroad reached some of the mining settlements in western Montana Territory. More white people were coming to Crow country on the Yellowstone to settle. The Crow still had many buffalo on their reservation, but they were unable to keep the white hunters from killing buffalo. The government did not protect the Indian reservations, as they should have, from the buffalo hunters. More whites were pushing into Montana Territory from both the west and the east.

The fierce Sioux, Cheyenne, and Blackfoot Indians were forced by the United States Army to stay on small reservations. This gave the white buffalo hide hunters free access to the great herds of eastern Montana. They killed the buffalo by the hundreds of thousands, took the hides and left the carcasses rotting on the prairies. Travelers in 1880 found the prairie littered with rotting buffalo carcasses throughout eastern Montana.

The slaughter increased to a frenzy in 1881 and 1882. It was a time of incredible greed and waste. The bleached buffalo bones and skulls lay in catastrophic numbers across the plains from the Rocky Mountains into the Dakotas. Crossing the prairies through endless bleached buffalo bones was a horrifying sight for Dan and all of the Indians. It was impossible for them to understand why the United States Government would allow such a terrible waste to happen, unless it was to annihilate the remaining Indians. For the Indians, it was now a life of hopeless grief.

One survey found fewer than two hundred buffalo in the entire West. The buffalo were within a whisper of extinction. It was the end of a romantic and colorful era. The nomadic Indian tribes would never again roam the great enchanting plains.

One day Dan and Lily visited the site of Custer's Battle of the Little Bighorn. It was so strange that here, at the top of the hill where Custer and his soldiers died, along with many Indians, was the same spot where so long ago Chief Red Bear had laid his medicine arrow to point the direction for the three white trappers to travel to the great stone tower, Mateo Tepee, that was now known as the Devil's Tower. Incredibly, it was the same place where Chief Red Bear saw the vision! There seemed to be something supernatural here on the top of this long, high hill.

As they watched from the top of the hill, a golden eagle spiraled in a quiet, blue sky over a lonely band of antelope. It spiraled much the same as the eagle had spiraled when Chief Red Bear saw the vision, but now the eagle spiraled above a scene of desolation where buffalo skeletons stretched across some of the little remaining land of the Indians, and the skeletons of many of the Indians lay upon their burial platforms. Only a broken and demoralized small Indian population remained. There was only a haunting memory of the enchanting Red Men and their mighty buffalo.

Dan exclaimed, "Everywhere we ride we find only dead buffalo, never a live one. It's madness. I didn't think it was possible that all of the buffalo could be killed just as Chief Red Bear foresaw. What a terrible fate for the Indians, and a sad world for all of us."

"Oh, Dan, it can never be the same again," Lily lamented.

The fulfillment of Chief Red Bear's vision was nearly complete. Only the puzzle of Dan and the buffalo calf remained unknown.

Dan said to Lily, "I still don't know what part I will play in the fulfillment of Chief Red Bear's vision, but now I believe there is something left that I am to do, and I don't even know what it is."

Lily replied, "Sometime I'm sure it will be clear to you."

For a short time, wide spaces of deserted, lonely prairie existed. To the far horizon, the undulating ridges of sagebrush and grass were empty. Dreary miles of bleached bones lay on the abandoned landscape to attest to its former magnificent, dark, shaggy herds.

Even before the last of the buffalo were gone, cattlemen and sheepmen were moving into northern and eastern Montana. Western Montana had been settled earlier. Foreign and eastern capital financed large corporate ranches from Texas to Canada. Strong and ambitious individuals grasped ranges of their own. In the early 1880s, numerous herds of cattle and sheep grazed where vast herds of buffalo once roamed.

In only twenty years time, from the 1860s to the 1880s, the land was changed from a beautiful wilderness with vast herds of buffalo, antelope, elk, and other wildlife, where happy and colorful nomadic Indians roamed, to a land named Montana, where eager, ambitious, hard-working cattlemen and farmers soon changed the very essence of the land.

Dan wondered if he could fit in and be happy after such a radical change from the life he loved so well, but he knew he must.

20

▼▼▼▼▼▼▼▼▼▼▼▼

RANCH BELOW
THE PEAKS

▲▲▲▲▲▲▲▲▲▲▲▲▲

Through the summer and fall of 1882, Dan Daily and his family moved with the Crow from the Stillwater River on the west side of the reservation to Pryor Creek. There were only a few small herds of buffalo, but they found enough to keep from starving. They hunted back across the reservation to the mouth of the Clarks Fork Canyon and around the mountains to the East Rosebud River. By late fall, the Crow and their white friends had enough dried buffalo meat to help them live through the winter. The Indian agency was able to furnish some supplies to the Crow.

The Dailys, LaFountains, and Jake Barnes, were not counted as Crow. So they were not entitled to any of the annuities from the Indian agency. In October, Dan, his son James, Jake, and Striking Hawk each led two pack horses to a new settlement on the Yellowstone, below the mouth of the Clarks Fork River. At this little settlement named Billings, they loaded up with flour, dried foods, and other supplies that were available. Dan and Jake bought the supplies with money from their gold.

The Crow managed to have food through the winter. The Crow and their white friends were able to kill some deer and other wild game to help supply them with food. The Crow still found a few small fur-bearing animals to trap that would help them buy food and supplies.

In the summer of 1883, many Crow hunting parties traveled all over the reservation looking for buffalo. They even looked in the mountains and beyond the boundaries of the reservation. Many buffalo bones were found, but the hunters returned with fallen spirits and empty hands. The hunters found some deer and antelope, but even these animals were becoming scarce. The Crow were forced more and more to depend on the annuities from the Indian agent at the reservation agency. It was frightening and disheartening to the Crow. Their morale continued to lower as more white people settled in the area. There was no escaping the reality that their happy, nomadic, colorful life was gone forever. It had vanished with the buffalo.

The Indian agent tried to get the Crow to learn to plow the ground and be farmers.

The great hunter, Gray Wolf, said to the Indian agent, "I don't want to be a farmer Indian, I just want to be an Indian Indian. We must find where our buffalo have gone and bring them back to multiply."

Striking Hawk said, "I think our buffalo are gone forever. We should have killed all the hide hunters."

Red Arrow said, "This is what the army did to us. They wanted all the buffalo killed so we would have to ask the agency for food. Now the white men will take all of the land."

The Crow village was along Rock Creek in September 1883. One day Jake came to Dan and said, "These are bad times. There will never be enough furs anymore for people to live by trapping. The buffalo are gone. Most of the elk are gone. There can never be enough deer and antelope to use to take the place of the buffalo."

"I'm sure you're right," Dan agreed.

Jake continued, "We both have most of the money left from the gold. We'll have to buy land and cattle to have a way to live."

"We should get all the land we can," Dan added.

"The time could come when we would need the gold in the cache. I'm getting too old to need it," said Jake, "but I have two squaws that are sure to need the money. We're camped here on Rock Creek only eight miles from the cache. We've made some new pouches because the old ones must be rotten after twenty-seven years."

238

"When do you want to go?" Dan asked.

"This September weather is just right. Tomorrow would be a good day to go."

"I'll get the horses and some tools ready to go in the morning," Dan agreed.

After Jake left, Dan rode out to the horse herd and got a pack horse. When he returned and passed by Striking Hawk's tepee, Striking Hawk asked, "Do you want some help to get the gold?"

"How did you know we were going after it?"

"Just a guess. After old Jake left, you went right out and got a pack horse. Looked like his squaws were making new pouches for gold."

"Jake's pretty old," Dan replied. "He's eighty now, but I sure wouldn't want to make him think he's too old to help. It's a short trip and Jake feels fine. It's good weather. I don't see any reason why we wouldn't be all right, but thanks for the offer anyhow, Striking Hawk."

The next morning Dan and Jake had a nice ride together down Rock Creek Valley.

Dan said to Jake, "It's just like old times, riding along together, Jake. We haven't been riding together for quite a while. One of these days we'll go hunting for a big buck together."

From the valley, Dan and Jake rode northwest to the lower end of a ridge that led to the high rimrocks. They followed a mile-long slope to the base of three layers of high, long sandstone cliffs. Pine trees lined the top of the long cliffs eight hundred feet above the valley floor. Other scattered groves of pines grew on the fifty-foot-wide ledges at the base of each layer of cliffs. Dan and Jake followed game trails that climbed from ledge to ledge up steep ravines between cliffs.

There were hundreds of scattered holes in the face of the cliffs that had been worn by erosion through the ages of time. There were holes of all sizes. Some were caves large enough for birds and animals. Others were large enough for men. Many were high enough up the face of a cliff that a man had to use a ladder to climb to the cave.

On the second ledge Dan and Jake rode their horses to the cave that held their remaining gold cache. Dan tied a ladder together with thongs. He threw a rock in the cave before he climbed to it. Jake laughed, "That oughta scare the owls out." Dan removed the sand and flat rocks that covered the gold pouches. The pouches were very dried and weak. Dan very carefully lifted them, one at a time, with a small scoop under them and poured their gold into the new pouches. A few of the old pouches were split, and some split when he moved them. He carefully gathered up all of the spilled gold with the scoop and got very little of the sandy dirt.

Dan handed the pouches of gold down to Jake. He climbed down and they loaded them on the pack horse. They dismantled the ladder, but they did not bother to wipe their tracks away this time.

Dan and Jake started down the same trail they had followed to the cave. On the bottom ledge, they came around the corner of a cliff and met two rough-looking characters that were standing there holding rifles pointed at Dan and Jake. Dan and Jake were leading their horses. The strangers ordered them to raise their hands, then walk over and face the cliff wall.

Dan thought the strangers could be the outlaws or horse thieves he had heard of who were operating north of the Yellowstone River. He sure had not expected to see such men here and did not think he and Jake would be left alive.

One said, "We watched you at the cave in the cliffs. You musta cached something pretty valuable there. We'll have a look at your pack horse. Just stand right still there and you might live a little longer."

One of the men untied the pack and said, "Sure enough. It's gold. Now where—?" The sharp crack of a rifle sounded from across the narrow ravine. Dan turned and saw the outlaw, holding the rifle, fall backward! The other one at the pack horse took three steps, stooped and picked up his rifle. He raised his rifle as he looked across the ravine, but could not see a target. The rifle across the ravine roared again, and the second outlaw fell backward!

Dan thought the rifleman across the ravine must be Striking Hawk, although it was even possible it was more outlaws. He did not run for his rifle. That could be a mistake.

Then Striking Hawk stepped from behind a cliff and called, "Think that's all of 'em, but watch. I'll come over."

Dan and Jake got their rifles and watched all around. Then, in a few minutes, Striking Hawk reached Dan and Jake.

Dan exclaimed, "Man, are we glad to see you, Striking Hawk."

Jake said, "I'm sure glad you came, Striking Hawk, or we'd be dead by now!"

"Figured I better follow you," said Striking Hawk. "If something like this happens, it's always when you least expect it."

"I wonder how they happened to follow us," Jake pondered.

240

Striking Hawk said, "Prob'ly they were just passing through here at the wrong time. They got suspicious when they saw you go up in the rimrocks. Prob'ly wondered if you had somethin' cached up there. Their horses are in the next ravine. My horse is hidden farther down below here."

"What are we goin' to do about killing these outlaws?" Dan asked.

"Just like always," said Striking Hawk. "Just like we did with the Cheyenne and Sioux. We'll let the magpies and coyotes take care of 'em. We'll leave their saddles up here and turn their horses loose. I'm not about to do a lot of explaining to the Indian agent or the army at Fort Ellis about these saddles and horses. You and Jake go on down slow. I'll go turn their horses loose and catch you in a little while."

They all left. Soon after Dan and Jake reached the valley floor, Striking Hawk caught up to them.

Dan said to Striking Hawk, "We're really grateful to you for saving our lives and the gold."

"Well, I kind of owed you for getting one of the hide hunters when they both drew on me," said Striking Hawk, "but I'd've done it anyway."

Dan, Jake, and Striking Hawk returned to the Crow village a few miles farther up Rock Creek. Dan and Jake each put their pouches of gold out of sight with some of their belongings in their tepees. Few people would know about the gold, and no one would molest it there.

Through the winter of 1883–1884, the Crow managed to live, but not nearly so well as they had in the days when there were buffalo. For a few years, they would have some moose, elk, deer, and antelope to help with their food and clothing. Sometimes the Indian Agency provided part of their food. As more white people came, they also used the wildlife for food, and there was not enough anymore.

In the summer of 1884, without any negotiations, the government told the Crow Indians that the size of their reservation had again been cut on the west end. The boundary would now be on the divide between Pryor Creek and the Clarks Fork River. This was another enormous cut of nearly one half of their remaining reservation. There were so many white settlers, miners, and stockmen wanting to take the west end of the reservation, that the government had again given in to their demands. The Crow Agency was now moved to the Little Bighorn Valley, and all of the Crow moved to the remaining reservation.

Very few of the Crow took any interest in farming. Some would try to raise a few cattle. It seemed impossible for them to adjust to the white man's ways. They knew their nomadic hunting life was destroyed forever. Their cultural heritage was badly shattered by the white authorities insistence that they learn the white people's ways. Much of their land was even sold in desperation to white people. The Crow lived in impoverishment as they tried to exist on their allotments. The sudden change was a terrible shock to their morale. It was the low point in the history of their existence. Now Dan recalled the old days, when the Crow, the Blackfoot, and Sioux always fought each other. He had wondered why they did, but anyhow, all of the tribes were a happy and proud people then.

When the Mountain Crow moved eastward to the smaller reservation in 1884, because Dan, Jake, and the LaFountains were white people, they stayed in the area of the East Rosebud and West Rosebud Rivers. Jake's two squaws stayed there with Jake. These white people would have a much better chance to manage to live where they were. They planned to immediately claim land in the area. Their Crow friends understood the reasons for this, and told them to take all the land they could get.

They knew which land they wanted in a place called Antelope Basin, at the foot of the Beartooth Mountains, between the East Rosebud and West Rosebud Rivers. A small creek ran through the center of the three-by-six-mile strip, and emptied into the East Rosebud River. It was a shallow basin of grassland, bordered on the east and west edge by evergreen and aspen trees. Brush and aspen trees lined the small creek that ran through the center. It would always be a secluded place because of its location between the Rosebud Valleys, where any future roads were sure to be. Antelope Basin did not lead into a huge canyon, as each of the Rosebud Rivers did. It stopped at the base of steep peaks, where only rugged mountainsides with steep ravines carried water to the small creek. Beyond the base of these mountains, there was nowhere to go but nearly straight up, therefore, there would never be any roads passing through Antelope Basin.

The gentle slopes through the middle of the basin could be used for hay fields, grazing, and even a place for raising oats. The rest was very good grazing land, some timber land, and some high, rocky places.

Dan knew that he would need to learn to like ranching, but he was sure to be happy here in one of the most splendid, beautiful places in the West.

The Dailys and LaFountains, including children of legal age, and even a few far-away relatives, from whom they would later buy their land, filed for homesteads under the Desert Lands Homestead Act of 1877.

Although Striking Hawk was half Crow and looked to be Indian, he used his white man's name of Leo LaFountain to file for his homestead claim. His two children and Dan's two children filed for claims. Lillian was just recently old enough to file.

Many of the huge cattle ranchers of Montana gained title to their land by having their hired men file for homesteads, and then buying the homesteads from their cowboys.

The Daily and LaFountain families were able to file for all of the land in antelope Basin. Their twenty-four sections was considered small by comparison to the large ranches of eastern Montana. The Dailys and LaFountains owned adjoining halves of the ranch and had separate houses on their own land, but they ran the ranch as one unit.

Jake said he was too old to start ranching, so he only homesteaded one section on the West Rosebud at the edge of Dan's land. One day while visiting with the Dailys and LaFountains, Jake said, "My squaws can't homestead any land, but they're allowed to stay here with me 'cause I call one of 'em my wife and one my sister. They look a lot alike, but most people don't think my sister and me look a bit alike," he grinned and laughed softly as the others laughed. Jake was getting old, but he looked and acted younger than he was, and he enjoyed life very much.

Dan and Striking Hawk went to Bozeman and bought fifty cows and two bulls. They also bought fifty yearling steers. The steers would grow, and then some would be used to butcher instead of buffalo as they used to. Some could be sold as three-year-olds, and many more yearlings would be bought as they developed their ranch.

Striking Hawk was raising some very good riding horses from stallions he had bred as the progeny of Sonny. Dan was happy and proud to see Sonny's traits carried strongly through the generations. He always had a soft spot in his heart when he remembered Sonny, the horse that had been such a great one, and had saved Dan's life so many times—those were the exciting times.

Dan was thankful that life was going so well for everyone here at the ranch. One evening he said to Lily, "We really enjoyed it when we found the gold and dug it out of the stream bed, and we thought it

243

would be useful some day, but now it's been even more useful than I would ever have thought it could be. The time came when we needed it for the money to get this land, and the cattle to put on it. I didn't expect such a thing when we found the gold. Our trapping would never have paid for much. It's good that we're able to pay for our half, and help the others get their half. The only way we can live in this real good basin is to own it."

"Yes, Dan, I thought you'd find a way for us to live in a place we'd like; and I'm really happy, living here in this nice log home you built for us. It's the first house I've ever lived in, and I really enjoy it. Thank you for building it for us, Dan. I love you," and she hugged him.

Dan replied, "We were always able to stay warm at night in our tepee in the winter. Remember some of those cold nights? Our buffalo robes are the warmest cover people can have to sleep under. This big log cabin is even warmer than our buffalo hide tepee was. We can't travel from camp to camp enjoying new scenery and fresh camping grounds like we used to, but we can sure enjoy our good home here. I'm really happy that we're all here together and have a place where we'll always have food. There'll always be some wildlife here, and we'll soon have some cattle we can butcher." He paused, and then, "My only real regret is that I can't help the Crow as much as I'd like to. Just a steer once in a while for a few friends. When I can raise more steers, I can help a little more, but all the Indians need help."

"Some day maybe you can help more."

The Dailys and LaFountains worked hard and lived very well on their ranch.

That fall, in 1885, Dan and Jake wanted to sell their last gold cache that they had brought out of the rimrocks two years ago. They still had plenty of money, but they wanted to get the gold sold and not have to care for it any longer.

Fort Union, where they used to trade, and where their gold had been shipped from, was no longer operating. There was only a small fur trade. Freight wagons had replaced the river boats, and now the railroad was replacing some of the freight wagons. The buildings of Fort Union had been sold to the army to use in building nearby Fort Buford.

It was decided to take the gold to Butte, where the big mines and mills were. The new Northern Pacific Railroad had recently been built up the Yellowstone Valley from North Dakota through Billings, Butte, and on across Montana. Dan was curious about the train, and thought he might like to try a ride on it.

Dan asked Gray Wolf and Lone Walker to come over from the reservation to help guard the gold on the trip. Striking Hawk would also help.

The gold pouches were carried in leather suitcases that Dan bought in Billings. They boarded the train in Billings, and no one knew what was in the suitcases.

Dan and the other men enjoyed their first ride on the big train that ran as fast as a horse and never got tired. They also enjoyed the fall scenery along the way. On the ride up the Yellowstone Valley to Livingston, the tracks paralleled the bright, blue water of the Yellowstone River that was lined with a wide border of yellow-leaved trees.

From Livingston the train crossed a mountain pass of lush green grass. Brilliant red chokecherry, thornbrush, and mountain maple bordered by white-trunked groves of golden-leaved aspen trees colored the canyon. The tunnel near the top of the pass was a real wonder to them.

As they rode down the west side of the Bozeman Pass, Dan recalled the escape in 1853 of Dan, Jake, and John from the fierce Blackfoot who had trailed them into this pass, but were evaded by riding to another pass during a snowstorm. Dan thought, things have sure changed since then. He certainly had not liked the Blackfoot Indians at that time, or when they killed John Daily, but in the last few years so much had happened. He reasoned that in 1853, most Indians had to fight hard to hold their land and survive. The Blackfoot had a reputation of hard fighting, and a viciousness that Dan had not liked. Now, as Dan considered what he had heard of the plight of the Blackfoot, he felt sympathy toward them.

Due to the failure of Congress to appropriate sufficient funds, and sometimes due to corruption or inefficiency, the Indian agencies did not provide sufficient food for the Indians on the reservations. As the buffalo herds vanished, many of the Indians suffered from malnutrition, cold, and starvation. It was exceedingly desperate on the Piegan Blackfoot Reservation in northern Montana. There, in the extreme winter climate, possibly one-fourth of the Piegan perished from starvation in 1883 and 1884.

In the past, Dan had not liked the Blackfoot, but now he was sorry they were treated so badly. He wondered if someday the white authorities would learn to treat the Indians as humans.

245

Beyond mountain-rimmed Bozeman, willows covered the wide river bottoms where the three rivers, the Madison, Jefferson, and Gallatin, joined to form the broad Missouri River. Dan and his pardners had dared not come here when they passed through this area so long ago. Dan thought it was an interesting place, but it had taken him a long time to get a chance to see it.

For awhile, they followed along the Jefferson River that ran down from distant mountain ranges and river basins to the southwest. Somewhere, far away in the distant landscape, lived the tribe of Bannock Indians that Lone Walker had been taken from in his dim past. Dan knew that Lone Walker would like to visit there to satisfy his haunting memories.

The train steamed up Pipestone Pass through huge granite boulders strangely fitted together. A plume of black smoke billowed from the engine as they chugged up the steep, twisting grade, around horse shoe bends, and bored through more dark tunnels while crossing the high Continental Divide. From the top, they raced down a long cut in the side of a mountain to the fabulous mining city of Butte.

The city was built on a hill beside the mines. There were tall brick buildings for hotels, banks, department stores, and various business houses. Saloons and gambling dens were located on all of the business streets among the assay offices, mineral offices, banks and stores. Tough-looking men and women mingled among boisterous, hard-drinking miners.

Dan felt ill at ease in such a wild and unfamiliar place. It worried him just to walk down the street among such strange people. He knew what Striking Hawk could do with a knife, in just a flash, if he was assaulted.

They sold the gold and received a $20,000 bank draft to deposit in a bank in Billings. With relief, they retired to a small hotel and cafe in a more quiet area at the edge of town. City life held no attraction for this group.

The following morning, the men boarded the train for their return trip to Billings. This time it was a longer passenger train. To help the train up the long grade to the top of the Continental Divide, a pusher engine was used at the back end of the train. Dan and his men were riding in the last passenger car, the one ahead of the pusher engine. It was a really disturbing experience for them. The front end of the big engine was very close to the back door of their car. The fast, hard

246

chugging of the heavy steam engine gave their light passenger car a rapid, hard pounding and shaking. As the grade became steeper, the pounding and shaking of the car increased.

A passenger opened the back door of the passenger car, and the chugging, blasting noise was terrific. It seemed the car would collapse between the long string of cars ahead and the powerful steam engine behind. Dan could see a grave look on the faces of his friends, so he said, "They do this every day, so it must be all right." They all stayed in the car, but they were relieved when the noisy engine detached at the top of the grade.

In the Bozeman area, they could see where some people were raising oats, potatoes, and hay.

When they reached Billings, Dan sent John's daughters in Missouri their share of the money. He also made arrangements to transfer the remainder of his money from the bank in St. Louis to the bank in Billings.

In Billings, Gray Wolf and Lone Walker bought food and other supplies with wages paid by Dan and Jake, and then returned to the reservation on their horses.

Dan and Striking Hawk bought some supplies and rode back to their ranch on their horses. It had been a successful trip without an incident. Dan wondered if sometime he and Lily may be able to ride a train to Missouri to visit his relatives.

The winter of 1886-87 was the worst winter Dan and his people had ever seen. The severe cold started in November. In January, the warm chinook winds partly melted the snow, and then turned terribly cold with temperatures as cold as thirty to fifty below zero. The melted snow turned to ice over the grass. It was bitterly cold work to haul hay to cattle, but with enough help, Dan and Striking Hawk were able to, with horses and sleds. There were some areas bare of snow on the hillsides, where the cattle could graze during the less severe days. Their small herd of three hundred cattle found protection from the cold wind among the trees along the west side of the ranch. The ranch, in an average year, should run five or six hundred cattle. Thankfully, they had not fully stocked their ranch yet, because their hay fields needed to be enlarged. The ranch was in an area where there was always much winter snow, and hay was needed each winter. Although it had been a dry year, they had enough grass and hay.

Because of the previous dry summer, the ranges east of the Rockies had been overgrazed by the huge herds of cattle that had been brought to Montana. The big cattle ranches that had hundreds or thousands of cattle on unprotected, windswept, open range did not have hay for their cattle. These ranches lost most of their cattle from starvation and freezing. When the snow finally melted in the spring, the Montana prairies were once again covered with the hideous sight of bloated carcasses rotting in the sun. Most of the cattle in Montana had died!

Dan saw that it was reminiscent of the carnage that had covered the plains only a few years before, when the hide hunters had slaughtered millions of buffalo. Again it was a shameful waste. He wished that it had still been buffalo on the prairies instead of cattle, and most of the buffalo would have survived. The hardy old buffalo with their thick hides, heavy coats of hair and strong constitutions had stood dry summers and terrible cold winters such as these for thousands of years.

Dan and Striking Hawk saw what happened to the ranches that did not raise some winter feed and vowed to never be caught in that situation. The big ranchers learned their lesson, and after this bad winter, most of the ranches were smaller, and they tried to have some hay for the worst periods in winter.

There was a store, a saloon, and a few other buildings near East Rosebud River, just above where it meets the Stillwater River. One summer day in 1887, Dan and Striking Hawk walked out of the store, and along the front of the saloon. A few men were sitting and standing while they visited there. As Dan and Striking Hawk passed by, a rough-looking character, considerably larger than Striking Hawk, and who had evidently drank enough to make him bold and defiant, stepped over to Striking Hawk and said, "Hey, Injun, how come you're not living on the reservation? I hear you even claim to own a big ranch up by the mountains. I oughta chase you back to the reservation."

Instantly, Striking Hawk gripped the man's clothing at his throat and jabbed his knife a little ways into his skin just below the breastbone.

The man shouted, "Oh, don't!" Then Dan said, "No, Striking Hawk, Please don't do it!"

A small stream of blood ran down the blade of the knife as Striking Hawk held the man for several seconds while the man gasped, "Oh, no, no!"

Striking Hawk spoke, "All right, I won't kill you this time, but I want you to leave here right now and never come back. If you do, I'll kill you for sure. I don't even want to see your shadow. I don't like to be insulted." He released the man with a push and said, "Now go!"

"Thank God!" exclaimed Dan, as the man quickly left on his horse.

"Don't let it bother you," Striking Hawk advised. It wouldn't bother me to kill him. People here think he was a hide hunter anyway. I sure don't need for him to live."

On their way home, Dan said to Striking Hawk, "I've seen you kill men before that needed to be killed and it didn't bother me too much. I really don't like to see it, but now days you'd probably have to stand trial for killing someone. Probably you would go free, but it would sure be a lot of trouble."

"Hell's bells," exclaimed Striking Hawk, "I didn't have time to figure all that out. I'm not a lawyer or judge, or something," and then he laughed and rode on.

Dan knew Striking Hawk was actually a very good fellow, but it had always been a bad mistake for a man to choose Striking Hawk to fight. Life was not usually dull for very long around Striking Hawk.

Dan and Striking Hawk were working at the lower end of the ranch one day in the fall of 1887. They were near Jake's log home, so they rode over to visit Jake and his two squaws for a little while.

Dan said to Jake, "You're eighty-five years old now, Jake. You feel good, and you don't have any trouble with your health at all. You even walk and act like a much younger man. You should reach a hundred! Tell me Jake, what's the secret for being able to live so healthy for so long?"

"Oh, it's no secret. Everyone knows I have two wives to take care of me. I figure if a man has one wife that cooks real good for him and he lives to be fifty or more, then with two good wives he should live to be a hundred or more," and Jake grinned.

Dan answered, "Well, I guess I can't argue with you about that. Anyhow, I'm sure glad to see it working so well for you, Jake."

21

A VISIT TO MISSOURI

The Northern Pacific Railroad was built up the Yellowstone Valley from Dakota in 1882. The Union Pacific had crossed southern Wyoming to Utah thirteen years earlier in 1869. The Utah Northern was built from Utah north to Montana. It connected the Union Pacific Railroad to Butte, Montana on December 26, 1881.

Dan had never returned to St. Joseph, Missouri to see his parents since his departure in 1855. Many times he had wondered if they were alive and all right. He longed to see them and have them meet Lily.

Because of the hostilities of the Sioux and Cheyenne with the army and all whites in the 1860s and 1870s, it would have been very dangerous to attempt to cross their land toward Missouri. At that time, it was also dangerous to cross Blackfoot land to get to western Montana and the Oregon Trail to Missouri. Many adventures had filled those years for Dan while he lived in Crow country.

In June 1888, Dan and Lily could now travel by railroad to Missouri. The only railroad traveling south from Montana Territory was the Utah

Northern from Butte to Salt Lake City. From there, the Union Pacific ran to Missouri.

This is the route Dan chose for a return trip to visit his parents, which would give Dan and Lily a chance to see some of the land that the three trappers had traveled through on their first trip to western Montana. They would see part of western Montana, Idaho, Utah, and Wyoming Territories. This would be an interesting and beautiful route. In June 1888, Dan and Lily started their trip to Missouri.

Dan and Lily did not have any children to bring with them on the trip. Their boy and girl were both grown long before now. Their son, James Louis Daily, was twenty-eight years old. He had married a nice Crow girl, White Swan, in 1881 at the Indian agency when it was still on the East Rosebud. James and White Swan's son, Robert Daily, was six years old now. The family lived on the ranch in Antelope Basin.

Dan and Lily's daughter, Lillian, was now twenty-five years old, and had married a fine white man a little older than her, named Tom Long. They lived a few miles down the East Rosebud River. They were married in June 1887, and were now expecting a child.

Dan and Lily boarded the train on the Northern Pacific rail line at Billings. They rode the train up the Yellowstone Valley to Livingston, a railroad town on the Yellowstone east of Bozeman Pass. They rode over Bozeman Pass where Dan showed Lily how John, Jake, and he had escaped the Blackfoot. As they rode the train through the basin of the Three Forks of the Missouri, Dan told Lily of the three men's escape from the Blackfoot by riding in a herd of stampeding buffalo to destroy their trail.

With black smoke spouting from the stack, they climbed the Continental Divide on a winding track so curved that they were able to see the rear coaches of their train emerge from the tunnels. From the top of the divide, they rolled down the long cut on the west face of the mountain to the copper mining town of Butte. At Butte, Dan and Lily left the Northern Pacific train and boarded the three-foot-wide, narrow-gauge Utah and Northern rail line for a trip almost five hundred miles southward.

Soon they crossed the Continental Divide to the east side again, then passed through the Beaverhead Valley to Dillon, and traveled the same area the three trappers had traveled in 1852. They rode over Monida Pass to the west side of the divide once more and stopped in Pocatello.

Dan recognized most of the area they had passed through as he recalled his first trip to the West. He pointed out to Lily some of the route he and his pardners had followed. Dan and Lily enjoyed the trip through this area. By evening they had reached Ogden, sitting at the base of the Wasatch Mountains.

After staying overnight in a hotel, Dan and Lily boarded the Union Pacific train for the long one thousand mile trip eastward over standard gauge tracks, fifty-six and one half inches wide.

Their train climbed a long pass up Weber Canyon and Echo Canyon through the Wasatch Mountains. In the canyon, Dan and Lily were uneasy as their train passed over the high, frightful Devil's Gate Bridge, and they looked far down onto the rolling, roily water of the Weber River swollen with snowmelt. With black smoke puffing violently from the stack, their train chugged and rattled up the spectacular Echo Canyon through three dark tunnels, alongside of a precipice, and below high rock walls.

This grade had been gouged from the canyon twenty years before with hand drills, black powder, pick and shovel, and the muscle and guts of men.

When the train finally broke out of the canyon at the summit, Lily expressed her opinion, "White men do strange things."

"They sure change things," Dan agreed. "Where we live, the Indians are not even using the wheel yet, and life is simple and quiet there. It's a real wonder what the white men built here, though."

Dan noted their crossing of the upper end of the Bear River. From farther down the river, the three pardners had followed it to the Snake River long ago. A few miles from the site of old Fort Bridger they left the mountains and crossed the dry prairie to a bridge across the Green River.

"This river's easy to cross now, but it was kind of a thrill to cross it on a little log ferry," Dan said.

That day they crossed a dry area of high, sandy plains where they rode over the Continental Divide to the east side again. It was almost unnoticeable because even though the elevation was over 6700 feet, there was no deep mountain canyon for a pass.

"That's the fourth time we've crossed the Continental Divide," John told Lily. "Now we're back on the side we started from."

As the train sped along at thirty miles per hour, they reached plains that were not as barren. There were no buffalo left on these plains, but there were many antelope that were seen from the train. One band of antelope was running alongside of the train, 150 yards away. The antelope sped up and ran closer to the train. Soon they stretched their bodies into a terrific burst of speed, twice as fast as the train. In less than a minute, they passed the train, crossed the tracks ahead of the engine and sped away. The passengers watched the race with excited wonder. One remarked, "Wow, look at 'em go!" A quarter of a mile from the tracks the antelope stopped, turned back and watched the train go by.

Dan said, "They just proved they like to run. They weren't afraid of being caught, they know they're the fastest things in the West."

The long days of June and a full moon at night provided enough light to see the land the travelers passed through. Quite often they stopped for water and coal for the steam engine. Sometimes there was a little town where they may have time for a quick lunch. The Dailys usually ate in the dining car where the meals were very good.

At night the seats were folded down and made into beds that were reasonably comfortable. The conductor distributed pillows and blankets that were rented to the passengers. The lights were turned low for sleeping. The pullman car was filled by passengers with reservations from San Francisco.

In the bright moonlight, the dark silhouettes of the mountains could be seen as the train passed around the north end of the Medicine Bow Mountains and chugged around the south end of the Laramie Mountains. Finally, the rhythmic clickity-clack of the rail car wheels and the steady rocking motion of the car lulled them to sleep. A broken rhythm and the long, lonesome whistle of the steam engine nudged them to life at dawn as they came to a stop at the depot in Cheyenne. It looked like a long, long way from home across the wide prairie, but some fragrant coffee and a hot breakfast soon raised their spirits as the bright sun blazed over the horizon.

After a two hour stop in Cheyenne, the train continued eastward into the great plains, and the mountains were left far behind in Wyoming. This time as the mountains faded from view, Dan was not sad and lonesome. Lily was with him, and he was sure he'd be coming back.

As the train traveled east from North Platte, Nebraska, the Dailys watched the countryside change from a land of dry shortgrass prairie to a land of moderate rainfall and tall green grass. It was a very noticeable difference that divided the continent between the high, wild, dry and rocky western half and the flat, fertile, well-populated eastern half.

254

They traveled on down the Platte River Valley, and that night the train lulled them to sleep across the corn fields of eastern Nebraska. The next morning they reached Omaha, where they would have to change trains for one to the south.

Dan was amused at the thought that this same long trip that he had taken riding a horse in 1852 had changed from trails to rails.

The following day, after they arrived in Omaha, they took the train that ran down the Missouri River Valley to Kansas City. They got off of the train at St. Joseph. Lily did not like the confusion of the towns of the white men.

It had been a very long 1700 mile trip. It was twice as far as a straight line from Billings to St. Joseph. The long way around to Ogden had added six hundred miles. The only direct route was by horseback as Dan, John, and Jake had gone through the north edge of the Black Hills long ago.

When they arrived at St. Joseph, Lily commented, "If I had known it was this far to where you were going when you left the Little Bighorn so long ago, I would have been even more sad, thinking you may never return."

After arriving in St. Joseph, the Dailys visited John Daily's daughters. Dan was fifty-three years old now, and John's daughters were just a little older. The daughters, Jean and Ann, were very thrilled to see Dan and Lily.

As they visited, John's daughters wanted to know how their father was killed. Dan told them about the battle with the Blackfoot, leaving out the worst details.

He told them about the location of the grave in the small canyon and described to them the quiet beauty of the peaceful canyon. He told them John had a Christian burial, but he did not tell them how short the service was. Dan told them of the nice stone he found and engraved for a marker.

The daughters thanked Dan sincerely for the care of their father's burial. They also were very grateful for the money they had received from the gold. Without going into great detail, Dan told them of finding the gold and working to get it, then of packing it to Fort Union.

The daughters fixed the most delicious dinner that Dan had tasted since he left Missouri.

The next morning, Dan hired a hack to take Lily and him the few miles out to his parents' farm. Dan and Lily were dressed in store-bought clothes, and looked about the same as other people.

Dan's father was fixing the yard gate when they arrived. He walked over near the buggy as Dan stepped down. For just a short time, Dan's father had a studied look on his face, and then exclaimed, "Danged if I don't think it's Dan," and reached to clasp Dan's hand.

"Yes, it sure is," said Dan as they shook hands and then even hugged. "Well, you're looking great, Dad," said Dan.

Dan's mother walked out of the house at that time. She ran to Dan with open arms. "Dan, it's really you. I thought you'd never come back. Oh, Lord, I'm glad you did," and as they embraced, "You left so long ago."

"Mom, I'm thankful you're both all right," and he reached a hand toward Lily. "This is my wife, Lily."

"Lily," and Dan's mother hugged her, "how pretty you are. Oh, I'm so glad you came with Dan."

Then, "Well, goodness sakes, come on in," said Dan's mother, gesturing toward the house.

The hack driver, Dan and his father carried the suitcases and followed the women into the house. Dan and the driver came back outside. Dan paid the driver, thanked him, and shook his hand.

They had a wonderful visit that day and the following days. Dan's father was seventy-five years old and his mother was seventy-four. Their health was fine. They were both spry and sharp, and they seemed younger than their ages.

As they visited, Dan learned that one of his brothers, Lewis, was farming their parents' farm, and the brother Ray, was farming the place their Uncle John had left to his daughters. Both men had also bought land of their own. Dan's sister, Eloise, had lived in Kansas City since her marriage. After a few days, Dan went to visit all of them.

In the following weeks, Dan and Lily visited their relatives and Dan even met people he had known here when he left thirty-three years ago. A few of the people he knew on sight, but many had changed so much that he had to be told who they were. Those he had known as young men or children had changed the most. His friend Clarence, who had curly hair as a young man, was still called Curly, though he did not have any hair at all.

One Sunday morning at the edge of the church yard where the sidewalk along the street met the sidewalk leading to the church, Dan and Lily met face to face with Dan's old friend, Elaine Elliot, the girl who had wanted Dan to stay in Missouri. She was walking with a rather dignified city dude that Dan assumed must be her husband.

As they met, Elaine exclaimed, "Why Dan Daily, I'm sure it's you. My goodness, what a pleasant surprise," and she reached her hands toward Dan in a rather lowered position, not as an invitation to embrace.

Dan took her two hands and held them momentarily with a friendly squeeze. "Elaine, what a pleasant surprise. How nice to find you still living here in St. Joseph, and still looking wonderful."

"Well thank you, Dan, for the nice compliment. Looks like you have weathered the years very well yourself." And then, "This is my husband, Charles Wellington. He is a financier from New York."

"How do you do," offered Charles Wellington.

"Pleased to meet you," replied Dan, "and this is my wife Lily."

Elaine nodded and spoke, "Lily, why how beautiful you are. When Dan left here, he told me of the yearning he had to return to the beautiful mountains in the west. Now I understand better why he had such a yearning. It's plain to see that the yearning he had was for a beautiful woman. Well, its all right now. It's so nice that we all found what we were yearning for," and she smiled at Dan.

"I'm glad that you and Mr. Wellington are happy, Elaine," replied Dan, and they all started toward the church.

After they had left the church and were riding home in the buggy, Lily said, "She's very pretty, Dan. I had a feeling that there was something troubling you here when you left the Little Bighorn for Missouri long ago."

"She never did trouble me, Lily. I honestly was never really in love with Elaine, and after I met you, there was never a chance that I would be."

"I think she was heartbroken for a long time after you left, Dan. You seemed important to her."

"She has exactly what she always wanted now; what she could never fashion me into. We're as happy as two people can be together, Lily."

"Yes, Dan, I'm sure of that," and Lily reached an arm around Dan.

Sometimes Dan used his father's buggy to drive Lily on sightseeing tours around the countryside or to shop in town. Dan and his father also drove the buggy around the area. It was a fertile farming area and had many good homes.

257

One evening, Dan's father said, "Dan, from what you've told me, you must have plenty of money from the gold. Have you considered buying a farm here?"

"Yes, I have," said Dan, "I've given it fair consideration. I have pictured myself living here on some of the best farming land money can buy. I'm sure it would be fine farming, but there is so much that would always be calling me back to the West. I could never forget the thrill of seeing a long ridge of high, snow-capped mountain peaks. Far up on their narrow ledges and crags, snow white mountain goats pick their way over dizzying heights. In the fall, the faint bugling of an elk drifts in on an evening breeze. Great herds of buffalo once roamed where I now have a cattle ranch at the foot of the mountains. I could never be happy living anywhere else."

Dan's father said, "Son, you've painted such an interesting picture with your description of the West that I can see how it must have a great fascination in its wild beauty. It seems to cast a spell on the men who go there, and put a wild, restless urge in them. Maybe some day your mother and I will go there just to see what it is, and have another good visit with you."

Dan said, "Many settlers are there now. The wild days are over, but the West will always have wide, lonely prairies and pretty mountains."

"I would sure like to see it," said Dan's father.

After three weeks, Dan told his parents he was getting restless to return to Montana. They were able to get Dan and Lily to stay another three days, and then they bid everyone good-bye. All of them asked Dan and Lily to come to visit again without waiting so long.

Dan's mother and father said they really hoped to go to Montana for a visit. They both were very sad when Dan and Lily left.

Dan found there were rail lines from Kansas City nearly straight north through Des Moines and on to Minneapolis. They stayed over night in each of those cities. It was a four hundred mile trip through beautiful farm land of rich, black soil, great corn fields and sturdy farm buildings. It was some of the best farm land that could be found, but it still held no appeal for Dan and Lily as a place to stay.

Dan and Lily were enjoying the sights, but they were happy when they headed west from Minneapolis. Now each mile they rode the Northern Pacific train brought them closer to home.

They continued to cross hundreds of miles of good farm land dotted by many ponds and blue lakes. In western North Dakota, the land began

258

to have the look and feel of the West. At the Bad Lands of North Dakota, they knew they had returned to the Wild West.

When they reached the Yellowstone they felt very close to home, although they still had over two hundred miles to ride up the valley. At Billings they were almost home.

From the depot, Dan pointed to the southwest, "Honey, just look at the snow-capped Beartooth Mountains."

"They're sure pretty, Dan."

Then still pointing, Dan exclaimed, "I can even see the base of the peaks just above our ranch; there by that widest canyon. The air's sure clear today. That's seventy miles from here. You just don't see like that in the east. This is God's Country."

"Yes, and when you're out of it, you fare worse," and Lily laughed, "This is Crow Country."

The day after arriving in Billings, they got their saddle horses and pack horses from the stable and started for home. Riding up the Stillwater River and looking toward the great mountain peaks gave them a wonderful feeling of happiness. When they reached Antelope Basin, they were relieved to be back home. They were happy to have made the trip, but after being gone, Montana looked even better than before to them.

22

▼▼▼▼▼▼▼▼▼▼▼▼

THE BUFFALO DANCE

▲▲▲▲▲▲▲▲▲▲▲▲▲

Each year the owners improved their ranch in Antelope Basin. More cattle and horses were added to the herd. A brand for the ranch was registered with the Territorial Government. Their brand was L D on the left ribs on cattle and the left shoulder on horses. It was a good simple brand that did not blotch easily. The brand was taken from the first letter of LaFountain and Daily.

More fences and buildings were built. Although the soil was good and the rocks were few, another field was picked of rock each year to establish another hay field or a grain field for oats. It was convenient to have oats to feed the riding horses. While living on the prairies with the Indians, before there was any farming, there were no oats for horses. They lived by grazing on the abundant, nutritious prairie grass. Oats and hay were handy to use for a quick addition of energy for riding horses that could not have enough time for grazing. Oats and hay were also necessary for the five milk cows that were brought to the ranch in 1889.

Now there was enough farming and small towns with general stores for people to be able to buy food, clothing, and most of the articles needed in a ranching community. Wagon trails spread like spider webs across the land. Ambitious, hardworking people were bringing great changes to most of the land. Where buffalo and Indians had roamed freely across the prairies only a half dozen years ago, there were now ranchers or farmers on nearly all of the land along the Yellowstone and along the foot of the mountains.

The people of western Montana, where the population was greater because of mining, had been pushing hard for Montana to become a state. In 1889, Montana was ratified as the forty-first state.

Although Dan was reluctant to accept the position, he was elected as a State Senator to the Montana State Legislature. He accepted the task because he felt that he was as well qualified and was as interested in the people's welfare as anyone in his district. Dan was not familiar with formal procedures of committees and the workings of the legislature, but he expected to be able to learn. It was a position that would give him some prestige to help him accomplish those things that he felt were important.

Dan suggested to Lily, "I don't think it could be as bad learning the procedures in the State Legislature as it was to ride in a buffalo stampede."

"I'm sure it wouldn't, Dan. You'll be a good Senator."

Each summer a band of Crow Indians would come over from the reservation and stop two or three days for a visit. There may be anywhere from fifty to two hundred Crow that came. Many rode saddle horses, and some came in small wagons, or maybe even a buggy. On rare occasions, there may even be a travois in the bunch. They always had some fresh venison from bucks they shot along the way.

The Crow set their tepees along the creek between Dan's house and Striking Hawk's house. This is where they had camped for generations. They set their tepees with the entrance to the east as they always had. When they awakened early, they could watch a beautiful new dawn of blue and pink slowly reach across the sky to begin the miracle of a new day.

Dan and Striking Hawk furnished whatever number of steers were needed for a big feast, with plenty more for as long as they wished to stay, and some meat to take with them when they left. These people were the friends they had lived with for more than thirty years. Dan and

262

Striking Hawk were glad to furnish the steers. They had over three hundred steers, and they were living on land the Crow had once owned for longer than anyone knew.

After some steers were driven near to camp, it did not take the Crow long to shoot and butcher them. Most of the beef was eaten fresh and some was dried. Nothing was wasted. They ate the marrow from the bones, and their dogs used the bones the Crow did not use.

The Crow had games and contests in the day time. In early evening, there was a powwow and storytelling. Later in the evening there was a dance, just as in bygone days.

Dan and Lily and the other people at the ranch enjoyed these visits of the Crow more than any event at the ranch.

After one such Crow visit in 1891, Dan rode out across the ranch the next day. He still seemed to hear the faint rhythm of tom-toms whisper to him memories of days on the old Indian trails. His mind was preoccupied with those old memories as he rode his saddle horse out to the high western edge of the ranch to look at their cattle grazing there.

After looking at the cattle, Dan stopped on a high knoll on the ridge. When he dismounted, he took note of his saddle horse, Flash. Flash was another of the descendants of Sonny. Like Shadow, Flash also looked nearly like Sonny. As Dan reminisced of the days of riding Sonny, and traveling with the Crow, he gazed toward the Crow Reservation.

While Dan stared in the direction of the Little Bighorn in deep thought, his mind recalled the image of Chief Red Bear's vision. Dan considered the way in which the vision was formed. Dan and the buffalo calf followed the soldier on the black horse pursuing the Indian skeletons and the buffalo skeletons that signified the end of the buffalo herd. End of the herd? Dan and the buffalo calf were at the back end of the herd. Another meaning of end? Suddenly it seemed clear to Dan. Dan was to find the end of the herd! The back end, the last end, the ones that remained living! That was his part in the fulfillment of Chief Red Bear's vision. He must find the remaining buffalo and return them to the Indians. Why had he been so long in understanding this? Probably because it had not been possible to return any buffalo to the Indians before now, but was it possible now? Dan would do his best to find out.

It had been reported that the buffalo were not all dead. There were a few privately owned, very small herds of buffalo in Texas and Montana. It was unlikely that anyone could buy any of these herds.

Dan had heard rumors of the presence of buffalo in Yellowstone Park. It had been designated a national park as early as 1872. Dan inquired at the Yellowstone Park Headquarters and was informed there were actually several hundred head of buffalo in Yellowstone Park. They said these buffalo were living in this high, remote, almost inaccessible mountain area when the buffalo herds were being exterminated on the plains. When the hide hunters destroyed all of the buffalo herds on the plains in the killing frenzy of 1878 to 1883, the buffalo in the remote area of Yellowstone Park were left to kill until last. When there were no buffalo left on the plains, some of the hide hunters went to Yellowstone Park and killed some buffalo. The army had been ordered to protect the buffalo in Yellowstone Park, so they stopped the killing of the buffalo after a few had been poached.

Because Dan was a state senator, he had respect and influence with government officials. He learned from the Interior Department that it was possible for the Indians to be given a few buffalo to start their own herd. Dan was influential in the decision to give the Crow some buffalo.

In early spring, Dan was in the Lamar Valley in Yellowstone Park as one of the members of a committee to help with the planning for transporting the buffalo to the reservation.

While he was there, he was shown a small buffalo heifer calf whose mother had just died. The rangers asked if Dan had a milk cow on his ranch. It was decided to have Dan raise the calf with a bottle and milk from his cows.

Soon the buffalo calf was following Dan around the small calf pasture.

Most of the buffalo were in the Lamar Valley. When all of the arrangements were made, the Park Rangers and employees transported ten buffalo cows and a bull from the Lamar Valley to the Crow Reservation.

The Crow had a big remote range ready for the buffalo between the Bighorn Canyon and the Bighorn Mountains.

The buffalo were transported from the Lamar Valley to the Crow buffalo range in early September. They were transported in large wagons with specially built boxes holding large cages. Five wagons were used to haul the ten buffalo cows with calves. Another wagon carried the big buffalo bull. Dan had weaned the buffalo calf from milk, so he took it to the Crow range to be freed with the other buffalo cows that also had calves.

There were many Crow Indians, and some whites gathered near where the buffalo were freed on their pasture. The pasture was strongly fenced at the north end where it would have been possible for the buffalo to escape.

It was very exciting to see the buffalo on Crow land once more. The buffalo would never again roam across the western plains by the millions, but the hoofbeats of buffalo would rumble once again over a wild Crow prairie by the hundreds or possibly more. Dan and Lily, with an optimistic Striking Hawk, were among those present when the buffalo were returned to the Crow land.

To celebrate the return of the buffalo, a barbecue was held that evening near the Little Bighorn River, below the Custer Battlefield and the hill where Chief Red Bear had seen the vision. This time, the Crow provided the steers from their own herd of cattle.

The Crow were gathered in the open center of their tepee village. At dusk, dressed in his traditional buckskin clothing, Chief White Temple told them, "We are glad that the last part of Chief Red Bear's vision has come to pass. Now we can understand the meaning of all of it. The first part of the vision foretold the destruction of the buffalo and Indians. The last part foretold the return of a small part of the buffalo herds."

Dan said, "I'm relieved that I finally understand the meaning of the vision that was haunting me for so long. Now I can understand what the symbols were. The Indian skeletons were a symbol of the Indians that perished. The buffalo skeletons were the symbol of the buffalo herds that perished. Custer's death was the event that hurried the conquest and the destruction of the Indians and buffalo, so in the symbol of Custer on the black horse, they were fleeing from that destruction. From the end of the herd, I helped return some of the remaining buffalo to the Crow tribe, and the buffalo calf was the symbol of the remaining small herds of buffalo. Chief Red Bear had the power to see this vision that foretold the future of the Indians and buffalo."

"I deeply regret that the vision actually happened, but I'm thankful that some of the buffalo and Indians survived."

The return of a small herd of buffalo was a wonderful event for the Indians, so they had a Buffalo Dance that evening. Even some Sioux and Cheyenne were there to celebrate.

As in the days of old, flickering campfires lighted the wavering dancers. Pulsating tom-toms stirred the Indian's spirits back to the enchantment of their wandering, wild existence. Quavering voices joined the rhythmic, stomping feet in cadence with the beat of the tom-toms.

The dancers wore buckskin costumes with embroidery of beads and quills, decorated with elk teeth and bear claws. Spinning, bobbing dancers, some with headdresses of buffalo horns, imitated the action of buffalo. The squaws joined the dance to help form groups that swung to and fro, and wove in ribbons as wandering buffalo. As the tempo quickened, glittering feathers quivered on leggings, fan bustles, and headdresses. Rows of happy dancers circled in the firelight.

Among the spectators, Dan and Lily sat on a blanket-draped log. With an arm around each other, they watched the colorful pageant as the new moon, flanked by a bright evening star, shone in the western sky. They felt great happiness as they recalled the scenes of their early love while they lived among the Crow Indians.

Dan told Lily, "I'm happy we live where we do. It's nearly as good as when we were living with the Crow in the land of the buffalo. It's good that the Indians now have hope for better times. Honey, I'm glad I found you when I came here. We've had a wonderful life together, but most of all, I'm happy for the love we've always had for each other," and he squeezed Lily a little tighter.

"Yes, Dan, our love will last forever."